NOTHING BUT THE TRUTH

Emma Williams

Prosimian Press

For Jasper

1

L and Rover, matching Barbour jackets, two black labs. Sarah Wilson watched in horror through the mullioned window of the vicarage as the couple disappeared into the village hall. Jesus Christ, she'd landed in enemy territory.

Sarah took off her Jezza for PM t-shirt. It, like her dreams of a Labour government, had long since faded to irony. Catapulting it into the wicker laundry basket, she scanned her new collection of plain pastel blouses that hung above the row of Marks and Spencer trousers. The salmon pink with navy combination would do for today. She pulled them on and glanced in the mirror; the mouse-brown bob that replaced her black spiked hair was truly hideous.

What the hell had she done? Could she really get away with this? A vicar, for Chrissakes, when atheism was one of the few things that she still believed in. She was so far down the rabbit hole she'd never be able to claw her way back out. Retain anything of her former self in this paleoconservative backwater and she'd be paraded through the streets on a ducking stool.

The flyer on the Parish notice board had announced that the monthly coffee morning was today. Her first test.

She took a shot of Lamb's Navy.

The church bells tolled eleven. A steady stream of woollens, tweeds and gilets made their way into the hall. An array of pastoral dogs whimpered in the four-by-fours parked askew on every verge; windows cranked open sufficient for a collie's head without thought for security. West Tillington was evidently not a high crime area.

Sarah practised a benign smile, adjusted her dog collar

and headed across Church Lane. She'd hoped to make an unobtrusive entrance but as she stepped through the door a sea of grey heads periscoped in her direction and a polite trickle of applause accompanied her to the tea counter. Jesus Christ. She clipped the length of the hall in her tight court shoes nodding like a crazed poodle.

The ancient women behind the serving hatch – one tall, one large, one tiny – could be characters from a Roald Dahl children's book. They formed an effective production line; the recent arrivals were already seated at Formica tables laden with flapjacks, cakes, and scones.

'Welcome, Vicar, we've been so looking forward to meeting you.' The tall one gave a horse-toothed smile. 'What would you like, dear? Tea, coffee, hot chocolate?'

The local accent was a rogue Somerset that had lost interest as it crossed the border. It triggered thoughts of inbreeding.

'Oh, I'd love a coffee, thank you.' Chirpy; she hardly recognised herself.

'I'm Eileen, this is Betty.' She gestured to the large rosy faced woman forcing a plunger into a cafetière. 'Just pop your donation in the jam jar, dear.'

Damn, she only had a fiver and it wouldn't do to fish out change. The closing balance on her bank account had been twelve pounds fifty-five.

'I'm Jean.' The tiny woman was warming a giant teapot, a gingham tea towel draped over one shoulder. 'Marvellous to have a female vicar.' She had the look of a startled hen.

Sarah employed her trusted visual mnemonic: she imagined Eileen leaning like the tower of Pisa, Betty spinning a roulette wheel and Jean wearing denim dungarees. It paid to remember people's names and she had a whole parish to learn. She posted her five-pound note into the jar.

'Very generous, Vicar.' Eileen beamed. 'Cake is included, all homemade. Mine is the lemon drizzle.'

'Call me Sarah, please.' She cut a large slab of Victoria sponge – it would do for lunch.

'Delighted to have you here at last,' said Jean, adding an alarming number of teabags to the pot.

'Normal service will be resumed as soon as possible.' Sarah

produced an accent as crisp as Jean's tea towel.

'Well, hello there.' A baritone voice boomed over her shoulder. 'You'll be a breath of fresh air. The last incumbent left under a cloud.'

The man was a badly reconstructed photofit. Jet black hair, prominent chin, improbably small nose. He wore a fitted tweed jacket and a Rupert the Bear waistcoat that accentuated rather than disguised his paunch.

'A cloud?'

'Very dark.'

Sarah was unsure whether he was requesting a strong tea or referring to the nature of the cloud.

'My usual, please, Mrs R,' he boomed. 'Charmed to make your acquaintance, Vicar, I'm Terence Johnson.' He affected an exaggerated bow. What a prat.

Eileen retrieved a small plate of chocolate brownies from under the counter. A white label bore his name written in a spidery hand.

Sarah fought the urge to resist as Terence took her elbow and steered her towards an empty table. Pompous tosser.

Jean tottered over and placed his tea and chocolate brownies unsteadily on the table. 'There you go, Mr Johnson. Eileen put extra nuts in for you.'

'Why thank you, my favourite girlfriend.' He flashed a veneered smile.

His sexism made Sarah bristle. Along with a strong musk aftershave he emanated a sickening self-importance but she was stuck with him. 'Were you alluding to an issue with the Reverend Gooseworthy?'

'I was indeed.' He broke off a chunk of brownie that was received by an unpleasantly coated tongue. 'But let's not dwell on unpleasantness.'

Sarah made a start on the sponge which was as light as a feather. 'Have you lived here long, Mr Johnson?'

'Terence, please,' he smarmed. 'I'm a permanent fixture. Turn left after the bridge and keep going until you're past the smell of the chicken farms. Eileen is my nearest neighbour. I'm a quarter-mile further up Bradbury Hill.' He poured the tea from his saucer back into his cup. 'I attend all the coffee mornings in the district. Our paths will cross.'

'An interesting pastime.' She smiled, her jaw already aching with repetitive strain.

'One of my many duties. Head of the council, have been for twenty-four years. I hope I can rely on your vote in the upcoming?' He chewed his brownie like a cement mixer.

Sarah suppressed an urge to punch him. 'That's a long track record.'

'Let's just say it's a two-horse race and one of them is a mule.' He winked.

He'd evidently honed his pitch down to memorable sound bites.

'You'll find your flock small but fervent. The usual births, marriages and deaths, particularly the latter.' He gave an unnervingly girlish laugh. 'Have you come from a large parish?'

'This is my first.'

'Sorry to butt in, councillor.' A man with halitosis and a prominent stye loomed over them cascading a shower of sour breath. 'Might I have a word about the potholes on the Midwardine road?'

Sarah took the opportunity to finish her cake and rose to mingle. She scanned the assembled figures engaged in joyless conversation. This was her life now. Jesus Christ, how would she ever survive?

2

Sarah awoke the next morning to an insistent hammering. The muted light suggested early dawn. She turned over and pressed her finger to her ear. The banging erupted again. Christ, it was worse than Smethwick.

Oh, maybe a parishioner in distress? She'd have to allay any expectation that she was on-call twenty-four seven.

Sarah padded downstairs in her blue bunny slippers and threw open the door. No one there. More urgent battering – the racket was coming from the living room. She grabbed a walking stick from the umbrella stand and wielded it above her head as she peered through the doorway. A great black bird was pounding its beak against the french windows. It lifted unsteadily on huge wings and flapped away. Its return to the oak tree was greeted by a cacophony of cawing.

Good God.

It was five-thirty.

The hammering resumed as she returned to her bedroom. She forced open the sash window, the paint flaking in her hands. There were now two of the bastards hopping around the patio like pantomime villains, squawking and pecking ferociously at the glass.

'Bugger off,' she shouted and immediately regretted it. Lord knows who was within earshot. The birds took flight.

The blast of cold air had destroyed any real chance of sleep but she retreated under the duvet and closed her eyes. Within ten minutes they were back; this time there were four. She was trapped in a Hitchcockian nightmare.

Resigning herself to wakefulness Sarah made a coffee, opened her laptop and clicked on her work in progress: Sunday service first draft. Another bird stormed the window, its assault like gunfire. She jumped knocking her espresso over the keyboard. Shit.

Grabbing the tea towel, printed with old English pig breeds, she dabbed at the keys. With a forceful finger she deleted the opening hymn *All Things Bright and Beautiful* and replaced it with *Make Me a Channel of Your Peace*. She reread her sermon. It was based on Matthew 25:31-46, the parable of the sheep and the goats. The story should appeal to the farming community, although on closer examination it presaged judgement day, with sinners and disbelievers being banished to hell. Well, that was her stuffed. She'd reinterpret the message: God loves everyone regardless of how they forage, the texture of their coat or the directional position of their tail. Very nice. And to end they could sing *Love Divine All Love Excelling* – clergyonline.com described it as rousing. Job done.

The kamikaze birds were gone but there was little point going back to bed. She might as well grasp the nettle and drive to Peaminster. Putting it off was increasing her anxiety. She stood up straight, smoothed her hair and addressed the imagined bank teller in her best ecclesiastical voice. As a kid she'd hated those Saturday morning elocution lessons; pronunciation, vocabulary building, accent reduction. Lessons in pretence. The art of deception. Who knew they'd prove so valuable?

'Proof of residence? Yes of course, will a gas bill suffice? I also have my tenancy agreement. I'm so fortunate that the vicarage comes with the job.' Pause for radiant smile. 'Oh, you need proof of identity too? Silly me, I did not think to bring my passport, does a dog collar count?' Cheery laugh.

Sarah had not been inside a bank since that day. Tuesday eleventh February. The day that changed her life. Hard to believe it was only six weeks ago.

Peaminster had two banks. Sarah peered through the window of Lloyds. The trick was to pick the right teller. Hmm, it didn't look promising; a choice between a young woman –

too junior she'd do things by the book – or a jaded looking man in his mid-fifties with half-moon glasses and monstrous eyebrows. No thanks.

Barclays on Bridge Street offered a relaxed thirty-something scrolling through his phone. Third time lucky. Sarah walked straight to the counter and asked to open a bank account in her best Home Counties accent. She stuck to her script. He was buying it.

'Yes, of course, Reverend. If you don't tell my boss ha-ha-ha. Who can you trust if you can't trust a vicar?' He turned to photocopy her documents.

Get on the floor.

Get on the fucking floor.

'Are you alright, Vicar? You've gone very pale.'

'I'm fine.' She gripped the counter and breathed. 'I shouldn't have skipped breakfast.'

'There's Molly's tearoom on Gallows Lane.'

'Thank you.'

'Your cheque book and debit card will be sent to your postal address within seven working days. Welcome to Barclays, Vicar.'

Sarah turned to the exit in slow-motion. The tick-tick of her sensible heels, the familiar weighted door, the heft of the handle in her hand. Then she was back on the street, breathing cool air, striding past Molly's tearoom. Going home.

3

Sarah surveyed the meagre congregation. Eileen, Betty and Jean were settled in the front pew. A hulking man with a ravaged complexion sat three rows back, his sparrow of a wife perched beside him. The sole occupant of the right-hand side was a woman wearing a camel coat and a look of disdain. The capacity was a ludicrous two hundred.

Sarah regretted not wearing thermals under her vestments. The chambered nave had trapped the cold of the winter and was yet to let it go. She checked her watch; the service should have started ten minutes ago. There was little point waiting.

'Good morning, everyone.' She raised her arms preacher-style. 'I am delighted to welcome you to my first service at St. Osmund's. I'm looking forward to getting to know you all and to serving our community for many years to come.' The thought sat like a stone; she ploughed on. 'Let us stand to sing hymn number two-six-one together.'

Betty clip-clopped to the piano, shrinking the congregation by one sixth. She was surprisingly spritely for a large woman. Eileen's reedy soprano clashed with the dissonant altos, while the lone tenor made halting progress to the chorus before losing heart. Fortunately, Betty's enthusiastic chords pumped up the volume.

The congregation resumed their seats and cast expectant eyes upon Sarah. It seemed unnecessary to take the pulpit but now was not the time to break with tradition. She delivered her sheep and goats sermon with as much fervour as she could muster, earning appreciative nods from the holy trinity at the front. The odd couple sat poker faced and the camel coat appeared to be writing her shopping list. Sarah bulked out the remaining service with readings from the Book of Common Prayer which elicited the same responses. Having already loaded the hymnal board it was too late to change the closing number to one less reliant on mass voices. They would have to endure.

At last, it was over. Sarah strode to the foyer to bid the congregation farewell – another handy hint she'd gleaned from clergyonline.com.

'Lovely service.' Betty shook her hand vigorously.

'Thank you for playing so heartily.'

'I did enjoy your sermon.' Eileen looked wistful. 'I kept a small flock of curly coated Cheviots when I was younger.'

'What beautiful diction you have, Vicar.' Jean clutched Sarah's hand between two mouselike paws.

As a teenager, Sarah's coached accent pinned a target to her back – Smethwick High was no place for outliers – she'd soon learnt to switch seamlessly between Brummie and Received English as the situation demanded. Her verbal dexterity was certainly paying off.

Eileen, Betty and Jean tottered away with their arms linked. They reminded Sarah of the spindly apple trees that had grown entwined and stunted in the rubble-strewn garden of her mother's house in Arden Row. Indistinguishable in character, the ladies were benign, benevolent and ready to put their trust in her. They deserved better.

'Interesting sermon, Vicar.' The woman in the camel coat evidently felt it unnecessary to introduce herself. The mascaraed eyes lingered disparagingly on Sarah's trainers as she walked on. Damn, she'd forgotten her vicar shoes.

'So kind,' Sarah called after her. Although it was evidently not intended as a compliment.

The barn door man appeared from the shadow of the vestry and engulfed her hand solemnly. 'Ernest Farmer,' he said.

Was he joking? He would definitely not require a mnemonic. He introduced his wife as 'My Nancy'. Patriarchal bastard. Astonishingly, the wife bobbed a small curtsey. Strands of crimson hair poked from beneath a floral headscarf. Sarah tried to picture a famous Nancy but nothing came to mind.

'I hope to see you both at our next service.'

'You'll see me soon enough. I'm the sexton. I'll be over to trim the yew hedging tomorrow.'

'Oh, you're not a farmer then?'

His face portrayed a slow cycle of computations. 'No,' he said finally.

'Perhaps you might have some idea how to stop those black birds pecking at the glass doors?'

'Rooks back then.' He was evidently a man of few words. His wife blinked impassively by his side.

'I thought they were ravens.'

'Rooks.'

'What on earth are they doing?'

'They attack their reflections. Territorial, see.' With the conversation apparently concluded he took his wife's hand and walked her to the church gate.

'Goodbye,' she called.

Neither replied.

For a place where very little happened, Sarah noted an almost obsessional marking of time. The church bells announced each fifteen minutes with one, two or three resonant clangs that culminated in the ponderous counting out of the hour. In the hall the grandfather clock clopped its way around a rust-spotted dial, its hollow tocks joined by the ticks of the carriage clocks that hunkered in every alcove. It was very irritating.

Sarah changed into her black jeans and Greenpeace t-shirt and opened a bottle of Budweiser Light. This Sunday working was a doddle. She swung her feet onto the chintz settee, flicked through the channels and settled on the box set of *Derry Girls* series two. Afternoon sorted.

The pompous chimes of the doorbell interrupted. Damn. She covered her tattooed arms with a cardigan and opened the door. A middle-aged woman in a pale green twinset and pearls – blimey, they actually did exist outside British sitcoms – thrust a casserole into her hands. It was the woman in the camel coat, sans coat.

'Mrs Carole Adlington-Wyndham, I've come in my capacity as chair of the Civic Society to formally welcome you to West Tillington.'

Sarah pictured carol singers; her ridiculous surname would have to remain elusive. 'That's very kind of you.' She eyed the casserole with dismay. 'I'd invite you in but I'm in the middle of writing my sermon.'

Carole looked past her to the living room from where emanated a tirade of Northern Irish invective. 'I see.' She narrowed her already thin lips. 'In that case I won't keep you from your duties.' She made no signs of leaving.

'Very kind,' Sarah repeated. She inched the door further closed.

'We're meeting this Tuesday, seven-thirty sharp. I expect we will see you there.'

'I'm sorry?'

'The Civic Society.'

'Oh.'

'Numbers are dwindling. Some people do nothing to support the parish. Apathy reigns.' Her tone suggested a supporter of corporal punishment.

'I'm not sure I can commit. I have a very busy schedule. Four churches.' According to the Dean the other three were pretty much historical legacies that padded out the job role.

'I'm sure we can trust you to do the right thing.'

Blimey. If only she knew.

Still, it was an opportunity to build goodwill to mitigate any slips in the façade. 'Of course, I'll fit it in. I'd be delighted.'

'Excellent. I'll induct you when you return the casserole dish.' Carole looked proprietorially towards the orange monstrosity that loomed beyond the hedge. 'I live at The Grange.'

'Thank you, but I'm afraid I can't accept this.' She handed it back. 'I'm vegetarian.'

'Vegetarian? Goodness.' Carole looked her up and down as if garnering signs for future reference. 'Well, never mind, we're very open minded in WT. My husband, Ted, owns the butcher's in Ardminster.' She cradled the dish as if it were an orphaned child. 'He has a special offer on short-ribs this week. You'll miss out.'

A jaunty advertisement for cat food blared into the silence.

'Thanks again.' Sarah attempted to close the door.

'I trust that you've been apprised of the situation regarding the Russets?'

Perhaps a variety of apple with which she should be acquainted – must be the ones in her garden. 'Are they communal? I'm happy for people to pick what they want.'

'The Russets are a local family, Vicar. You will have met Eileen. She's taken in her grandson, little Benjamin, only seven, poor mite.'

Sarah was already on information overload. Why on earth was this woman standing on her doorstep telling her all this? 'Well, it's been lovely to meet you.'

'The boy's mother ran off.' Carole shook her head to emphasise the heinous nature of the crime. 'Quite dreadful.'

'Very sad, but I suppose if you're not happy –'

'Then Eileen's son Melville Russet, the boy's father, disappeared on Valentine's Day. Left no trace. The whole of West Tillington rallied of course but the search party drew a blank. As did the police.'

'Goodness.' That was actually pretty shocking.

Carole, evidently satisfied that she'd made her mark, gave a last withering glance towards the source of an Irish rebel song. 'I'll leave you to your work, Vicar.'

Alone at last, Sarah threw herself onto the settee and downed her lager. Well, that was news. News that nobody else had mentioned.

4

M onday. Sarah had nothing in her diary. If she could just keep her head down, this might turn out to be the perfect job. The sunlight filtered through the fleur-de-lys curtains and cast a line of swaying shadows across the bedroom wall. It was not a pleasant room in which to wake. She'd opted to take the vicarage fully furnished, her own boxed-up possessions barely filled the back bedroom, but living with the previous incumbent's taste was creeping her out. The shady forms loitered on the duvet – to her sleep-addled brain they resembled strange hanging fruits. She recalled the Billie Holiday song and shuddered. At least the bloody rooks hadn't pitched up this morning.

Sarah drew back the curtains. The shock a crashing chord. She reeled back clutching the fabric. A row of dead rooks hung from the guttering, suspended by their feet. Their empty white eyes staring into nothingness. She dropped onto the bed, suppressing the urge to vomit.

From the distance came the whirr of Ernest Farmer's chainsaw. Shock gave way to fury.

Okay, she was tough. She could handle this. She might be a townie but surely this brutal massacre could not be considered reasonable? Even in West Tillington. So, how was a novice female vicar going to tackle a Neanderthal murderer armed with a chainsaw? She grabbed her bible and headed for the yew hedging.

Ernest was brutally severing branches. He acknowledged her presence with a nod and continued his work. A volley of expletives exploded in her head. She closed her eyes and waited for Sarah Wilson, vicar-of-this-parish, to step up. The long hours spent annotating and colour-coding biblical quotations had been well spent. She turned to 'Nature' marked up in Genesis 1:21.

'God created every winged bird according to its kind. And God saw that it was good,' she shouted above the roar.

Ernest shut off his chainsaw and fixed her with a puzzled look; the expression in which his face seemed most at home. 'What?'

'The rooks are God's creatures. You had no right to kill them.' There was a waver in her voice.

'Genesis 1:28: "God said unto them to have dominion over the fish of the sea and over the birds of the heavens and over every living thing that moves on the earth,"' Ernest said with uncharacteristic loquaciousness.

'He meant us to look after them, not to massacre them.' Sarah brandished her bible in evidence.

'You said you wanted rid.'

'I thought you might make a scarecrow or something.' She followed his expression on its meandering journey before it settled once again on puzzled. 'Would you please remove the rooks and give them a decent burial?' She became aware that her attire – a short nightie decorated with rainbow coloured sheep and fluffy slippers – was inappropriate for the occasion. 'And in future please consult me before undertaking any activities likely to result in harm, serious injury or loss of life.'

She stomped back to the vicarage with as much dignity as she could muster.

Sarah took the Tillington Times into the kitchen. The sunlight through the leaded windows cast a scatter of crucifixes over the huge oak table. She flicked the pages of the newspaper. Boring drivel. A plea for a replacement bell ringer due to Miss Flowerdew's nasty fall. A talk on eighteenth-century farm machinery at the Civic Society. Ted Adlington-Wyndham's meat raffle: first prize a rack of ribs, second a ham hock, third a cockerel 'delivered dead or alive'. Jesus Christ. How had her moment of madness led to this slow suffocation?

What was this? *No stone unturned in hunt for Melville Russet.* A photograph of Terence Johnson sitting beside a tower of paperwork, grinning like an idiot with those ridiculous white teeth. *Councillor Johnson is prioritising all available resources to find his friend and former business partner.* Interesting, 'former' suggested a rift. The adjacent editorial, *Tragic wait for news,* highlighted the emotional toll on all concerned. Praise for the police blah, blah, blah, followed by some simple sound bites from Chief Constable Jericho, evidently designed to appeal to the unsophisticated Tillington Times readership. Mr Russet's desertion by his wife, his international business dealings, the pressures of being left to care for Ben, his young son. The intimation was suicide with a hint of murder mystery.

The paper's back page listed the times of Sarah's services, refuse collection dates and contact details for the Neighbourhood Watch. She resisted pouring herself a consoling rum – it was only nine-fifteen.

Through the lens of temporal and geographical distance, Sarah's Smethwick bedsit and previous dreary job did not seem so bad. She'd liked the diverse array of high street food shops and, since the brothels had closed down, the low-rent flats had attracted a bohemian student population. Her own had overlooked an Edwardian building that bizarrely paired the municipal baths and the public library. The road was noisy, there was an unresolved rodent problem and the upstairs tenants were active in the Mongolian throat-singing community. But still.

Living one hundred miles from her friends, with no pubs or clubs and literally nothing to do was seriously depressing. Her parishioners were either bland, irritating or maniacs, she had a row of dead rooks dangling from her guttering and she was tied to a parish that expected her to participate in events of mind-numbing tedium. In short, she was trapped in a tangled web. A web of her own making.

5

Sarah headed for the empty fourth row but her flock insisted that she come and join them at the front. At least her attendance had tipped the balance in favour of attendees over committee members. Carole Adlington-Wyndham waited stone-faced behind a trestle table flanked by two small figures. Nancy Farmer perched to her right; her hair a shocking purple. She had been deposited by Ernest who had settled her in and left her as if she were an abandoned puppy. To her left a pale woman leafed through a notebook, her foot and arm sheathed in plaster casts. Presumably it was the luckless Miss Flowerdew.

Mrs Adlington-Wyndham stood as if poised to address the United Nations. 'I call the meeting to order.'

The holy trinity looked disappointed. Betty rubbed Sarah's arm to signal their intention to catch-up later.

Carole tapped the table briskly with a sheaf of papers. 'May I welcome the Reverend Wilson to the Civic Society.'

'Sarah, please,' she said to the ripple of applause.

'I do hope that you've settled in. I suspect the vicarage needs a woman's touch. Nancy did clean but refused to return.'

Nancy flushed but said nothing.

Sarah had no idea how to respond to this bizarre introduction.

'I do have an exciting announcement this evening,' Carole continued, suddenly buoyant. 'Terence Johnson has made a very generous donation with which to purchase designer curtains, velvet seat cushions and cashmere throws to make the Civic Society warm and welcoming to all.'

Eileen raised her hand. Sarah guessed that the gesture was

ironic – there was a touch of maverick about Eileen. 'Would a more diverse range of speakers not be more attractive?'

'Of course, the choice of design is to be agreed with the council so I shall be meeting with Terence Johnson next week.' Carol cooled her face with the agenda.

A litany of looks was exchanged on the front row.

Carole resumed her seat. 'Item one, unallocated tasks.' She scanned the front row accusingly. 'The following remain undesignated: raffle tickets, litter pick, keeper of the flag, fruitcake competition, and village-in-bloom subcommittee.'

A prolonged silence ensued. Sarah took the trinity's lead and gazed into the middle distance. Keeper of the flag didn't sound too onerous but she assumed the role also involved raising and lowering it so she kept quiet.

Carole clenched her jaw. 'Honestly, the committee cannot do everything.'

Surely Eileen should be exempted, given her recent catastrophic life events. Why should the poor woman be burdened with sweeping up discarded dog-ends and selling raffle tickets when her son was missing?

Miss Flowerdew struggled to dislodge her incarcerated leg from between the chair and table. 'Actually, Carole, I'm standing down. I've reached the end of my tenure and it would be wrong to deprive others of the opportunity.'

Carole met this bombshell with a menacing scowl. 'I assume you will see fit to continue until a replacement is found?'

She grimaced and scribbled the minute.

Carole turned to Nancy and dared her to speak. 'Any financial update?'

Nancy closed her ledger and shook her head. Her hair was the exact colour of her cardigan, it actually looked rather good.

'May I remind you that the post of treasurer is not time limited.' Carole gave a cold stare. Nancy shrank further into her bird-like frame.

Sarah offered her a sympathetic smile. Nancy was timid, seemingly knew her way around a balance sheet and was beyond suspicion. She was perfect.

A shrivelled man in a long mac appeared at the door. Sarah rose and delivered her fabricated apology. It would not be possible to retain the will to live during a talk on derelict farm machinery. Her flock looked bereft. She was starting to warm to them.

It had been worth putting in an appearance. Nancy Farmer was an absolute gift.

Having escaped the Civic Society Sarah rooted through her boxes and retrieved a bottle of Lamb's Navy and six shot glasses. She lined them up, knocked back the first three and opened her laptop. It was time to bite the bullet. The 'Fund My Charity' site seemed far too easy to set up; why wasn't everyone doing it? Maybe they were.

Name of Charity: hmmm, something that people wouldn't feel inclined to support; she could do without actual donations being paid in. Bats freaked her out. Save Our Bats; SOB had a ring to it. She found the ugliest looking bat on the internet – the close up of its hideous snub nose and vampiric teeth made her recoil. Ideal for the cover image. The tagline needed to be equally uninspiring: Your donation will help to increase the number of these endangered bats. Full stop.

Set target goal: Five hundred thousand pounds. No, that sounded ridiculously ambitious, ten thousand – donations could always exceed expectations.

Name of trustee: Mrs Nancy Farmer.

Sarah linked the donate button to her new deposit account. Now she could drip feed the money. Inconspicuous anonymous donations, street collections, cash from raffles, bike rides and bring-and-buy sales. She took another shot and pressed launch. Easy.

There was one more task that she'd been putting off; erasing her social media presence. She deleted her Instagram and Twitter accounts. She hesitated over her Facebook page. A skinny, wild-eyed woman grinned back at her, asking her as usual WTF she was doing. She scrolled through last year's posts; there she was camped out on London bridge with Extinction Rebellion, drunk with Maz on the Isle of Man ferry, waving a banner at Birmingham black lives matter, dancing with Maz, Callie and Denny at Glastonbury. That was the thing with social media, you could be anyone you wanted to be, even yourself. But it was too risky to leave an electronic trace. She savoured the images one last time and deleted her account. Her life.

The telephone trilled.

'Sarah? Geoffrey Tibble here, just wanted to see how you are settling in and to formally welcome you to the diocese.'

She regretted downing that fourth shot. She carried the phone out into the garden for some sobering air. The garden path glistened with slug trails, spiders' webs clung to the bushes, gnomes lurked in the shrubbery. The faint moon shared the sky with a pallid sun; West Tillington really did feel like another planet.

'That is extremely thoughtful of you, Dean. Yes, yes, everything is absolutely excellent thank you.' Perhaps she was overdoing the superlatives, but she'd noted this tendency in the religiosi – unwarranted enthusiasm was the norm.

'Good-oh. Now, I have sent over your parishioner list.'

Sarah strolled past the herbaceous borders. The surviving rooks called vengefully from the old oaks. 'Parishioner list?'

'I'm afraid your predecessor rather let the side down vis-à-vis ministering to the lame and the needy. Took his eye off the ball as it were. Goosers preferred to tend to his own flock if you get my gist.'

Sarah had no idea what he was talking about, the mixed metaphors were hard to untangle. Seeking clarification regarding the Reverend Gooseworthy appeared to be strongly discouraged. 'I'm very much looking forward to meeting them all. Church attendance was a little disappointing, I only had six on Sunday.'

'My goodness, that's an excellent turnout, practically a full house!' His laugh evoked a braying camel. 'Also, I might have neglected to mention the probationary period.'

'Probationary?' She caught her breath as the yew hedges transformed into spectral shapes. Country life was as creepy as hell.

'Twelve weeks. Just a formality. Don't commit a sin, cardinal or otherwise, or we'll have you out on your ear before you can say, Let God be my judge!' He bellowed with laughter.

Three months best behaviour. Okay, she needed to stay focussed. Not upset the locals. She could do this. 'Well, if there's anything I can do, Dean, please don't hesitate.' She felt unnerved, as if some watchful creature was prowling the undergrowth. Did badgers attack?

'Actually, I do have one tiny favour to ask. I'm sure you must be rattling around in that old vicarage. We have a parishioner in need of temporary respite.'

Sarah stopped in her tracks. The hedge morphed into an elegant flamingo with one leg raised in classic pose. 'Wow.'

'Yes. He lives in the parish. Not a church goer but the poor chap has fallen on hard times. Nowadays, of course, it's our duty to wrap the arms of fellowship around all and sundry!'

She felt that she'd missed something important. 'All and sundry?'

'Just until he's back on his feet as it were.'

Beyond the flamingo stood a giant peacock, its tail in full fan. It was absolutely stunning. She had misjudged Ernest, the man was a genius, the Edward Scissorhands of West Tillington. 'I'm sorry, what are you proposing, Dean?'

'The parish has some making up to do after old Goosers.' He released his camel laugh.

Perhaps he'd been at the port.

'Two- or three-weeks tops. Jack Stretton and his son Jesús. Should we say the day after tomorrow? Charity begins at home and all that.'

A third figure rose silhouetted in the fading light, an owl, no, a rook, its majestic wings raised to the salmon-pink sky. Bless him, Ernest had made amends in the most endearing way.

'It does indeed, Dean. It does indeed.'

'Jolly good. Cheerio then.'

Sarah returned to the living room and finished the shots. What the hell had she just agreed to? House guests would be a disaster. It seemed that the arm of fellowship did not extend to the six-acre Deanery. It was a fait accompli. Checkmated by her distraction and neat rum. Damn, she could have played the gender card. A single woman inviting two men into her home? Not only did she know absolutely nothing about Jack Stretton and son but she would now have to be the Reverend Sarah Wilson twenty-four hours a day. What a total nightmare.

6

B orten Wood Farm was perfectly positioned behind an arc of chestnut trees on the leeward side of the hill. With its red brick walls, grey tiled roof and blue front door, it was a happy child's drawing of a house. It stood sentinel over its fields; a colour chart of greens that sloped down to the malachite darkness of Borten Wood. The triangle of woodland had been severed from Montague Forest to allow an access road for heavy potato trucks to deliver their weekly cargo and disgorge the loads of packaged crisps.

Jesús hung out of his bedroom window and trained his binoculars on the afternoon convoy. He counted each lorry as it passed; eight, an average day. The rattle of a struggling car engine made him jump. He leaned further out as the car coughed into life. His mum's old mini. That was weird. It had stood unused by the side of the house for a whole year because Dad said it would freakthebejesus out of him if he saw it being driven around by someone else.

Dad had gone a bit fruit loops. Not scary crazy like Mum had been but he was acting pretty strange. Now he was bumping across Top Meadow in the mini and leaving snaky tyre tracks on the grass. Fortunately, all the goats were down in Bottom Meadow or they'd have been freaking out. Dad skidded to a halt dead in the middle of the field. He jumped out and left the door wide open. Jesús shook his head the way Miss Bickerstool did when she couldn't believe someone's silliness but wasn't actually going to tell them off.

The car was pretty beat up after all the reversing into walls and going too close to scratchy hedges and not stopping in times.

Dad did his funny lopsided trot back to the house; like a crazy penguin. He was doing pretty well because he wasn't good at walking over rough ground. There was the tock, tock, tock of his stick on the stairs. Jesús shoved the yellow digger back under his bed. It had been a present from Mr Johnson but he and Dad didn't like him anymore.

'Hi, Dad.' He gave his most innocent smile.

'Put your coat on, mate. We're going to have some fun.'

Uh oh, that's what he'd said about football practice.

They walked slowly towards the car. Jesús examined the two milk bottles Dad had given him to carry. The liquid was clear with just a tiny bit of yellow and there was a rag stuffed in the top of each. They smelled funny, like that smell you get when you have to wait in the car at the petrol station. His tummy told him that something bad was going to happen.

Dad was sweating with the effort of walking, or of going mad. 'Hold them tight. Be super careful.' But Dad's own bottle was sloshing around like crazy because of his gammy leg. They reached the car and Dad opened the boot and took out the green plastic can.

'Right, mate, stand well back.'

Jesús walked slowly backwards as Dad splashed the petrol all over the roof and the bonnet and emptied the rest on the front seat. This did not look good. He waited, a snake of anxiety curling in his stomach.

Dad kicked at the passenger door. It had never opened again after the time Mum drove into a ditch and a tractor had to pull it out. Jesús had survived because he'd been strapped into his booster seat. People have nine lives, like cats do, but it was a shame to lose one so early. He had to be extra careful now. Back when Mum used to take him to school, he'd have to squidge past the steering wheel and crawl over the handbrake and the gear stick. It was fun unless you got caught on something and Mum went all shouty. *Estúpido maldito idiota.* Mum had often shouted at him. Jesús knew it didn't mean anything. She shouted at Dad too. She'd definitely be shouting at them now.

Dad clicked his lighter and held the flame to the rag in his bottle until it caught. He lobbed it into the car. Bam, like a bomb. Flames shot up from the front seat. Super scary. Jesús held his bottles out in front of him as far as they could go. The heat on his face was nice but not nice. Dad came back and took the bottles, one in each hand and disappeared into the thickening smoke.

Oh no, what if Dad died too? Bursting into flames like Guy Fawkes on bonfire night. He'd be an orphan. Most people had two parents and he'd have none. He'd have to become a pick-pocketer like in Oliver Twist. He would hate it in London. It wasn't fair.

And then Dad was back. All sweaty and red but smiling. He came over and stood beside him and put his hand on Jesús's shoulder.

Woosh! The fire lit up the whole car. The paint turned from red to grey to black. Chunks of burning metal flew into the air. Yellow and blue flames shot from the empty windows.

Wait! For an instant Jesús wanted to run forwards. What if Mum had left something important inside? But he remembered it didn't matter. It was okay, she didn't need stuff anymore. Dad's hand gave his shoulder a little squeeze. He could relax and enjoy the crackles and pops and the crazy coloured flames. Sparks flew way up into the sky. The passenger door fell off; they cheered. Dad was right, it was fun.

Jesús poured the remains of the coco pops over his Ready Brek. It was their last day so anything the food bank wouldn't take would be wasted. Dad was scrambling eggs with chopped-up cabbage. The smell made Jesús feel a bit sick. Or maybe it was the thought of having to say goodbye to the goats after breakfast. Either way it was putting him off his cereal.

Dad pulled up a chair beside him and shovelled the green and yellow mess into his mouth with a teaspoon. They'd been a bit hasty clearing all their possessions into the charity bags and only had three pieces of cutlery left; all spoons. Jesús had been pleased to get rid of some things, like his abacus that he'd never really understood, and his big wooden clock with the blue hands because it was so babyish. He had a cool watch now anyway, glow-in-the-dark so he could see the time when he woke up at night.

'Not hungry?' Dad phutted the last of the tomato ketchup onto his eggs.

'Nah, not really.' He'd miss the shiny cooking pots that hung above the stove. He'd miss Dad banging his head on them and saying 'Geez'. It was hilarious. It was safe to laugh with Dad.

'When big things change, it's helpful to think about things that are still the same.'

'Like that I'll still be at Bridge Street primary?'

'Yes, for now.'

Jesús stirred the coco pops into the porridge and watched it turn a muddy brown. 'I'm not good at making friends. I'd have to start from scratch. I only have two friends and I don't even like Marky that much.'

'The forest will be the same, we'll still walk in it, just on different paths. The forest won't ever change.'

Jesús put down his spoon. 'What about the climate catastrophe?'

'Well yes, but don't dwell, mate, I'm trying to cheer you up.'

They finished their breakfast. Dad chucked the dishes in the sink and put his coat on. Jesús struggled into his boots. They were a bit tight but it wasn't worth getting a new pair now that he wasn't going to be a goatherd anymore. He slipped his hand through the oval grooming brush for the last time and followed Dad down to Bottom Meadow. Grooming wasn't a priority but Jesús wanted them to look their best. He listened out for Beyoncé because she'd had a cough. He couldn't hear her so she must be better. Or dead.

It had taken a while to find them good homes. They wouldn't let them go for meat – they weren't the right type of goat anyway but you couldn't be too careful. Some were going to Wales where people went for holidays and the others to Shropshire. Jesús wasn't sure what happened there.

He caught up with Dad. 'Maybe we could go and visit them?'

Dad just looked away.

Beyoncé was standing under the big maple so she wasn't dead. She was a British Saanen so could be a bit bitey. Jesús brushed her neck with long gentle strokes. It was nice the way she leant into him. Adele and Pixie came tumbling over doing their long maaah sound.

'Hi from Ben,' he said. Ben was always saying 'Say Hi to Adele and Pixie for me.' Ben had got to know them when he started coming over after his mum left. They'd sit with the goats and stroke the goats and talk about the goats. It stopped Ben being too sad that she'd just buggered off without so much as a byeyourleave. Ben still came over after his dad disappeared and he went to live with his granny Eileen. Then he'd bring carrots and pears and spinach. Granny Eileen was the best. Now Jesús wouldn't be able to say 'Hi from Ben,' anymore. Pixie looked at him sort of questioning with her long rectangular pupils.

'Don't worry, everything will be alright. Wales is very nice. You'll get to see the sea and hear seagulls and maybe go and play on a nice sandy beach, one with rock pools. There'll be fish and chips and ice cream.'

Dad ruffled his hair. 'Right, mate, let's move the Wales group up to Top Meadow.' He hobbled back up the hill rattling the treat box.

Jesús counted the goats as they pushed their way through the gate. Twenty-four. All present and correct. Nothing was as nice as walking with your dad and your herd of goats, even if it was for the very last time. He hummed *The Lonely Goatherd* and Dad joined in with the yodel. Lay ee odl lay ee odl lay hee hoo. Shakira and Taylor had a good explore of the burnt-out car. Then the others all started crowding around it, wary but brave. You could learn a lot from goats.

'Are we going to leave the car here for Mr Johnson?'

'Yep.' Dad kept walking.

'Where exactly are we going to live?'

'Don't fret, little fella. Leap and the net will appear.'

Jesús gave him his best smile. It was nice that Dad said things to try to make him feel better. He had another question but he didn't ask it because he was pretty sure he knew the answer. 'Does the net appear if you've been pushed?'

7

Sarah was on edge; she knew almost nothing about her imposed houseguests but they would be a major risk. It wasn't even possible to indulge her last hours of freedom with Netflix and caffeine. She had things to do. Things to hide. She peeled the three post-it notes from the fridge door and stuck them in her page-a-week diary. Conceal mattress in back-bedroom. Increase donation rate. Revise church festival days.

The name Jack Stretton conjured a down-to-earth guy in overalls, maybe holding a tool box with a pencil propped behind one ear. Annoyingly blokey. Probably a whistler. 'And son' was a scant clue – she hadn't caught his name; his offspring could be anything from a sulky teenager to a never-left-home forty-something. Either would be dire. For all she knew Mr Stretton had been fired for misconduct, become bankrupt through online gambling or be a Skid Row alcoholic. Well, at least she'd have a drinking partner. Whoever they were, she'd have to get rid of them as soon as possible.

In spite of the heavy oak furniture the cavernous second bedroom felt empty and devoid of all charm. Forty-eight hours of airing and incense sticks had failed to remove the taint of farmyard and rotten apples. It had permeated the depressing mustard walls, woven into the plum curtains, the wine-red carpet and the honey-coloured chaise longue. The room was a veritable grocery list of doom.

Sarah made up the twin beds with linen that still emitted its camphor smell despite the hot wash cycle. She sprayed a liberal coating of Pledge across the bookshelves that housed a bible, an assortment of livestock manuals and several well-thumbed copies of *Farmer's Weekly*. The Reverend Gooseworthy had clearly thrown himself into the world of his farming parishioners.

A Maybelline lipstick 'Divine wine' rolled in the drawer of the bedside cabinet. How bizarre. Perhaps Gooseworthy had a sister. She straightened the picture of *St Francis with Fawn* hanging above the dressing table and stood back. Dismal. Perhaps she should pick a bunch of daffs from the front garden and stick them in a vase? Oh well, at least no one would overstay their welcome in this hideous room.

The sound of crunching gravel. Sarah ran to the window to see a battered jeep and trailer bouncing up the driveway. A slim muscular man in a beanie hat emerged followed by a small boy holding a toy sheep. Despite his athletic build the man moved with a dragging gait assisted by a walking stick. He stopped to point out various plants in the border.

Sarah opened the door before they'd rung the bell. The man removed his hat to reveal a fountain of corkscrew hair that fell around an unshaven face. He emanated a sense of calm and a sense of loss. A captive otter pining for the sea. The boy peered warily from behind his leg with the deep brown eyes of a bear cub. The man wore a *Clangers* t-shirt, the boy a *Rebel for Life* hoodie. They produced matching smiles. She liked them immediately.

'Jack Stretton.' He held out his hand. 'And my son Jesús, J-E-S, accented U, S. Pronounced Hay-sous not Jees-us.'

'Sarah Wilson.' She resisted touching the boy's wavy black hair.

They stepped inside. The boy was minute in the huge entrance hall. He stayed close to his father clutching his toy.

'Does your sheep have a name?' she asked, bending down.

'Paloma,' he said seriously. 'She's a goat.'

'Cool name. Come on, I'll show you your room.'

Sarah climbed the stairs, batting dust motes and adjusting the paintings as she went. They followed in silence; the man's stick clicking on the polished oak. She gestured to the open door and stood back apologetically.

'It's lovely, thanks.' Jack's gratitude appeared genuine. 'Which bed do you want, mate?'

'I don't mind, you chose.' His voice tiny.

'You take the one by the window so you can look out in the morning.'

The boy stroked Paloma as if to reassure her and moved her in an arc to show her the room. He was adorable.

'Do you fancy a drink and a biscuit while your dad sorts out the luggage?' She'd like to give him a welcoming hug but it wasn't appropriate.

The boy waited for a nod of permission before following her. He took her hand as they went downstairs. Was it normal for kids to be so trusting? Had nobody told him about stranger danger?

'We used to call these dead-fly biscuits.' Sarah handed him a plate.

'We still do,' he said, 'but they're named after Garibaldi who was an Italian general.'

'Blimey, how old are you?'

'Seven-and-a-half.' He stuffed a biscuit into his mouth. 'But I'm a bit small because I had a trauma.'

Sarah carried two rum and cokes through to the living room as Jack limped behind. Apparently Jesús had fallen asleep five pages into James and the Giant Peach.

Jack took the chair by the french windows. 'I didn't think vicars were allowed to drink, well apart from sherry and communion wine.'

'Holy communion is the other lot, but yes, everything in moderation or not at all is the general message.' They clinked cheers.

'Some place you've got here.' He glanced up at the coffered ceiling. 'It's really nice of you to put us up.'

His accent was hard to locate, somewhere north of the Midlands, south of Yorkshire. Not a born-and-bred local; a definite bonus.

'To be honest it's Geoffrey Tibble you should thank. He set it all up.'

'Set you up more like.' He gave a broad smile. Perfect teeth. 'I only met the guy once. We had a long chat when I delivered a palette of goat's cheese for a dinner party. Nice bloke, arranged a standing order.'

'He seems to do a lot of entertaining. I haven't had the call yet, small mercies, clerical gatherings can be pretty dire.' And they definitely didn't help with her imposter syndrome; although it wasn't a syndrome if you were actually an imposter.

Jack laughed. 'You don't seem much like a vicar. You know, in a good way.'

'Thanks.' She put down her rum, she needed to watch herself.

'I'll get on with finding us a place as soon as possible.'

'Yes, that would be good. If you don't mind me asking, how did you end up needing refuge?'

'Long story short, I got injured. I couldn't work. Got evicted. Borten Wood Farm.' He looked through the window at the row of small white crosses beside the lawn. 'Pet cemetery?'

'No, just the sexton taking a rook burial a bit far.'

'Ah.' Jack pressed his finger into the hole in the worn armchair. 'It turned out there was a clause in the tenant farmer contract. Fitness for manual labour.'

'Oh dear.' She didn't know that tenant farmers still existed. It sounded very feudal.

'The bastard wasted no time. Sorry for the language. I literally got notice to quit the day I was out of hospital.'

'That's terrible.' A familiar pang of injustice stirred. 'Who's the landowner?'

'Terence Johnson, local bigwig.'

'Oh, I've met him. Total weasel.' She managed to filter out the expletive.

'That's insulting to weasels but yes, I agree.' He indicated to the pouffe. 'Do you mind, my leg's killing me?'

'Go ahead.'

Jack removed his shoe and propped his foot up with a wince. His big toe had worn through the darned hole in his hiking sock.

'So, how's Geoffrey involved?' She sipped her rum.

'I told him about it because I had to cancel his cheese order. I got the impression he wanted to redeem the church in some way.'

A light rain mottled the window. 'Do you know anything about Lionel Gooseworthy? The previous vicar.'

'No sorry, religion is definitely not my thing.' He drained his glass. 'No offence.'

'None taken. Fancy another?' Something about his hippie aura resonated. Let her breathe. It was going to be a challenge to retain the religious façade.

'Sure, thanks. Neat please. Don't want to support the Coca-Cola plutocrats.'

Sarah preferred shots too but they'd give the wrong impression. 'How did you get injured?' She gestured to the bowl of twiglets.

Jack knocked back his rum in one. He could be a dangerous drinking partner. 'The ward doctor identified the hoof prints on the back of my shirt. The medical records say that I was kicked by a roe deer.'

'Gosh, impressive. If you're going to have a freak accident it's certainly up there.' Something dark crossed his face. Strangely it made him even more attractive. 'The thing is, I'm pretty sure it wasn't an accident.'

'What, the deer did it deliberately?' Oh God, the guy was a nutter.

Jack stretched his foot back and forth like that ballet exercise she did as a kid. Good toes, naughty toes. 'I was bird watching, crouched in a bush trying to locate a woodpecker through my binoculars. I woke up in hospital with a head injury, fractured phalanges, a dislocated knee and a broken scapular.'

'Okay, that does seem pretty gratuitous for a deer.'

'I think it was Terence Johnson.'

'What? He planted the deer?' She could really do with another drink.

'I know it sounds crazy but I think I was whacked on the head. After I passed out someone gave me a good kicking and then stamped hoof prints on my shirt.'

'To be honest that does sound a bit nuts.' She was trapped in her own house with a paranoid conspiracy theorist.

'The thing is, the doctor reckons I'll make a decent recovery. Fit enough to work anyway. The eviction papers must have been drawn up while I was still in hospital. Johnson wanted me out.'

It did actually sound pretty suspicious. 'Is there anything you can do?'

'No. The tenancy contract is clear. The law is on his side.'

They sat in silence and watched the drizzle turn to hard rain. 'Why would he want you out?'

'No idea, always paid the rent, kept the place in good order. He seemed to like us, even bought Jesús presents.'

'Very odd.'

Jack rubbed his leg. 'We've been there since he was born.'

'He's a lovely boy.'

'Thanks. And thanks for not asking about his mum, most people do.'

'In your own time.' Although, actually, he didn't have long. Nice as he was, she was plotting her own eviction.

'It seems you're quite vicary after all. Even without the confessional you're very easy to talk to. You haven't told me one thing about yourself.'

'Confession is the other lot. And my life is very uneventful.'

8

Sarah had only known them for twenty-four hours but their presence had stirred something, reignited a little of her old self. The self that a convincing Reverend Sarah Wilson had to keep buried.

Jesús was endearing, there was a spontaneity to him that she recognised in herself. And an underlying turmoil. She knew the aetiology of hers but what could have happened to a seven-year-old to have acquired such an emotional load? Could you be born with a tendency to foreboding? She saw it in his father too. Oh God, maybe it was just the view through her own distorted lens? Projection. Onto this sweet little kid, who probably didn't have a care in the world. But what the hell was the trauma all about? Whatever their story, something powerful had entered her house.

But she needed them out. If she could dig up some evidence that their eviction was illegal, maybe they could move back to the farm. Why on earth would Terence Johnson want to turf Jack off the land and lose the steady rent?

From her brief stint at Citizens Advice, Sarah knew that information was king. She opened her laptop, searched for the minutes of West Tillington district council meetings and clicked on a random sample from successive years. God, they were depressing. Sporadic refuse collections, lack of WIFI connectivity, nursery closures, day centre demolition, sale of school playing fields. There had been a relentless downward slide under Terence Johnson's leadership. Perhaps the changes were so incremental that people hadn't noticed – or they'd become resigned to it. Interesting that Reverend Lionel Gooseworthy attended several meetings but his contribution had been redacted.

There was no mention of tenant farmers in general or Borten Wood Farm in particular, just the usual local planning applications: conservatories, barn conversions, extensions. She scanned the change of use applications. Bingo! The land had been sold 'subject to contract' for an undisclosed sum a month ago and with no mention of sitting tenants. The change of use was unspecified. The buyers' names were redacted. Highly suspicious. She put in a Freedom of Information request for the missing details.

Terence must have been waiting for an excuse to evict them, when none came and with the contracts prepared, he took it into his own hands. Jack was right, he'd been deliberately attacked. Terence was a dangerous man, seemingly benevolent but beneath beat the heart of a shark. Maybe it took one to know one.

Sarah transferred ten thousand pounds – raised by a particularly successful Land's End to John O'Groats cycle ride – into the Save Our Bats account and closed the lid.

The afternoon's duty loomed before her; how lovely it would be to meet Callie and Maz for a catch-up at The Fat Cat in Smethwick. God, that was a lifetime away. This was her life now. Sarah had to suck it up – she'd put off full-bore vicaring for long enough. Bracing herself for her first parishioner visit she snapped on her dog-collar and grabbed the car keys.

Within ten minutes she was lost. The local nomenclature was ridiculously unhelpful. For a start, there were no other Tillingtons. While she didn't expect a representative of every compass point there was not even an East Tillington to lend balance. The place names might have been drawn from a handful of scrabble letters; Lingen, Lingsley and Lingsland were on her patch, as were Borten and Bortenfield. Bortenwood and Borten Wood were two different places. Upper Wychwood and Lower Wychwood were nowhere near Wychwood Cross. In a conversation with the bin men this morning she'd discovered that an unfathomable pronunciation also conspired against incomers. Even the shortest and apparently obvious name sat booby-trapped.

'Prepare to navigate off-road' is not an instruction one wants to hear, particularly when driving a 2006 Renault Clio with a dodgy clutch. Sarah turned off the Satnav and continued down the narrow track that snaked through Bortenfield – apparently she'd missed Borten altogether. Isolated houses squatted at the end of long driveways that possessed neither names or numbers. The high hedges formed a labyrinth concealing any landmarks. She'd entered a video game that had levelled up beyond her ability.

Nick Cave's *Murder Ballads* CD, at full volume, kept Sarah's panic at bay. She rounded a blind bend and slammed on the brakes as a mud-shedding tractor idled towards her. She backed up for half a mile, the Clio whining in protest, before edging into the narrowest of passing places. At least she could ask for directions. But no, the driver ignored her frantic gestures and rolled past, throwing clods of red mud onto her windscreen.

God, she hated this place.

Of course, there was no bloody phone signal. Sarah checked her scribbled notes; over the hump bridge, couple of miles, small pond, past the five-bar gate, stone pillars on the left. The instructions had sounded fool-proof when standing in her kitchen but the whole district was riddled with hump bridges, five-bar gates and bloody stone pillars. She hadn't noticed any small ponds. The letter box leaning at an acute angle looked ominously familiar. Yes, she'd definitely been down this lane before. Perhaps more than once. A royal mail van idled behind a scrubby hedge, the occupant enjoying a crafty cigarette. Salvation.

Sarah drew level and wound down her window. 'Hi there, I'm looking for the Old Lambing Barn?'

'You the new vicar? Sarah Wilson, The Vicarage, Church Lane, West Tillington?'

'Yes, are you my postman?'

'Aye, Pat Mallard. You've not had much mail, Vicar. Just the one letter, local postmark, quality envelope.'

Postman Pat, he had to be kidding. 'Yes, my parishioner list.

I'm on my way to my first visit.' She had no idea why she was telling him this.

'I hope you've redirected your mail from your previous address, Vicar.'

'No, I never really have much.'

He took a long disapproving draw on his cigarette and stubbed it out on the wing mirror. 'Ardlingly or Winsmoreton?'

'Sorry?'

'There are two Old Lambing Barns.'

'I've no idea.' She showed him her notes.

'It's on my way.' He revved the engine and sped off.

Sarah weighed the risk of a hideous car crash against losing her convoy and floored the accelerator. It was a pinball ride of manure avoidance, swerving fallen branches and dodging cavernous potholes. Eventually, hazard lights flashing, Pat slowed momentarily pointed to a set of stone pillars and accelerated into a bend.

The Old Lambing Barn was beautiful; a solid rectangle of thick stone walls, long-slit windows and lichen-encrusted roof tiles. A glistening brook snaked through the wildflower garden alive with birdsong. Even by West Tillington standards Sarah felt that she'd stepped back in time. She clanged the old bell that hung from a weathered brass hedgehog.

Jean cracked open the door then flung it wide. 'Oh, Vicar, do come in.' She showed small yellowed teeth.

Sarah followed her into a high-ceilinged living room clutching her bible. She shoved it back into her bag; it was probably a bit much. Jean removed her hairnet and turned on the electric fire. The bars crackled alarmingly and released the taint of burning dust.

Sarah settled into the armchair. 'No need on my account, I'm very comfortable.' God, it was a relief to finally be here.

'Are you sure, dear?' Jean peered at the thermostat on the wall. 'Sixteen degrees, you're not meant to let it go below eighteen according to the radio.'

'Honestly, I'm fine.'

Jean poured two shots of what looked like sinister urine samples.

'Limoncello from our last holiday in Amalfi, 2015. We don't get over there anymore, not with my knees.' Jean switched off the fire, its orange glow fading to grey. The comforting aroma of home-cooking replaced the singed dust.

'Betty's watching the soup.'

'So sorry, I didn't know you had guests.' Sarah sipped the liqueur. It was strangely invigorating despite the parochial surroundings.

'Betty lives here.'

'Oh.' Sarah took a moment to process the information. 'So, how have you been?'

'Very well, thank you, Vicar. Would you like to see the cats?'

'Perhaps later, I was wondering if you had anything you wanted to discuss?' She already felt out of her depth. 'Of a pastoral nature.'

'No dear, just shifting the cats!' Jean let out a surprisingly hearty chuckle.

Perhaps living in a rural backwater had eroded her conversational ability or else Alzheimer's had taken a toehold. 'As I said on the phone, the Dean advised that I visit.'

'Is he wanting a cat? He has poodles I believe.'

'No, not that I'm aware.'

'They don't tend to be cat-friendly, poodles.' Jean drained her limoncello. 'Care for a top-up, Vicar?'

'No, I'm driving.'

Betty poked her head around the door. Disembodied from her substantial frame her perm-frizzed hair, rosy cheeks and beady eyes conjured a cabbage patch kid. 'Are you here to see the hedgehogs?'

'No.' Perhaps they were both losing their marbles.

Betty returned to the kitchen from where the *Crime Watch* theme-tune started up.

Jean folded a plaid blanket across her knees. 'Nancy tells me you have an interest in bats. She's so excited to be the trustee of your charity.'

Oh God, she'd had a quiet word with Nancy to secure her retrospective permission but she'd failed to factor in the unnerving rural interconnectedness. 'Yes, I befriended one as a child.' She really needed to work on her backstory.

'How unusual, I can't imagine they're particularly tameable.' The television blared from the kitchen.

Investigations continue into an armed robbery at a branch of NatWest bank in Birmingham. Police are appealing for witnesses.

Shit. Shit. Shit. Okay, everything's fine. Block it out. Nobody saw anything. Nobody knows.

'Are you alright, Vicar?'

'Yes, fine. Thank you.'

'Did you want anything in particular?' Jean looked at her watch. 'It's just that we have online bingo at two. Betty likes her routine.'

'You requested a parishioner visit.'

'No, I don't think so.'

The masked gunmen made off with over five hundred thousand pounds in used notes.

Five hundred and eleven thousand to be precise. Every last note in the vault. Okay, focus on the task in hand.

'It might have been some time ago. I understand Reverend Gooseworthy was somewhat behind.'

'Oh, it must have been last year when my brother passed. I wanted advice about funerals.'

'He must have forgotten to cross you off the list. Did he provide a nice service?'

'We went for a humanist in the end. We're only recent churchgoers. It's more social than anything. Does you good to get out occasionally. No offence, dear.'

Thought to be in their twenties, the men are armed and dangerous and should not be approached.

Maybe they were showing photofit images. No, they wore masks, no one saw their faces.

'Should I take you off the list?'

'Yes, but do pop by anytime, we're practically neighbours.' A small grey cat scaled the back of Jean's chair and landed silently on her lap. 'Careful with my drink, Binky.'

'It took me an hour to get here.'

'Oh, go back on the Borten road. Five minutes tops.'

Perhaps it wasn't an entirely wasted journey; she could

garner some information on the shark.

'You and Betty seem to get on well with Terence Johnson.'

Jean roared with laughter. 'Lord no, entre nous he's a prime snake.'

Blimey, she hadn't been expecting that. 'How so?'

'I shouldn't sully your view of him but tread carefully Vicar he has more than a touch of the malevolent.'

Police are asking for any suspicious cash payments to be reported via Crime Stoppers.

Keep calm. She hadn't made any suspicious cash payments. She'd spent thirty-five pounds at Aldi, the rest was in the mattress. Talk about Terence. 'I notice he sits on both the conservation group and the planning committee. Conflict of interest, one might say.'

'He has his sticky fingers in many pies.' Jean stroked the cat vigorously. 'This is the mother by the way.'

'Sometimes people need to ask questions.'

'Lionel Gooseworthy did. He was a nice man, whatever people say.' Jean opened her purse and pressed a twenty-pound note into Sarah's hand. 'For the bats, dear.'

'No, please I can't accept this.'

'Bingo in ten minutes,' called Betty.

The cat sprang from her lap as Jean rose unsteadily to her feet. 'You might as well see the kittens before you go.'

Sarah left the twenty on the hall table and followed Jean down to the kitchen.

9

Jack suspected that Jesús would have preferred to stay at the vicarage and play with the new kitten but they should give Sarah some space. He limped through the leaf litter releasing the dormant smell of last year's autumn. From a time when he couldn't have imagined he would be jobless and homeless and crippled. Jesús let go of his hand and bent to examine a bracket fungus.

The heavy rucksack awoke the stab in Jack's shoulder. Pain punctuated every step. Bloody. Terence. Bloody. Johnson. Their first camping trip since the 'accident' and he'd forgotten to bring his paracetamol. And his dope. Well, he could survive for twenty-four hours. It was good to be out in the forest.

A break in the canopy revealed a bank of dark clouds rolling in from the north. Damn, he hadn't packed their waterproofs. Or fixed that tear in the tent. Jesús skipped ahead, unburdened by rumination, regrets or camping equipment. Oh man, to be seven again. Although come to think of it, that was the age he'd lost faith in his own father; he wouldn't let that happen to Jesús. The precious little guy was waiting for him beneath a gnarled sycamore.

'How about here, Dad?'

Jack examined the foliage. 'Nice spot but sticky stuff would drop on us.'

'Out of the leaves?'

'No, secretions from aphids.'

'Cool but not cool.' He raced ahead to scout for another location.

The lad's enthusiasm was a tonic. He even liked it at the vicarage. It was the last place he himself would have chosen, but Sol's shepherd's hut was now occupied by a woman he'd met at Treefest and he couldn't face renting a caravan on the soul-sucking holiday site.

Jesús was waiting under a sweet chestnut tree with his arms outstretched. 'Here is perfect.'

'I think you're right.' Jack shrugged off the rucksack and dropped it by the twisted trunk.

'Is it very old?'

'Ancient. If it can avoid being in the way of a road or a railway line it'll be here for another few hundred years.'

'So, it'll still be alive when I'm dead?'

Geez, the boy was dark. 'Why don't you collect some kindling, mate? I'll set up camp.'

It was good to keep Jesús busy; keep him out of his head. God only knew what went on in there. Jack slung the blanket over a fallen bog oak. Maybe he wouldn't mention to Jesús that the log was fossilised, no, he'd focus on things that were living, thriving. Or at least not dead.

The methodical laying out of equipment and counting of poles brought a sense of calm. Erecting a tent with only two fully functioning limbs was a challenge but at least Jesús wouldn't see him struggling. He'd lived on his own long enough to have forgotten what it was like to see yourself through someone else's eyes. Sarah must think he's a total loser. She was nice to talk to; his usual shyness with women had evaporated with her. But she was a vicar so she didn't really count.

Still no sign of Jesús with the kindling. The ground was littered with masses of dry twigs brought down in last year's storms. Where the hell was he?

Jack clicked the last pole into position. 'Jesús, Jesús,' he yelled. A waver in his voice.

Shit, he shouldn't have let him wander off alone. He didn't know this part of the forest. Anything could have happened. It was easy to become disorientated, to panic, to stumble into a mire. To get your skinny leg caught in a snare. To be abducted by fricken perverts. What the hell had he been thinking letting him out of his sight? The crack of wood underfoot. Jack spun round.

There was Jesús trotting through the undergrowth with his arms full of twigs, wild nests of dry moss spilling from every pocket, grinning with pride. The best lad in the world.

The evening held the hush of resting birds. Jack and Jesús sat together on the bog oak which now doubled as a bench and dinner table, and watched the fire lick up the teepee of logs. The clouds had swept south as the sun dropped so there would be no rain. The sky was tinged violet.

Nothing could beat eating hot food in the twilight. It didn't matter that the Quorn sausages had disintegrated in the pan and the potato cakes were charred black. Jack scraped out the last of the baked beans and dropped them into his son's mess can.

'What do you reckon to the vicar then?'

'She's nice.' Jesús chased a piece of squashed sausage with his spork. 'She's just like a normal person.'

'And she pronounces your name right.' It was cool that she hadn't made a big deal out of it like most people.

'Jesus is a major player in church so she'll know the difference.' He stopped pursuing his sausage. 'Is a lady vicar a bit like Jesus's mum?'

'No, not really.'

'You said she'd be banging on about God all the time but she hasn't mentioned him. Not even once.'

Jack took a swig from his bottle of Owd Bull. 'That's true.' She must have sensed his anti-religion vibe. Maybe he should turn it down a bit.

'It was nice that she let me name the kitten. His fur is the exact same pattern as a grey dagger moth. That's why I called him Moth. There's also an actual moth called the puss moth that has very fluffy legs. I'm going to teach him to –'

'Mate, it's just for a little while, right. Until we find somewhere to rent that isn't a shithole.'

'Oh, okay.' Jesús looked at the fire.

The soft call of an owl came from far away. Jack positioned more branches in the fire and poked at the tinder. 'You're right, she's not very vicary, but even so it's best behaviour, yeah?'

'A wasp was doing that half-crawl-half-fly thing up the window this morning. It would've been dead easy to squish it like Mum used to.' Jesús ran his finger around the bottom of his mess can and licked the sauce from his finger. 'Then bam, it stung Sarah right on the head and she said the F word.'

'Oh.'

'I ran at it with my shoe and she said "Hey, don't kill it." I said "Is it because it's one of God's creatures?" And she said "No, it's because they're part of the ecosystem, even if they're total bastards."'

Jack laughed. She was surprising, that was for sure. Pretty too. He pulled out a bag of pink and white marshmallows. It had been hard to source the type that didn't contain horses' hooves but campfires demanded marshmallows. He skewered a couple on a stick and handed it to Jesús. 'We should be tucked up in our tent by ten.'

'Tell me a story.' Jesús dangled the marshmallows over the flames.

The umber of the fire illuminated the crescent of black trees. Sparks spat into the sky.

'A long time ago there was a wicked landowner who exploited his workers.'

'Oh, Dad, not this one again.' He pulled a blackened marshmallow from the stick and stuffed it into his mouth. 'Ow. Hot.' He spat it into his hand.

'No, this is a different one. It's called The Beast of Bradbury Hill.'

'Cool.'

'The workers revolted, they captured the wicked landowner and cut off his head.'

'Wow.' Jesús drew closer and sucked at the marshmallow.

'His fearsome hound hurtled through the blood-soaked forest and scooped up his master's head with its slavering jaws.' Jack loaded more skewers. 'The hound galloped off to the top of Bradbury Hill, the hideous head hanging from its teeth. They buried the headless body in an unmarked grave.'

'What happened to his head?'

Jack slowly turned the spray of marshmallow in the fire.

'Nobody knows.'

'Maybe it is right under our tent,' said Jesús, wide-eyed.

'Strange things started to happen. Wagons overturned, horses spooked and ran away, cattle drowned themselves in the river. The huge black dog stalked the forest.'

Jesús leaned heavily against his arm.

'Finally, the workers trapped and killed the hound. The ghost of the beast still haunts the woods to this day. Ready to carry off your head.'

Jesús looked scared. 'Do you think that's what happened to Ben's dad?'

Maybe he'd gone too far. 'No, mate, it's a made-up story.' He handed him a perfectly toasted skewer. 'Nothing can hurt you in these woods.'

'Dad, if you break a mirror are you in for seven years bad luck?'

'No.' He chewed a marshmallow. 'Superstitions are for people who don't understand cause and effect.'

'That's as long as I've been alive.'

'Did you break a mirror?'

'The one in our new bedroom. It's a crack in the corner so maybe that's one year's worth.'

'Don't worry about possessions they can be replaced. I'll buy her a new one.'

'I'm trying to be on my best behaviour so we can stay. Thinking about the mirror makes me feel sick.'

Jack put his arm around his skinny shoulders. 'Well, that is cause and effect. Try to stop thinking about it.'

Jesús lay warm against his chest. He carried him into the tent and held him until his breathing deepened into sleep.

10

Sarah poured the tea as her guests settled themselves around the kitchen table. It was nice to have company; the vicarage had suddenly felt empty. They were a pretty weird bunch. Eileen's hair was highlighted in a strange turquoise that coordinated with her jacket – apparently Nancy had a diploma in tints and colours from 1984 and had a small but loyal clientele. Betty and Jean wore matching cardigans with a hedgehog motif.

The bone china tea-set, decorated with frolicking farmyard animals, had been ingrained with a layer of sticky dust. Gooseworthy had evidently not been one for home entertaining. But really, what else was there to do here? The last time Sarah had entertained she'd set out a variety pack of craft beers and opened a bag of twiglets. Today she'd Googled 'afternoon tea' and followed the *Good Food Guide* suggestions to the letter. She could do this.

'What a treat.' Betty made a beeline for the brie and cranberry triangles arranged on the three-tiered cake stand.

'Wonderful,' said Eileen, eyeing the scones. 'I must put you on the rota for the coffee morning.'

'I'm not quite up to coffee morning standard.' Her first three attempts now languished in a double bin-liner under the sink.

'Nonsense, these are perfect.'

There was no point prevaricating, she needed information. 'I'm interested to learn more about local history.'

'Carole will be delighted.' Jean piled several strata of crustless sandwiches onto her plate. 'The Civic Society talks aren't well attended.'

'Perhaps you could tell me something of the history of

45

Borten Wood Farm?'

'Oh yes, the farm up at Borten Wood.' Eileen added three sugars to her tea.

'It's always been part of the Borten estate,' said Betty. 'They own most of the land around here, have done for centuries.'

Moth crept from behind the Aga to a chorus of admiration.

'Oh, he looks well,' said Jean, delighted.

'He's made himself quite at home.' Sarah stroked his skinny flank as he slinked passed. 'So where does Terence Johnson fit in?'

'I'm sorry, dear?' Betty looked bewildered.

'Borten Wood Farm?'

'Oh, he won it in a poker game years ago. Twenty acres and the farmhouse.'

'Good grief.'

'Takes a good rent by all accounts,' said Jean. 'Money for nothing, Jack Stretton was a marvel, did all the maintenance.'

'Then why would Terence want to sell it?'

'Good question, he likes playing at being landed gentry.' Jean worked her way through a large scone. 'Collected the rent personally I believe.'

'There's a no-housing covenant on the land, so he won't get a lot for it.' Eileen spoke with evident dislike. 'He's up to something.'

It was odd how they had all fussed over him at the coffee morning.

'We heard that you've rehomed Jack and Jesús. It's very neighbourly of you.' Betty started on the stilton and grape. 'One in the eye for Terence.'

'Charity begins at home,' said Sarah. Especially when you're backed into a corner and didn't know what the hell you were signing up for.

'You would have liked Sofía, Jesús's mum, a little crazy but aren't we all?' said Betty.

'Was she a local woman?'

'No, Mexican, from the place the tiny dogs come from.' Betty stopped to search for the name that never came. 'They met when Jack was in Central America. What's that called when you walk around with a pack on your back?'

'Backpacking,' said Eileen. 'He was helping with the tequila bat project I believe.'

'Impressive.' Sarah imagined him knocking back shots in a taberna, swaying in time to a mariachi band. Suntanned and gorgeous in an open-necked linen shirt. God, get a grip.

'I hear you have a special interest in bat conservation.' Eileen fished in her in handbag and brought out a cheque book. 'I'd like to donate.'

'Please, there's absolutely no need, honestly the money's pouring in.'

'It would help to assuage my guilt. I once sprayed a pipistrelle with L'Oréal extra firm hold.'

'You killed a bat with hairspray?'

'Poor creature survived but was rather disorientated. Middle of the night, I thought it was an intruder, grabbed the first thing to hand. Stiff as a board it was. I revived it with a damp flannel.' She wrote a cheque for fifty pounds.

Sarah took it graciously. She could destroy it later.

'Delicious scones, what's your secret ingredient?' asked Jean, a globule of cream on her lower lip.

'A healthy glug of Pimm's.'

'Oh dear.' Eileen spat hers into a paper napkin. 'I'm afraid I'll have to pass. I had a little trouble with the sauce. Haven't touched a drop since 1995.'

'So sorry, I didn't realise.'

'No reason you should, dear. I'm pleased I don't look like an ex-alcoholic.'

Betty rubbed her friend's arm. 'Of course you don't, love. Anyway, pass it over, waste not want not.'

Sarah replenished the cake-stand with fairy cakes. 'Jesús's favourite.'

'It's so kind of you to take them in.'

'I'm sure the vicarage has always been a place of safety,' said Sarah.

The guests exchanged glances.

'It seems that you haven't been apprised of the Reverend Gooseworthy situation.' Betty's expression lay somewhere between surprised and not surprised at all. 'I don't wish to speak ill of your predecessor but it doesn't seem fair that you've been kept in the dark, dear.' She glanced around warily. 'Especially as it happened here.'

'What happened here?'

'Lionel was always an odd fish, but Judge not as he would say.' Jean took Betty's hand.

Sarah was unsure whether the 'he' had a capital letter.

'You must come and visit me at Vespiary cottage and bring Jesús, he and Ben are great friends.' Eileen took a fairy cake. 'It's lovely now with the daffodils out. I'm half way up Bradbury Hill.' She gestured a steep incline.

'You don't mind being so remote?'

'Not at all, it's safer than being in a town with bank robbers and such.'

Talons gripped Sarah's gut and held tight. A swell of acid pumped to her throat. Focus on the kitten. Look at its soft fur. The sheen of its silky body. Its slowly blinking eyes. She took a sip of tea. Say something. Anything.

'How do you find looking after your grandson?'

'He's good company. I've lived alone for years. Father moved in when I was on two bottles of Pernod a day. Said he'd stay until I was sober. That was some incentive to get off the sauce, I can tell you.' Eileen's laugh showed her horse's teeth to full effect.

Sarah recovered herself. She tried to picture this docile elderly woman swigging from a bottle of Pernod. She could not. The conversation had veered away from Lionel Gooseworthy.

'Would you like to remain on the parishioner visit list by the way?'

'No need dear. Anyway, we're glad he didn't visit.' Betty shuddered, stirred her tea and took a steadying sip.

'So, the Reverend did something pretty bad?'

The door chime was followed by an unnecessary rapping of the brass knocker. Damn.

Sarah returned with Carole Adlington-Wyndham holding a large boiled ham.

'I didn't realise that you had guests.' Carole nodded a curt acknowledgement. 'I thought I'd fill you in on the fascinating talk that you missed.' She looked pointedly at the cakes and at the empty chair.

'Thanks.' Sarah took the meat. 'You must have forgotten I'm vegetarian but I'm sure the food bank would love it.'

Carole relinquished the ham reluctantly. 'It's one of Ted's finest.'

'Sarah has been fully updated on the joys of eighteenth-century farm machinery.' Betty winked at her as Carole settled at the head of the table and waited to be served.

'Didn't you spot our car in the drive? The big green thing next to the front door.'

Carole ignored Jean and glanced critically around the kitchen, her mouth a drawstring purse. 'Lionel wasn't one for domestic duties. Busy with other things.'

'Ted supplied him, didn't he?' asked Eileen pointedly.

'How are your houseguests settling in, Sarah? Must be such a burden especially when you've just moved in yourself.'

'Very well.'

'Imagine a Jesus living at the vicarage!' Carole looked delighted with herself.

'It's pronounced Hay-sous.' Sarah poured Carole a stewed tea.

'I stand corrected. Terrible shame about the mother. Suicide is such a selfish act.'

Blimey, another revelation that no one had mentioned.

'The poor boy being raised by a homeless single parent who appears hardly able to look after himself.'

'Jack's doing a very good job.' Sarah bristled. 'They'd been at Borten Wood Farm for years I understand.'

'I hardly know the man. He doesn't attend any civic events and Ted has never seen him in the shop. We suspect a vegetarian.' Carole pulled her pashmina tight. 'And I do wish he'd cut his hair it's very unmanly.'

Sarah gestured to the picture of Christ holding out his arms above the sink. 'I think Our Lord might disagree.'

The silence that followed held the delight of suppressed laughter.

'Do you know why Terence evicted him?' Sarah tried to sound casual.

'Terence is a businessman. Business is business. Anyway ladies, I wanted to inform you that the fabrics for the

Civic Society makeover have been ordered.' Carole's audacious change of subject suggested knowledge, if not complicity.

'I thought the allocation of funds was a mandatory voting decision,' said Jean crisply.

'As the meetings are moving temporarily to The Grange the constitution rules do not apply.'

Sarah stared in disbelief. Public funds were going to refurbish Carole's living room. How the hell was she getting away with this?

An outburst of chimes and church bells erupted. 'Goodness, is that the time? We must be going.' Jean was evidently livid.

Sarah walked them to the door. Masked by the general hubbub of collecting coats and retrieving handbags Betty hugged her and whispered three shocking bullet points. 'Reverend Gooseworthy. Offences against piglets. Terence turned him in.'

11

The camping trip had been fun but it was back to school tomorrow so Jesús had to have a bath. He had to be as brave as a goat. He poured a glug of Sarah's passionfruit bath gel under the running tap and watched the foam cloud rise. It smelt like you could eat it. Even with both taps full blast the water crept slowly up the giant slipper bath. Dad took showers but Jesús didn't like them because you could slip over and hurt yourself quite badly. He'd always enjoyed bath-time until Mum had ruined it. Now he couldn't splash about like a dolphin, bob like a seal, or float like a basking shark without her turning up and freakinthebejesus out of him. Maybe it would be okay here. No one had suicided in this bath as far as he knew.

There wasn't much to do in the bathroom. The little mirrored cabinet just had plasters and cotton buds and those pills that stop ladies having babies. It would've been nice to have had a little brother or sister to muck about with but his mum didn't need another parásito. It looked like Sarah didn't want babies either, although it wasn't her name on the label. Ms Jess Walters must have lived here before and forgot to pack her pills.

The big weighing scale looked ancient. The pointer zoomed around crazily before settling on forty-one pounds and three ounces. The school nurse had said he was underweight and his dad had said bollocks-to-that.

Jesús dipped his hand in the water. It was lukewarm, not nice. He turned off the cold tap. The smooth feel of the white floor tiles under his feet was comforting. If Sarah had a lipstick, he could've drawn out a hopscotch grid but she wasn't the type to wear makeup. She was really pretty anyway. Out on the landing he could hear Dad and Sarah chatting away downstairs. It was nice. They were discussing who was the better songwriter; Leonard Cohen or Nick Cave. Jesús didn't really like either. He would have voted for Adele.

The bath was still only half full but he couldn't wait any longer. He stepped in and slid down into the bubbles. The temperature was just the wrong side of nearly right. It didn't really feel like being in a slipper. More like a giant gravy boat. That was the silver thing they had on the table now that they were living in a posh vicarage, although Sarah put tomato ketchup in it because they were all vegetarians and didn't bother much with gravy. He closed his eyes and pretended he was a chip covered in tomato sauce.

Mum lay dead beneath the surface. Her face a shocking white in the red water. Her long black hair floating like seaweed. Mouth open. Eyes open. Neck open like a second mouth.

Jesús leapt out, cascading water onto the bathmat and curled up tight like a hedgehog until Mum disappeared. He hugged the big towel around his body to stop the weird shaky thing. Mum had followed him here. Not fair. He was being haunted. Only bad people got haunted. To teach them a lesson, for example Ebenezer Scrooge. Jesús must have done something really bad but he couldn't remember what.

Monday morning, the first lesson was usually English but a very big police officer was standing in front of the white board and he didn't look like he was getting ready to talk about adjectives. The class hushed. Miss Bickerstool clasped her hands together all excited and smiley so they knew they hadn't done anything wrong. Jesús and Ben sat at the front with horrible Craig who'd been separated from his mate Barry for being a 'disruptive influence.' The policeman stroked his enormous beard as if it was his favourite pet. He smelled a bit funny.

'Good morning children,' said Miss Bickerstool.

'Good mor-ning, Miss-Bick-er-stool,' they sang.

'Now, we are very lucky to have Constable Keith Dweller with us this morning and he is going to tell us some very important things about how to keep ourselves safe.'

'My uncle,' said Marky, all boasty.

Horrible Craig made a snuffling noise like a pig, someone sniggered from the back – probably Barry.

'Right, let's get started.' Constable Dweller surveyed them as if they were alien lifeforms. 'Who's heard of Stranger Danger?'

Jesús had but he didn't want to put his hand up in case he got it wrong – the copper looked pretty scary. It was something to do with not taking sweets from strangers. Not that any strangers ever offered him any sweets. There was that one time on a bus when an old lady gave him a bag of mini chocolate buttons and Dad said that was fine and to say Thank you very much. Mr Johnson gave him sweets but he wasn't a stranger.

The policeman pointed to Katy who was waving her arm like mad. 'Don't go home with a stranger because they could be a peedo.'

'Exactly right, spot on,' said Constable Dweller. 'There are lots of people who want to hurt children and they don't all look dangerous, so you need to treat everyone as a potential danger.'

Miss Bickerstool stopped smiling. 'Perhaps don't frighten them too much,' she whispered.

'Better safe than sorry,' boomed Dweller. He wasn't using his inside voice. 'Unfortunately, we see the reality of stranger danger every single day. Well, not every day but a couple of times a year. It does happen boys and girls, so be vigilant.'

'What are they talking about?' Ben asked Jesús.

'No idea, mate.'

'I'm talking about people touching you in inappropriate places.'

'Like in Tesco's car park?' said Katy.

Miss Bickerstool had gone very pale. She rifled through her handbag. She shrieked and threw it to the floor.

'Everything alright, ma'am?'

She held up her lace hanky. A large black slug clung to it. 'Who did this?'

Gasps. Giggles. Nobody said anything.

'It's left a horrible slimy trail all over my personal belongings.' She waved the slug in evidence. 'Do you think this is funny? DO YOU?'

Jesús looked at the floor. Probably everyone else was too. You're not meant to answer that sort of question because it was just to make a point. That sort of question had a special name but he couldn't remember it. Now wasn't the time to ask. Miss Bickerstool held the slug at arm's length and dropped it theatrically out of the window. The poor thing would not like it out there by the bins. He'd go and find it at break and carry it to a place of safety. Maybe the big nettle patch by the bike shed where they threw Donny that time when he wouldn't share his Monster Munch.

'Perhaps you could move on? said Miss Bickerstool crisply.

Constable Dweller looked at his notes. 'Alright, kids, what is the thing to do if people make you feel uncomfortable?'

'Tell them to back off,' called a boy from the corner.

'Push them,' shouted another.

Miss Bickerstool was looking twitchy again. She coughed and looked at her watch.

Constable Dweller wrote on the white board in very scrawly handwriting: 'If someone is making you feel uncomfortable...' he paused for a long time and added the three things to do.

Tell them that you don't like it.

Tell them to stop doing it.

Tell an adult what happened.

The sound of tapping, shuffling and whispering indicated that Year Three had reached the limit of its attention span.

'Right. Who wants to put the blue light on in my police car?'

Everyone shot their hands up.

'You, you, you and you.' Dweller pointed at Jesús, Ben, Marky and Katy.

The class moaned as the chosen ones stood up. It wasn't really fair to pick Marky – he could put the nee-naw on any time he wanted.

'He only chose you because you're a charity case,' hissed Marky.

They trailed out into the car park and took it in turns to press the siren and pretend to speed away to catch the baddies. It was pretty good fun. When it was time for him to go, Constable Dweller ruffled Jesús's hair which made him feel very uncomfortable but he didn't say anything.

Back in the classroom it was hard to settle. Everyone was overexcited from hearing the siren. Miss Bickerstool said that they could spend the rest of the lesson drawing a picture of what they had learned. Then she changed her mind and said to just draw anything that made them happy.

Jesús drew a picture of himself, Dad, Sarah and Moth watching *Blue Planet.*

Ben made Jesús a card. On the front he wrote Welcome to your New Home, in his best handwriting and drew a church, a shining sun and some day-flying moths. 'I was going to draw a goat, probably Adele, but I thought it might upset you.'

'It wouldn't have but it's a nice thought.'

Jesús slipped it into his blazer pocket. Oh no, he still had the special letter for Sarah. Pat the postman asked him to sign for it because she was still in bed. It was cool because it had an Irish stamp. He tore it open without thinking. Very weird; inside the letter was another envelope. Like those Russian dolls. It was addressed to Mr and Mrs Wilson, Il Mulino, Via del Mulino, San Gimignano, Italy. They must be Sarah's mum and dad. He put it back in the envelope and stuck it down with Sellotape. It didn't look too bad.

12

Piglets. Sarah reeled. Sweet little piglets. It was sickening. She knew exactly where the offences had taken place. Jesús was going straight to a sleepover at Ben's and Jack was visiting friends in Lingen field. Perhaps it was the crime-scene room that was driving them out.

Sarah braced herself outside the door and made a dash for the window pushing it wide open. A gust of purging wind rattled the ornaments. Who was she kidding? This called for more than fresh air – it practically required an exorcism. The grim furniture cast porcine shadows. The thick velvet curtains had absorbed the pungent odour of distressed piglet and clung tenaciously to their evidence. She unhooked them and folded them into flat carcasses. The stained carpet would also have to go.

Jesús had arranged a line of sea animals along the shelf; octopus, shark, turtle, stingray, four different whales. The orange patterned skull money box looked traditional Mexican. Maybe a birthday present from his mother. It was empty, of course he'd have to smash it to get the money out. She cleared everything into a cardboard box.

From the window Sarah watched Ernest forking tangles of dry bindweed onto the bonfire. His gardening; pollarding, strimming and cutting back, seemed to be a constant battle against encroachment. She dragged the curtains downstairs and hauled them onto the smouldering fire. Ernest made no comment. They stood and watched the flames etch their way across the musty fabric. To what unthinkable atrocities had they borne witness? Thankfully Ernest still had nothing to say.

'I wonder if you could give me a hand with some

redecorating when you're finished here?'

He nodded his assent.

Sarah returned to the house and entered the back bedroom. All her worldly goods fitted into the small room; the loaded mattress and a tower of packing boxes unhelpfully labelled 'Miscellaneous but useful'. Several pots of unopened paint and the dust sheets from her abandoned bedsit project were, inevitably, in the last box that she opened. The mustard walls would require two coats of Smooth Hound – the B&Q alternative to Farrow and Ball's prohibitively priced Pale Hound.

Sarah exhumed her mother's curtain collection and held up each in turn. The William Morris *Strawberry thief* would be perfect. She recalled her mother's excitement when she hung them in the living room, the sunlight illuminating the larcenous thrushes. She'd seen them on a home improvement show and had saved up for months. 'They'll see me out,' she'd said in justification of the expense. An accurate pronouncement as it turned out – she was dead within the year. Their faded perfume sent Sarah reeling back to her childhood home. They'd been happy there, mostly. She had been an angelic child who transformed into a feral adolescent before taking a sharp turn into a feisty young woman. But through all those changes she had remained true to herself. Trustworthy. Moral. Ethical. That is what she had lost. Her mother would be appalled at what she had done. One day, one hour, that overshadowed everything that came before. Anyone would have done the same given the circumstances. How many times would she tell herself that? Would she ever believe it?

Sarah carried the curtains through to the bedroom where Ernest stood silent in the middle of the room; a bemused Frankenstein's monster.

'How's Nancy?' Her chirpy voice.

He shouldered the wardrobe away from the wall and paused to think. 'She's okay.'

'I hear she's a very diligent treasurer for the Civic Society.'

Ernest manoeuvred the wardrobe through the door. The turn-taking of conversation eluded him.

'Maybe she could present the accounts at the next meeting?'

'Maybe.' The whistling through his nose was off-putting.

'I understand she used to clean for Lionel.' The irony of using Nancy's name to launder the money had not escaped her.

He rear-ended the beds. 'A while since.' A yellow JCB digger and a pink tutu lay in the dust beneath Jesús's bed.

Sarah sponged the walls with sugar-soap. It was rather therapeutic. Ernest continued his work without comment, expertly navigating the rest of the furniture through the door then returning to stand silent in the corner. He was a helpful man, if a little unnerving.

'What did you make of Lionel Gooseworthy?' she asked.

Ernest turned to the task of ripping up the carpet, which required his undivided attention. Perhaps the reason for the reticence to speak about her predecessor was a shared shame that this could have happened in their community, in their vicarage. She could see no other reason for continuing to cover for the abominable Reverend.

Ernest examined the floor boards. 'Not everything's as it seems.' He spat on the floor and rubbed it with his finger.

'In what way?'

He kept his eyes lowered. 'There are many vices in the world.'

Sarah recognised the lines from Corinthians' – she'd been looking for quotes for her sermon on inclusivity. There were actually some pretty cool messages in the bible but most had been misinterpreted. She was pretty sure it was voices not vices but she didn't correct him. 'That's true.'

'I've got rent to meet. Needs must.' He stood up and wiped the dust from his hands. 'Oak,' he announced. 'I'll need my sander.'

Sarah stood in the doorway, hands on hips and admired the transformation. Ernest had varnished the floorboards beautifully and left them to dry overnight. The crisp walls off-set the indigo curtains and brought out the warmth of the stunning floor. The furniture was now painted a soft white and the fussy table lamps ditched for moon globe nightlights, delivered courtesy of Amazon Prime. Jesús's sea creature collection and orange skull looked great on the white shelf. It was the nicest room in the house.

But the curtains hung like an albatross of memories around her neck. Why had she lugged the box of her mother's belongings all the way to West Tillington?

She knew why. The Victorian terrace in Arden Row had been her home for over twenty years. The two-up two-down adjoining the playing fields had been offered at a bargain price in Thatcher's sell off. Her mother had declined on moral grounds. She told her then six-year-old daughter that the policy would be the death of council housing. 'A Trojan bloody horse!' she would yell at the television and she, unable to see any horses, worried for her mother's sanity. Later of course, she agreed with her mother's decision to shun the Right to Buy debacle but it led to her own unceremonious eviction. When her mother died the council acted with unseemly haste. She inherited seven George Michael CDs, a collection of porcelain whippets and a hundred pounds worth of premium bonds. She took the curtains.

By the time Jack and Jesús returned Sarah had changed out of her paint-splattered clothes and was lying on the sofa reading *Vernon God Little*.

'Hard at work I see.' Jack smiled.

'Homework.' She brandished the book. 'How was the sleepover?'

'We saw bats in the garden and I helped to cook dinner.' Jesús looked exhausted and rather grubby.

'I'd keep that quiet, mate, or you'll be consigned to the kitchen.'

'Eileen says "Hi" and gave me some gooseberry jam for you.' Jesús scanned the living room distracted. 'Where's Moth?'

'Last seen hurtling upstairs. Why don't you take your stuff through to your bedroom and we'll have a drink?'

Jesús dashed off. Jack threw himself into the armchair by the window. 'Thanks Vic, a beer would be lovely.'

'You know where the kitchen is.' She opened her book.

Jack returned with two beers and an elderflower cordial. 'Sorry. Cheers.' He clinked his glass against hers. 'And a little treat for later.' He produced a bottle of tequila from his rucksack. 'I'll make you one of my famous sunrises.'

Jesús raced into the living room and skidded to a halt, his eyes shining. 'Our room has been replaced by a better one! Come and look.'

Jack made a quizzical face and allowed Jesús to pull him to his feet. 'Okay, mate, lead the way.'

Sarah finished her beer and stared out of the window. They were taking a worryingly long time. Maybe Jack was annoyed that she'd been in their room and had moved their possessions. She should have waited and asked them. Impulsivity was a bitch. Still, she'd made worse decisions.

Finally, they appeared at the door. Jack approached, put his arms around her and hugged her very tightly. She could smell the warm draw of cannabis in his hair. Jesús ran forward and embraced her leg. It was the longest hug she had ever had.

13

The club bar at Lingsford Downs golf course was dark and cheerless. Jack leant against the patterned wallpaper and polished a wine glass. The same one he'd been polishing for the last five minutes. Why the hell had he opened a bottle of tequila the evening before starting a new job? Well, he hadn't expected to finish it. Sarah was a constant surprise. The wall clock seemed not to be ticking. Ten pounds per hour. Twelve noon. He hadn't even earned the price of his mandatory white shirt. It was costing his soul but he was going to pay Sarah for board and lodgings even though she said not to worry.

Joe was cool but there was barely enough work for him let alone a deputy barman. The plan was to get on the payroll, then request a move to green maintenance but it'd be a long wait. He could die of boredom before then.

Joe predicted it would get busier if the rain held off; the big guns favoured Fridays for networking on the links. Then there were the fair-weather golfers, not to mention the new ladies enjoying the recently bestowed privilege of partial membership. The club represented everything Jack despised. He was just going to have to suck it up and think of payday.

A frazzled woman in a blue tabard was making heavy work of vacuuming the green flecked carpet. She banged the brush head against the baseboards as if exacting some terrible revenge. Jack gave her a nod and she returned a tired smile. The door swung wide and in strode a portly man in a Pringle golf jumper and mustard trousers. Shit. Terence Johnson.

Jack ducked behind the bar, crawled over to Joe and tugged at his trouser leg. 'Can you serve him,' he mouthed.

'What can I get you sir?' Joe asked above the thrum of the

Hoover.

'Let me think, a white-wine spritzer perhaps, no wait, a fruity Malbec, or maybe a cheeky little Glenfiddich might hit the spot.'

Joe's foot tapped in irritation.

Jack inched towards the mixer crates where he had a clear view of the entrance. An imposing guy with a military gait led a small group who sauntered through patting each other on the back. The vacuum cleaner fell silent. Soft jazz arose once more from the speakers.

Joe abandoned the prevaricating Terence and straightened his tie. 'What can I get for you, gentleman?'

'Four black coffees, four whiskey chasers please, Joseph.'

'Certainly.' He set immediately to his task. Jack kept flat against the crates.

'Make that five.' Terence addressed Joe's back. 'On me gentlemen.' The creep was here to do some schmoozing.

'Very decent of you. Have we met?' The trumpeting of a nose being vigorously blown.

'Several times, Chief Constable Jericho. I'm Terence Johnson, head honcho at the Council.'

'Oh, I don't usually forget a face.' The copper mustn't have seen Johnson since his nose-job. It had morphed from pendulous to Michael Jackson.

'Good round, Chief Constable?'

'Julian, please. Robbed on the eighteenth, four under par.'

'A brave man who'd rob a Chief Constable!' The remark elicited a ripple of ironic laughter.

'And how did you fare, Terence?'

A general hubbub arose from the men who had not been introduced.

'I haven't ventured out yet. Just popped in for a snifter.' As predicted. He probably didn't even own clubs.

Joe set eight drinks on a round tray and left Terence's on the bar. 'Shall I take these to your table, sir?'

'Yes, the bay window if you will. Cheers, Terence. Enjoy your game.'

'Oh, before you go, any news on Melville Russet?'

Jack cocked his head and strained to hear over the growing

banter above him.

'What is your view, councillor?' said the copper through a mouthful of bar-nuts.

'He was taking the desertion by his wife very hard. And of course, the burden of being a single father must have been onerous, I imagine little Ben was a handful.' A ricochet of laughter competed with Terence's opinion. '… my money is on suicide.'

'I'm not a betting man, councillor. Also, we're investigating a disappearance not a death.'

Jack slid along the floor keeping close to the bar. The plod's companions had moved off to their table.

'Of course, but as time goes on one would have to assume – '

'We deal only in facts.' Julian sounded stern. 'Actually, he had a lot to live for, his boy, his business, a remarkably robust bank balance.'

'The council is very keen to help in any way.'

'We have adequate resources, thank you.' Curt now.

'I do have some good news. We've organised a substantial donation to the Constabulary Benevolent Fund.' Smarmy git.

'Very kind.' The copper's voice more distant now. Must be walking away. The remark sounded sarcastic. His following inaudible wisecrack elicited loud laughter from the bay window.

Terence's phone pinged. 'The bill, please,' he said coldly.

He paid and left.

Jack unfolded himself from between the barrels. 'Nice one, mate. I owe you.'

'The man's a puffed-up prat.' Joe counted the money. 'No tip. Mind you forty-five quid and he didn't even touch his coffee. Do you want to drink it?'

'No thanks, mate, I think I'll have a whiskey.'

14

U n-bloody-believable. Sarah turned up Apocalyptica's Worlds Collide and ironed her primrose yellow blouse as if tanning a carcass. She'd been summoned to see the Dean. Three weeks in. There had been 'concerns'.

Being the Reverend Sarah Wilson was not getting any easier. She inserted her dog-collar and resolved to listen attentively to the evidence, nod humbly and apologise for whatever purported misdemeanour she'd committed. As long as it wasn't the cash donations pouring into the bat charity she could wing it.

The letter from Ireland had also unnerved Sarah. She'd told her it was a bad idea; they needed to leave no trace between them. But Sarah had softened and finally acquiesced – relentless crying will do that. They'd agreed to one letter per month, special delivery, and she would send the enclosed letter on to Italy from West Tillington. It was relatively risk-free. Of course, they hadn't factored in an omniscient bloody postman.

The Clio was shiny for the first time in years; cleanliness is next to Godliness. Sarah crawled down the long driveway to the Deanery to allow time for her transformation into a beacon of calm and reverence. The ivy-covered mansion stood behind an enormous leylandii hedge. To the left an ornamental lake glistened between water lilies, to the right a regimented soft-fruit orchard was coming into leaf.

Sarah slammed on the brakes.

What the hell? A huge blue bird strutted in front of the car, its tail dragging behind it and disappeared behind the parked Daimler. A peacock, are you kidding? She pulled up beside the pristine lawn set with white hoops. Oh Christ, her curriculum vitae.

Geoffrey Tibble skipped down the stone steps, a large wooden box in one hand, a croquet mallet in the other. 'Sarah, old girl, welcome to my humble abode.'

'Lovely lawns, Dean.'

'Aside from a touch of plantain and a little adverse camber on the near-side hoop it is indeed a fine lawn.'

Sarah made a mental note to Google how to play croquet.

'We are looking forward to you joining our circle. I'm afraid the standard might be rather low for you.'

'I'm really a novice.' She matched his cut glass accent.

'Nonsense, I heard from the clerical panel that you were tournament standard. Probably what landed you the post!' He released his camel laugh. 'Care for a game?'

'I'm afraid I need to be back by three. I have a hymn book delivery.' God, she really needed to work on her apologies.

'Next time then. Bring your mallet.'

The Dean seemed to be very genial for a man who was about to dispense censure. He led her into the panelled entrance hall and through to the drawing room. It revealed a panoramic view of a yew maze and yet another lake. Three apricot poodles sprang from the antique leather sofa.

'Settle down boys, friend not foe!' He lowered himself into a wing-backed chair, retrieved a stubby pipe and tamped down a generous pinch of Golden Virginia ready rubbed. 'Don't mind if I puff on the old nose-warmer do you?'

'Not at all.' She took a chair embroidered with an ancient hunting scene. A poodle flopped onto her lap – it smelt vaguely of Pedigree Chum. 'Nice lake.'

'I keep ornamental fish.'

'Koi carp?'

'No, actually they're quite outgoing.' Geoffrey roared his camel laugh. He was a difficult man to read.

'The maze looks wonderful.' She sounded such a sycophant but he was lapping it up.

'Ah yes, Ernest is a marvel.'

'He seems to work for everyone.' The poodle gave her neck an enthusiastic lick.

'I'll cut to the chase, old girl. It seems that the contents of your recycling bin have not gone unnoticed.'

What the hell? She tilted her head in what she hoped was a receptive rather than sarcastic manner. 'Really?' she managed.

'Rum and tequila bottles and an impressive collection of beer cans I believe.'

Jesus Christ, someone had been rooting through her bins. 'Oh yes, all recyclable.' She smiled. The poodle wriggled onto its back exposing its pale underbelly which she stroked gently.

'I fear that it's the quantity, not the ecological impact, that is of concern.' He drew vigorously on his pipe and spent several minutes relighting it.

Must be bloody Carole Adlington-Wyndham. 'I do of course have a houseguest.'

'Ah, yes, yes. Jack, the goat-man. Bit of a drinker is he? Can't say I blame him.'

'Just the recommended daily limit I believe.' Another poodle leapt onto her lap and jostled for position.

'Jolly good. Now, what else?' He frowned into the middle distance. 'Oh yes, I understand there have been reports of behaviour unbecoming to public office.'

God, what on earth was this? Could support for a bat charity be considered too left field for a vicar? 'Go on.'

'It is alleged that you were talking to the sexton in your nightwear.'

Good grief, not only had Carole rooted through her bins but she must have binoculars trained on her garden. 'Ernest and I were having a discussion about God's creatures.'

Geoffrey inhaled vigorously and released a series of unexpected smoke rings. 'I'm sure there was nothing improper vis-à-vis extra curricula liaison. Appearances, dear thing, appearances.' He examined his pipe, apparently trying to summon the next point.

The third poodle hurled itself onto the sleeping pair provoking a competitive spate of jostling before they settled into a Jenga of furry bodies. The gaseous odour of undigested dog food arose from her lap.

Geoffrey's grimace indicated that he'd recalled the issue and it was causing him some discomfort. 'And lastly, concerns regarding, shall we say, well, the acceptance of sexual deviance.'

What the hell was this? She stroked the poodles and tried to recall making any remotely offensive comments. Perhaps she had inadvertently said something in support of Lionel Gooseworthy before she knew of his offence? 'Could you elucidate, Dean?'

He struggled to position the arms of his round spectacles behind his ears. They were so clouded with finger prints it was unlikely they would enhance his vision. He thumbed through a thin leather-bound notebook, squinting at every page.

'Ah, here we are: *God loves everyone regardless of how they forage, whether their coat is straight or curly and whether their tail points up or down.*'

Her very first sermon. 'But that is correct, Dean, is it not?' Her finest plummy accent with a hint of confusion.

'Oh, quite so. I fear it is more the sexual implication that gave offence.'

'I was not endorsing the behaviour of Lionel Gooseworthy.'

'That was not the nature of the complaint, but yes, it is a rather unfortunate metaphor in the circumstances. No, the parishioner in question was concerned that the message endorsed alternatives to heterosexuality.'

Jesus Christ, she was not going to let this one slide. 'As I am sure you know, Dean the parable references our Lord's unconditional love. The message is tolerance.'

'Indeed. Sadly, West Tillington is not known for its embracing of the LGBTQ+ community. Best it remains behind closed doors as it were.' He gave her a conspiratorial wink.

'I'm afraid that I disagree, the church should be setting an example should it not?' A glimmer of her real self. She liked it. 'Perhaps it is Carole, sorry, the parishioner to whom you should be speaking?'

'Let's not upset the apple cart, old girl. Probationary period. Friends in high places and all that.'

'I would have thought that our friend was in the highest place of all.'

'Ha. Very drôle, dear girl.'

'So, empty bottles, a nightie and an inclusive sermon.' She struck the perfect note of hurt indignation. 'It hardly competes with piglet abuse, Dean.'

The poodles looked up in shock.

Geoffrey removed his glasses and pressed the bridge of his nose. 'That was indeed a very dark day for the diocese. But all the more reason to set an impeccable example.'

'I think we need to hold our ground on inclusivity, Dean.'

'Ah yes, perhaps you are right.' He took a long draw on his pipe and released a perfect smoke ring.

'I will do my utmost not to cause any offence.' She produced her most beatific smile. 'But I will not pander to prejudice.'

'Quite. Well now, perhaps we could schedule a game? I'll get a four together. How about next Thursday?'

Damn, she could summon no reasonable excuse. 'I'd be delighted.'

The poodles accompanied her out, their tails wagging. Geoffrey waved as he closed the door.

What on earth had that been about? A caution of sorts, albeit a toothless one. A friendly warning shot? At least the Dean was a man who could be easily swayed; it had been surprisingly easy to dodge the bullets. Now she had a week to learn croquet to tournament standard.

The peacock was launching a full-scale attack on her car. It flapped its ridiculous wings in vertical take-off and drew its claws down the shiny door of the Clio. She ran at it waving her arms. It retreated to its spot behind the Daimler. What the hell was it with birds attacking their reflections? Although her own reflection currently elicited a hostile response when it caught her off guard.

A Land Rover careered past throwing up a cloud of dust; Terence Johnson raised a hand in greeting or apology. In the passenger seat sat a flushed-faced Carole Adlington-Wyndham. She was holding a croquet mallet.

15

Jesús touched on his bedside moon lamp.

Oh no. That's why he'd woken up. A warm dampness clung to his pyjamas – he'd wet the bed like a little kid. An adult would probably say that he wet the bed because he'd had a trauma but it was probably because of the three cartons of Ribena and the hot chocolate he'd had before bed.

Although, maybe it was because he'd been worrying about Dad dying. When you only have one parent you don't have a spare. Dad said he was like a cat with nine lives but Jesús calculated he'd already used up five. Six if you count the deer. And he was only thirty-four. If they were God botherers he could've asked God to keep Dad safe but they weren't so he'd asked Sarah instead. She said she'd light a candle in church. She'd looked a bit teary so she must be worried too.

Laughter came from downstairs. Dad and Sarah were either telling each other jokes, or smoking Dad's happy tobacco that Jesús couldn't tell people about, or maybe both. He struggled out of his pyjamas and pulled off the sheet. Ew, the mattress was soaked. At least the duvet was dry.

Jesús bundled the washing into the bath, squirted in a load of shampoo and ran the shower. He got in too. Standing on the sheet stopped him from slipping. Mum wasn't in the bath this time; she probably didn't want to be in with smelly washing. It was fun treading up and down like those people who trample grapes in films about Italy. And it smelled nice now, like flowers. He turned the shower off.

More laughter from downstairs. Sarah was hilarious. When he'd told her what he'd learnt from his library book *How to care for your kitten* she said he was an expert in animal husbandry which meant looking after animals not marrying them. Dad never laughed with Mum. Perhaps they did before he was born. Jesús had probably ruined everything. Maybe that was why he was being haunted. After Mum died Dad said 'It's just you and me now kid.' But he didn't mind sharing him with Sarah. Jesús squeezed and twisted the sheet and pyjamas until his arms hurt but they were still wet. He hung them over the radiator.

Perhaps he could swap his mattress for the one that was leaning up against the wall in the back bedroom? He crept across the hallway and cracked open the door. Moth dashed through quick as a fox. Oh no, Moth wasn't allowed in there. Actually, he wasn't either, and now Moth was crawling into a hole in the mattress. He was a naughty rascal.

Jesús crouched down, shoved his arm inside the mattress and felt around for something furry. No, nothing but slippery paper. He didn't know that mattresses were stuffed with paper; it must be a budget one. He wiggled his arm further in. Still nothing that felt like Moth and now his shoulder was wedged so tight into the hole that he couldn't get it out. It was cold in here, probably because he didn't have any clothes on. Perhaps if he shuffled backwards he could pull the mattress with him and drag it over to his bedroom.

Argh. Ow.

Now the mattress was lying on top of him and it was really heavy. Moth yowled from deep inside. He could feel him with his fingertips but he couldn't move. Moth was scrabbling and screaming like a trapped badger. Footsteps on the stairs. Clop, clop, clop.

'Oh Christ.' Dad dashed in. 'Don't move.' He tore the hole wide open and heaved the mattress off him.

'Thanks.' Jesús rubbed his arm. It was very red.

'What's going on?'

'Moth got stuck.'

A floss of grey fur appeared through the hole and Moth emerged wild-eyed and hissy with a fifty-pound note speared in his claws. A pile of fifties slid out after him.

'Whoa, Sarah is rich.'

Dad stuffed them back in and took his hand. 'Okay, mate, let's get you back to bed.'

'It's wet. Sorry.'

'Okay. No problemo.'

Dad held a hairdryer above the mattress as Jesús put on fresh pyjamas. 'Sorry, Dad.'

'Don't worry. Listen, maybe don't mention the mattress money to Sarah. It's not really our business.'

'Can I mention it to Ben?'

'No, mate, don't mention it to fricken anybody.'

16

Sarah stared out of the vicarage window at the steady drizzle that dampened the gravestones and her spirits. The quiet life was becoming tedious. Be careful what you wish for. Ha! That was one of the phrases she'd had to practise at elocution lessons. The irony.

If it hadn't been for those sessions she wouldn't be here – they certainly opened doors but not in the way that her mother had imagined. After individual tuition, students met for 'conversational enunciation.' The girl she was paired with was podgy, ginger and corpse pale. As if her appearance didn't single her out sufficiently, the girl played the harp. She was cowed, stuttery, timid. Ruthlessly bullied at her twenty-grand-a-year private school. Posh but not quite posh enough. Sarah's sense of injustice overrode her hatred of the Abercrombie and Fitch brigade. She rounded up a posse from Smethwick High and waited outside the ostentatious pillared entrance at the end of the school day. They greeted harp-girl with a chorus of unruly whoops and high-fives. That was all it took for the bullying to stop. They were never really friends but they kept in touch; helped each other out a few times. Ironically, the girl turned into someone else entirely.

Sarah turned from the window, oh well she was here now and, despite the apparent surveillance hotline to the Deanery, filling Lionel Gooseworthy's shoes was not too onerous. No one on the parishioner list wanted a home visit. She had nothing in her diary until Sunday. Could she become a competent croquet player in five days? She recalled seeing a croquet mallet sticking out of the umbrella stand at Eileen Russet's when she'd called to collect Jesús. Getting a ball through a hoop; how hard could it be? Eileen said to come right over.

Sarah took the boys' trampled crow-flies path that led straight to the back garden of Vespiary cottage. There was Eileen fully absorbed hunched over the garden tap.

'Hello,' called Sarah.

Eileen stifled a scream.

'Sorry to creep up on you.'

'Gosh, you did startle me. World of my own.' She dried the mallet on an old towel and handed it to Sarah.

'It's so kind of you to help me out. I'm afraid I'm rather rusty.'

'Not at all.' Eileen disappeared into the shed and returned with six hoops and a set of balls. 'We'll have to share the mallet.'

Sarah stood square over the ball as demonstrated in the 'Croquet for beginners' YouTube video and whacked it hard. It sailed past the first hoop and into the shrubbery. 'I think I need a little help with technique.'

'And perhaps a reminder of how to hold the mallet, and the rules of the game. Blue, red, black, yellow, remember.'

Sarah had skipped the mind-numbing introductory video on the correct grip. 'Eileen, I have a confession to make.' She couldn't look her in the eye. 'I've never played before. The Dean got the wrong end of the stick, no pun intended, he thinks I'm professional standard.'

'In that case we'd better get you up to speed, dear.' Eileen lined up the balls.

'You're a life-saver.'

'Now, most beginners tend to be hoop-centric. Dead giveaway. You need to aim to be in a good offensive or defensive position for your next shot, rather than hog the hoop.'

Eileen turned out to be an excellent teacher; a perfect blend of distilling the key points without extraneous explanation. She explained the principles and practice of running hoops, roquet shots, stop shots, jump shots, split shots and various techniques to stymie the opposition. She showed her 'cheats' to give the impression of a seasoned player. Sarah had imagined croquet to be a genteel game played with courtesy and civility but no, it was a blood sport for the devious, the ruthless, the unflinching. She loved it.

'You must take the set and practice daily,' Eileen insisted.

Sarah had nothing to give in return. Perhaps only the opportunity to talk about her son. From dropping into the virtual clergy-r-us forum, she knew that the best contribution to a conversation with a parishioner was to shut up and listen. She'd honed it to a fine art. Start with a lowkey opening, throw in the occasional psychotherapist nod and encouraging vocalisation, mmm, mmm, mmm and you were considered a wise, supportive and caring vicar.

'You have a lovely garden.'

'Thank you. I try to keep it low maintenance.'

They strolled past the grapevine trained along the south wall. 'And your son?'

'Oh, Melville wasn't one for gardening.'

Sarah noted the use of the past tense. 'An unusual name.'

'After my favourite author, have you read Moby Dick?'

Blimey, at least it wasn't Woolf, or Kafka. Or Pasternak. 'I started it a few times.'

'Melville wasn't much of a reader. Preferred numbers.'

'You must be worried sick.'

'One has to soldier on.'

'Mmm, mmm.'

Eileen stopped and examined a gooseberry leaf. 'Greenfly. I don't like to spray.' She rubbed them off with her fingers. 'Do you garden?'

Sarah's only attempt at horticulture was a cress hedgehog she'd grown when she was ten and the three cannabis plants that she'd kept in her bedsit window. 'Not really, and now I have Ernest of course.'

'It is good to have a hobby, passes the hours.'

'You must miss having Melville around.'

'He didn't visit often.' Eileen bent to retrieve a small red dinosaur from the rockery. 'Ben will be missing this. Goodness he'll be back from school soon.'

'It's lovely of you to give him a home.'

'Anyone would do the same, like you have with Jesús.'

'At least he has his father. How is Ben coping?'

'They're resilient at that age, aren't they? He rarely mentions him.'

'Mmm, mmm.'

'Talking of which I'd better get the tea on.' Eileen hugged her goodbye. 'Practice, practice, practice.'

Sarah headed back through the wood, the croquet mallet over her shoulder humming like a Disney dwarf. Well, she'd given her the opportunity to talk; Eileen was evidently not one for personal disclosure. Fair enough, neither was she.

17

Jesús had planned to climb out of the bedroom window but in the dark it looked very high up. The rose bushes wouldn't be a nice place to land. Also, he might wake Dad because the window squeaked like a startled mouse when you pushed it up.

He crept downstairs and turned the big key in the back door. It creaked open like in Scooby Doo, very cool. Moth was going crazy scooting up and down the kitchen floor; cats can get over excited at night – his kitten book said it was to do with circadian rhythms – also, he'd gone to the toilet on the floor but never mind.

Outside the air was cool and silent and clean like he'd stepped into a magical world. There was a three-quarters moon, a waxing gibbous. A good sign. He walked quickly through the churchyard scanning for night-flying moths. It was so beautiful; he should go out at night more often.

Ow. A sharp pain shot through his shin. A tombstone. He dug in his rucksack for his torch and continued into the field.

A barn owl ghosted the length of the meadow keeping close to the hedgerows. The shapes of the cows were scary; they looked much bigger at night and there were cow pats everywhere. The soft squelching beneath his feet was revolting. The dark hedgerows were creepy too, no bird song, not even an owl hoot. Dad would say 'I don't give a hoot, like a mute owl,' it always made him laugh out loud. It was a relief to get into the forest although the roots were a trip hazard and there was a risk of walking into a branch and knocking yourself out. The sound of his breathing was like a little dog panting.

Jesús reached the bog oak at exactly eleven-thirty as planned. No sign of Ben even though he only had to go out of his backdoor and along their track straight into the forest. It was cold just hanging about so he sloughed off his rucksack and did a little dance.

They had been planning tonight since the sleepover when he retold Ben the story of Dad being trampled by the deer. It was Ben's favourite story; he'd told him it at least ten times. Jesús always added bits from his imagination to make it more fun. Like that the deer had huge velvet antlers and it picked Dad up and trotted off with him into the deep dark forest. The deer told Dad it stole him because it was afraid of the dark. Dad told the deer to befriend other forest creatures like owls and bats because humans didn't make good pets. The deer thanked him and let him go and he found his way back home.

Ben reckoned that his own dad could be lost in the forest because he'd gone to visit granny Eileen and went for a walk up Bradbury Hill and never came back. He might have been trampled by wild ponies, or a wild boar or even a tame one. Perhaps he was concussed and didn't know where he was and he'd been wandering around in circles living off berries and mushrooms and stuff. The police search had been a bit rubbish; only two police turned up and they walked up and down the hill and looked in the pond and then went home. In the police dramas that Jesús's mum used to watch they always spread out in a line and walked forward very slowly looking down and picking up evidence with their blue gloves and if there were trees they also looked up.

Jesús snapped open his Swiss army knife. The best piece was the sharp blade with the long groove – he wasn't really sure what the others were for. The bog oak was difficult to cut but he had a go at carving a good luck charm. It didn't harm the tree because it was long dead and getting ready to be a fossil. The tip of the knife caught his finger as he pushed the blade closed. Damn-it-to-buggery. Fortunately, there was no one there to hear the swear words. A bead of dark blood swelled and dripped onto his trousers. It hurt like hell. He picked a dock leaf and wrapped it tight around his finger.

He'd wait another ten minutes and then go home.

His sandwiches were nice; crunchy peanut butter, a bit too thick. The detectives on TV always went to fast-food places but Dad said they were cow genociders and the pity-me of corporate greed.

Yey, there was Ben at last running through the trees like a spindly deer with his headtorch bobbing up and down.

'Sorry, Gran was up listening to a programme about hedgehogs.'

'It's okay. I did this for luck.' Jesús shone his torch on his carving.

'A starfish. I didn't know they were lucky.'

'It's a four-leafed clover.'

Ben took out his compass and unfolded their map. The bog oak was crayoned in the bottom corner and marked with an X to show where they would start and finish. The main broadleaf trees and birch copse were drawn in and a line of pines going all the way up to the top of the hill. Jesús had added a sketch of the Beast of Bradbury Hill, the way ancient sailors drew cool sea monsters on their maps. It looked brilliant.

They were going to describe a square like they had done with Miss Bickerstool on the playing field. It didn't mean saying what a square looked like, it meant walking. If you went at the same pace north, south, east and west for the same amount of time you ended up back at the start. They'd be back at the bog oak by five am and home before the grownups woke. They knocked on the wood three times for luck and started dead on midnight.

The compass pointed due north past the birches and up Bradbury Hill. It was hard to keep in a straight line because the brambles were prickly and the undergrowth was crazy thick.

The ground was squelchy with mud. Jesús felt the wet seep into his socks; he should have worn his wellies. The mixed woods gave way to rows of planted conifers so they had to walk in single file. Ben up front. The ground was drier here but the trees were close together and the dead lower branches were scratchy. At least the fresh pine smell masked the cow poo on his trainers. Ben's headtorch made weird jumpy shadows as he walked. If only Dad hadn't told him the tale of the Beast, and he shouldn't have told it to Ben because he was sticking very close and was as jumpy as a wren.

Jesús hummed *Rolling in the deep*. 'Alpacas hum to reassure each other,' he said. It felt nice when Ben joined in.

The slope was steep now, Jesús was panting and his rucksack was digging into his shoulders. He probably shouldn't have bought his binoculars and his moth book and Paloma, although she wasn't very heavy. A fallen pine looked like an excellent spot for a break.

It wasn't very comfortable. The moss made it look soft but the wet soaked into Jesús's trousers making him shiver. Ben brought out a Tupperware box and shone his headtorch on four butterfly cupcakes. 'Ta Dah!'

They made exaggerated 'mmm' noises as they ate. The sponge was so soft and the icing tasted like ice cream. One of the little silver balls got stuck in Jesús's back tooth but they finished off the cakes. It would make the bag lighter.

A weird rustling sound came from very nearby; it was far too big to be a squirrel or even a badger. Jesús flashed his torch between the pines. A dark figure was creeping from tree to tree. It looked human but with a big hump on its back. It disappeared into the blackness.

'What the hell?' Ben jumped to his feet.

'Probably a deer.' Jesús knew it was definitely not a deer. It could be Quasimodo but they were a long way from Paris.

'Damn. We forgot to time our stop.'

Jesús looked at his watch. 'I reckon about ten minutes.'

'I'd say more like twenty.'

They agreed on fifteen. It was a quarter to one. They kept walking north, Jesús in front now. Could it have been the Beast of Bradbury Hill? Ben's headtorch scanned quickly from left to right. He must be thinking about the Beast too. The figure didn't look like a massive dog. Maybe it could shape-shift into a camel, although a camel would not do well in these woods. Jesús imagined the Beast carrying off his head between slathering jaws. Sometimes his brain was annoying.

His dimming torch light was a worry too.

'D'you think we're walking more slowly because we are going uphill?' Ben had lots of good ideas. Ideas that he didn't have when they were lying on the carpet in his bedroom planning the search.

'Probably,' said Jesús over his shoulder.

'So, the problem is, we might not be describing a square. Probably more like a rectangle, or a rhombus.'

Another good point. 'Or a trapezium.'

'Or a parallelogram or an irregular quadrilateral.'

They laughed.

Ben's light went out. 'Ow.' He walked flat into Jesús. 'Let's stop and think of our options.' Ben's voice sounded wobbly.

Ben didn't say much but when he did it was usually a good idea. He looked so weird in the torchlight; as if he had no blood.

'Maybe we should go back?' Jesús was thirsty now after all the cake but he'd left his apple juice in the kitchen. How long did it take to die of thirst?

'Gran says if you lose something you should retrace your steps. I guess it's the same if it's you who's lost.'

A fluttery sound came from above, like when a moth gets caught in a lampshade. Now it was buzzing, sort of mechanical. That meant people. People could be scarier than animals.

A scream sliced through the air. And again, nearer now. It had to be a human. A terrified human.

They were off, running full pelt down the hill, slipping and sliding on the dry pine needles, going somewhere – where? – it didn't matter as long as it was away from whatever was in the forest. Run! Run! Don't stop! Ben up ahead, fast as a greyhound, his arms out for balance. He went down.

Jesús skidded to a halt beside him and helped him to his feet but Ben's knee was bashed and made him wonky. There was no sound except the wind in the leaves and some skittering noises. Probably a squirrel. But now there was no chance of retracing their steps. His torch went out. The forest was pitch black. He linked his arm through Ben's and kept walking. It was important to keep moving but he wasn't sure why. Maybe singing would help. Britney, to keep their spirits up. *Toxic*.

The snapping of branches. He jerked Ben's arm to hush. His own hand was sticky with blood. A beast could smell it.

Horrible laughing.

Then talking. Four or five people. Adults.

Jesús signalled to crouch down. It was stingy, must be a nettle patch, it hurt like hell. Tears rolled down his cheeks but he wouldn't make a sound. He crawled after Ben into a scratchy bush.

The talking came closer. Something about ghosts and ghoulies, more laughing. A group of legs stopped. A strong beam inched along the ground.

'Come out, come out wherever you are.' Like a sing-song but not very nice.

Jesús closed his eyes and kept as still as a hedgehog. Not even breathing.

The smell of cigarette smoke. A man's voice, very close. 'We know you're in there.'

A spotlight hit his face, blinding bright. He was a rabbit about to be squished.

'Hey pipsqueaks.'

Ben was curled up tight. Trembling.

A big face peered into the bush. A fat man with a baseball cap. Two more loomed in. They were wearing hoods. Jesús screamed and pulled Ben to his feet.

'Run for your life.'

18

The bedside clock flashed five-fifteen. Jack didn't know what had woken him but he knew that something was very wrong. The lump on the twin bed was too big. Jesús's silhouette usually evoked a prostrate whippet not a hefty labrador.

Jack swung out of bed and pulled back the dinosaur duvet. Pillows. Was this a prank? Under the bed, in the wardrobe, behind the curtains. No sign of Jesús. The carved oak chest contained only musty blankets and a couple of mothballs. He limped across the corridor and hammered on Sarah's door.

'Hey. You awake?'

'I am now.' Her voice groggy. 'What's going on?'

'Jesús is gone.'

Jack hobbled downstairs and into the kitchen where an acrid smell hit him. Something soft and wet between his toes. Cat poo. He hopped out of the back door and wiped the offending mess onto the grass. A chaos of footprints shone in the dew. Child-sized. His gut writhed as he followed them through the graveyard. The prints led across the field and stopped at the forest margin. From the vicarage came Sarah's voice shouting Jesús's name. The silence heavier with each unanswered call. He hurried back, his heart thumping.

'There are three cartons of apple juice on top of the dishwasher.' Sarah looked panicked.

He rushed past her into the hallway. 'His coat and shoes are gone.'

They had planned to be up early this morning. Moth was having his vaccinations at eight-thirty and it would take time to confine him to the cat box and drive to the vet in Peaminster.

Had Jesús looked a little sheepish when they were discussing the plan? With hindsight, yes.

'I think he went into the forest.' His own voice that of a stranger.

'Okay.' Sarah picked up the phone.

'Eileen, hi, is Jesús with you?' She was trying to sound casual but the catch in her voice betrayed her. 'Oh Lord, Ben is missing too?' Eileen's response was inaudible. 'Stay where you are, I'm calling the police.'

Jack stood with his hands by his sides as she dialled nine-nine-nine. She set the phone to loudspeaker but he couldn't trust himself to speak. The officer gave unhurried advice; check the wardrobes and under the beds. They would send a car from Peaminster but it might be a while. Fricken useless.

'I'm going to walk through the woods towards Eileen's. Could you double check all the rooms?'

'Sure.' She touched his arm lightly. Like a blessing.

Jack pulled his jacket and waterproof trousers over his pyjamas and went out. The summerhouse door was ajar. Jesús's absence filled every corner – a drawing of a moth lay on the table, a pair of laughing-goat socks were discarded on the floor, a yellow digger still held a mound of soil in its claw-bucket. It was the digger Terence Johnson had given him for his birthday. Jack hadn't seen him play with it for ages. Must have been hiding it so as not to upset him. Man, he was kind, thoughtful, underestimated.

The dawn held a shroud of mist. The gathering moisture rinsed away Jesús's footprints, eliminating his last traces. Jack made his way slowly through the forest poking at brambles with his stick, scanning every tree, alert to any clue. Every shadow brought a glimmer of hope followed by a lurch of defeat. *Estúpido. Inútil. Patético.* Piss off, Sofía.

Might he have gone to find the goats? No, he didn't know the addresses. At least Ben was with him. Wherever they were. He pictured them huddled together, cold, lost, frightened. The old pond was partly obscured by bracken; its surface an unbroken sheet of algae. They could be lying at the bottom, their lungs filled with stagnant water as the ruptured green veil resealed above them.

'Jesús. Ben. Jesús. Ben.' He called softly, then louder, then urgently.

The sycamore that Jesús had suggested they camp beneath stood alone. The sweet chestnut was forlorn. Jack sat on the tomb-like bog oak and ran his hand over the smooth wood. His fingers found a knobble of grooves, newly carved – a flower perhaps, or a moth. It certainly looked like Jesús's work. He must have taken his Swiss army knife; good lad.

Jack followed the deer paths up Bradbury Hill into the conifers. The only prints were cloven. It was hard going, almost impenetrable. Here it was too dry to leave tracks. He made it to a clearing. Ah, there, a muddy cluster of footprints; several boots with different soles. At least four people, maybe five. A gang who stopped to confer? Fading beams of orange light shone up ahead; must be security lights on Terence Johnson's house. Might the boys have gone there? It seemed unlikely, unless they were desperate or lost. Or injured. But why wouldn't he have phoned him? He would go and check.

Deep within the pines something white was fluttering from tree to tree like a small ghost. The mist was dissipating. Hidden birds called through the damp air. Jack prayed that Jesús and Ben could hear them too, giving them hope that help was on its way. The thing caught in the dead lower storey. Jack skidded down towards it, ducking through the brittle branches and lunged as it flew again. He smoothed it out – a crude map with a square of arrows marked in red felt-pen. The bog oak had been drawn with care in the corner and a misshapen open-mouthed dog roughly coloured with heavy black crayon. The Beast of Bradbury Hill. Dark smears smudged the page. Oh God. Blood.

'Jesús. Ben. Jesús. Ben.' Sarah's voice called far below.

A scream. The calling stopped dead.

Jack tumbled towards her, sliding on the needles, back towards Vespiary cottage. Silence except for his puffing and the snapping of twigs beneath his feet. Ahead a broadleaf maple held its branches high, its sombre canopy black against the grey sky. He skidded to a stop and stared in horror. Sarah lay face down beside a pool of vomit. Jack turned her over; she was breathing. He arranged her limbs in the recovery position and scanned around for the cause.

Beyond the maple stood a wizened oak. A lifeless figure, the size of a small boy, hung from a lower branch by a noose. The rope creaked in the gathering breeze.

19

The ancient oaks of Montague Forest had doubtless borne witness to many terrible events over the centuries. Grown strong on nutrient-giving graves, unfurled their leaves as plots were hatched. A highway man might have been hung from this very oak. The hoary tree was wise to the follies of man. If it could escape the relentless creep of development it would continue to flourish amid the human misery.

The sense of endless time that stretched before and after helped Sarah in moments of crisis. Perspective was needed to cope with the hand grenades of her life. This too will pass. The oak seemed grateful to be relieved of its new burden.

Sarah stood by the small grave that Jack had dug with his bare hands and took a moment before speaking.

'We thank you for everything you were and all that you gave. The joy you spread, your loyalty and unconditional love. May you rest in eternal peace. Amen.'

Sarah threw a small posy of dog violets before Jack pushed the peaty soil over the stiff body. She was glad not to have to look at it anymore. The rictus grin, the clumps of missing fur exposing patches of white skin. It was hard to determine the breed, maybe a large terrier or perhaps something crossed with a corgi. He must have been a lustrous apricot colour during his lifetime and doubtless quite a character. Somebody had loved him.

The image of it swinging from the branch would be hard to erase. At least Jesús and Ben – found huddled together in the nearby undergrowth – had been spared the sight.

Who could have done such a thing?

Jack had examined the corpse with forensic detail – the

parched skin, the clear beaded eyes, the light droplets of moisture on the very tips of the fur – and deduced that it must have been strung up that night. The navy-blue plaited rope was unusual. There was nothing else to go on.

'Don't you think we should call the police?' Sarah murmured. Contact with the cops was the last thing she wanted but it was what a vicar would ask.

'And say what? We found a stuffed dog hanging from a tree. I don't think that's a crime.'

'But it's wrong and immoral and unethical.' Now she was the champion of virtuous behaviour. What a joke.

'The police didn't even bother to come out to search for the boys.'

'He must have been someone's special pet, taxidermy costs a fortune. They'd want to know.'

'I doubt it was microchipped.' Jack smoothed the soil into a satisfying mound.

'We should have taken a photo in case someone could identify him.'

'You'll have to draw a photofit. I'm not digging him up again.' Jack collected a pile of large stones and placed them around the grave. His hands were shaking.

'At least the boys are safe now, back with Eileen,' she said. 'It was just a bad idea, well-intentioned but poorly executed.'

He patted down the soil. 'They could have died.'

'No harm done, well apart from a twisted knee, multiple bruises, cuts, grazes and slight dehydration.'

Somewhere within the cluster of birches came the hint of an eavesdropper. She scanned the trees for signs of movement, eyes, feet. Nothing. She must calm down; she was becoming paranoid.

Jack stripped two small branches and fashioned them into a cross. He knocked it into the head of the grave with a rock. 'There, at least he's had a decent burial, poor mangy bastard.'

Sarah ran her hands along the bog oak. 'Another West Tillington mystery.'

'How'd you mean?'

'Ben's dad's disappearance.'

'Oh, Melville.'

'What do you really think happened to him?' she asked.

'He's probably sunning himself on a Spanish beach by now. The guy was a bit of a git to be honest.'

'Really?'

'Pinstriped suit, cufflinks, played golf.' He sprinkled a handful of fine soil over the grave.

'That doesn't necessarily make you a bad person, but yeah, I know what you mean.'

'The coppers interviewed me after he disappeared. I didn't tell you, didn't want you thinking I'm a nutter.' He didn't look at her.

'What are you saying?'

'Melville came over to buy some goat's cheese. I was just out of hospital, in pain, stressed out over the eviction, off my head on Tramadol...'

'Okay.' Oh God, what had he done? 'And?'

Jack craned his neck to watch a croaking raven flap overhead. 'Melville was going on about women. Called his wife a slut and my Sofía a nut-job. I hit him.'

'Blimey.'

'Not hard, I had a broken scapular. Hurt me more than it hurt him. The prat just picked up his cheese selection and walked out. Didn't even pay me.'

'Are you still a suspect in his disappearance?'

'I guess.'

There was something exciting about Jack swinging a punch. Thrilling even. She wished he'd hit him harder. God, what was wrong with her?

'He dobbed me in for assault even though there was no visible injury. Then he disappeared.'

'That doesn't look good.'

'I can understand why his missus ran off. She was nice, always friendly whenever I dropped Jesús off. Stupid, but I never asked about her life, just said "You alright?" and she'd nod.'

'We never really know what's going on in other people's lives.'

Jack rubbed the soil from his hands and watched the ravens flying west. 'My wife killed herself.'

'I'm sorry.' It was nice that he finally trusted her.

Her mind cycled through the possible scenarios: swallowing handfuls of pills, drinking herself to oblivion, jumping into the river with her pockets full of stones. There was no easy way. It took real courage.

'Jesús found her. He ran in to use the toilet. She was in the bath. Cut her neck and wrists real deep. He just came out and stared at me and then he called nine-nine-nine.'

'Poor Jesús.'

Jack joined her on the bog oak. They listened to the hammering of a distant woodpecker.

'So, that was the trauma.'

'Yes, a pretty horrific sight. I haven't forgiven her for that.'

'Sometimes people just don't think things through.' She knew that alright; she had replayed her actions on that day so many times that it ran like a film reel.

'I should have seen it coming. Sofía hated her life. She told me often enough.' He picked at the dog's mercury sprouting from under the log. 'The doctors were no bloody use.'

Sarah waited for him to continue but he had nothing left to say. The woodpecker resumed its drumming. A beam of sunlight warmed the freshly dug grave. 'You've done a lovely job.'

'If it's worth doing and all that.'

'Thanks for looking after me. I've never passed out before.'

'It's okay, women faint on me all the time.'

She punched his arm. 'Come on, let's retrieve Jesús, Eileen will be feeding them like baby birds.'

20

Dear Dad and Sarah,

It must have been very horrible and scary to find that I was missing and you probably thought that I had been stolen or something. Then you had to go out and look for us and you would have been sick with worry.

Also, Moth missed his vaccinations and has to be rebooked and it's all time and trouble. Plus, half the parish was searching for us and lots of people were distressed and most of them are very old and don't need that kind of upset. Or any kind really.

I know I should have told you that we were going to search for Ben's dad and not to have been so bloody stupid, although it was our behaviour that was stupid not us.

It is also sort of my fault that Mr Johnson came round with flowers and Eileen had that asthma attack from the pollen because she is allergic to lilies. Dad, I am really sorry that you had to speak to him again because he is so annoying and he didn't even ask how we were or how the goats were getting on.

When you found the dog hanging in the tree it must have been a trauma. I feel very sorry for you and for the dog. I don't know what conclusions to draw about the dog. I promise not to say anything about that to Eileen who is a big fan of dogs. It would make her very sad on top of everything else.

I have sat and thought and this is what I have learnt from this experience:

1) Always make sure that an adult knows where you are.

2) Some things are best left to adults even if they didn't actually do a good job and someone could be out there injured and lost.

3) Wind-up torches are better than battery ones.

4) You can squeeze water out of moss if you are really thirsty.

5) Knowing which fungi are edible is not that helpful if you haven't got any way to cook them.

Thank you for finding us and for carrying Ben all the way back with his knee.

I promise not to scare you like that again.

Yours sincerely,

Jesús Stretton

21

J esús slept the whole of Sunday. Going to school on Monday morning felt like the first day back after the holidays. Everything felt weird, the same but different. Or maybe it was he who had changed. Ben met him by their hedge and held out his little finger to renew their pinky swear. They'd been through something that had made them stronger. More grown up.

Somebody who looked like Mr Johnson but in a pale grey coat with a black velvet collar, was standing in the playground gazing around like he was in Narnia. He waved at them but they didn't wave back. Oh no, it was Mr Johnson and he was coming over.

'Back from the jaws of death.' He ruffled Jesús's hair.

He had the sort of hair that adults liked to ruffle. Maybe he should have it cut really short like Craig's. Mr Johnson clicked his phone onto a selfie-stick and took some photos of the three of them. Happy. Sad. Relieved. Jesús didn't mention the goats. Mr Johnson was standing so close that he could smell his aftershave, sort of flowery, sort of lemony.

Mr Johnson gave them both a bag of Jelly babies. 'They're all boys, because they have a tiny bit more jelly.' He did a slow kind of wink.

The bell rang. Phew.

The whole school had to attend a 'special assembly.' It was about the risks and dangers of being outside unsupervised. Miss Bickerstool looked all serious like that time someone had drawn a willy on the school sign and everyone had to stay behind until someone confessed and no one did so eventually she had to let them go.

Miss Bickerstool was talking about things that could happen to children in the woods. Jesús fidgeted with the frayed cuffs of his blazer. The Teddy Bear's Picnic tune played in his head. The song had pretty much the same message as Miss Bickerstool – it's safer to stay at home.

Jesús exchanged glances with Ben. They both knew what was coming.

'Two boys have been very reckless and silly and spent the night alone in Montague Forest.' Gasps. Horror. Pretend shock. Everybody already knew. Jesús sat very still, eyes down, trying not to catch the stares of the kids who turned to gawp. Probably everyone.

'Stand up Benjamin Russet and Jesús Stretton.'

An explosion of chattering. The single word 'Silence' shut them all up. Jesús got to his feet. He stood close enough to Ben to feel his arm against his. She went on for ages about fatal accidents (ooh-ahh) and exposure (te-he-he) and stranger danger (ew). Jesús tried not to think about needing the toilet – if you were desperate you were meant to think about deserts. Kalahari. Sahara. Gobi. Namib. The Antarctic and the Arctic were also officially deserts but they didn't help. When would she stop talking? The little kids sitting crossed-legged at the front were getting twitchy, the ones behind were shuffling. Someone poked the back of his leg with a sharp pencil. Probably Jason from Year Four.

'A lesson to you all.' Hung in the air as they filed out for double maths.

At break Jesús and Ben were heroes. Everyone crowded around wanting to hear about how they'd survived. Jesús sat next to Ben on the wall by the bins and told them how they'd built a log cabin out of logs and put pine branches over the top to keep out the rain. How they sat up all night telling each other creepy ghost stories because nothing frightened them. That they made a delicious stew out of roots and mushrooms and dandelion leaves. How they started a fire by rubbing sticks together and Ben roasted insects on flat stones because he isn't a vegetarian.

Jason and Craig pushed through the crowd.

'Did you see your dad's ghost?' said Jason.

Ben jumped up and hit him right on the nose. Jason reeled back. Craig shoved Ben hard in the chest with both hands. He fell over the wall in slow-motion. Everyone formed a circle.

Fight, fight, fight.

Jesús had never been in a fight before. Jason grabbed his shirt ripping off the buttons and dragged him to the ground. He scrambled to his feet and clutched at Jason's jumper. A sudden sharp pain went straight through his eye. Ow. A finger. Bam into his other eye. Ow. He couldn't see anything. Somebody tripped him up. The ground was dirty. It was hard to crawl and it was making holes in the knees of his trousers. He rubbed his eyes and there was Ben lying flat on his back with Craig standing over him. Someone pulled Jesús to his feet. He launched himself at Craig, they both fell sideways crashing to the concrete. Ben rolled to safety. Now the crowd was chanting again.

Jesús. Jesús. Jesús.

He ran at Jason and punched him hard in the nose like boxers do.

'Everyone stand back. Now.' The playground assistants.

They looked pretty scared. This was what could happen when children were left unsupervised outside. Craig was sitting very still holding his head. Jason was lying on his back. There was a lot of blood on the tarmac.

Jesús had never been sent home from school before. Fortunately, no one was badly hurt – the blood was from Jason's nose. Miss Bickerstool had taken statements from them all and called their 'parents or guardians.' The size difference and the record of previous altercations had both been on their side.

There was a lady in the living room wearing a grey and white woolly jacket that reminded him of his goat Beyoncé. She looked very serious, so did Dad and Sarah. She held one of those plastic clipboards that people write on when they don't have a desk. They all stopped talking and looked at him. Dad winked, Sarah smiled, the lady didn't.

'You must be Jesus,' she said.

'It's pronounced Hay-sous,' he muttered under his breath. He hoped she wasn't going to make an annoying joke. His knees were stinging and he smelt of TCP and he hadn't had any lunch.

The lady took a long hard look at him. At the gap in his shirt where he'd lost the buttons, the bloodstained rips in his trousers, the big blue plaster on his finger from the knife cut, the bruises from walking into gravestones, the scratches from the hawthorn and the blotches on his arms where he was allergic to something in the forest. She would be good at that game where you have to spot the difference.

'This lady wants to ask you a few questions.' Dad flashed his eyebrows like those warnings that baboons give.

'I'm sorry about the fight,' said Jesús.

'What fight?' asked the lady.

'Oh, that was nothing.' Dad turned to him. 'This lady is from social services.'

Sarah left and came back with a glass of milk. Jesús drank it although he usually had squash. She disappeared again and he could hear her doing the washing up and humming a little tune – that one from the Fairy liquid advert. He sat down on the sofa next to Dad.

'I wonder if I might speak to Jesus alone,' she said. It didn't sound like a question.

'It's Jesús,' said Dad. Dad looked at him and did his baboon eyes. 'I'll be in the kitchen if you need me.'

Maybe he was saying don't mention the dog. Over the last few days 'Don't mention the dog' had become their little joke, like when Dad said 'I mentioned it once, but I think I got away with it,' and he and Dad and Sarah had laughed so hard.

The lady had a big hole in her tights. Her hair was tied up but straggly bits had fallen out and she kept tucking them behind her ears. She scribbled something on her board. She didn't tell him her name. That was the thing with grownups.

'How old are you Jesus?' It was annoying when adults got your name wrong but you couldn't correct them. She didn't need to ask his age because he could see his date of birth on her form right next to his name and address.

'Seven-and-a-half.'

'You're quite small for your age.'

That was a bit rude but he didn't say anything.

'What's it like living at the vicarage?'

'Very nice, thank you.'

She tilted her head to one side like a parrot. 'Now, Jesus I came to see your father because the police told me that you had run away.'

He had no idea what she meant because he'd never run away. There was a long silence.

'Your father said that you share a bedroom with him. How do you feel about that?' She said it in that voice people use when they are talking to babies.

'Fine.' He hoped Moth would come in so they could talk about him.

She tilted her head to the other side. 'If you had a magic wand and could have three wishes, what would they be?'

That was a better question. 'Like in Aladdin? But without the lamp?'

'Yes, just like Aladdin.' She looked at the hole in her tights and crossed her legs and uncrossed them and touched it with her finger and tutted.

Jesús thought about it carefully. He didn't want to make a mistake in case it actually came true and he'd wasted it on something like gummy bears. 'I would like my goats back, please.'

'Anything else?' She tapped her biro like she was in a big hurry.

'Oh, I know, I'd like to see all the moths in the world, not every single actual moth, I mean every species.' Jesús was pleased with his answer but she looked disappointed.

'How about something closer to home, maybe something we could actually change?'

'I thought it was a magic wand.'

'Well yes, it is.'

'I can't think of anything else I want.' He did want whatever Dad and Sarah were making for lunch. It smelled like barbeque flavoured Super noodles and veggie sausages.

She wrote something down and did her head tilt thing again. It was quite annoying. 'If you could live with anyone you wanted, who would you live with?'

'David Attenborough, no contest.'

'No, I mean people in your family.' She tapped her biro on the board again. Tap, tap, tap.

'I thought it was still the magic wand thing.'

'No, not this time.'

'Dad and Sarah.'

There was another long silence. Jesús could hear chopping sounds. Maybe they were making fruit salad for pudding. It was his second favourite after chocolate cracknell hedgehogs.

'Do you miss your mum?'

'No.'

'Do you get upset about your mum?' A big chunk of hair fell down and she twisted it back into the scrunchie.

'No.' He swung his legs.

'Has anything happened to upset you?'

'The goats.'

'What happened to the goats?'

'They went to Wales and Shropshire.'

'I see.' She turned over to a new sheet of paper. 'Jesus, why did you run off into the forest at night by yourself?'

'I was with my best friend.'

'But without an adult and without telling anyone.'

That wasn't a question so he looked out of the window. Moth was sitting near the flower pots in a little patch of sun. He looked very happy. He liked being warm.

'You had no one to protect you.'

That wasn't a question either. 'I had a knife.'

She looked a bit freaked. 'A knife?'

'Yes, Dad gave it to me. It's very sharp.' He held up his finger in evidence.

'Do you feel worried about anything?'

'A little.'

She leaned forward and nodded her head. 'Can you say more. I'd like to help you.'

'There's a maths test on Friday. I'm not good at division.'

'I see,' she sighed.

She must also struggle with division because she didn't offer to help.

'If there was something really wrong, who would you tell?'

'Probably Ben.'

'What about your dad? Or Sarah? Or a teacher?'

That was three questions. He wasn't sure if he was meant to pick one or if he had to answer all three so he just shrugged. Also, he was starving. 'Can I go now?'

'One more question. Remember I'm here to help you, Jesus.' She held her hands in her lap. 'Has anybody ever hurt you?'

That was a big question. He probably shouldn't mention the fight again. There was that time Craig gave him a Chinese burn. Ben opened a door onto his head once when he was putting his shoes on but that was an accident. Mum hurt him by suiciding without saying goodbye. He didn't want to talk about that. 'Can I go now?'

'Okay, Jesus. I'll see you again.'

He dashed out as fast as he could.

22

Nothing had happened in West Tillington for bloody centuries and now a bestial vicar, a suicide, a suspicious disappearance, two lost children and a hanging dog in the space of twelve months. Yet the headline in the Tillington Times this morning was Prize-winning artichoke, accompanied by a photograph of the winner dwarfed by her spikey bouquet. At least it demoted the story of Jesús and Ben to a short paragraph on page seven, Local boys safe and well. How bloody Terence Johnson got in on the photograph Sarah did not know. But it had been worth buying the paper for the one-line announcement in the small print notices. Public consultation Borten Wood Farm, Council offices, Wednesday 17th April 2.00 pm. She would be there.

But she was currently entering a parallel universe. She watched herself cruising down the lime-tree arbour, watching out for stray peacocks, off to play a croquet match with the great and the good of the parish; her eccentric boss, a potential violent offender and spy-of-the-month. With the image of a hanging dog still imprinted in her mind.

What with Jesús's disappearance, the dead dog debacle and the intrusive social worker, Sarah had had little time to practise croquet. The alarming clunk-clunk-clunk of the engine and the relentless rise of the temperature gauge were not helping her state of mind.

Geoffrey, Terence and Carole were already on the lawn practising shots. The sound of their convivial laughter filtered into Sarah's car and made her want to turn it around. Or drive straight into them. The crazy poodles bundled over to greet her as she climbed out, pogo-ing on their hind legs, all fluff and tongues. Their fur shone orange in the morning sun – maybe the hanged dog was a poodle? She really needed to stop thinking about it.

Geoffrey strode towards her with an outstretched hand. 'Ah, there you are, old thing. We tossed for partners. I got you. Lucky me, eh?' He showed tobacco-stained teeth. 'I'll start.'

Terence made his ostentatious bow. He was wearing a pink and white Pringle golf jumper and tight mustard trousers. Good God. Sarah managed a smile. 'I heard that you were re-elected.'

'They will keep voting me in. Better the devil you know and all that. I suspect they'll be wheeling me out in a box!'

'Well, congratulations.' She could get through this.

'I do hope that we can join forces.' His smile was more of a leer. Smarmy git.

Carole stepped between them, a vision in a white trouser suit. 'So sorry to hear about dear Jesus. I do hope he was unscathed.' She could not look less sorry.

'It's pronounced Hay-sous.'

Geoffrey struck his blue ball with a pleasing twock. It curved and stopped directly in front of the first hoop. He puffed out his chest as if he had accomplished nuclear fission.

Carole bent over her ball, displaying to Terence like an ageing sex-kitten, wetting her lips, shimmying her hips, penduluming the mallet between her legs. Her ball rolled to block Geoffrey's.

'Excellent manoeuvre, partner.' Terence winked.

Carole flushed pink.

Sarah placed her ball on the far-edge of the starting arc. 'I saw your photograph with Jesús and Ben in the newspaper.' She studied Terence's face for a sign of embarrassment or contrition at making the boy homeless. There was none.

'I caught up with the boys at school to check they were okay.'

She focussed on the line between her ball and the target and slowed her breathing as Eileen had instructed.

'I noticed the young woman from social services called at the vicarage,' piped Carole. 'They must have to check up on him, what with the nasty business of finding his poor dead mother. So damaging to a young mind.'

Sarah took her time. Eileen had warned her about trash talk

and spoiler tactics but using Jesús and his mother's suicide was a whole new level. She recalibrated the angle and followed through, her black shunting Carole's ball out to the boundary.

'Oh, lovely shot,' sang Geoffrey.

Terence knocked his yellow wide leaving Geoffrey to clear the first hoop and sail towards the second. Phew. One hoop down, eleven to go.

Carole retrieved her ball and eyed the long-distance shot.

Sarah approached and waited until her backswing. 'Why would you assume that she was a social worker?'

Carole caught the ball with the corner of her mallet and watched it roll hopelessly off line. She stalked after it muttering.

Sarah repeated Eileen's mantra: head down, adjust, relax. The ball ran wide, bumped like a pinball off a lump of freshly excavated soil and veered straight through the second hoop. Wow, what a fluke. Squirrel assisted, but still. She stopped herself from doing a little victory dance; it would not be expected of a tournament level player.

Geoffrey high-fived her. 'Two-nil.'

Sarah was beginning to like him despite his dubious choice of friends. Terence badly miss hit and struck his mallet into the ground leaving a hollow divot.

'Steady on old chap, the lawn was freshly rolled this morning,' called Geoffrey. He leant towards her. 'The old fool spent a fortune on a customised Woody, the milled endplates give an advantageous weighting. Now he has no excuse for losing.' He winked. Geoffrey knocked his blue behind the third hoop to defend her ball.

The unspoken teamwork felt good.

Carole aimed prematurely for the hoop and languished beside the pin leaving Sarah with a clear shot. She stalked the hoop, weighed the angle and got into position.

'Yea, though I walk through the valley of the shadow of death,' said Terence, hovering at her shoulder.

'I'm sorry?'

'Psalm one hundred and two. My favourite, what's the next line again, Vicar?'

What was this? A test? She steadied her grip. Was he

suspicious of her credentials? 'I don't memorise psalms, fortunately, they're all written down.'

'I think you'll find it is psalm twenty-three, Terence. The Lord is my Shepherd,' said Geoffrey. 'I will fear no evil.'

'Ah yes.' Terence smiled. 'Sorry, I didn't mean to distract you.'

Eye on the ball, line to the hoop, angle the mallet for top-spin, hit and follow through. Yes.

'Three-nil,' sang Geoffrey.

'By the way, I heard about the burial.' Terence stood unnervingly close and made the sign of the cross on his Pringle.

Sarah looked up. No one knew about the dog except Jack, Jesús and Ben and they were watertight. 'Burial?'

'The rooks.'

'Oh yes.' She held his eye. The creep was just trying to put her off her game. 'Ernest went to a lot of trouble.'

'You're lucky he didn't stuff them.' A malevolence in his tone.

'Sorry?'

'Your sexton has an interesting hobby.' Terence tapped his ball firmly towards the fifth. 'Not for the fainthearted.'

'How so?'

'Rather like your predecessor. He stuffs animals.'

'What?'

'Our Ernest is a taxidermist.'

Geez. Ernest, a taxidermist. He must have stuffed the hanged dog. He'd know the owner. Sarah made a hasty excuse; an elderly parishioner – weren't they all – wanting to discuss global poverty and injustice. Her exit also avoided the suggested best-of-three. Croquet mission accomplished. She had not made a fool of herself. Indeed, Geoffrey had been delighted with their convincing win.

Sarah sped off narrowly avoiding the death-wish peacock. In a rare moment of self-disclosure Ernest had mentioned that he lived in the only house in Lingsland with seven-thousand neighbours but they were all chickens. The car-radio masked the low growl that the Clio had added to its repertoire of protests.

Reggie 'the dice' Jones, who was arrested in Smethwick yesterday, is said to be known to the police. He claimed that although he had entered the bank wearing a ski-mask and gloves it had been a prank and he had not taken part in the robbery. He remains in custody and is likely to be charged later today. Police continue the hunt for his accomplices and for the stolen money.

What an idiot to think that the police would buy such a ridiculous story from a man with a criminal record and a dodgy nickname. The guy deserved everything he got. She turned it off.

The Farmers' dilapidated house hunched at the end of an unmarked lane seemingly embarrassed by its weed-cracked driveway. Sarah rang the bell, no reply, she rang again. Perhaps she should have phoned ahead. The rancid smell of droppings from the neighbouring chicken farms was infusing into her new wool coat.

The front window revealed a seventies museum set, complete with box television, teak furniture and shagpile carpet. Sarah followed the path around to the kitchen. There was Nancy in a yellow apron with one arm raised to the ceiling and the other extended as graceful as a swan's wing. She gyrated past the cooker. Their eyes locked, Sarah waved. Nancy stopped dancing. Her hair was a beautiful cornflower blue.

A battered Volvo pulled into the drive and Jean and Betty appeared carrying a basket of rhubarb and a bottle of damson gin. 'Ah, Vicar! Are you joining us?'

Nancy opened the door, her apron now removed. 'Come in everyone.'

'It seems that I am.'

The kitchen table had been pushed back against the wall leaving an expanse of scrubbed quarry tiles but nowhere to sit.

'Sorry if I startled you.'

'I don't always hear the bell.' Nancy received her gifts with a flurry of excitement. 'Oh lovely, thank you.' She opened the damson gin and poured four shots without asking for preferences.

'Ernest not home?' Sarah stared at a stuffed tawny owl who stared back with glassy eyes.

'No, he was up at the Deanery doing the lawns first thing, then over to Mr Johnson's for hedge cutting.'

She wondered if Nancy made use of her time alone because Ernest forbade drinking and dancing. He seemed the puritan type.

'Riddled with divots apparently after last weeks' match.' Nancy distributed the gin. 'Did you need him?'

'I just wanted to ask him something. It can wait.'

'By the way, I checked Save Our Bats this morning, twenty thousand pounds already.' Nancy sounded astonished.

Spoken aloud it did sound a ridiculous amount. There was that five grand from a fictional mass skydive at Hope Bagot nursing home and two thousand from a charity whippet race in Ribblesdale. 'Amazing.' Perhaps she needed to slow down the donations.

Jean plucked a cat hair from her cardigan. 'I thought I might go pink this month.' She patted her hair.

'I have just the shade for you,' said Nancy.

Sarah was glad the conversation had moved on from bats.

Betty put the rhubarb in the fridge. 'For your crumble.'

'Thanks, Bet. I always make a crumble for horror-film Fridays.' Nancy knocked back the gin. 'We enjoy the ones where people get killed by chainsaws.'

Blimey, she had completely misread Nancy.

Jean put on a pair of red slippers.

'Right, are we ready?' Nancy turned on the CD player and stood with her arms raised. Sparse drumsticks marked the beat before a jazz-funk fusion filled the kitchen.

Sarah watched in astonishment as the three women launched into a choreographed dance sequence. They threw themselves from side to side, twisting and turning to the beat. It reminded her of a documentary she'd watched with Jesús about the courtship ritual of grebes that they had later recreated holding lettuce in their mouths as a substitute for river weed. Nancy two-stepped in her fluffy slippers wearing an expression of pure delight. They strutted and swayed and shimmied to a saxophone solo. The rhythm changed to a Cuban beat.

Betty held up her hands as if clicking castanets. 'Come and

join us.'

Sarah recognised the Buena Vista Social Club, an album she'd listened to incessantly the summer she'd left school.

'Arriba arriba,' called Nancy.

They circled each other like matadors, rotating and snaking their arms. They promenaded in pairs, changing partners after each circuit between the fridge and the cooker. They spun in crazy circles until they were giddy with disorientation and excitement.

Ernest loomed in the doorway with a hammer-head pick over his shoulder. Nancy turned off the player. They stopped dancing.

'Bloomin' heck, Vicar, not you as well.'

He dropped the contents of his old leather bag on the kitchen table. A recently deceased Shih Tzu, its neck adorned with a pink bow.

23

S arah was glad to be home. She was exhausted from the croquet and the dancing and the readjustment of her views about her parishioners. A nice cup of tea and a digestive would sort her out. God, no. Who was she becoming? She'd have a shot of rum.

What the hell?

It had been a week of shocks and surprises and now a bald man was hunched at her kitchen table with his back to her, eating a bowl of Honey Nut Loops. Where was Jack when she needed him? Damn, the job interview at the crisp factory – he could be gone for hours. She grabbed a frying pan, the heft of it making her brave. That smell of steel.

Hands on your head.

Get on the fucking floor.

Wait. What sort of burglar would break-in, sit at the kitchen table and study the ingredients of a cereal box at three in the afternoon?

'Oi, you.' She held the pan high.

The man turned.

'What the f –?' Milk-soaked loops splattered across the table.

'Jack?'

'Yes.'

'What the hell happened to you?'

He ran his hand over his shaved head. 'Nits.'

'Oh, Christ. I could have killed you.' She was shaking.

'Hey, no harm done.' He took the pan from her and gave her a hug. 'Sorry, I should've warned you. I don't do chemical warfare and I didn't fancy raking a nit comb through my mop.'

Sarah sat for a moment to recover. His stubble gave him

a roguish look and the pleasant ovoid of his head offset his muscular neck. 'A bit drastic.'

'Seven to eleven is peak nit-fest age. Another four years and I'll grow it back.'

She ran her fingers through her own hair. Hopefully the itching was psychosomatic. 'What about the job interview?'

'It doesn't look that bad, does it?'

'I mean, I thought it was his afternoon.'

'It's been pushed back to four-fifteen.' He retrieved a loop from his t-shirt and ate it. 'Apparently there was a fight in the waiting area and then a long wait for the ambulances.'

'Geez.'

'So much for "seeking team player with a positive attitude." Still, it sounds like it's taken out most of the competition so I'm in with a shot.'

'I know you hate the golf club but at least they're not animals.'

'The longest three weeks of my life. I'd opt for standing beside boiling oil over serving Tories in lambswool jumpers any day.'

'I can see to Jesús so if they offer you full time go for it.' Blimey, this whole vicar thing was getting to her, next she'd be delivering sermons about the importance of gainful employment.

'What about ole curtain twitcher next door?' Jack said through a mouthful of cereal. 'She'll be clocking me in and out and sending a dossier to social services.'

'I can't imagine they'd have a problem with a vicar providing afterschool care.' She held her hands in praying position. 'I'm a pillar of the community.'

Sarah took her fleecy blanket into the living room and positioned it in a shaft of sunlight. It was time to get back to some of her own interests; although would a vicar be into eastern meditative practices? What the hell. She lay on her stomach, her cheek to one side and allowed herself to sink into the floor.

Don't move a muscle.

Stop fucking crying.

She scrambled to her feet and sat rigid in the armchair. God.

Now she couldn't even meditate.

Jack poked his head around the door. 'So, this is where you got to.' He looked from her to the blanket. 'Just building up to lying down?'

'I might just sit here awhile.' Her voice wavered.

'You okay?'

'Fine.'

'You're kind of pale.'

'There's a lot going on at a cellular level.'

'I'm really sorry I frightened you before.'

'No problem.'

'I wanted to say thanks for choosing the bat charity, Jesús is so happy. They're one of his favourite animals, top three I think.'

'Don't mention it.' Word was spreading, bats were not such an ideal choice after all; they seemed to have become a talking point.

'Anyway, I'm off to the interview, wish me luck.'

'Don't hit anyone.'

Suddenly the house felt empty. Jesús was going straight to Ben's. Ridiculous to feel lonely. Get a grip. She consulted her to do list: Revise funeral services – there were so many over eighties it was best to gen-up. Prepare pre-marriage sessions for couple from Cadmonley. As if she had anything to offer given her disastrous relationship record. Officiate dispute resolution for church flower-arrangers; there had been an unseemly argument over the rota which led to the destruction of the lily-of-the-valley altarpiece. Was her new life in the country, a house and seventeen grand a year really sufficient recompense for this crap?

A firm knock on the patio door; it was Ernest holding a bucket, his forehead smeared with soil.

'Alright, Vicar?'

'Yes. Everything okay?'

'Aye.'

'Do you want to come in?' She glanced at his muddy boots.

'No.'

The reason for his visit was far from clear but it certainly wasn't for a chat. 'Did you want something?'

'Best boil the water.'

'Sorry?'

'Looks like dysentery. Up Bradbury Hill.' He looked north for clarification. 'Terence Johnson, not Eileen.'

'Goodness. How did that happen?'

'Contamination. Most likely the spring, but boil just in case it's mains.'

'The spring?' The man was talking in riddles.

'Johnson's got it bad both ends.'

'From drinking water?' God, it was like Jesús's favourite game; Twenty questions.

'Sank a borehole so he don't have to pay water rates.'

'Oh, what could have caused it?'

'Chicken farm maybe. Or dead animal. Leaching, see.' Ernest turned and walked away.

'Thanks for the head's up,' she called after him.

Oh, God. They were going to have to dig up the dog.

24

Jesús sat next to Ben on the fallen gravestone of Elias Brown, died 1755. It wasn't possible to make out any other details but Jesús imagined Mr Brown had lived a happy life, smoking a pipe, dancing jigs and looking after sheep. It must have been nice to live back in the olden days. Back before social workers and football practice and long division.

Sarah waved through the kitchen window. He waved back. He had to stay in full view at all times. Goats always kept their kids in line of sight too; prey animals couldn't be too careful.

It was pretty cool to be sitting on top of dead bodies. Some of them were hundreds of years old. So old that other bodies were buried on top of them. Some had died of plague and some were lepers – that was a disease where bits of your body dropped off so the olden days weren't all positive. It was a good place to tell Ben what he'd overheard. It was dead weird. The hanging dog was stuffed.

Ben puffed out his cheeks. 'Cool.'

'It died years ago, probably before we were even born and Ernest, the giant man who works in the garden, stuffed it.'

Ben poked a stick into the crack in the gravestone. 'So, the dog probably had a better death than being hanged. Like maybe it was woofing its way through a big juicy bone and it had a heart attack.'

Jesús waved back at Sarah again. 'He's got loads of dead animals in his house. Even an actual owl and a tortoise. A tortoise must have been pretty easy to stuff. And a big ginger cat that the owner wanted stuffed and then changed their mind when they saw it.'

Ben did his amazed face. 'I'd really like to see the owl.'

110

'Same.'

'Who owned the dog?'

'Ernest couldn't remember because he's stuffed so many but he remembered doing an apricot cross-poodle. That's something that's half-poodle-half-something-else, not an angry one.'

'It's weird to think there are dead animals all over the place, sitting in people's living rooms or bedrooms or the downstairs loo.' Ben traced the date of death on the tombstone with his finger.

'I like the idea and don't like it at the same time.' Jesús wouldn't want a stuffed goat – it wouldn't be the same if it wasn't trotting or jumping or maaahing for carrots.

'Granny Eileen had her dog Peachy stuffed. The thing was she couldn't relax when she was watching Coronation Street because he kept staring at her, so she keeps him in the garden shed. He was an orange colour.'

Eileen didn't know that a stuffed dog had been found hanging from a tree so they couldn't tell her it was probably Peachy and that his dad had buried him in the woods. That was why you shouldn't keep secrets.

'Should we check in her shed?' Jesús got to his feet.

'Yep.'

Jesús wasn't allowed to walk to Eileen's anymore so Dad dropped them off even though it took longer in the truck.

The garden shed was massive and spidery and packed with stuff. It smelled of soil and oil and old things. The shelves were crammed with jars full of nails, dusty bottles and rusty tools. Ben found the light switch. It didn't make it any better.

'Peachy, Peachy, Peachy,' called Jesús.

'He's stuffed, remember.'

'Oh yeah.' It was sad that he'd been in here all alone for so long. Getting dusty. Maybe with spiders running across him. 'Is he sitting or standing or lying down?'

'I only saw him once. He was sitting on a blanket with one paw raised up and his head to one side like he was waiting for a biscuit.' Ben looked behind a pile of blue ropes. 'Kind of sweet but kind of icky.'

Jesús picked up a blanket with a paw print pattern. A huge

spider clung to it. He flung it down, leapt back and crashed into a stack of old plant pots. The spider scuttled across the floor. 'Let's get out of here.'

'Hang on.' Ben was rummaging through a box of papers. 'Look.' He flicked through an address book. 'It's Dad's.'

'Take it. Come on, let's go.'

Eileen had made shortbread biscuits sprinkled with sugar; Jesús's second favourite biscuit. It must be nice to have a granny.

She took off her pinny and handed Ben the plate. 'You can take them through to your room as long as you don't drop crumbs.'

'We'd prefer to sit at the table.' Ben took a seat and nodded to Jesús.

'Would you like to join us?' Jesús did his best smile.

'What's got into you two?' Eileen was using her suspicious voice but she looked pleased as she sat down.

'Tell us about your dog, Gran.'

Jesús gave him a 'that's way too obvious' look. You had to lead up to these things.

'Let's think. I've had five dogs in my life. When people say "A dog is for life not just for Christmas," they mean the dog's life, not yours.' She looked sad. 'How's Moth getting on?'

She must've thought Ben was going to ask if they could get a dog. Adults always changed the subject when they didn't like what was coming next. 'He's great. He plays with his ball of wool like a cartoon kitten.'

'Do you ever go and stroke Peachy?' asked Ben.

Jesús kicked his shin under the table.

'Ow.'

'Peachy is happy sitting on his blanket in the shed and doesn't need to be disturbed.'

Sunday morning. Dad's first day at his new job. Jesús spread a thin layer of Marmite on his toasted soldiers. It was nice to have breakfast together like proper families in adverts.

'Is that what you're wearing?' said Sarah, buttering a triangle of toast.

It was what Jesús had been thinking too. Dad was wearing jeans and his Grateful Dead t-shirt.

'Yep. It doesn't matter because they give us blue overalls. Also, I have to wear a hairnet even though I haven't got any hair.'

Hilarious.

Dad had got a brilliant job. He would be making crisps. Not just the humble spud; he'd be sorting and frying root vegetables too. Pretty cool. There were even blood red crisps made from beetroot. Jesús was going to have them in his lunch box. He'd eat them with Ben in their hole in the hedge so they didn't get stolen.

Jesús was trying to be extremely well-behaved because when Dad told Sarah about the shift pattern, she'd pulled her Oh My God face like the shocked emoji. Dad said they rotate, like the potatoes, but she didn't laugh. Rotate means four days on, four days off, including weekends and night shifts – crisps never sleep. Dad drank his coffee and set off for work like a normal dad. Everything would be okay. Sarah would look after him. He didn't really need much looking after.

It was agreed that he and Ben could stay in the vestry as long as they were as quiet as church mice. The vestry was disappointing; it was basically just a back room that needed dusting. It was almost as bad as Eileen's shed. Jesús sprinkled the Cornflakes from his parka pockets onto the floor to attract church mice. They weren't special mice, just normal ones that happened to live in a church, but it would be nice to see them anyway. Jesús crept over to the door as Sarah started her sermon and squeaked really loud to make her laugh.

Ben had brought his dad's address book and some paper and a pen to write to his friends and ask for help. Jesús searched the cupboards for something to do. There were stacks of bibles and hymn books and some fancy goblets like they have in Harry Potter. At the back under a pile of white dress things was a computer. He pulled it out and plugged it in. It took ages to load up. He squirted his Ribena cartons into the goblets and passed one to Ben. 'To seeing a church mouse.'

'To finding my dad.' They clinked goblets.

It tasted special enough for their wishes to come true but that might have been the dust.

Ben flicked through the book. There weren't many names but three of them had a red star next to them. They didn't have phone numbers or home addresses. Or last names.

Jesús looked at the computer screen and pressed the Gmail icon. 'Wow! It's all set up, you can send them emails.

They'd had a whole lesson on how to write a letter. Jesús looked over Ben's shoulder as he typed with two fingers.

Dear First name,

My name is Ben and my dad is Melville Russet. You probably already know that he disappeared. I am looking for him. Do you have any clues? Even a wild guess would be good.

If you can help, please write back.

Yours sincerely

Ben Russet.

It took ages because they couldn't remember how to do cut and paste so Ben had to type it out three times. They had a long discussion about whether it was Yours sincerely or Yours faithfully if you were using someone's first name but you didn't actually know them or whether it's neither if it's an email but best wishes sounded wrong.

Jesús wanted to look up some stuff about moths but *All Creatures of Our God and King* started up, which Sarah liked to end on, so he shut down the computer.

Now they just had to wait.

25

The dog sat stiff and filthy in the hall. His mouth clogged with mud, his mangy pelt further depleted, missing an eye. Sarah felt sick. It was hard to look at, hard to look away.

Jack had been a star, doing the disinterment on his own despite his painful shoulder and knee. He'd bundled his clothes straight into the washing machine and spent half an hour in the shower. It had been worth it. Poisoning your ex-landlord, who had recently had you evicted, was not a smart move. It was also not ideal for a fake vicar who was trying to keep a low profile to poison the head of the council.

But now there was the problem of what to do with the exhumed remains of a contaminated dog. It wasn't something that she could Google. The dog's gaze followed her with its one eye – judging or beseeching it was hard to tell. Sarah laid out bin bags, tape and rubber gloves as if enacting a crime scene reconstruction. She double bagged him and took him upstairs. She'd ask Jack to put him in the attic until they came up with a better idea.

At least it had given her a topic for her next sermon: The raising of Lazarus from his tomb. According to clergyonline.com the story illustrated Our Lord's power to grant eternal life. More macho hubris. It was also a foreshadowing of Jesus's own resurrection. Perhaps too heavy for a spring Sunday; Easter stories were such a downer. Sarah felt sorry for Lazarus, he was a pawn whose own wishes were never considered. She decided on a series of rhetorical questions for the congregation to ponder. Did Lazarus want to be raised up from the dead? What would he do with his second chance at life? How might the experience have changed him?

What would you do? Become a vicar in the land that time forgot?

Blimey. She needed a drink. She treated herself to a single shot of Lamb's Navy. The Borten Wood Farm public consultation was this afternoon and Jesús would be back from school at four. She'd imagined that temporary, part-time parenting would be all kittens and sock-puppets, she hadn't signed up for packed lunches, homework and bedtime stories. This was her second chance at life and she'd just swapped one straitjacket for another. Although this one was growing on her.

There was only one bus a day to Peaminster and it left in eight minutes. She grabbed her coat and ran down the drive. Pat was leaning out of his van waving a letter. 'Wait up, Vicar, need a signature.'

'Perhaps you could just pop it in my mailbox?'

'No signature, no delivery.'

She stopped and took the envelope. 'Thanks.'

'Nice that you've got an Irish pen pal but the traffic seems a little one-way if you don't mind me saying.'

She did mind, actually. Everyone around here had a bloody opinion. 'I prefer to phone.'

'I see you sent a letter to Tuscany. We all like a foreign post down at the sorting office. Rare these days.'

Sarah checked her watch. 'Sorry, I have a bus to catch.'

'Heard your car's given up the ghost.'

Blimey, it wasn't possible to cough around here without someone filing an all-points bulletin.

'Jack said my Clio was worth about ninety quid and that was because I'd just filled up with petrol.'

'I could get you an ex-post-van. A real bargain.' He looked both ways and lowered his voice. 'Cash in hand mind.'

Sounded dodgy but a cash deal would be perfect. 'Thanks, I'd be very grateful.'

'I'll pop it round later. You can take a look.'

'Great, must dash. I'm catching the twelve-fifty-eight.'

'You've plenty of time, it arrives at one-fifteen.'

'Better safe than sorry.' She hurried off.

Sarah had not shifted down to the low gear which life in West Tillington demanded. She waited for the bus for fifteen minutes. Its imminent arrival was signalled by two teenage lads who turned up at one-fifteen holding a whippet and four cans of Stella. The bus was empty. The boys leapt on first. She took a seat a few rows back. Oppressive hedgerows blurred past the grimy windows revealing occasional glimpses of potato fields or rows of stubbly brown stalks.

Raucous laughter erupted from the teenagers who were scrolling through their phones. Sarah craned to see what they were looking at. Wow, it was a photoshopped image of Terence Johnson with a large sausage emerging from his head. Oh God, it wasn't a sausage.

'They reckon he's got food poisoning or something.'

'Hopefully nothing too minor.' They laughed again.

'Is that on Facebook?' Sarah called.

'What's it to you?'

She pushed up her sleeves; her tattoos might help. 'I'm not a big fan of Terence Johnson.'

The blond boy scanned her with curiosity. 'You the new vicar?' His eyelashes were so pale they were almost invisible.

'Yes, I'm keen to get involved in local issues.'

'Pray for us you mean?'

'No, change things. It looks like things have gone downhill.'

'Johnson sold off the playing fields. Promised all sorts but the money got stuck outside a fence or something.'

'Why do people keep voting for him?'

'Dunno.' He pressed the bell although there seemed to be nothing outside but potato fields.

The one with the whippet got to his feet and gave a toothless smile. 'Facebook group is westtillingtonwtf, all one word.'

They jumped from the bus and lifted their hands as it pulled away.

It was another twenty minutes to Peaminster. Sarah set up a Facebook account Hellsangel and joined westtillingtonwtf. It was a revelation. A barrage of savage Terence Johnson memes. She clicked on the links from spotlightsam and garythesheep. They opened cans brimming with worms. Councillor Johnson had recently been admonished for neglecting to pay his council tax for the past three years. The final ever EU grant had been squandered on 'town twinning' trips to Thailand. And what was this? Terence Johnson's face superimposed on a picture of Norman Bates, knife in hand: 'Who killed Melville Russet?' Another showed the poster for The Shining, Terence's face photoshopped onto Jack Nicholson's. It leered through the axed door 'Here's Terence!' Wow.

The driver dropped her directly outside the council offices despite there being no bus stop. His response to her inquiry about the return journey was less welcome; there were no buses to West Tillington until tomorrow morning, she'd have to take the three-ten to Borten Wood and walk across the fields. Damn, and she was wearing her stupid court shoes.

The town of Peaminster promised much but delivered little. It was faded and dirty. Smethwick was positively vibrant in comparison. The council offices were housed in a seventies concrete block that overshadowed the charity shops, off-licences and bookies that cowered around its periphery. A pock-marked security guard made a cursory rummage in her bag and waved her through. Fortunately, there were no sniffer dogs; Jack's pungent cannabis was infusing into her clothes.

There was no information about the public consultation and the three people Sarah asked had no idea. She walked the four bleak corridors of the ground floor and returned to the front lobby. The closed grey doors of the second floor were no more enlightening. The third floor looked entirely unused, the fourth housed deserted meeting rooms. She was beginning to lose hope. But wait. What was that in the alcove behind the store cupboards? A noticeboard. It displayed a badly photocopied site map: Proposed Borten Wood Farm Development. Jack's farmhouse did not feature in the architect's drawing. It had been replaced with a new vehicular access point with an HGV turning bay. A large crosshatched rectangle took up the remainder of the land. One word squatted in the centre of the block.

ABATTOIR.

Oh my God. It was enormous.

According to the brief description the abattoir would serve the whole county. No relief road would be necessary as removal of the hedgerows along West Tillington road would allow passage for even the largest live animal trucks. Their carcasses would leave via Peaminster Old Road thus avoiding Bradbury Hill. Objections to be lodged by 18th of April – tomorrow. Bloody outrageous. She took a photograph, posted it to the Facebook group and made a hasty exit.

A light drizzle had started up. Sarah's first month's salary should be in her bank account by now. It was a Midlands tradition to spend it on others although that was probably in the days of the weekly pay packet. She tapped her PIN into the ATM. The young man behind her was standing too close. She shielded her request for the maximum daily withdrawal – three hundred pounds. She could smell spearmint gum, could hear him chewing.

Hands on your heads.

Hands on your fucking heads.

Heart pounding, she revoked her card and headed for the bus stop.

'Hey. Miss. Oi.'

She turned in slow motion, her fist clenched.

'You forgot to take your money.' He thrust a wad of twenties into her hand.

'Oh, I thought I'd cancelled it.'

'Nope, definitely yours.'

He was younger than her, twenty-five maybe, black beanie, cheap jacket, missing a tooth. Were there no dentists in Peaminster?

'No.' She tried to hand the money back. 'You have it. I want you to have it.' She really did.

He stood with his arms by his sides. 'I'm not a charity case, Vicar.'

'It's not for charity. It's for your honesty.'

'It's too much.'

'Please.' She pressed the money into his hand and walked away.

'Thank you,' he called, his voice choked.

As Sarah stepped from the bus at Borten Wood the first fat raindrops spotted the road. Even in the grey afternoon the view over Jack's old farm was stunning. How lovely it must have been for Jesús to wake up to the green patchwork and watch his goats safely graze. Their fields were now devoid of animals and grasses grew in scrubby clumps. In the distance cows dotted the hillsides. Clean white sheep followed each other along the hedgerows. The thought of this beautiful landscape being covered by an abattoir was unthinkable.

The warning drops were joined by a roll of thunder as the clouds darkened. Sarah put her head down and lengthened her stride. A crack of lightning. She started to jog, unseemly for a vicar but what the hell. Ten minutes of steady trotting and she was out of breath and her feet were aching. She crossed into the meadow and hurried to the shelter of the single huge beech. Jesús was teaching her the names of the trees. The band of rain drove towards her, whipping over the hunkered cows, lashing the leaves, finding an angle sufficiently acute to negate the shelter of the canopy. So heavy that it made her laugh out loud. She stepped from beneath the tree and raised her face to the sky. She whooped, turned and surrendered to the onslaught. It was like wild swimming but without the hassle.

As the downpour slowed to persistent rain and returned to drizzle the joy of the moment turned to regret. The story of her life. Freezing water ran down her neck, seeped into her underwear, plastered her hair to her head. What a bloody idiot.

Sarah would be passing Bridge Street Primary at letting-out time. By the time she arrived the rain had stopped. Now she was shivering. A pride of mothers stepped from their cars and assembled at the gates. She hadn't seen any of them before. A few nodded.

'Hello, I'm Jesús's ...' what was she exactly?

'Fiona and Mary's,' said a stout woman in a startling pink jumper.

'Donald's,' said another wearing a headscarf from which protruded a row of prickly blue curlers. She didn't know they still existed.

Sarah stood beside a woman holding the hand of a sickly-looking child. 'By the way, are there any afterschool activities?' She couldn't believe how short the school days had become; perhaps they always had been.

The women exchanged glances.

'This ain't Eton,' said the pink jumper. 'There's a homework club but it's really just sitting in a room.'

The first trickle of children appeared, some locating their parents, others starting the slow walk home.

'There used to be a school bus,' said the woman with curlers. 'That was a Godsend.'

Now the women perked up and drew closer, each trumped the next with their contribution to the catalogue of what-used-to-be.

'And a toddler group,' said a woman struggling to put her daughter's arm into an oversized blazer.

'Are you on westtillingtonwtf?' Sarah asked as if she were a seasoned contributor. Several nodded as the sea of children washed around them. 'Check out the new posts.'

There was Jesús heading home across the field. Sarah ran after him waving. A sudden slow motion backwards sensation. She was vaguely aware of the comedic image of a sodden vicar, arms flailing, sliding rear-first into a cow-pat. A small circle of mothers stood over her. Pink jumper extended her hand. Sarah's ankle buckled. She sat back down and watched Jesús disappearing into the distance.

26

The 'stay in sight' rule had eased up but Dad and Sarah worried if Jesús wasn't back on time so he walked quickly like a fast-walking bird, a sandpiper maybe. Being a parent-slash-adult seemed to be pretty much all about worrying. Same as being a child.

It was Ben's turn to clean out the stick insects after school so he was going to meet Jesús back at the vicarage. The stick insect monitor had to take out the old foliage, add new privet and triple check that none of them had ended up in the bin. Jesús always worried he'd missed one so he'd make sure he could count Adam, Bess, Carl, Dave, Emma, Fred and Gill safe in their tank before he gave the all clear. Ben would be extra careful too so he didn't have to fret.

It was nice to walk through the fields after the rain, everything was shiny and clean looking. The middle of a field was a good place to practise whistling because people didn't laugh if he just made blowing sounds. A ring of mushrooms shone pure white in the green grass. He crouched down and gave them a good sniff; cucumber, they were St George's mushroom. He picked ten and left a few for the field mice. Sarah would be pleased because sometimes she forgot to go shopping and they ended up eating beans on toast. Mushrooms on toast would be a nice change.

Jesús was looking forward to seeing Sarah's face when he gave her the mushrooms 'Wow, Sweetie, aren't you clever.' But nobody answered the door when he did his rat-a-tat-tat. No one came when he held his finger on the bell. The downstairs toilet window was cracked open. If he went in at an angle, he might be able to squidge through. He emptied the garden bucket and tested his weight on it like Dad did. Wriggling in head first was the best bet. He pressed his legs together and moved them up and down to get momentum.

Maybe he should've taken his blazer off because now he couldn't move at all, he was stuck like Winne-the-Pooh after he ate all the honey. Winne-the-Pooh didn't panic, he just waited until he'd digested. That wasn't going to work for him. He squirmed and twisted and waved his arms in front of him inching forward, forward, forward to reach the sink. He grabbed the taps and hauled himself through. Ta dah!

All the mushrooms were squished to buggery in his pocket.

'Sarah! Dad! Sarah! Dad!' Nope. No one home.

Moth scampered around his feet as he poured two glasses of Ribena and put out the bourbons. Maybe Dad was asleep. He crept upstairs and peeped into their bedroom. No, he must be at work. A big black binbag had appeared on the landing. Whatever was inside smelled funny, kind of soily, like a chestnut mushroom. It was a strange shape and firm to touch and sounded sort of hollow when he knocked on it, like a weird drum. The thing was wrapped up tightly with the type of brown tape they had in the craft cupboard. He could re-wrap it, no harm done. It took a few hard tugs to rip the bag open. A row of dirty teeth grinned at him from a snout of faded apricot fur.

The doorbell. He re-covered the face and ran down two at a time.

'You'll never guess who I've found.'

Jesús and Ben sat cross-legged next to Peachy and considered their options. Option one: wrap him back up and pretend that they never saw him.

'That would be very hard,' said Ben through a mouthful of bourbon. 'We'd be desperate to find out what had happened to him and we could die of curiosity. Like a cat.'

'Okay, option two, we ask Dad and Sarah why they have a dead dog in a bin bag and why isn't he still buried.'

'That might sound a bit rude.'

'True, and I shouldn't have been poking around and it's probably something that they don't want to talk about.'

'Option three, put him back on his blanket in the shed where he belongs.' Ben stroked Peachy's head. 'Granny Eileen's been sort of funny recently. Jumpy. If she found out he'd been stolen and hung and cut down and buried and dug up again she'd be dead upset.'

'She'd also think it was us that took him because we'd just been asking about him.'

Okay, so it was option three.

Peachy wasn't heavy but he was awkward to carry. They bumped him down the stairs trying to avoid Moth, a major trip hazard, weaving crazily in and out of their legs. They placed him carefully in the hallway and covered him up as best they could. Moth slinked closer, inch by inch, daring himself to attack. He wriggled his hind quarters and sprang onto the bag, his claws tearing at the plastic, his fur fluffed, biting and yowling. Jesús threw his blazer over him and pulled him scrambling and hissing off the defenceless Peachy. It was definitely time to go.

They took their shortcut through the woods going as fast as they could – a black bag with bits of dead-looking fur poking through the holes would be tricky to explain. Jesús worried about maggots but maybe they didn't bother if there were no insides. They sat for a while and watched Eileen's house for signs of Eileen. All clear. They were about to make a run for the shed when the rattle of an engine revving up the hill announced the arrival of Betty's car.

'Betty and Jean come over to play poker on a Wednesday,' said Ben, his arm around Peachy.

'It's Wednesday.' Jesús dropped down behind a rosebush and covered the bag with dried leaves. He calculated how long it would take Betty and Jean to get out and walk to the front door and say hello and go through to the living room. Then he added another five minutes in case they stopped to admire a flower or something. It seemed like a very long time.

'I reckon the coast is clear.'

Jesús liked the way Ben talked; it was like a detective.

Peachy looked very soily when he came out of the bag. He didn't look like he'd ever been alive. They couldn't leave him in the shed in that state. Jesús retrieved an old sweeping brush from beside the compost heap and brushed him as if he was grooming a goat. It just spread the dirt around more. Ben stuck a twig between Peachy's teeth and poked about to clear the mud. A couple of teeth came out too. Poor Peachy.

Jesús carried him over and sat him under the outside tap. It was too risky to sneak in to get shampoo so he just turned the water on really fast, like a power-shower. It was nice to watch the dirt wash away. Peachy looked a bit cleaner, then bits of fur came off and he didn't have that much to start with. The water was sort of seeping into his body and misshaping him like a creepy magic act. And now he was dead heavy. Jesús tried to dry him off with his jumper but it didn't really help. They dragged him into the shed and put him back on his blanket. His one eye hung loose looking down at the puddle of water trickling out of him. It was pretty sad. Jesús closed the door tight.

Hopefully Peachy would dry out and be dog-shaped by the time Eileen saw him again.

27

S arah hobbled through the front door with her arm strung limply over Miss Bickerstool's shoulders. The living room held the risk of empty bottles from last night not to mention Jack's spent roaches in the ashtray. Perhaps the kitchen would be safer.

They bumbled their way down the corridor. Sarah lowered herself onto the nearest chair and propped her leg on another. Miss Bickerstool busied herself opening cupboards and drawers and set out two mugs. Oh, good grief, she was staying.

'There's really no need. Jack will be back any minute.' She scanned for contraband and cat mess. All clear.

'You can't be left on your own.'

'It's very kind of you but – '

'Gets me out of cloakroom duty.' She prepared the coffee like a barista. 'I'd just finished the stick insects.'

Sarah didn't ask. 'Jesús must've gone over to Ben's. Those two spend all day together, it's a wonder they have anything left to talk about.' The pain had morphed into a dull throb that boded well for a quick recovery.

'Right, let's get you some dry clothes. You'll catch your death.'

God, the exhumed dog was on the landing. 'Don't worry, I'm fine.'

But she'd already gone.

'First door on the left,' Sarah called after her. She imagined Miss Bickerstool stumbling over the bin bag, revealing the wretched creature in all its grimy horror. She'd explain that she had taken up taxidermy and the dog was her first attempt. She'd been disappointed with the result and had decided on a less challenging pastime. Flower arranging, perhaps.

The minutes ticked by.

Miss Bickerstool bustled into the kitchen with a clean towel and a pile of neatly folded clothes. 'Do you need help changing or should I start on the washing up?'

Thank God, she hadn't investigated the bag.

'Honestly, I can manage from here.'

'Nonsense.' Miss Bickerstool clattered last night's dishes into the sink and squirted an alarming quantity of Fairy liquid under the running tap.

It was comforting to put on dry clothes, Sarah pulled her rapidly expanding foot through the trouser leg. Miss Bickerstool had selected a baggy tracksuit; the woman was evidently familiar with the care of those with soft tissue injuries.

'How's Jesús doing at school?'

'Very well, it appears. They seem to take it all in their stride at that age.' She rinsed the cutlery under the tap. 'Time will tell of course. Do you have any frozen veg?'

'Don't worry. It's Jack's turn to cook.'

Miss Bickerstool pointed to her foot. 'Cold compress.'

'Ah.' She nodded at the freezer. 'Did you know his mother?'

'A little.' She folded a family bag of garden peas into a tea-towel and packed it around Sarah's swollen ankle.

Miss Bickerstool's age was difficult to determine; somewhere between forty and sixty. She looked as if she bought her clothes from a budget catalogue and didn't bother with returns. A hint of Parma violets took Sarah back to her own school days. Her poor mother summoned to hear about another transgression and to plead for a further final warning.

'Jesús must miss her terribly. It's really tragic.' The icy draw of the peas leached into her foot.

'The doctor dismissed Mr Stretton's concerns about her mood swings.'

'How appalling. So she was never diagnosed or treated?

'Sadly not.' Miss Bickerstool dried the cutlery. 'She hated England, hated goats, seemed to hate children.'

'Poor Jesús.'

'Probably bipolar disorder.' She wiped down the surfaces.

'Not that I'm an expert, but I've read Stephen Fry's autobiography.'

'Poor Jesús,' Sarah said again.

'He's unlikely to come out unscathed, even if the environmental factors don't get him the genetic loading will.'

Blimey, she was a prophet of doom. 'Well, as you say, kids are resilient.'

'Will he be staying with you long?'

A good question. 'It was meant to be a temporary arrangement.' She couldn't ask Jack about his plans; he'd interpret it as notice to quit. Now that he'd landed the new job he could find a place to rent. It would be a shame for Jesús to be uprooted again but this was becoming much more than she'd bargained for.

A firm knock on the door. Miss Bickerstool obliged.

Sarah strained to hear. Two male voices that she didn't recognise. A low measured cadence, authoritative, perhaps a set of questions. It sounded serious. A two-way radio crackled. Oh God, the police.

'I'm afraid he is not at home.' Miss Bickerstool's voice in full school ma'am. 'You'll have to come back later, officers.'

Wheels on gravel. Jack's car. The voices accusatory now. Something about digging.

Oh Christ.

Sarah levered herself onto her good foot, manoeuvred the chair into a makeshift walker and clunked her way down the corridor.

'Can I help?'

The police officers ignored her. She glanced at Jack, who looked shaken, at the police with their deadpan expressions and back to Jack. Was it further enquiries about the disappearance of Melville Russet? Or perhaps someone had seen Jack burying the dog and Terence's dysentery had been traced to the water course.

'What is going on?' she asked, more forcefully than she meant to.

'We're here to check out reported concerns and to ask Mr Stretton a few questions.' The thin officer had an odd bluish tinge to his skin and a tapered face that put her in mind of a fish.

'This is ridiculous.' God, her loaded mattress was propped up in the back bedroom. No sniffer dogs. But still.

The fish's heavily bearded consort flashed a cold smile. 'Won't take long, Vicar.'

She couldn't bar their entry, it would look too suspicious. 'What are the grounds?'

'A video recording has been handed to us. It shows Mr Stretton digging up a deceased dog in the woods.'

'How is that an offence?' Jack bounced on the balls of his feet like a teenager. He wasn't helping.

'Are you admitting to the desecration of a grave, Mr Stretton?'

'No comment.'

'What are you expecting to find?' Sarah feigned outrage. 'A dead dog sitting on the landing?' When in a corner it was best to come out fighting.

The officers walked past her into the hall. Miss Bickerstool gave her an 'I'm here anytime' look and crunched away across the drive.

Sarah sat with Jack in the kitchen and discussed their strategy in hushed tones. The officers' heavy footsteps creaked on the floorboards upstairs. At least the dog was in an obvious place so they wouldn't need to go poking around in the bedrooms. In the face of the overwhelming evidence – a video recording and Exhibit A one recently exhumed dog in a bin bag – Jack would admit to coming across the dog when digging for truffles. Realising that it was buried on a water course he'd dug it up to prevent possible contamination. Hopefully there was no evidence of them actually burying the dog in the first place. A disappointed looking officer poked his head around the door.

'Right, we'll be off.'

Nothing made sense.

28

Jesús searched for signs of church mice. There were no visible holes or droppings but every single cornflake had been eaten so they were definitely en casa. It was nice to get out for a while, Dad seemed a bit stressed. Sarah did too. There had been lots of whispering.

'My dad nearly got arrested.'

'Cool.' Ben turned on the computer 'What for?'

'Not sure, but Dad said the pigs in blue have been sniffing around the vicarage like blinking beagles.'

Ben's cheery laugh made Jesús feel better. Dad wouldn't do anything wrong. The police had said that he needed to watch himself. Probably because they didn't have enough officers to watch him themselves. He wasn't going to be locked up like Reverend Gooseworthy or horrible Craig's dad.

'The worst thing is the police told social services something and now I've got to talk to that lady with the hole in her tights again. Next Wednesday after school. Dad said she's called Miss Walker.'

'Oh, the one who does the weird neck thing?' Ben puffed out his cheeks and stared at the screen. 'I had to see her once. She was very annoying.'

'I'll miss my turn with the stick insects but Miss Bickerstool said I could do it on Thursday instead.' She was being extra nice to him, kept saying he could talk to her anytime. He didn't know what he would say.

'Whoa,' said Ben.

Jesús leant over the screen. Two new emails. A sixty-six percent response rate was excellent, although the first one wasn't that helpful:

Thanks for your message lad but do not talk to men you don't know on the internet, or even men you do know, from John 666.

The one from Dave 101 was dead friendly.

Hey, Ben, how are you doin'?

I'm great mates with your dad. I'd love to help.

You must be lonely and sad without him. Maybe I could cheer you up. How old are you? What do you like doing?

Maybe we could meet up and have some fun? Loads of love, Dave.

PS Send me a photo of yourself.

'Cool,' said Ben.

The email gave Jesús a funny feeling. It was weird that the man asked more about Ben than about his dad's disappearance. Best not to say anything though because Ben was so pleased.

There was a file attached. Maybe some information about Mr Russet. No, it was a photo of Dave 101. He was standing on an empty football pitch wearing a Manchester United shirt. He had one foot on the ball trying to look super sporty but he had a porch and was quite podgy. That didn't make you a bad person – people came in all different shapes and sizes and had different coloured skin. Dave 101 had red skin. It was hard to see his face because of the shadow from his baseball cap and his sunglasses.

Peter 123 had not replied. Maybe he was on holiday.

Ben typed out a reply.

Dear Dave 101,

Thank you for your email.

Please can you help by searching your local area and maybe put up posters like we're doing?

Dad might have a concussion and not know who he is.

Thank you from Ben.

PS I am seven.

PPS Yes, I can meet up but I don't really like football. Can my friend Jesús come too?

Send.

A strange sound, like a trapped goat, came from within the church. Jesús pressed his ear against the door. The service had stopped. There was a bit of a kerfuffle followed by worried voices. He stepped back from the door as Sarah and Betty came bundling through all het up with Eileen slumped between them. They half-carried, half-dragged her into the vestry with Jean waving a hymn sheet in front of her face.

'Incoming, make way,' called Sarah.

Jesús wiped the dust off a chair with his hand. Ben shut down the computer and covered it with his jumper.

Eileen was not like normal Eileen. She looked very white. Betty patted her hand.

Ben gave her his goblet of apple juice. 'You alright, Gran?'

'I'm fine. There's no need for such a fuss.' She took a sip of juice. 'I fainted, that's all. People faint all the time.'

It had probably been Sarah's sermon about Lazarus being raised up from the dead that had made her feel woozy. Jesús had heard it yesterday when Sarah read it to him for comments. It was really good but it might have been too much for an old person. There were some scary bits like rolling away the stone from the tomb and Lazarus coming out all wrapped up in bandages like a zombie – she didn't actually say that but that's what he pictured.

Oh no.

He exchanged glances with Ben. Maybe Eileen had found Peachy all covered in soil like he'd risen up from the dead and the sermon freakedthebejesus out of her.

'Shall I put the kettle on?' asked Jean.

Jesús tidied away the goblets as the adults bustled around trying to locate cups and saucers. Ben took Eileen's wrist like doctors do on the TV. Everyone seemed to feel better when they were holding cups of tea because they started talking about other things rather than asking Eileen if she wanted to lie down, or perhaps she should be checked out by a doctor to be on the safe side, or be driven home.

'I think I've been resurrected by the tea,' said Eileen. They all laughed, especially Ben, because they knew she was going to be okay.

29

J ack was hot and exhausted. The stink of the factory in his
clothes. He should have a shower but it was so good to
be outside and there was Sarah sitting in a deckchair reading
some papers with two glasses and a jug of something with
ice cubes. She looked wicked in her sunglasses and bucket hat.
Her rainbow warrior t-shirt was cute. She'd be more at place at
Glastonbury than in a vicarage garden.

'How was your shift?' Her smile so welcoming it felt like
coming home.

'It's over.' He'd be back in the hell-hole soon enough, he didn't
need to think about it in his free-time. He repositioned the
deckchair in the mottled shade of the cherry tree. Man, he was
beat.

'Elderflower pressé?'

'Ta.' They were on a virtuous living drive until social services
put down their spotlight. He plucked a leaf from above his head
and rubbed it between his fingers. 'Powdery mildew,' he sighed.

'What's up with you?'

He tossed the leaf aside. 'I'm homeless, I work in a crisp
factory and the child snatchers are stalking my kid.' Also, she
was seeping into his soul.

'You live in a vicarage, you're in full-time employment and
you're a brilliant dad.'

'Thanks.' He sipped his pressé like a small child. It tasted
good. 'By the way, Jesús reckons he hasn't seen the dog. God
knows what happened to it.'

'Yes, He does,' she smiled.

'What?'

'God. He knows what happened to it.'

Man, he was losing his sense of humour too; it was being buried under boiling oil and visits from cops and stressing about Jesús. At the factory everyone was a bloody comedian but he couldn't get into the banter. Being inside all day watching conveyor belts of potatoes roll past was sapping his spirit.

'Jesús seems fine to me.'

'I hate the idea of him being grilled by social workers.' He went to run his hand through his absent hair and put it down forlornly. He was losing himself.

'It's not like there's anything to unearth. They'll be used to dealing with all sorts of horrors. Jesús isn't being neglected or abused.'

'They can put words in their mouths at that age, suddenly two and two make forty-six.'

'But there is no two and two.' Sarah lit a roll-up and offered him one.

'Healthy living, remember.'

'Sorry.' She stubbed it out in the overflowing ashtray.

It was nice of her to play things down but she didn't get how this shit worked – outliers like him didn't stand a chance against Big Brother. 'Seven-year-old finds his mother dead in a bath full of blood. Spends night alone in the forest. Father – with two previous convictions – is filmed digging up a dead dog. Jesús ends up in care before you can say Wicker Man.'

'You worry too much.'

'Aggravated trespass and resisting arrest by the way. Protesting the road being bulldozed through Lingen common.' He didn't want her to think he was an actual criminal. 'He misses the goats. It breaks my heart.'

'He showed me the photo album you made together. Very sweet.'

'We were doing okay until bloody Johnson and his land grab.' He tracked a lazy bee cruising the pink and white flowerbed. 'Any word on his condition?'

'Recovering, according to Ernest. At least we're out of the woods on that one.'

Jack didn't want to wish him ill, but he did. His humanity was being buried too. 'Anyway, how's the post-van working out?' Pat had told him she'd handed over a Tesco bag stuffed with twenties, no questions asked. It was nice to know she wasn't completely virtuous. The dosh in the mattress was a little disturbing but it was not his circus, not his monkeys.

'Drives like a dream after the Clio.'

'Well, you deserve a decent motor.' The elderflower was reviving him, or maybe it was Sarah.

'Would you go back to the farm? You know, if we could reverse the decision?'

'You trying to get rid of us?'

She took the papers from her knee. 'The Freedom of Information response. It's dynamite. Dynamite with which to blow Terence Johnson out of the water.'

Bless her, she was so optimistic. Came with the job of course. Must be nice to have an unshakable belief, even if it was all bollocks. 'Oh yeah?'

'Proof that he sold the farm, subject to contract, to Bowman Brothers Meat Inc the day after you were attacked.'

'Okay, that's cool.'

'Not only that, but the council approved change of use before the public consultation, so the abattoir contract is null and void. By the way, once people knew about it there were over fifty objections.'

'But they'll just ignore all that and redo the contracts.' He couldn't share her enthusiasm.

'We should go to the police.'

'It's circumstantial evidence, the cops won't investigate.' A lawnmower started up in the distance, somewhere a dog yowled. 'Johnson's bullet proof.' The toady creep was tucked up in bed with the babylons. Nothing would shake him out.

'There's more.' Sarah brandished a sheet in triumph. 'Lionel Gooseworthy was removed from the council chamber after protesting against the abattoir. He apparently held up a banner of baby piglets.'

'All very interesting, but none of this is against the law.'

'Melville Russet was Johnson's business partner, right? He just disappears without a trace, without telling his elderly mother or taking his son? Johnson has got to be behind it.'

Her eyes shone crazy green when she was excited.

'Just parts of a jigsaw.'

'Yes, exactly, with the two most important pieces missing. We need to prove that Johnson had you hospitalised and that he got rid of Melville Russet.'

'The guy's got half of West Tillington in his pocket.'

'Then we start with the other half.'

A crow cackled from the oaks. This crazy vicar, sitting in a deckchair sipping elderflower cordial and smoking roll-ups, made anything sound possible. 'Okay, so we need to do some more digging.'

'We need to find someone who's not scared to speak out against Johnson.'

'When you ain't got nothing, you got nothing to lose.'

She smiled; she must recognise the Bob Dylan lyric. She was pretty damn cool for a vicar. So, who had nothing to lose?

'The Reverend Gooseworthy,' they said together.

30

Jesús felt small in the big room. The bright red carpet was stained with dark patches just like on the crime scenes programmes Mum used to watch. There were big chairs, medium chairs and small chairs like in Goldilocks and a pile of beanbags scattered on the floor. Enormous weather pictures had been painted straight onto the wall but they were a bit rubbish. Fluffy white clouds, dark rainy clouds, a sun with pointy yellow triangles. A horrible cloud with puffed-out cheeks and pouty lips like it was whistling was probably meant to be the wind but it was as creepy as hell. Jesús chose the medium-sized blue chair by the wall so he'd have his back to it but now he was looking at a rainbow that only had five bands.

Miss Walker sat on the big orange chair and put her mini-suitcase on the floor beside her. She smiled but she didn't look friendly. 'Would you like to play with any of the toys, Jesus?'

There was a big box of Lego that looked a bit sticky, some creepy dolls, a family of grubby teddies, a tray of grey plastic soldiers and a ball of plasticine with the colours all swirled together.

'No thank you, Miss Walker.' All polite, just like he'd practised with Dad.

'Now that we know each other you can call me Debbie.' She didn't look like a Debbie, more like an Alexa.

Jesús swung his legs and looked at the rainbow. He'd like to add the orange and the indigo but there weren't any paints.

'I have a special game called My Family and Mr Nobody.' She didn't ask if he wanted to play, she just took out a set of white boxes and a pile of cardboard figures from the mini-suitcase and unfolded a little table. Maybe it was a magic trick. He hated magic tricks. Miss Walker propped a man in a grey suit against the first box. 'This is your dad.'

Jesús laughed. Dad never, ever wore a suit; they were for bankers. That's what Dad called people he didn't like. Prince Andrew was a banker, so were all Tories and Justin Bieber. Mr Johnson was a total banker.

'Who else is in your family?' Miss Walker was all serious now to show that it wasn't really a game.

'Just me and Dad.'

She picked out a lady in a brown dress. 'Shall we put your mum next to your dad?'

'No, because she is dead.'

'That doesn't mean she's not important.'

'Okay, but put her on the other end.' Mum wore bright colours like her tight red dress with the white zig-zags that made people stop and look at her.

Miss Walker spread out the other figures like a fan. 'Who else should have their own box?'

Her breath smelt minty, like after Dad had had a sneaky cigarette. Jesús picked out a lady wearing trousers and put her on the box next to Dad. 'Sarah.'

Miss Walker did a weird half-smile-half-frown thing so perhaps he'd done it wrong. He reached for a boy in a stripy jumper. 'Also Ben and Moth.'

'No, because they're not in your family, are they?' She let out a puff of air and took the boy back. Jesús was on his best behaviour so he didn't say anything.

She added a man with no face. 'This is Mr Nobody.'

He was creepy as hell.

Miss Walker placed a pile of cards in front of him. 'You're going to read each card out loud and post it through the slot of the person it belongs to.'

This person cares about me.
This person can get angry.
I wish this person wasn't in my family.
This person makes me laugh.
I don't like this person.
This person loves me.
I am scared of this person.

This person can make me cry.

It was fun posting the cards but it was all a bit random. He couldn't put any bad ones in Mum because you shouldn't be mean about dead people. Or about your mum. He couldn't put all the bad cards in Mr Nobody because you were obviously meant to spread them around a bit. Dad scared him with his stories but that was fun-scary. There wasn't a fun-scary box, so scary would have to do. He'd cried when Dad told him that the goats were going to new homes. So that was Dad too.

No, he wasn't doing it right. Maybe he should start again. But Miss Walker was checking her watch. She took out her clipboard and her biro. She hadn't tidied away the boxes. It was polite to be helpful.

'No, just leave it.' A snappy voice.

He dropped Dad's box. 'Sorry.'

She smoothed down her skirt. 'Tell me about your mum.'

Jesús preferred the sort of questions where you could just say Yes or No. It was hard to remember. It seemed like years ago. Mum was a terrible driver. Like, really terrible. Everyone knew to stay out of her way; not even to park next to her. Sometimes she went out at night and drove like crazy around the roads. She said she was running away but she always came back. One time she hit a badger and it died and Dad had to clean the fur off the bonnet. Not nice.

'Jesús?'

He remembered something else. 'There was this one time we went to the zoo and a big llama spat at her and I laughed and she hit me.'

'Dear oh dear.'

Jesús wanted to say, 'No, it was a llama, not a deer,' but it wasn't the place to make jokes.

'She could be nice too, Dad told me she used to sing to me in Spanish when I was a baby. But I can't remember.'

'Can you tell me about another time that she hit you?'

There had been a few times, always when Dad wasn't around, and a lot of near misses because he'd got good at ducking. 'This one time, Dad told his mate he was worried that Mum was losing her marbles. So, I put my best bag of marbles under her pillow and she went mad and threw them at me one by one. I was zoom, zoom, zoom, like a ninja but a shooter hit me really hard right on the forehead. Lucky it didn't go in my eye.'

Miss Walker took a long look out of the window. Maybe there was a squirrel. 'It must have been scary being out in the woods all night.'

It was good not to have to talk about Mum anymore. 'There were people in hoods and they all gathered round and were probably going to kill us or torture us or something.' Oh no, he'd forgotten it was a pinky swear secret.

Miss Walker was very still. She didn't even do her parrot-neck thing. 'Who were these men?'

'One was a woman.' She took hold of his hand. 'Jesus, have you ever told anyone about this before?'

'No, it's our secret. Actually, I shouldn't have told you. I promised.'

'You have been a very brave boy.'

She wiped her hand on her skirt when she thought he wasn't looking. It was a bit sticky because he'd been eating a peanut butter sandwich in the car.

31

Sarah sat behind a grubby Formica table and felt all joy drain from her. There was a crowd of other visitors, mainly women, some heavily pregnant. Children coughed. Babies cried. Nobody spoke. They shared a collective mourning for the loss of their mobile phones and cigarettes. From beyond the safety glass a cacophony of shouts, jeers and hollow laughter spilled into the expectant hall. The sound of criminals.

Put your fucking hands up.

You want to die today?

She couldn't survive prison. The noise, the food, the people. Criminals were a breed apart; impulsive, dangerous, amoral. Not like her. Who was she kidding?

The visiting order had come through before she'd had time to change her mind. Selecting the right clothes was tricky; she wanted to strike the right balance between trustworthy colleague and don't-mess-with-me-mate. She'd vacillated on the dog-collar, eventually deciding in favour to prevent any Clarice Starling type impropriety and to smooth the admission process. Instead, she'd been subjected to increased scrutiny, confusion regarding whether the visit was personal or professional – and therefore required rebooking – and bombarded with dark sarcasm at every stage.

'A bit late for confession, Vicar, he's doing five years.'

'You here for his last rites?'

'Hope you haven't got any loaves and fishes in that bag.'

Having endured the vetting, photographing and searching she was herded into a waiting room for a forty-five-minute ostracism. Perhaps they knew the Reverend Gooseworthy's crimes and had condemned her by association. Or maybe they just distrusted the clergy. She couldn't blame them.

The hall hung heavy with the smell of sweat, cabbage and poverty. The visitors looked up whenever the door opened and hung their heads when yet another officer brisked through. Sarah battled the impulse to leave. Perhaps she should come back next week when she'd planned her approach? But how did you prepare to face a piglet abuser, let alone get him onside? There were no textbooks.

There really were bars on the windows. Beyond the curved external wall she could see one corner of the visitors' car park. What a miserable view. A shiny bronze Mercedes stood out from the old bangers. The same type that Carole Adlington-Wyndham drove. It must be the car of choice round here for the pretentious middle-classes.

The doors burst open admitting a swarm of men who hugged their partners under watchful eyes. Her empty seat remained empty.

Anger, relief, disappointment. She caught an officer's eye. He looked at his clipboard. 'Name and number?'

'Sarah Wilson, West Tillington 835466.'

'No, the prisoner.'

She dug in her bag for the paperwork although he had the information in front of him.

'Gooseworthy 4219.'

'Coming from the hospital wing,' he said with a mirthless smile.

Oh God, he must have been beaten up. That's what happened to sex offenders. The officers would turn a blind eye, encourage it even, there would be a six-on-one in the shower block. As the minutes ticked by she imagined ever more grotesque injuries. A wave of nausea hit. What would happen to a skinny weakling like herself in a women's prison? Actually, if it was anything like Orange is the New Black, she might enjoy the camaraderie.

A side-door opened and the Reverend Gooseworthy limped into the hall, gave a tight bow and took his seat.

'How charming to receive the gift of visitation. You are my first.'

Lionel Gooseworthy was not what she'd expected. She'd imagined a balding man in his fifties with a ring of neatly trimmed hair, a plump face ruddied by port. The man opposite was gaunt, his hair coloured a light auburn, his eyebrows shaped.

'I understand you've been attacked.'

'Only by the press, my former friends and the prosecution, dear thing. One learns to live with it.'

'Aren't you in the hospital wing?'

'Just overnight, plantar fasciitis. It comes from years of standing at the pulpit in soft-soled footwear. Vicars beware!' His teeth were small and crowded.

She could detect a splash of Paco Rabanne; the thought that he'd applied it especially for her visit made her unaccountably sad.

'One assumes that this is not a social visit, Vicar. How may I be of assistance?'

'I've come about Terence Johnson. A friend of yours I believe.'

'Hardly. We had a mutual understanding for a while.' He adjusted the cuffs of his baggy grey sweatshirt. 'He crossed a line.'

'That line must have been pretty wide coming from you.' She was going to add 'no offence' but did not.

'Judge not, Vicar. What is given in evidence is not necessarily the truth, the whole truth and nothing but the truth.' His intonation and cadence belonged in a church not a prison. It was rather disorientating.

'You were convicted of a horrible offence.' She lowered her voice – however vile his crime she didn't want to be responsible for making him a target.

'Fear not, they all know. One has to endure endless oinking and snuffling not to mention jokes about saveloys and pork scratchings. Then there are the creative recitations of 'this little piggy' in which the piggy in question engages in evermore diabolical activities.'

'We seem to have drifted off topic. What was the mutual understanding you had with Terence?'

'I am afraid to say that I succumbed to the lure of riches. Well, not riches exactly but a nice little supplement to the stipend.'

'Is that how he holds such sway?'

'That and ferreting out the chinks in one's armour. Alas, we all have a few bones if not entire skeletons piled in the closet.' He attempted to adjust the waistband of his tracksuit bottoms. 'I do apologise, I fear I have been allocated an extra-large jogger. Very unflattering, not to mention impractical.'

'Bribery and blackmail?'

'Indeed. The man is a master puppeteer. Greases the right palms, massages the right egos. They prop each other up like a circus act.'

She tried to ignore the raised voices behind her. 'Do go on.'

'If one does not sing from the same hymnal sheet one's penalty can be harsh.'

'And you chose a different hymn?'

'Indeed. A solo acapella. I vehemently opposed his abattoir scheme and was summarily set-up and sacrificed. Made an example of in order to demonstrate the power of his wrath.' He looked suddenly bereft. 'Alas, who would take the word of a piggy-fiddler?'

'Are you claiming that you are innocent?'

'Not entirely, I did invite piglets up to my rooms. Solely for company you understand.'

A table was overturned. A deafening alarm sounded. Someone wielded a chair. The officers ran from their stations, separated the prisoners, twisted their arms behind their backs and marched them headfirst through the double doors. Her heart was racing.

Evidently accustomed to the violence, Lionel waited calmly for the alarm to stop. 'I was gathering support against the abattoir. Et voilà.' He raised his hand in a balletic flourish. 'Terence conveniently comes up with an incriminating video. I was framed.'

Sarah allowed her nerves to settle. 'They were dressed in tutus and wearing lipstick,' she hissed.

'Exactly, Janice and Janet were not naked. It was all very tasteful.'

'But dressing them up, that cannot be right.'

'In the finest tulle so as not to irritate their delicate skin. Cruelty-free lipstick, never tested on animals.'

She couldn't quite believe she was having this conversation.

'I haven't come to ascertain your guilt or innocence, Reverend.'

'My darlings never suffered.'

'Really? They consented?'

'It was purely talking. A one-way conversation admittedly but I treated them like princesses.'

'What about the explicit video?'

'The video was shot at a compromising angle. Clever cutting. Image manipulation. He must have paid someone. Quentin Tarantino perhaps.'

Another heated argument was escalating behind her. It centred on a question of paternity.

'You were found guilty beyond reasonable doubt. There must have been convincing evidence.'

'I am afraid that the offensive conclusions were drawn solely by deviant inference and arose entirely from the perverse minds of those within our criminal justice system.'

A woman in a lime-green tracksuit stalked past them and demanded to be taken back to the gate.

Sarah checked her watch. They were veering off-track again. 'Do you have any information on the forced eviction of Jack Stretton from Borten Wood Farm or Terence's relationship with Melville Russet?'

'I would love to help, Vicar, but I'm afraid it is not in my best interests to do so.'

'What have you got to lose?'

'I am appealing my conviction. Terence Johnson is a dangerous man to cross. He could certainly scupper one's dream of release.'

'Could you at least give me a lead?'

A bell blared. 'Two minutes. Say your goodbyes, folks,' bellowed an officer.

'Check out Terence's finances. They were rising like the good flood until somebody pulled the plug.'

'Time gentlemen please!'

'What about Melville Russet?

A scraping of chairs and final farewells ricocheted around the hall.

Lionel stood to leave. 'Melville knew much more than was good for him. Then he 'disappeared."

The inverted commas were implied.

'And the line Terence Johnson crossed?'

Reverend Gooseworthy looked her straight in the eye. 'Murder.'

32

M urder.

The single word that suffocates all others.

Sarah paced the living room. The downpour had finally stopped, leaving the tock, tock, tock, of dripping guttering. It was getting on her nerves.

What the hell should she do? Go to the police? But Lionel wasn't willing to testify and it was true that as a convict he now lacked any credibility. She had no actual evidence to link Terence to Melville Russet's murder. Or to the attack on Jack.

Terence was a man who exacted revenge. Sarah was out of her depth. Terence had a web of cronies. She had no one apart from Jack and he was so anti-establishment he wouldn't deal with any form of authority. Eileen, Betty or Jean might have some ideas but she didn't want to plant thoughts that Melville had been murdered without definite proof.

Lionel had indicated that Terence's motive was financial betrayal. She needed documents, bank statements, something. She paused her patrol. Through the window Ernest was forking grass cuttings onto the compost heap.

What was it that he'd said the day they were clearing out the bedroom? Something about not everything being as it seemed. A hint about his employer. Maybe it wasn't Lionel Gooseworthy he was referring to; he also worked for Terence. And he had access to his bins.

Ernest acknowledged Sarah with a nod and continued with his forking. She scanned in search of an introductory compliment: close-cropped hair, grubby checked shirt, baggy trousers; there was little to go on.

'The lawn looks good.'

'Aye.'

'That old mower's seen better days, perhaps I should update?'

He spat a gob of phlegm. 'Does the job.'

'I'm guessing that Terence Johnson has a better one.'

The smell of rotting mulch rose as he stabbed the pitchfork through the lower layers of compost. Sarah stopped herself from further comment. It paid to wait for Ernest.

'Sit-on,' he said eventually.

'Ah, they must be pricey. Are they worth it?'

He mixed in the grass cuttings. 'Don't do the edging. That's what makes a lawn.'

She nodded. Her tolerance of lawn-based conversation had reached its capacity. 'Have you worked for him long?'

'Few years.'

'What do you make of him?'

'Work's work.'

She suspected that this was as close as he ever came to open criticism. 'I need to ask you a favour. Nothing illegal.'

Ernest stopped, wiped his hand across his brow and leant on his pitchfork. His eyes were the disconcerting amber of a stuffed fox. 'Oh?'

'It concerns Terence.'

'Aye.' His countenance remained taciturn.

'Say no, obviously, if you don't feel you can.'

'There's risk.' A statement given without inflection.

'It would pay to be discreet.' She waited for a response. None came. 'Acquisition of information.'

Ernest picked up a handful of mulch and rubbed it through his thick fingers. 'He's out Wednesdays,' he said brusquely.

'Would you be able to look through his bins?'

'For evidence of wrongdoing?' He gave an almost imperceptible movement of his head.

'Well, yes. Anything that might be of interest.'

He scratched his cheek with his stubby thumb leaving a smear of green. 'Aye, alright.'

They had agreed that Ernest should come straight over to the vicarage first thing but there was still no sign of him. Sarah hadn't slept all night. Her concentration was shot. When had she become such a worrier? Jack hadn't helped, pointing out that Ernest was just as likely to be in the pay of councillor Johnson as anyone else, or to be cowed by his threats. He could be spilling the beans right now. Were he to be caught rifling through his bins, or whatever the hell he was doing, she would be responsible for him losing his job. Or worse. Either way, it had the potential to be a catastrophe.

Sarah drained her third cup of coffee and checked her phone again. A sudden forceful rapping on the window took her back to the rook assaults. She let Ernest in the back door.

'From Johnson's.' He slung a bulging bin bag onto the kitchen table.

'There's a lot of it.'

'Been through the shredder. Bank statements and such.'

'That's amazing.'

'Usually dig it into the compost. He'll not miss it.'

'Wow, brilliant. Cup of tea?'

'No.' He turned to leave. 'Nancy said the bat charity has reached fifty thousand.' He went out to tend to the manure.

33

Jack's childhood hadn't been the happiest. So many moves, so much crap to deal with. It was tough being the only lad whose father didn't have a gun. Non-combatants were pussies.

He placed a canister of glue and a stack of transparent paper on the kitchen table and laid out three bowls of vegetable crisps; beetroot, parsnip, carrot. Rejects were free at the end of the shift. Jesús hadn't had the best start but he'd make it up to him. Frankly, craft time was a drop in the bucket but it was something.

Jack would be a better father. Better than his own dad. Not a hypocrite. Not a walking feckin contradiction. Could there be any more fraudulent an occupation than army chaplain? Praise the Lord and pass the ammo. He'd left home at sixteen – his father's blessing of the 'shock and awe' campaign the final nail in the coffin – and never spoke to him again.

Being an outsider was a heavy load to haul. He had survived. He'd ploughed his own furrow until he was happy with it. But would Jesús be able to rise above the silage being sprayed on him? His size and parentage already singled him out. Now he'd been uprooted, lost his goats and his home, had to see a social worker, had to cope with his own absence working crazy long shifts. Poor lad. And over it all hung the shroud of his mum's suicide.

So yeah, craft time was a grain of sand. Sarah had come up with the idea – something she'd heard on Women's Hour. It was also an opportunity to show evidence of excellent parenting, even though the bar was apparently set at the ominously sounding 'good-enough.'

Jack called them through. 'Okay guys, so today we're going to make stained-glass windows.'

'Cool.' Jesús stuffed a handful of parsnip crisps into his mouth, chewed briefly and coughed them violently onto the tabletop. 'Ew. Not nice.'

Jack tasted one. 'Ah, double salted. Rookie error.'

'Disgusting.' Jesús wiped at his tongue with his t-shirt.

'Remember what Buddhists say, mate, "Never take anything that is not freely given". I guess Christians say the same, right, Vic?'

Sarah nodded. 'Thou shalt not steal,' she mumbled through a mouthful of beetroot crisps.

'Anyway, lay out your designs on the tracing paper. When you're happy we'll glue them down.' He turned on some background music. The melancholic suffering of Nick Cave's *Skeleton Tree* seeped into the room. That was some dark vibe – Sarah had some pretty bleak tastes for a vicar. He swapped the CD for Billie Eilish, who sounded positively upbeat in comparison.

Jesús fashioned the carrot and beetroot crisps into the shape of a moth. He nibbled an orange disk for the moon, placed it in the top corner and sprinkled a handful of crunched up crumbs for the background.

'Elephant hawk moth?' Jack guessed.

'Yep. Ready for the glue.'

Jack sprayed the picture and held it up. The moth was flying over an ancient desert. It took his breath away.

Sarah turned hers around to reveal a still-life with root vegetables.

'Wow, I thought you'd do baby Jesus or God or something, like in real church windows.' Jesús was wide-eyed. 'That's way better.'

'Thanks, Sweetie.'

Jack decided on a goat in deep red and yellow with orange hooves and ears. He added a background of radiating lines to give depth. 'What do you reckon?'

'It looks like it's at a rave,' said Sarah. 'He just needs some shades.'

Jack added a pair of dark glasses. Jesús leant across for a better look, laughing like a cartoon character.

'The winner of best picture goes to...' Sarah drum rolled her fingers on the table. 'The moth by Jesús Stretton.'

They applauded and Jesús took a bow.

'Come on, let's put them up.' Jack led them through to the living room and hung the pictures on the south-facing window. The sunlight transformed them, throwing rainbow prisms across the room.

'Wow. Can we make some more?'

'I think we're out of crisps, mate.'

'We could make something else.' Jesús peered into the black bin bag. 'Let's use this.'

Jack looked to Sarah for an excuse – he was no good at making things up on the hoof the way she could. Come to think of it, a dodgy skill for a vicar.

'Sure, okay.' She tipped the shredded documents onto the carpet. 'This will be a good exercise for developing patience and concentration.'

'Really?' Jack pulled at the neck of his t-shirt.

'It'll be like doing a giant jigsaw puzzle.'

'I'm not sure this is such a good idea.'

'Please, Dad, it'll be fun.'

'We'll sort them by colour first.' Sarah gathered them into piles. Some had simply been ripped into eighths. 'Then line them up and if they match you stick them onto the card. The picture of the black horse goes in the top right-hand corner.'

It was hardly a wholesome family activity but Jesús and Sarah were already engrossed. Jack left them to it and went to clear the kitchen table. So much for excellent parenting, now he was letting his son piece together stolen documents for a vicar who planned to use them to discredit the head of the council. Jesús was enjoying himself though – squeals of delight came from the living room. Whooping and a round of applause signalled the completion of a letter or bank statement. They were getting quite unruly. Well, it was good for the lad to have fun.

Jack started on the washing up. Sofía never played with Jesús, even when he was a toddler. Truth was she neglected him; shoving him in front of Cbeebies for six hours a day was not good parenting. Still, he had learned to count and to recite the alphabet by age four although he still said zee not zed. Sofía's occasional efforts at mothering were misjudged; she would interrupt him when he was playing happily by himself and redirect him with a caustic criticism. That woman could suck the pleasure out of anything.

Shrieking erupted from the living room. It sounded like Moth had skidded through the papers. Jack rinsed the Fairy liquid from the plates and stacked them on the draining board. Now there was stomping and cheering. He poured three cordials and carried them through. Sarah and Jesús were lying on the carpet howling with laughter. Shreds of paper sticking to their hair, their eyes shining with glee, tears running down their cheeks.

'What's going on guys?'

Sarah waved a sheet of paper, unable to speak, and burst out laughing again. Jesús scrambled to his knees and rose unsteadily to his feet. Numerous completed documents lay drying on the chairs, the sofa and the coffee table, their surfaces shiny with glue. A strong smell of fish hung in the air. Jack inhaled sharply. Bloody hell.

'What did you use to stick them down?'

Sarah pointed weakly to the empty bottles of glue discarded on the carpet. He rushed to open the windows and doors.

'Repositionable glue, Dad. It's so cool.'

'Come and sit outside.' He took Jesús's hand and led him onto the patio.

Sarah was now crawling on all fours towards the open door. 'I don't feel so good.'

Jack helped her into a deckchair. 'You'll be okay now you're in the fresh air. Take deep breaths.'

It wasn't her fault – how would a vicar know about the effects of aerosol glue followed by a heavy dose of Copydex? At least Jesús wasn't too badly bombed.

'You okay, mate?'

Jesús drank his juice and swung his legs under the chair. 'Yep. The letters were easy to put together. And guess what? Some are from Ben's dad. Mr Russet.'

'Okay.'

'They're all about money but some have been pterodactyled

out in black pen. Maybe there's a clue to why he disappeared.'

Jack looked to Sarah who sat glassy eyed. She was no help. 'Look, mate, don't mention the letters to anyone, okay? Not even to Ben.'

'I thought you weren't meant to keep secrets.'

'It's not a secret, it's an omission.'

Sarah sat upright and vomited in front of the deckchair.

'Maybe keep that a secret too.'

34

I t was the first time Sarah had ever been in a police station. It was disappointing. Except for the smell of urine and the distant offkey singing of O Sole Mio, she could have been sitting in any shabby municipal building from the seventies. The heavy box-file was causing an alarming numbness to spread down her legs but she didn't want to risk putting it on the empty seat. The officer at reception was pleasant enough but had not shown the interest that she'd anticipated, he'd merely asked her to wait, someone would be through shortly. That had been forty-five minutes ago.

Her fellow incumbents included two teenage boys with cheap trousers and expensive trainers and a woman with the look of Myra Hindley. The boys spent their time watching what sounded like pornography on their mobiles, flicking their tongues at her and laughing like drains.

Finally, an officer appeared through the swing doors and called Reverend Wilson? Oh no, it was Fish. She adjusted her dog-collar and followed him through to an office that was as dismal as the reception area but with computers. He sat in front of one studded with Lego police figures and gestured for her to take the plastic chair opposite.

'What can I do for you?' He glanced at the clock.

The elephant of the desecrated dog grave and her inhospitable reception of him lumbered through and sat quietly between them.

She cleared her throat. 'I have information about financial impropriety.' No, that didn't sound strong enough. 'Fiscal offences.' She indicated the box-file on her lap.

'Are you turning yourself in, Reverend?' He produced a

hoarse laugh.

She swallowed hard. Would she ever be so burdened that she'd walk into a police station and confess? No, it had been a victimless crime. She had to keep telling herself that. Another lie.

'No officer but the illegal transactions were indeed committed by someone in public office.'

'Name?'

'Councillor Terence Johnson,' she said with relish.

'I'm guessing he's a town councillor, not a therapist counsellor.'

Why was he feigning ignorance? Everyone knew Terence, not least from his constant appearances in the local paper. 'The head of West Tillington district council.'

Fish clicked his mouse, squinted at the screen and tapped at the keyboard. 'Okay, and what do you allege he's been up to?'

'He's been syphoning off money to benefit his cronies and awarding illegal contracts.'

'Misuse of public funds is a very serious allegation, Reverend. I hope you have some evidence.'

She held up the box-file. 'His accounts, bank statements and various letters detailing the transactions. All colour-coded and indexed.'

'You have been busy.'

'So has he.'

'For example?'

'The Grange, Church Lane had a recent two-storey extension paid for by the Go Green initiative, triple-glazed with ground source heating.'

'Carole Adlington-Wyndham is your next-door neighbour I believe.'

'You know her?'

The officer busied himself with more inexpert typing. 'Please continue.'

'The Deanery has benefitted from a croquet lawn, an Arthurian maze and a deluxe floating duck-house all courtesy of a community improvement grant. Terence Johnson himself has enjoyed several all-expenses-paid town twinning trips to Khao Lak, Thailand. What a tropical beach resort has in common with land-locked West Tillington I do not know. It's basically theft.'

Stuffing the notes into the bags.

Stack after stack.

Heart pounding.

'Those are potentially libellous accusations.'

'Slanderous.' She patted the file. 'But it's all in here.'

Now he was ticking boxes in the electronic notes. He stifled a yawn.

'I also believe that Terence Johnson was behind a serious assault that hospitalised the tenant of Borten Wood Farm.'

'And why would he do that?' The fish stopped typing.

'He wanted the tenant off the land so he had him badly injured and unable to work.'

'I see.' He folded his arms.

'I further believe that Mr Johnson is involved in the disappearance of Melville Russet.'

'Wow, you really do have it in for him. Did he also kidnap Shergar?'

'This isn't personal, it's just that all the evidence points to Terence Johnson.'

'The evidence being?'

'A lot of circumstantial evidence that all adds up. The timing of the deal with Bowman Brothers Meat Inc, for example. It's all in the documents.'

'How did you come by these documents?'

'Freedom of Information request. Most are in the public domain.'

'Quite the amateur detective.' He evidently had little time for people who thought they could do his job. He leafed through the file with unconcealed disdain. 'And how did you acquire the personal financial statements?'

'I'd rather that remain confidential.'

'Hmm.' He rose and left the room.

Sarah stared out of the window. One of the youths from reception was urinating on a police vehicle while the other ran a key down the side of a Volkswagen Polo, oblivious to the CCTV. Perhaps she should have taken Jack's advice and waited until the case was watertight. Maybe his paranoia about the police was justified.

Fish reappeared and took his seat. 'I'm afraid we're not able to act on evidence that has been illegally obtained.'

'It's all above board. The documents had been binned.'

'Theft includes dishonest appropriation of property belonging to another with the intention of permanently depriving the other of it,' he quoted in a monotone.

'But Terence had thrown it away.'

'If it can be proven that the property discarded had a rightful owner, it would be illegal to take it.'

'Are you accusing me of theft?' Bloody hell, the irony.

'I'm just telling you the law. It's the same as prosecuting Tesco bin-divers.'

'That is also ridiculous. What about the FOI documents?'

'Leave them with me, I'll see what we can do.'

'I don't think so.' Sarah clutched the file to her chest.

He stood up. 'We cannot open an investigation without any evidence.'

'Then perhaps you could get some.' She headed for the door.

Fish blocked her exit. 'The DI has instructed me to seize the paperwork.' He prised the file from her fingers.

Sarah slumped on her kitchen chair and opened a bottle of Peroni. What an idiot she'd been. Terence Johnson was completely bloody bombproof. Of course, he would have fostered relations with the local constabulary; from the Grand fromages to the Dairy Lee triangles. And now she'd shown her hand. Everything she did either drew complaints, risked her arrest or made things substantially worse. She had pulled the pin and was still holding the grenade. Terence would hear about it. He would make her pay.

Maybe she could go back to Birmingham? No, she hadn't just jumped from that particular ship, she'd set it on fire.

Now she had started another one.

35

Jesús sprawled on a beanbag which looked comfy but wasn't. He scrunched around to spread the beans into a better position but it didn't help. Miss Walker perched on her chair holding her own hand.

Waiting.

Jesús had had some "homework". Yes, she actually did that double inverted commas thing with her fingers but not in the funny way like when Ben did it. He'd pucker his lips, pretending to be Miss Bickerstool and say "expert" or "accident" or "parental situation" using her best teacher voice.

'Don't worry, Jesus, take your time,' she said in a way that made him feel hurried.

He looked up at her and tried to remember what he was meant to have done for homework. She had new glasses with red frames that made her look friendlier than she was. No, still nothing. She came and sat next to him on the orange bean bag. She'd regret that, it was the really lumpy one that smelt of wee.

'Can you tell me one thing from last week that you'd like to explore some more?'

Oh, that was it. He was supposed to write-down-slash-think-about anything that he had never told anyone else. There were loads of things. Moth had done a poo in Sarah's shoe; it wasn't his fault he was only little. He'd got a star in his English book for his poem about bats but you're not meant to show-off so he hadn't even told Dad. He got called a Beaner by horrible Craig. Mum was in the bath again – it was best not to think about that.

'The woods?' she prompted.

No, nada. Ben had got another message from Dave 101. He

could tell her about that but it was nothing to do with the woods. Dave had attached another photo of himself, this time he was sitting by the side of a swimming pool. He was wearing mirrored sunglasses and in the reflection was the person taking the photo. It looked like a little kid. Dave 101 had asked if they wanted to go on a bike ride. Ben reckoned it wouldn't be polite to say no so it's all set up. Ten-thirty next Saturday morning, meet at Adfordley Cross. Dave said best keep it their secret because everyone nowadays was obsessed with stranger danger. It would just be an omission.

'Perhaps something you remember about the men and the lady in the woods?' said Miss Walker.

But that was also a secret with Ben. Dad and Sarah would go batshit crazy if they knew they'd been chased by scary people in the woods – he'd never be allowed outside again. Miss Walker seemed very interested in woods, maybe she liked moths too. Anyway, it would stop her going on about the people.

'Yes, there is something I'd like to tell you about.'

'Go on.' She tried to sit forward but beanbags didn't work like that.

'The giant wood moth is the largest species of moth in the world.'

She smoothed her skirt over her knee and let out a little puff of air. He waited for a minute – for what Miss Bickerstool called dramatic effect – before revealing the best thing about them. 'Some of them are too heavy to fly.'

She did her head-tilt thing that meant keep talking.

'They spend a lot of time sitting on logs in the woods by themselves.'

Miss Walker looked up at the little camera in the corner of the room. Jesús waved at it.

'Too heavy to fly,' she repeated.

'Yes.'

'Goodness. What must that feel like?'

That was an interesting question actually. 'Erm, lonely and disappointing I guess.'

'Tell me more about the feelings, Jesus.'

Wow, she really did want to know about moths. He closed his eyes. He was a giant wood moth – a female because they were the biggest – crawling along a branch with her antennae twitching. She picks up the scent of a flower on the other side of the pond. Maybe it's a water lily full of delicious pollen. She spreads her mottled grey wings trying to catch a breeze but the air is still. She folds them back in and walks along the branch until she can't go any further. Unable to eat, unable to explore the beautiful woods from the sky, she knows she only has days to live. 'I feel very sad and upset and trapped.'

Now she really perked up. 'Would you like to lose the heaviness and fly away?'

'I can't, it's not possible.'

'Perhaps in time, if you tried, we could find a way.' Her moth knowledge was very poor. They don't live long.

'I'm already preparing to die.'

Miss Walker clamped her fingers together. 'It doesn't have to be this way. We can get you to a place of safety.'

'No, that wouldn't work.' The wood moth's adult life was short wherever it lived.

Not much is known about giant wood moths so he'd run out of information. A creeping numbness seized his leg. Argh. Pins and needles made his eyes water.

Miss Walker looked a bit shocked. She wrote it all down. At least she was learning things.

Jesús rode his bike over to Ben's because it was only twenty minutes to Adfordley Cross from Vespiary cottage. They planned to leave at ten-past-ten to go and meet Dave 101. It was polite to be punctual. Jesús reckoned Dave wouldn't be much help, he never even mentioned Mr Russet in his last email, but Ben was dead excited.

The thing with Ben's dad was he wasn't that nice a person. He was nice to him and to Ben but he wasn't nice to his wife like you're meant to be. Ben said that he'd shout at her for not trying her best with the cooking and cleaning and maybe that's why she went to live in Missen-in-the-Marsh with a financial advisor. Ben really liked living with his gran but he also wanted to know what happened to his dad. Now he was getting worried that he might be found and he'd have to go back and live with him. Life is pretty complicated.

Jesús braked hard and skidded across the gravel in front of Vespiary cottage. He tooted his horn for Ben. There was just enough time to go and see if Peachy had gone back to normal after his power shower.

It was not good news. Peachy was slumped on his blanket all swollen like he'd been pumped up with a foot-pump and it wasn't nice to say but he was very smelly. Loads worse than before. He had collapsed forward onto his nose because his front legs were all soft. Wet sawdust poked through the holes in his skin where it had been over stretched. He was way beyond fixing.

Peachy's glass eye lay on the floor looking up at himself. Ben pushed it back into one of the small holes in his head. Now he was looking straight up at the ceiling.

'Granny Eileen shouldn't see Peachy like this. Especially after that whole fainting in church thing.' Ben plucked out the eye and tried it in another hole. It looked a bit better.

'Yeah. She could faint again and bang her head, or have a heart attack, or die of shock.' Jesús picked up an old sack with the end of a stick and shook it to check for spiders. All clear. 'We should bury him.' He lowered the sack over Peachy.

'Agreed. I'll go and tell Gran that we're off to play in the birch copse and we'll be well behaved.'

Jesús peered at Peachy through the top of the sack. 'Sorry about this, fella. We're going to take you somewhere nice now.' He wondered whether dogs ever came back to haunt you. If Mum ever came back as a walking-around ghost, not just a lying in the bath ghost, she'd just find empty cupboards and empty fields and no sign that they ever lived in Borten Wood Farm. She might be wandering around there now. She'd be dead annoyed about her burnt out mini. He would definitely not want to be there for that. Dad didn't believe in all that spiritism shite. But Dad hadn't been haunted.

Ben was back, carrying a big spade. 'She's making a Victoria sponge. She said to have a lovely time.'

Peachy was heavier than before. Probably heavier than he'd ever been in his life. It was important to find a nice spot for his final resting place; somewhere he'd know from when he was alive. Not too near the tree where he got hanged – he wouldn't have known about that, but still. The ground was nice and flat beyond the birch trees. It was the sort of place where there might be squirrels and there was the faint sweet smell of dog violets. A patch of undergrowth had already been cleared as if it had been waiting for him. Perfect.

The ground was softer than the hard earth all around but even so it was difficult to dig with such a big spade. They took it in turns; one to dig, one to reassure Peachy. It just needed to be deep enough to cover a puffed-up dog.

'Should we leave him in the sack?' Jesús didn't want to have to look at him again.

'Yes, it's more respectful.' Ben took a corner of the sack and dragged him into the hole.

'I hope you had a good life, Peachy.' Jesús made the sign of the cross. 'Rest in eternal peace.'

Ben waved goodbye as he covered him with soil. 'Enjoy it here in the woods, dearly beloved.'

It was funny but also not funny at all.

'Time for cake.' Jesús looked at his watch. Oh no, it was eleven-thirty. They'd forgotten about Dave 101.

36

A man – not exactly incognito in mustard trousers and Rupert the Bear waistcoat – checked that the coast was clear before ripping the Stop the Abattoir poster from the church notice board. He had evidently not considered the possibility that the incumbent vicar would be standing on a chair by the window checking the burner phone that was secreted in the curtain pelmet.

Bloody cheek. How dare he?

Sarah replaced the phone and ran outside. 'Hello, Terence,' she called over the gravestones.

He scrunched up the poster and tossed it into the bin. 'Oh, Vicar, I wasn't expecting to see you.'

'By the church and the vicarage? Well, I do like the element of surprise.' God, he looked rough. Those scarlet flecked cheeks signalled something sinister. A dysentery relapse perhaps.

'Very drôle, Vicar.' Terence raised his hands in mock surrender. 'Safe to approach?'

'Of course.' She was getting good at this.

'I thought perhaps a little chat to clear the air?'

'The air seems perfectly clear to me, councillor Johnson.' She turned the hose pipe onto full soak and drenched the border.

'Oh, come now, let's not fall out over a trifle.'

It seemed that he didn't yet know about the dossier lying on the police sergeant's desk in Sheet Street.

'An abattoir in the middle of West Tillington is hardly a trifle.' Look at her keeping her cool.

'Outskirts, Reverend, outskirts.' He waved his hand to indicate a far-away location and gave a sickeningly magnanimous smile. 'I thought you'd be in favour of such an unprecedented opportunity to bring jobs to the area.'

'It's not jobs I'm worried about, it's the cows and the sheep and the pigs going to untimely deaths, the stench of carcasses and the inability of people to enjoy their daily lives.' She adjusted the nozzle and sprayed a fine rainbow over the terracotta pots. How she'd love to douse the patronising little shit.

'You must understand that rural jobs are very hard to come by. This will be a huge boon to the youth of the area.'

'Training, jobs, prosperity? People don't buy those sound bites anymore. No one wants to live next door to an abattoir.' She smiled her most benign smile. 'Normal people wouldn't choose to slaughter animals for a living.'

'I think you're swimming against the tide with this one, Vicar, people here are barely eking out an existence.'

'I'm sure many would start up their own small businesses if funding was available. It seems all the EU grants went to established businesses. For example, builders and butchers.' She held his gaze. She'd done her homework.

'The church might not look favourably on you becoming so publicly involved with political agendas.' He examined his nails.

'By the church I assume you mean Geoffrey. He, like myself, is on the side of fairness, justice and community.'

Terence came closer and sighed with a practised resignation. 'May I offer an olive branch? I'd like to fully understand and consider your objections.' He produced his card like a magic trick. 'My direct line. Please phone or text anytime. No issue too small.'

'How very kind.' She didn't buy it for a minute. What was he up to?

'Entre nous of course. One doesn't want to be hounded by all and sundry.'

She slid the card into her back pocket. 'Are you alright, Terence? You look rather sickly.'

'A bout of gastro-intestinal turmoil. The price one pays for being a gourmand.'

'Not nice.'

'Anytime, day or night.' He strolled back to the lane.

What trap was he setting? Maybe his buddies at Sheet Street Station had indeed tipped him off about the chunk of evidence languishing in the in-tray. Evidence that she'd been rooting through his bins. Ah, maybe he was angling for harassment?

She Googled it. The Protection from Harassment Act 1997. *Repeated making of false and malicious assertions. Repeated attempts to impose unwanted communications and contact upon a victim.* It seemed that the key was repetition. He was attempting to lure her into quicksand of her own making, the more she struggled the worse her predicament would become. The offence carried a maximum of six months' imprisonment. God, he was trying to get rid of her. He must be covering up something major. Like murder. Lionel was right.

37

Today Jesús was in a different room that was pretty much empty. The walls had been painted white a long time ago and one side was just a whole massive window that you couldn't see through. He put his nose right up against the glass. It was a giant mirror. If anyone broke this one it would be a hundred years bad luck. His hair was wild because Sarah had dried it with her hairdryer. It made him look taller.

'Come and sit with me,' said Miss Walker.

She didn't seem very comfortable in her bean bag. They were the same ones from the big room that someone must have brought through. Just the red and green one – the orange one was probably in the wash. Maybe it had swollen up because of the beans, like Peachy.

Miss Walker put her hand flat on the floor for balance. Her pink nail varnish was chipped. She didn't have any rings. 'Aren't we lucky? We have a special longer session today.'

He pulled a face which wasn't very polite but now he wouldn't be back in time for Nature's Weirdest Creatures. Maybe Dad would find it on Catch-up.

'Don't worry Jesus, now we've got to know each other it will be easier.'

She was always saying that. He didn't know anything about her except she was a social worker and she worked with the safe-guarding team. They must be like the security people in bank robber films who always got tied up or shot. He hadn't seen any safes but perhaps there was an underground vault that she went down to guard. The job didn't really suit her.

Miss Walker put a pile of white index cards on the floor. It would have been easier on a table. He had to read the word printed in the centre and say what it meant.

Good. Dead. Truth. Scared. Abuse. Care. Safe. Bad. Sad. Alive. Happy. Lie. Relaxed. At risk.

It was hard to know if he'd got them right or not because she just said 'mmm.'

Then he had to find pairs of opposites. Miss Walker kept saying that there were no right or wrong answers. There were, for example, dead and happy don't go together. Truth and lie were kind of opposites but it was more complicated than that.

Flippin' heck, now he had to group them together into sets of three and Miss Walker had written some new cards out herself, and not even in her best handwriting. Luckily, he knew which of those went together because of Sarah testing out her sermons. Ritual, Rite, Sacrament. Miss Walker nodded. Devil, Satan, Lucifer. She was breathing like she was running out of air. Must be what she did when she was dead impressed. She asked if there were any words he wanted to add. For the churchy pile he wrote 'stained-glass windows' so he could talk about craft time which showed Dad and Sarah in an excellent light. A red and orange and yellow light hahaha. But she didn't ask about stained-glass windows. He racked his brain for another devilly word. Ah, got it.

'How do you spell Beelzebub?' It was from a Queen song that he and Dad sang along to in the truck.

'Golly, how do you know all these big words?'

'Because of Dad and Sarah.'

The red blotches were travelling up her neck. Jesús moved back in case they were catching.

She spelled the word out for him, snapped elastic bands around the piles and put them in her bag. 'Can you tell me one thing you do with your dad that you don't do with anyone else?'

Another chance to talk about craft time. He wasn't meant to mention Sarah because of the vomiting thing. 'We sniff glue and it makes us laugh.'

Miss Walker's rash was really red now. With any luck she'd have to go to sick bay and he could go home. Or she might ask him to guard the safes.

'Are you ever taken into the church?'

Going to church was probably an example of excellent parenting, although Dad thought it was an opium. 'Oh yes, all the time.'

'What do you do there?' Her voice was sort of shaky.

Maybe it was the spewy lurgy that spotty Lottie had last week. He lay back into the beanbag and inched away with his feet. 'We go into the vestry and have to be as quiet as church mice.' He made his best squeaking sound but she didn't laugh.

'What happens in the vestry?'

It wasn't a good idea to tell her about the computer. 'We drink out of the sacrificial goblets but don't tell anyone because we could get in trouble.' Actually, Sarah wouldn't mind.

Miss Walker looked at the big mirror. People seemed to be moving behind it but maybe it was just shadows. 'Jesus, is anything you've told me a lie?'

'No.'

'Is everything you said the truth?'

That was what Miss Bickerstool called labouring the point which is something you're not meant to do in written English; you make your point and move on. 'Yes. There might be some omissions.' There were always some omissions because if you said everything that happened it'd take the same length of time to tell it. You have to summarise. Miss Walker reached over and took his hand. Hers was all clammy; she definitely had the spewy lurgy. Jesús wriggled free and tried not to breathe her air.

'I can see how uncomfortable all this is making you. I hope you'll be able to tell me more when you're ready.'

After a short break for a digestive biscuit and an orange juice without bits Miss Walker brought out a box full of weird soft dolls. They had black hoods made from felt and held up with elastic bands tight around their necks. Their starey eyes made them look like they were being strangled. Jesús laughed.

'It's alright Jesus, don't be nervous.'

He wasn't.

'I'm going to leave you to play for a while.' She banged her knee hard on the floor as she struggled from the bean bag. That must be how she got the holes in her tights.

There was nothing to play with except the dolls. If horrible

Craig was here, he'd call him a poofy wuss. Jesús lined them up in height order. There were two smaller ones who didn't have the black felt. He sat them all in a circle and put the small ones in the middle back-to-back linking arms so they didn't fall over. Still no sign of Miss Walker. He tried to see through the cloudy mirror again – yep, there were definitely people in there. Maybe it was a tearoom.

Miss Walker came back in with a form. 'Jesus, I forgot to mention that these sessions are video-recorded.' She read out the form very quickly – it had lots of difficult words like disclosure and transparency and confidentiality. He signed it to say that she'd read it out loud. Maybe she was working towards her vocabulary badge.

'Right, now Jesus, you remember the people with hoods in the woods that you told me about? I'd like you to show me what happened with the dolls.' She spoke very slowly and clearly.

'Do you mean like on Crimewatch UK when they do a recreation?'

'A reconstruction. Yes, exactly like that.'

It sounded fun.

Jesús took the small dolls and walked them around between the bean bags. It wasn't much like a forest. He sat them down to have their cupcakes then walked them around some more. The people watching behind the window would be very bored. He grabbed the big hooded dolls and shoved the small ones under a bean bag to hide. They were shaking and wailing for dramatic effect. The hooded ones made creepy noises and did sinister laughs like the baddies in Scooby Doo. Much more fun than the little ones just sitting very still and then legging it. The hoodies danced around in a circle, kind of witchy, kind of native American Indian, to the theme tune from Jaws. Two of them dragged out the small ones and pinned them facedown and the others took it in turns to jump on them. The small ones wriggled free and fought back with karate kicks. The baddies shouted after them as they ran away wailing.

It must have been a good show because Miss Walker had tears in her eyes.

38

The doorbell was persistent. Sarah looked through the spyhole.

Oh God. The fish, the beard and that annoying bloody social worker.

She pressed her back against the door, buying time. They wouldn't come mob-handed if it was to update her about Terence Johnson. Either they'd uncovered the money laundering operation, were pursuing the theft of Johnson's bank statements, or had concocted some charges about dysentery dog. Whatever it was, she should start on the front foot. She flung the door open.

'Have you come to return my box-file?'

'No, Reverend Wilson, we have a warrant to seize property.' Fish flashed his ID; his mugshot was practically a pollock.

Beard held up a document. It had been issued that morning. Thankfully she'd made a big donation to SOB yesterday – thanks to a remarkably successful fundraising dinner in Pinner – and her laptop was now wrapped in a tartan blanket under the floorboards of the back bedroom. But the mattress still held the majority of its incriminating stuffing.

'I'm Debbie Walker.' The social worker gave an officious smile. 'I'm here to ensure that Jesus is not distressed.'

'Jesús,' she corrected, 'is at a friend's house.'

Debbie looked crestfallen.

'We are acting on information regarding the potential commission of very serious offences,' said Fish.

'In relation to Terence Johnson?'

'No.'

'Are you actually investigating the offences of Terence

171

Johnson?'

'Alleged offences. I'm not at liberty to say. We're here on another matter.'

'Not the dog again?'

'There are several avenues of inquiry.' Beard's radio crackled; he ignored it.

'Why, what's been said?'

'We have reason to believe that a minor is at risk.'

Sarah imagined a dilapidated coal mine but didn't make the joke. Her eye caught Carole straining to see over the privet hedge.

'What sort of risk?'

'There are a number of grounds for concern.'

'Such as?'

'Your recent visit to a known sex offender.'

Carole was now searching for non-existent weeds on her driveway.

'You'd better come in.'

Debbie, now superfluous, followed them in. They stood awkwardly in the living room while the radio requested a response vehicle to Weatherspoon's in Peaminster. Fish scanned her bookshelves, peered at the paintings of farmyard animals and the bottles of lager arranged in a ten-pin bowling formation on the sideboard. Thank God Jack had smoked his stash in preparation for the perfect-parent detox.

Beard studied a photograph of Jack and Jesús in the woods. 'Was this taken recently?'

'Last month.'

'Why has Mr Stretton changed his appearance so dramatically?' He stuck a red spot on the back and put it in a zip-lock bag.

'I'm not allowed to remove rubbish that has been thrown away but you can come into my house and take our property?'

'If you wouldn't mind answering the question, Reverend?'

'He had nits.'

Debbie took a scrunchie from her wrist and tied up her hair – she was evidently prepared for the occupational hazards of working with children.

'A little extreme, don't you think?' Fish thumbed through

her notebook.

'Excuse me, that contains confidential parishioner information. It has nothing to do with...' Sarah waved her arm, 'whatever this is.'

Moth sprawled in a shaft of sunlight on the Persian rug surrounded by an array of cat toys, setting the violation of her home in clear relief.

'I'm afraid it's not only Mr Stretton who is under investigation.' Beard dropped her notebook into another evidence bag.

'You seriously think that I'm a risk to Jesús?'

'Specific concerns have been raised.' Fish scratched his head with his biro.

'What the hell are you talking about?'

'Interesting turn of phrase for a vicar.' He pursed his lips like a guppy.

'I've been more than cooperative but this is getting ridiculous.' She shouldn't have let them in. Would they have kicked down the door? No, that was for drug dealers. And armed robbers.

'Your laptop please, Vicar.'

'I don't have one.'

'You must be the only person in the country without one.' Beard sounded pleased with himself. The space he took up was disproportionate to his contribution.

'Do you use the church computer?' Fish gave a cold stare.

'No.'

'Some disturbing correspondence has come to light.'

'I've never even turned it on.' Perhaps it contained links to some dodgy piglet-based chat room.

'It has been in use recently. Following intelligence from a parishioner and having viewed said computer's history, the concerns are credible.'

'This is crazy. I'm being set up. Why aren't you focussing on serious issues like the disappearance of Melville Russet?'

'You don't regard child grooming as a serious issue?' Fish unhooked her vegetable crisp stained-glass window. 'Interesting.'

'I'd love to chat about crafts, officer but I'd prefer to keep to the subject of this investigation.'

'Very phallic.' Fish blinked his slippery eyes.

'That's a parsnip, a beetroot and a carrot, what is wrong with you?'

Fish took a photograph of the offending picture and of Jack's rave-goat which he presumably interpreted as a drug reference.

Beard flicked through Jesús's wild mushrooms book. 'The poisonous ones are marked with a skull and crossbones,' he announced to the room.

Fish strode the living room like a gestapo officer. 'You might be aware that councillor Terence Johnson has been very unwell. He has expressed concerns that he is the target of a vendetta. Fears he has been deliberately poisoned. Your name was mentioned.'

'I hardly know the man. I've only been here two months.'

'And yet you've spent much of that time building a case against him.'

'You can't possibly think that I have anything to do with his illness.'

'You were very determined when you came into the station. Obsessed almost.' Fish blinked at her. 'I think we have all we need for the time being. We will find your laptop, Reverend Wilson. Your non-cooperation has been noted.' He tapped his notebook with his biro.

'Do tell Jesus that I was here and I look forward to seeing him very soon,' Debbie piped as if arranging a tea-party.

39

Man, Sarah was one cool fricken cucumber. Calm as a
clam. Getting on with things as if nothing had happened.
Jack stabbed at his peas. He had declined the social worker's
request for Jesús to have a medical examination. Something
dark was going on. His life was becoming a Scandinavian noir
without subtitles.

Sarah was munching away on her side-salad as if she was
at a fricken picnic. What did he actually know about her? She
never talked about herself. He'd put it down to an occupational
quirk but she was definitely hiding something. She had made
an extra effort with dinner – guilt makes good cooks. Fat chips,
runner beans and tofu nuggets; not the horrible ones from
Spar, homemade from scratch, even the breadcrumbs. Jesús
pushed his nuggets around the plate. Must be picking up the
frosty atmosphere. It was hard to miss.

'Don't you like your dinosaur legs?' Sarah asked.

'They don't have feet.'

'That's because they've been attacked by other dinosaurs.'
She sent a squirt of tomato ketchup across his plate. 'The poor
things have lost a lot of blood.'

Jesús smiled and took a mouthful. Jack eyed her. The woman
was very inventive – she had to be to keep up whatever pretence
was going on with the dosh in the mattress and the lies to the
cops about not having a laptop. What the hell was she up to?
She'd recounted today's storm-trooper home-invasion in some
detail but God knows what she was omitting.

'Hey, Jesús, how's it going with Debbie?' Her false cheeriness
was annoying.

'Meh.' Jesús added bean eyes to the T-rex he'd constructed

from his nuggets.

'Something you want to tell us? Anything on your mind?' She had the same blind Christian righteousness as his father.

'Nope.'

'Sure?'

'Geez, leave the lad alone.' He slammed down his fork.

'It might help to know what we're dealing with,' Sarah said through tight lips.

Now she was projecting the blame on to Jesús. She was the liability. What sort of idiot would grass up Terence Johnson without watertight back up? And why the hell had she left Jesús and Ben unsupervised with a computer containing God knows what perverted content? Not to mention allowing her visit to Lionel Gooseworthy to become public knowledge.

'How is this all my fault?' she said coldly. The woman could read his mind.

Jack bounced his knee under the table. 'I've got a lot to lose here.' He nodded at Jesús.

The scraping of cutlery on plates grew louder. Moth crept from under Jesús's chair and slunk away through the cat-flap. That was another thing. What was with getting a kitten the week they moved in? Asking Jesús to name him. It would be hard to leave; another loss for Jesús. What the hell had she been thinking?

'Please may I leave the table?' Jesús asked softly.

'There's chocolate mousse.' Sarah collected the plates.

'Oh.'

She placed a tub and spoon gently in front of Jesús and banged Jack's tub down next to him. He went to get his own spoon.

Jesús examined the label on his mousse. 'Me and Ben used the church computer to email his dad's friends.'

Jack ran his hand over his scalp, the moleskin regrowth was vaguely comforting. 'Did they email back?'

'One did but we never went to meet him.'

'Did you look at anything dodgy?' asked Sarah

'What are you asking him that for?' Jack snapped.

'Nope, just stuff about moths.' Jesús peeled off the lid and licked it. 'Also…' He looked sheepish.

'Go on, mate, it's okay.'

'We found Eileen's old dog, Peachy in a bin bag upstairs and we buried him again.'

'What?' Jack tried to soften his voice. 'Where?'

'Up by the birch copse near Eileen's.' Jesús scooped up a loaded teaspoon of mousse.

'That's tough ground to dig. Did you bury him deep?'

Sarah glared at him. 'Oh yes, because that's the only thing that's wrong with this.'

'We found a spot that was easier to dig.' He was much too young for such a worried expression. 'It was shaped like a rectangle the size of a big adult. We just dug a hole in the top.'

'A softer area?' Jack looked at Sarah and emphasised each word. 'As if someone had already been digging there?'

She stifled a gasp. 'D'you think?'

'Thanks for telling us.' Jack stood up and pulled on his black hoodie.

'Are you going to check?'

'Could you put him to bed?'

'You're doing it now, in the dark?'

'Yep. And tomorrow I'll look for a new place to live.'

40

It was hard to sleep knowing that Dad was in the woods digging up Peachy. Again. And knowing they would have to leave their home. Again. And leave Moth when he'd only just learned to jump up onto his shoulder. No one had explained why but it had definitely been a big mistake to bury Peachy. Sarah had looked extra shocked. She must be a real animal lover or maybe it was something to do with reincarnation although that was Buddhists.

It was funny how all the things he tried not to think about came creeping into his brain at night. Dave 101 would be angry with them for not turning up. He'd probably waited at Adfordley Cross for ages. Getting cross. Maybe he'd brought a picnic or some information about how to find Mr Russet.

Jesús turned on the bedside lamp and looked through his goat album. Goats were a great healer. It was nice to remember the day he and Dad took a photograph of each goat and printed them out and wrote their name, age, and whether they were a wether or a whether they were a doe. They were nearly all girls but he liked saying whether it's a wether. The album was like his memory box with stuff about Mum but he looked through the goat book more. It was too sad to think about Mum. He tested himself by covering up the names: forty-eight correct out of fifty-two. Not bad because Avril and Alicia and Milly and Miley were identical twins. He used to get them mixed up in real life.

Jesús closed his eyes. The goats trotted passed one by one to be patted and be given a carrot. Still he couldn't sleep, well, maybe he'd slept for a bit because he was lying face down on the album. He unstuck his cheek from Beyoncé. It was twelve-thirty. He tiptoed downstairs to get some juice. Sarah was curled up on the sofa in her blue rabbit onesie watching something in French on Netflix. Must be waiting up for Dad.

She shuffled over to make a space for him. 'It's about an agency in Paris that looks after actors.'

It sounded dead boring but it was series three, episode five, so she must like it. He lay down and put his head on her lap. The subtitles flashed by. They were hard to read from the side. It was nice to listen to the French accents and not talk about school or social workers or the police or Peachy or Mum. The gentle stroking of her hand on his hair was nice too. It must be a sad story because Sarah was crying but pretending not to. He closed his eyes. He was a sleepy dog. Not Peachy.

When Jesús woke up he was back in bed and Dad was getting ready for work.

'I have to hurry because I've got to wash my hair.'

Dad made that joke a lot now that he didn't have any. But today he sounded as if he was trying too hard to be funny and he seemed sort of off. Sarah looked terrible too – probably from being up all night watching the French thing. It was all a big rush to get to church on time. The clocks chimed ten. Sarah grabbed his hand and they ran out and across the lane. They didn't stop to look left, then right, then left again but there weren't many cars on a Sunday, or any day really.

Ben was sitting in the front pew with Eileen, Betty and Jean. They put their mobile phones down and said hello. Betty had been showing Eileen how to do online gambling on her new App. They were hilarious. Jesús waved a packet of chocolate chip cookies at Ben and headed into the vestry.

Oh no. There was a big empty space instead of the computer. Now they wouldn't be able to tell Dave 101 that they were sorry they missed him because they were held up by a dog. Things had been moved around; even the goblets had gone. Must have had a big clear out.

Ben had an animals dot-to-dot book so that was something to do. Jesús lay on his front on the dusty floor and flicked through the pages. Tiger, zebra, elephant, giraffe. He could see what they were before joining the dots. If he was going to make his own book he'd choose an anteater, platypus, tasselled wobbegong and star-nosed mole. He'd ask Dad and Sarah if they could make one in craft time. Oh, except they were leaving.

Jesús cracked open the door to listen to Sarah's sermon. He hadn't heard this one before because she was busy yesterday with all the polishing and hoovering and wiping the leaves of the rubber plant. She was getting pretty het up, just like one of those preachers you get on American God channels. She was not herself. Going on about not murdering and not stealing and not bearing false witness, although she didn't really explain what that meant. Then some stuff about camels and eyes and rich men. Probably she hadn't had enough sleep. She seemed very stressed. Being alone with Mum when she was stressed had been super scary. She got weird and started licking the cheese, opening all the cans and pouring the milk down the sink.

'Can I come over to your house this afternoon?' he whispered to Ben.

'Yep. Good idea, Sarah's gone mad.

41

According to Jack the body had been rolled in an Axminster rug. His eye for detail was disconcerting. At least he had been spared the full horror of viewing the corpse. The feet, still wearing shoes, protruded from the roll and he'd removed one for identification. Sarah had imagined the monstrous removal of a foot with the forceful stab of a spade but no, it was the shoe he removed. Like some macabre Cinderella. It was now in a Tesco bag-for-life under their sink. Under her sink. He'd cut himself with the spade. Leaving one's blood on a murder victim was not a great move. The enormity of the ramifications was all too much to take in. And then he'd just gone to bed. Perhaps he was in shock.

Nothing had been said the following morning. Neither of them could eat breakfast. They could hardly look at each other.

Sarah applied another squirt of shower gel and turned up the temperature to uncomfortably hot. She'd gone rogue in church. It had been heart-breaking seeing Eileen smiling in the front pew, blissfully unaware that she was living only minutes away from her son's mutilated body. No, he hadn't been mutilated, that was just her crazy imagination. Get a grip. It was a shoe. Just a shoe. And it might not even be Melville. She couldn't blame Jack for not uncovering the face. Just shovelling the earth back over him. She wouldn't want to look at a decomposing head. It was too revolting to think about.

And poor Ben. Thank God the boys had dug such a shallow grave for Peachy; the very idea that he could have unearthed his own father's body. She put her hand against the tiles to steady herself. Just stop thinking about it. The water ran cold. She stepped shivering onto the bathmat.

Sarah cleared the sink of dishes and put on a pair of yellow Marigolds, a faded *God is Love* apron, and a pair of ski goggles from the back of a cupboard. Even at arm's length she could smell the foetid stench of decay. With one swift movement she emptied the bag under the running tap. The water gushed into the inner shoe where it pooled and spouted like a macabre water-feature. Water spilled over the tongue and seeped through the eyelets making the laces dance like tiny snakes. She couldn't look away. The soil bled to reveal conker brown leather. A man's dress shoe. Quality. She nudged it over with a wooden spoon. Clods of earth detached themselves from the sole. Thomas Bird Made in Italy. Size nine. She zig-zagged a generous quantity of Fairy liquid over the shoe and watched the foam rise to engulf it. Best to leave it to soak. She needed to talk to Eileen.

The boys were playing with a bat-shaped kite in the garden, making it dip and soar and crash and start again. Everything was a bloody metaphor for her life.

Eileen was in her new summer house, bought and furnished with an online bingo win. The woman was a constant surprise. The sunflower yellow walls and cheerful polka-dot curtains were deeply incongruous with the message she was about to deliver.

'My new hobby.' Eileen gestured to the row of bonsai trees on the shelf.

'I always seem to over water.' Sarah dropped into the egg-shaped wicker chair suspended from the ceiling.

'The best ones thrive on neglect.'

'Tell that to social services.'

'Oh, I keep them at arm's length. They wanted Ben to talk to that Debbie Walker but she was no help last time so we declined.'

Damn, she hadn't known refusal was an option. 'Last time?'

'I had concerns, they dismissed them.' She offered Sarah a polo. 'Absolutely hopeless.'

'I don't think the sessions are helping Jesús either.' She took a mint.

'Haven't they given him the all clear yet?'

'Quite the opposite. They seem to be compiling a dossier. I'll be accused of stockpiling weapons of mass destruction next.'

'I suppose they can't win.' Eileen felt the soil under a tiny Japanese elm. 'They're always accused of doing too much or too little.'

'Anyway, Jack is moving out, probably for the best.'

'That's a shame, Jesús seems so happy at the vicarage.'

She liked the way Eileen just accepted things at face value without digging for detail. She needed to tell her about Melville. 'Did you have any contact with social workers when Melville disappeared?'

'Some girl phoned and asked if I needed any assistance. She sounded pleased when I declined.' Eileen cracked a polo between her back molars.

They watched the boys disentangle the kite from a blueberry bush.

'Does Ben talk about him much?'

'No, I suspect he thinks it might upset me.'

'I'm sorry. I'm being insensitive.'

'Not at all.' Eileen touched an arthritic finger to her eye.

It was a stretch to bring the conversation around to foot wear, shoe size or a penchant for Italian designer loafers.

'Could I use your loo?'

'Upstairs, second door on the left.'

The living room mantlepiece held a string of photographs: Ben as a baby, Ben and Melville sitting beside a river, Ben with Eileen holding coconuts at a country fair – the equine family resemblance spanned three generations.

The cupboard under the stairs was a jumble of shoes, hats and scarves. A pair of polished court shoes, warm ankle boots and a lone Wellington boot, green size five. Ben's trainers, muddy football boots, scuffed school shoes. Ah, bingo! A pair of fleece-lined plaid slippers, hardly worn. Size nine.

Sarah returned to the summer house to find Eileen slumped in her chair, mouth open, her head lolling back against the wicker work. Oh God, no.

'Eileen, Eileen.' She shook her arm.

She opened her eyes. 'Sorry dear, must have dozed off.'

She looked so tired in the harsh sunlight. Her eyes haunted. Sarah owed it to her to tell the truth.

'Eileen, I don't want to alarm you but a body has been found.'

'A body? In the lavatory?'

'No, in the woods behind your house.'

'Oh lord.'

'Jack found it. He covered it back up. Wanted time to think before calling the police.'

Eileen watched the boys who were now fencing with bean poles by the raised beds. 'Is it Melville?'

'I wonder whether you might be able to identify a shoe?'

'I'm not sure I can go to the grave.'

'It's in my kitchen sink. Brown leather, size nine.'

'Oh.'

Ben and Jesús careered into the summer house waving their sticks. 'Careful lads, you'll have someone's eye out.' God, she was becoming her mother.

Eileen rose unsteadily to her feet. 'I'll get my coat.'

42

Jesús raced ahead with Ben leaving behind the calls of Sarah and Eileen telling them to wait. It was nice to be naughty and to know that you wouldn't be told off. Nice to run like a dog who'd slipped his lead but would be welcomed back with hugs.

A very shiny red car with a long bonnet was parked outside the vicarage. The man who opened the door looked way too big for the car. He unfolded himself out of the driving seat. The man smiled at them but it didn't look like a proper smile. Also, his teeth were too white. His cheeks were very spotty and bumpy – like that rash you got if you fell in nettles – and his skin was grey. Jesús felt a bit sick just looking at him. He wore sunglasses although it wasn't sunny. When he took them off it was Mr Johnson the total banker.

'Hello boys.' He leant against the car and put his hand in his pocket. 'What are you two up to?'

'We went to church, then we flew a kite, then we had a sword fight and then we came back here,' said Jesús, still out of breath.

'What a delightful life you lead.' He smoothed his black hair across his bald spot. It was like a raven's wing.

'Good to see you've recovered from your night in the woods.' Jesús stepped back to avoid any hair-tousling.

'You know I live up the hill from Eileen's. You're both welcome to call in for cookies anytime.'

It was weird that the man who took their farm and goats could be so nice. Nice but creepy. Jesús stepped from foot to foot not knowing what to say. Phew, here were Sarah and Eileen at last. Everyone did fake smiles; even Eileen. Sarah didn't invite him in, instead they stood by Mr Johnson's car.

Jesús pulled at Ben's sleeve and walked over to the funny

tree in the pot by the front door. It had been shaped into balls like a clipped poodle. If you're doing something, even if you're quite close by, adults don't think you're listening. He'd learnt that from Mum and Dad. Mum talked pretty loud anyway, Dad always going 'Shush, geez.' She wanted more out of life than bloody goats and vegetarian hotpot. She said that a lot. Also, that her life was empty and not worth living. But she had Dad and the goats. She had him.

Jesús picked up a stone and threw it into the plant pot. Ben did the same. Sarah was asking Mr Johnson if he was feeling okay because he looked pretty sick, but he didn't answer. Instead, he was talking about Ernest being a tenant and not knowing how to make sandwiches. He didn't seem to know which side to butter, although it was obviously the one that goes on the inside. It was a weird thing to be telling Sarah. Dad had been Mr Johnson's tenant but he never had to make him sandwiches. Hopefully he wasn't going to take his house off Ernest. He was sure he could learn.

Each time they got a stone into the pot they levelled up the game by taking one pace back. Sarah and Eileen were not saying much. They both stood with their arms crossed in front of them like Miss Bickerstool did when she was waiting for silence and you just knew she was going to wait until everyone felt ashamed of themselves.

'I know about the allegations and the freedom of information request.' Mr Johnson hissed like a super scary snake.

'Freedom of information request' sounded nice and polite. Not something to be annoyed about.

Mr Johnson was now doing that whisper-shout that adults did when they were getting properly angry.

Sarah was skating on dangerously thin ice.

She needed to back off.

People disappear.

Jesús looked at Ben. If they were still pretending to be dogs they'd be barking and baring their teeth. Maybe Mr Johnson made Ben's dad disappear. Jesús picked up a handful of gravel and chucked it. It clattered all over Mr Johnson's car. They legged it.

43

S arah held her hands out flat – she was actually shaking. The threats had been issued so coldly. In the next breath he was talking about his role as jams and pickles judge at Lingsland produce fair and she should try the damson jelly. She'd done well not to retaliate. She was learning to play the long game. So was Terence; he hadn't even lost it about his car – just said he'd send her the bill and that Jesús should come to apologise.

Eileen filled the kettle as if on automatic pilot. She must be thinking about Melville. 'People disappear.' What could Melville possibly have done? What terrible secret had he uncovered that sealed his fate? That had him killed and buried in a shallow grave? Had he too been warned off and ignored the threats?

Sarah and Eileen stood side-by-side at the sink and looked at the dark shape lurking beneath the grimy water like a shipwreck. Sarah pulled gingerly at the metal chain until the plug swung free. The water drained to reveal the shoe squatting on a layer of grainy mud. Neither spoke. The kettle boiled and turned itself off. Eileen seemed very calm, resigned.

The sound of Jesús and Ben laughing and clomping around upstairs came from another world. One where little boys flew kites and played with kittens, where no one had been murdered and buried in the woods by a psychopathic killer.

'He bought the shoes in London,' Eileen spoke slowly, almost to herself. 'I don't know why, he could've got similar in Peaminster for half the price.'

'I'm so sorry, Eileen.' Her parishioner, her neighbour, her friend.

'He was always terribly extravagant. Meals out, cars, fancy

clothes.'

'At least he enjoyed himself.'

'True.'

'They'll find whoever did this.' She rubbed Eileen's back. 'You will get justice.'

An upbeat reggae rhythm pulsed from upstairs, accompanied by the syncopated squeaking of floorboards. The boys dancing.

'What will I tell our Ben?' Her eyes still fixed on the shoe.

'Maybe wait until his dad can have a proper funeral. It's not nice to think of him lying dumped out there where they've been playing.'

Eileen suddenly looked very frail. She spoke into the middle distance. 'There'll be press coverage, an investigation, a post-mortem.' She gripped Sarah's arm. 'I'm not sure I can deal with all that.'

'Yes, you can. You'll get through this. I'll be here every step.'

'Can't we just let him lie in peace? The thought of him being dug up and photographed and chopped about on a slab is too awful.'

'Melville needs justice.'

'Do you really think Terence has something to do with it?'

'He's certainly capable of criminal behaviour. And threats. Perhaps Melville had something on him.'

'Betty and Jean always said he was a catfish.'

'A catfish?'

'Or was it a shark? Yes, a shark.'

But how they all fussed over him. Overcompensating perhaps to disguise their true feelings. It seemed that everyone was hiding something.

'I think Betty and Jean are right. He doesn't scare me, well he does, but if he's responsible he needs to be locked up.'

Eileen turned from the sink. 'He and Melville did have a big falling out, some sort of business deal.'

'What was it about?'

'Currency, I think.' She wrung her age-spotted hands. 'Do you mind if I have a day or so before the police come for him?'

'Sure, you can stay here if you like.'

'No, I'll be fine.' Eileen smoothed her hair and applied a thin layer of apricot lipstick before calling cheerily to Ben that they were going home.

She really was a remarkable woman.

44

Poor Eileen must be dealing with the devastating news by avoidance. It had been two days and she hadn't answered any of Sarah's calls. But really, how could you begin to process the murder of your son? She would give her more time, maybe pop over with a casserole. Good grief, what was she thinking? She'd never made a casserole in her life and she wasn't going to start now.

Anyway, she had to go to the Deanery, she'd received another summons from Geoffrey Tibble. The only thing worse than an autocratic boss was an autocratic boss who never clocked off. What the hell had she done now? Still, it got her out of the vicarage. Jack and Jesús were packing up. The pain was physical.

Sarah slowed and turned into the Deanery. Oh God, the last person she wanted to see; Terence was speeding down the driveway in front of her, spraying newly laid loose chippings in his wake. A few more missing paint specks would enhance his claim for a full respray.

The front door had been left open; more ominous than welcoming. Sarah followed Terence through to the drawing room where Geoffrey sat hunched over a chess board.

'Terence, dear fellow, do take a pew. Are you a chess man?'

The poodles emitted feral growls as he stepped gingerly passed them, their eyes following like those of a family portrait. 'Afraid not.'

'I'd imagine thinking three steps ahead was par for the course in local politics.' Geoffrey moved his white rook to queen four and turned the board. 'Ah, Sarah, there you are. Would you like to take black?'

She raised her palm to decline. The poodles leapt onto her lap the moment she sat down. At least they offered some protection.

'You're looking rather peaky, dear boy. Would you care for a nourishing crumpet?'

'Delicate stomach.' Terence grimaced. 'Still a tad off kilter.'

'I heard you had a touch of the V and A.'

'D and V. Yes, very unpleasant but I'm over the worst.'

'I do like a toasted crumpet,' muttered Geoffrey to himself.

Merely being in Terence's presence was making Sarah's hackles rise. His slicked down hair, his ridiculous gold-buttoned blazer, the smell of Extreme Men aftershave. She stroked the bundle of poodles to steady her nerves.

'I'm guessing our invitation isn't strictly fun and games.' Terence stood with his legs apart his thumbs tucked in his waistcoat pockets. What a prat. 'Is it about our little tête-à-tête?' Clever; he was getting in first.

'I think you mean contretemps old chap.' Geoffrey frowned at the board with his finger on the black knight.

'I felt Sarah needed some guidance, a little nudge to keep her grazing with the flock as it were. Can't risk another maverick after Lionel.'

Geoffrey exhaled. 'We don't want church and state coming to fisticuffs.' He retreated his queen back to its starting position.

'Not at all. I was merely making the point that Sarah might wish to reconsider her opposition to the abattoir.'

Sarah realised she had yet to speak. She'd been focussing all her reserves on not punching him. 'Actually, your intimation that people "disappear" was very threatening Terence.' She wasn't going to be cowed by this idiot.

'Oh, come now, I was merely suggesting that taking a stance against the town council was damaging our previously harmonious relations with the church.' He propped his elbow on the mantelpiece Cary Grant style.

Unbelievable. She imagined whacking him with the carriage clock but focussed instead on the poodle licking her hand. 'My opposition is a matter of moral not religious conviction. I am allowed to express personal views, am I not?' Take that, cockroach.

'I understand that she even has the old biddies crocheting carcasses to display in the village hall. Most distasteful.'

It was astonishing how he continued to talk to Geoffrey as if she wasn't there. Sexist git. And actually, Eileen, Betty and Jean had produced those startling creations completely of their own accord. They'd hung the red and white monstrosities in the foyer next to a stand detailing the abattoir plans. So life-like they made her feel sick.

'Old Goosers was opposed to the abattoir if I recall.' Geoffrey moved his knight and sat back. 'Bishop sacrifice,' he announced with glee.

'Well, his opposition turned out to be for other reasons.' Terence ran his tongue over his shiny uniform teeth. 'Hence, he is currently languishing in HMP Orleton dreaming of piglets.'

Geoffrey put on his glasses. His mole-like eyes transformed to those of an owl. 'I want to make it absolutely clear that I am not taking sides. However, we simply cannot have key representatives of our community brawling on church property. In future I would ask that all social intercourse remains cordial.'

Sarah couldn't trust herself to remain cordial even when sitting in a chair under a pile of poodles. 'Of course, Geoffrey, I quite agree.' She couldn't look at Terence a moment longer. She rose, scattering the poodles across the oak floor. They regrouped and followed her to the door.

'One more thing.' Geoffrey kissed the air noisily and waved a cooked sausage from his pocket. The poodles trotted back. Fickle friends. 'I understand that your recent sermon raised an eyebrow.'

God, she knew exactly whose manicured eyebrow was raised and how high. 'Oh?'

'Not so much the subject matter, more the vehemence of the delivery.'

'Forgive my enthusiasm, Dean. I'll try to strike a more moderate tone in the future.' It was true that she had gone rogue but the teachings were creeping into her soul. The message was simple and true: do the right thing, live the right life, be a good person. Conversion by stealth; she'd better watch herself. She backed out of the room as if retiring from the presence of a monarch. She left the door ajar and observed through the crack.

'Anything else, Terence?' Geoffrey moved his queen to threaten the king.

'I'm not sure it reflects well on the church having a female vicar shacked up with an ex-goat farmer turned crisp-fryer and his wayward son.'

Outrageous. She should walk straight back in and give him hell.

'Sarah is very charitably giving them a home. At my request actually.' He studied the board with a look of cautious optimism.

'I'm afraid social services are now involved with the boy.'

'You turfed him off the land, old chap. Reap what you sow and all that.' Geoffrey checked the black king.

Yes, you tell him boss.

'I have to travel to Peaminster to get my cheese now and it is of inferior quality. Quite an inconvenience.'

The low grumble of poodles filled the pregnant pause. Terence stalked to the french doors and spoke with his back to him. 'I understand that she's still in her probationary period.'

'What are you getting at, old boy?' Geoffrey retreated the king. 'Spit it out.'

'She is in a hole and needs to stop digging. It's perhaps time for her to be let go.' What an utter slimeball.

'Oh, I'd hate to lose her, excellent croquet players are hard to find. And the boys like her.'

'The boys?'

Geoffrey gestured to the mound of poodles now slumped mournfully on her vacated chair.

'They're no judge of character, they liked Lionel I seem to recall.' Terence waited as Geoffrey made his move and turned the board. 'I see that the duck-house, the maze and the lawns are looking splendid.' He turned and showed his full veneers. 'I understand that you've put in a request for a crown green bowling lawn.'

Geoffrey took the threatening rook with a flourish and leant back in his chair. 'Message received and understood, old chap. Very well. I'll give her an ultimatum.'

'I knew you would agree.'
'It rather feels like checkmate.'

45

The shepherd's hut down at Lingen fields was loads better than it sounded. Jesús liked the bed inside the cupboard and the wildflower meadow and the trees behind. The best thing was there wasn't an actual shepherd living there. Phew. Shepherds could be creepy. There was less to worry about here. Mum wouldn't be in the bath because there wasn't a bath. Dad's leg was getting better although he still couldn't walk that well over rough ground and all the ground around here was rough. Probably why he was so sad.

But he really missed Ben. It was five miles to Vespiary cottage – might as well be one hundred. Dad said it was good to learn to enjoy your own company because you had to spend your whole life with yourself. Jesús tried but sometimes he annoyed himself.

Dad was sitting at the table polishing his walking stick with linseed oil. It was excellent. He'd carved it out of ash wood the first week he was home from hospital when he couldn't walk at all and took handfuls of pills and sat around with his leg up on a pile of books. The handle was a badger's head – although badgers freaked Jesús out a bit – below that a raven, then a fox and a deer. It was nice of him to carve the deer considering what happened. The smell of the oil was icky. Jesús climbed up into the bed and closed the cupboard door behind him. It was all painted white inside, like a bathroom, to stop the damp. The branches waved outside the window and cast watery shapes on the glossy sheen.

Arghhh. Mum was lying beside him, naked and white, wide-eyed, staining the sheets with her pooling blood. Jesús pressed his knuckles into his eyes. Blackness. Flashing stars. He opened them. Mum still there. Still dead on the scarlet bed. He banged his head hard against the wall.

'You alright in there, mate?'

A pain exploded in his head like he'd been shot. The pain made Mum dissolve.

'Yep.' Jesús crawled down inside his sleeping bag and zipped it up over his head.

Everything was okay. He was a puss moth pupa. A healthy specimen and an excellent chewer. Busy making its cocoon of silk and bark. The cocoon was perfect; delicate but tough and camouflaged.

Now it was time to lie still and pupate. Enjoy the quiet. Enjoy the dark. Enjoy the cracking cocoon. Heart racing, dizzy, hard to breathe. That's what happens when your body is dissolving and reforming. Crawl out, twitch antennae, stretch crumpled wings. Take a deep breath. Jump and fly. Ow.

Jesús landed splat on the floor. His arm scraped the rough wood of the chair that Dad had brought in for sanding.

'What the hell, mate?'

'Sorry. I forgot I can't actually fly.'

Dad rummaged through the first aid box and dabbed at his arm with antiseptic. 'You'll live.'

'I was enjoying my own company.'

'Maybe we'll get Ben over soon.' Dad glanced at his watch. 'Oh Christ. Grab your coat, mate, it's time for Walker the stalker.'

Jesús zipped up his parka and pulled the hood right over his head. He was a pupa again.

Jesús had marked todays' last session on his Moths of the World calendar with a big smiley face. But Miss Walker was all serious and had a new clipboard and said because of 'developments' they were going to keep meeting. Weekly. Not fair. Dad was very upset too; said she was moving the fecking goal posts. Miss Walker told him to wait outside until he'd calmed down.

'Goodness, what's happened to your arm?' She used a new posh voice. 'And your forehead?'

'Nothing.' It was too difficult to explain and Miss Walker was all bustley and professional. Not like her.

They were back in the room with the clouds. Jesús had to look at the horrible one with the blowy lips because there was a man in the medium blue chair facing the crap rainbow. He looked funny all scrunched up – he must be dead tall because his knees were sticking right up to his chin.

'This is officer Fletcher. He's a policeman.' He didn't have a uniform so Jesús wasn't definitely sure that he was a policeman. His eyes were very close together. He looked more like a bank robber. He could pull out a gun at any moment and Miss Walker wasn't even guarding the safes.

'Graham.' He raised his huge hand and nearly toppled off his chair.

He was the sort of man who didn't say much but looked way serious. It was all pretty weird. 'Do you want to sit on the orange bean bag, officer Fletcher?' Jesús said. It was a bit mean of him but he was upset about Dad being told off.

'No thanks, lad.'

Miss Walker walked over like she was on a tightrope. She was wearing black high heels. She sat opposite him; at least she was blocking out the horrible cloud. 'Jesus, we have seen the emails that your friend Ben sent to a man called Dave 101.'

It wasn't a question so he just carried on looking at her. She had loads of makeup on today. Maybe it was to hide her blotches but it wasn't working because they were creeping up her neck already and her cheeks were very pink.

'Were you there when he sent them?'

'Yep.'

'Have you met the man? Or sent him photos or videos? Has he asked you to do anything? Or talked about anything that made you feel uncomfortable?'

What was making him uncomfortable was all her questions and the way she kept sniffing. You're meant to blow your nose. 'No, no, no and no.'

Miss Walker uncrossed her legs and tugged at the hem of her skirt. She should buy a longer skirt. 'I'll ask you again, Jesus. You are not in any trouble. Even if the man has told you to keep it a secret, it's very important that you tell us the truth. Have you met with him?'

'No.'

'What about at ten-thirty on the morning of Saturday 27th of April at Adfordley Cross?' said the policeman.

'Nope.'

Miss Walker looked at officer Fletcher and sighed. Her neck was one big blotch.

'If you could no longer live at the vicarage, is there anyone who you'd like to live with?'

'We don't live there anymore. We're shepherds without sheep.'

'What? You've moved?' All huffy. 'What's your new address?'

Jesús didn't think they had an actual address because the hut didn't have a name or a number or a post-box. He shrugged. Miss Walker and officer Fletcher looked at each other.

'If you could live with anyone, who would you choose?'

This was her favourite question. She asked it pretty much all the time.

'Dad and Sarah.'

'Are you sure?'

'Abserfuckinglutely.'

They looked at each other again. Maybe they were boyfriend and girlfriend.

'The thing is, Jesus, you might need a place of safety.'

Maybe it was something to do with Mr Johnson. If he made Ben's dad disappear, he could make Sarah disappear, or Dad, or him. Maybe they should move back to the vicarage to keep Sarah safe. Who would feed Moth if Sarah disappeared?

'Isn't the hut safe?' he asked the maybe policeman.

'That's what we are trying to establish,' said Miss Walker in her new posh voice.

Maybe she thought it could get blown away in a big storm like those caravans at Upper Wychwood that ended up in the lake.

Now she was talking about who he would tell if he was worried about something. 'Ben, Dad, Sarah.'

She did that face that made a vertical line between her eyebrows. The one she did when she didn't like his answers.

'Jesus, remember that you can tell me anything and also

officer Fletcher.'

'I haven't ever met him before.'

'It's okay, Jesus, I believe you.'

'No, I mean officer Fletcher.'

'Anyway, we are going to have a big meeting about you. Where we'll make some very important decisions.' She was out of breath although all she had been doing was sitting in a chair. 'Do you have any questions?'

'Can I go to the big meeting?'

'No, it's for adults.'

Dad was waiting out in the truck. He put Bohemian Rhapsody on really loud. Usually, they'd sing along but Jesús didn't feel like singing, he guessed Dad didn't either. He drove faster than usual. Jesús put his head out of the window like a dog to feel the wind pulling back his hair.

'Tractor,' Jesús shouted. It pulled out of a gate throwing clods of mud from its tyres.

Dad braked and crawled along behind it.

'Thanks, son.' He wound down his window and lit one of his happy cigarettes.

Jesús scanned the hedgerows for birds. Nothing much; a couple of sparrows and a wren.

'The lead guitarist of Queen does a lot of work for hedgehogs,' said Dad.

'That's cool.'

They played 'What animal am I?' Twenty yes or no questions. Jesús was a Jolly's mouse lemur. Dad didn't get it even though his second question was 'Are you a lemur?' Then Dad was a Canadian goose. Easy. They had another round (Hummingbird hawkmoth and hammerhead shark). It was so they didn't have to talk about Miss Walker or Sarah or Moth.

46

Sarah went out to check her post-box. A gloat of Range Rovers were strewn across the verges of Church Lane. One had even parked in her driveway. Bloody cheek.

Oh no, today was Carole's garden party. Sarah had received a formal invitation card although there had been plenty of opportunity for Carole to ask her in person. The woman had been loitering on the patio with some regularity – if Sarah waved at her she would feign interest in some spindly bush. It was pretty weird.

What was this? A sheet of paper had been folded and clamped under her windscreen wiper. She opened it. A colour photocopy of an article on Cambridge Theological College. Oh God. It included a graduation photograph of last year's ordinands, their names in row order. Shit. Shit. Shit. Third row, second from the right, Sarah Wilson was ringed in biro. Plump with long red hair. The word DESIST was printed above her.

Busted.

Sarah ran back inside and swallowed a shot of rum, then another. She held a match to the paper and dropped it into the grate. Total bloody disaster. What was the deal? Blackmail? Exposure? Public humiliation?

Don't panic. Evidently it was a warning to back off. They wanted her to know that they knew. The nature of the demand and the word choice pointed to one person. Terence Johnson.

Sarah hadn't been planning to attend the garden party but Johnson would be there. Better to face him; that was the way to play bullies. Show no fear.

It would delay her plan to go to Vespiary cottage but needs must. It had been three days since the identification of the body and still no word from Eileen. The poor thing must be in shock. Or denial. But they had to do something. Today. She'd make an appearance, talk to Terence and give her excuses.

A herd of bland couples grazed around the manicured lawn of The Grange one-upping each other's outfits, children and holidays with competitive condescension. Fake laughter pealed from Carole as she butterflied from guest to guest topping up glasses of warm prosecco. Even without the warning and the whole body-in-the-woods scenario, remaining convivial to Carole and her insipid guests would have been a push. Fortunately, no one was yet to approach. A dog-collar and a scowl were powerful protectors. An open-mouthed piglet turned on a spit above the fire pit. She was indeed in hell.

No sign of Terence. Sarah stood upwind of the piglet and examined the vista. Carole's garden afforded a perfect view of the whole vicarage and if she stood on the top step of the newly laid patio, she could see through her own kitchen window. She must put those net curtains back up. A whirring from above distracted her. What the hell? There, tucked beneath the eaves was a video-camera making a slow-motion trajectory between the church and her front door. Outrageous.

'Care for some delicious pork, Vicar?' Terence Johnson stood too close and offered her a plate of pallid meat like a taunt.

'I'm vegetarian.'

'I wanted to apologise. I do hope you didn't misinterpret my words.' Was he alluding to Desist? No, that was a single word.

'The words about Ernest and thin ice and people disappearing were pretty clear.' No way would he smarm his way out of this again.

'I misspoke. I've been under a lot of stress, I wasn't myself. Just recovering from another bout of something nasty.'

'Not your usual self? Really?'

He moped his forehead with a sodden handkerchief. 'Some sort of coliform bacteria, apparently. Severe diarrhoea and vomiting are prone to make one a tad paranoid.'

This was not a conversation she wanted to have while inhaling the stench of smouldering pig. 'You do look rough.'

'Getting there, a course of penicillin seems to be doing the trick.' He looked at her with a disconcerting intensity. 'I had hoped you'd call to discuss the abattoir.'

'Somehow the not-so-veiled threats put me off.'

'Come now, Geoffrey wants us to kiss and make up. Please do send me a text or an email anytime.' He gave the slimiest of smiles.

'I'm surprised that you take the Church of England magazine.'

'Sorry?'

'The cutting you left me.'

'Not I, said the fly.' He was an accomplished liar but he did look genuinely confused. He headed off towards a gaggle of women in floral dresses.

Sarah sat on the bench in the shade of a spreading magnolia. A good place from which to observe proceedings. Most of the guests were councillors and their wives; Carole would probably be submitting a bloody invoice. There was nothing Sarah could eat; they'd only catered for carnivores. Carole flirted with Terence only feet away from Ted who was hacking hunks from the decimated carcass.

'You can eat every part of the pig except its squeak,' cried Ted, but no one was listening.

A man with a baseball cap and a cadaverous complexion drew Terence to one side. It was Fish. So that was why she'd been invited – it was a conspicuous display of connections. Well, Terence might be able to buy protection from dodgy financial deals but murder?

If only Jack was here, they could have joked about the guest list, made fun of Carole's outrageous flirting, shared a lager.

The hideous hog-roast looked as if it had been ravaged by vultures. What would poor Lionel Gooseworthy have made of it? The unexpected letter she'd received from him had been warm and honest. He had described his bizarre but platonic attachment to pigs in some detail. She believed him. Lionel had been set up, another of Johnson's victims. At least the poor man didn't have to witness the slow turning of a butchered pig, droplets of fat hissing into the fire. She vowed to help with his appeal. The irony of Lionel serving his prison sentence while the man who put him there ate dead pig did not escape her. Plus, Lionel knew about the murder. He was the key with which to get Terence locked up. But God, she had to tread carefully now, the whole pretence could be exploded.

Sarah had endured the meat-fest long enough. It was time to nudge Eileen.

Sarah took the shortcut through the woods. The path trampled by the boys' frequent forays between houses was already showing signs of regrowth. Eileen sat in the summer house knitting a red and white carcass. Two lithe squirrels skittered across the tree trunks, chased each other through the branches and disappeared into the birch copse. The birch copse where Melville lay decomposing in his shallow grave. She took the chair beside Eileen.

There was no way to sugar coat this. Sarah waited for her to put down her knitting. 'Eileen, it's time we told the police. I can do it if you prefer. Or I could go with you to the station.'

'I know you're right. I'll telephone them.' She patted her newly tinted blue hair. 'I need to gird my loins.'

Sarah had never seen her so anxious. 'It's best to do it now. You know, to preserve evidence.'

'Goodness, you sound like someone from a crime drama.' She resumed clattering the thick needles.

'Sorry.' It was certainly not something a vicar would say. She was rubbish at this. 'Perhaps if you did it while I'm here.'

'I fear they'll erect one of those big tents you see on News at Ten and the place will be teeming with men in white paper suits rolling out crime scene tape.'

'You could always come and stay at the vicarage.'

She shook her head. 'Who would make them hot beverages?'

'I'm sure they bring their own flasks.'

Eileen put down her knitting and stroked her neck with arthritic fingers. 'I'll stay put. Perhaps if you could take Ben for a few days? Just until it's all over.'

'Whatever you prefer.'

'Very well. I'll telephone them now.' She struggled from the deck chair.

Sarah waited with her face raised to the sun. It was a

beautiful tranquil spot; the distant church bells, doves cooing, the chatter of starlings. She could see why people stayed for generations in the same family home. And how the disruption of a murder would rock this precious world.

Eileen returned with Ben who was carrying an overnight bag decorated with green and blue dinosaurs.

'Hi Ben, I really need you to come and help me look after Moth.'

'Sure.' He looked proud.

Sarah hugged Eileen. 'Are the police on their way?' she whispered.

'Answer phone. I left a message to call me back urgently.'

'Okay. Let me know the minute you hear. Call me anytime.' Eileen felt as frail as a bird.

47

Jesús was happy. Two brilliant things. First, Dad said he didn't have to go and see Miss Walker anymore because 'the more you give them the more they fricken twist it.' Second, he was having a marathon sleepover at Sarah's. Yay. Dad had back-to-back shifts and Eileen needed 'a little break' so he and Ben were indoor-camping at the vicarage. It meant he could sleep snug as a bug on a pug without bloody Mum turning up; literally.

The bag of marshmallows Dad had given him didn't taste so nice heated up on the radiator. Jesús had bought a packet of cat treats with his pocket money but there was something wrong with Moth. He wouldn't jump on his shoulder. He didn't do the cheek rubbing thing. He didn't want his fishy nibbles. He just sat under the chair in the corner and stared. Jesús thought at first that Moth had died and that Sarah had had him stuffed but it turned out that he was just being sulky. It was probably because Jesús had moved out and he felt abandoned and let down and hurt. He couldn't blame him. Jesús would make it up to him. Sarah said to give him time and space but he only had a few days.

Jesús and Ben decided to make a moth trap. The white sheets from the cupboard on the landing smelled of mothballs – not ideal for a moth trap – so Sarah washed a big one in eco non-bio and hung it outside to dry. Jesús disagreed with mothballs because the larvae of the common clothes moth and the case-bearing clothes moth were adapted to feed on natural fibres. It wasn't their fault, it was how they evolved, they weren't going to change. He'd hoped they'd nibble cool little holes in his jumpers but they hadn't.

Sarah said he could chuck out the mothballs because Reverend Gooseworthy wasn't coming back. Jesús rummaged through the cupboard and collected thirteen mothballs. One of the pillow cases felt sort of wiry. Inside were two pairs of pink fairy wings and two lacy skirts.

'That's weird, Reverend Gooseworthy didn't have children.'

'And they definitely wouldn't have fitted him,' said Ben.

There was something else wrapped up in a cloth; a small pink photo album with a red heart on the cover. Inside were photographs of very clean looking piglets with very red lips.

'Whoa, look at these.' Jesús flicked through the pages.

Ben peered over his shoulder. The same two piglets appeared in every photo. They were very cute. One had floppy black ears, the other a pale face with a white snout. They wore different outfits like the ones in the drama box at school but piglet-sized: little waistcoats, frilly aprons, velvet hats. In some they were wearing the wings and the lacy skirts. Their trotters were painted with bright red nail varnish. In one the piglets were eating fairy cakes on the red carpet that used to be in his and Dad's bedroom. They had crumbs all over their snouts. In others they lay on the honey-coloured long thing with silky scarves down their backs like Superman capes. The last were close up shots of each piglet tucked up in bed with its head on the pillow. So sweet.

'Blimey,' said Ben. 'The Reverend Gooseworthy was crazy about piglets.'

'You be white face. I'll be black ears.'

They pulled the tutus over their trousers and put their arms through the straps of the fairy wings. They chased each other across the landing snuffling and oinking. They bounded downstairs and crashed into the living room.

'Ta Dah!'

Sarah screamed with laughter.

'Oh my God, wait here.' She returned waving a CD. The *Dance of the Cygnets* from Swan Lake blasted into the room. The three of them lined-up shoulder to shoulder and Sarah showed them how to cross their arms and hold each other's hands in front of them. They trotted sideways on tip-toes up and down the room laughing and snorting with delight.

'Again, again,' Jesús and Ben shouted.

At the end of the third dance, they collapsed exhausted on the carpet crying with laughter. The best day ever.

As dusk fell Jesús and Ben turned off all the lights and directed their torches onto the sheet on the washing line. Moth came out and crept along the patio keeping close to the plant pots.

'We've attracted one moth already.' Ben's torch picked up the glow of the kitten's eyes.

Moth slunk away into the shrubbery. A gust of wind rippled the sheet sending him scurrying back to Jesús.

'Hey, boy.' Jesús held out his hand. 'Don't worry. I'll look after you.'

Moth inched closer and allowed himself to be stroked. It was good to be friends again.

Jesús had learnt how to identify the common moth species by sight because you could hurt their wings if you stuffed them into a jam jar. As well as cinnabars, brimstones and rustics they got two blood veins and an apple leaf skeletonizer. A good night's mothing.

Sarah shouted from the open window. 'You nearly done?'

'Five more minutes,' called Jesús. 'You want to see a skeletonizer?'

'No thanks.' Maybe she was scared of moths.

'What's the plan for tomorrow boys?'

'We thought we'd go and look for jelly ear fungi in the woods.'

'Okay, but stay close. Don't go near Eileen's, she needs peace and quiet.' Sarah closed the window and held up five fingers.

It was lovely sitting in the deck chairs at night. An owl hooted. Bats dropped from the eaves and flapped away into the darkness.

Ben craned to see the emerging pipistrelles. 'Want to hear something very weird?'

'Always.'

'You can't tell anyone because she could get into serious

trouble.'

'Okay.' Jesús was getting good at keeping secrets.

'One time I went into the kitchen and Granny Eileen was grinding up spiders and maybe also moths, it was hard to tell, with a pestle and mortar which is what they used to grind things up with in the olden days.'

'I thought she was an animal lover.'

'Same. She put the spidery mix into a jar.'

'That's pretty weird.'

A cloud of bats flittered over ahead and circled west towards the river.

'Then when she was making chocolate brownies for the monthly coffee morning, she added three heaped tablespoons to the mixture along with the nuts and the chocolate chips.'

'Yuck.'

'She said brownies were Terence Johnson's favourite.'

'Crikey.'

'Yeah, I know right.

An ambulance blared down Church Lane followed closely by a police car.

Sarah banged on the window. 'Alright boys, time for bed.'

48

Sarah listened to the sound of the boys' laughter filtering through the ceiling. How lovely to be seven years old and lying in a cosy tent with your best friend and a kitten. She tried not to think about the wider context. The moth sheet flapped in the strengthening wind. She should go and take it down but she'd watched too many Hammer horror films to think that walking around a graveyard at night was a good idea.

Eileen must have spoken to the police at last. But why would they blue light an ambulance to a corpse? Unless they were speeding to the crisp factory to attend a horrible accident with the deep-fat fryers. God, get a grip. Her imagination seemed to have recalibrated to catastrophic.

An hour passed. Still no word from Eileen, she hated to think of her dealing with all this alone. A slasher movie face loomed at the window. Jesus Christ. Ernest with a torch on his face and his sternness dialled up to maximum.

She cracked open the window. 'What's happened?'

'Not good.'

'Do you want to come in?' She was hardly breathing.

Ernest shook his head. He was an unhurried man but always on the way somewhere. 'Terence Johnson's very sick.'

'What?'

'Found him slumped in the toilet. Unconscious.'

'Oh God.'

Ernest ran his hand across his face. 'Nasty red marks on his skin. Haemorrhagic bullae apparently.'

'Oh God.' She must stop saying that. The cold breeze caught her hair.

'He'd phoned the coppers earlier to report he'd been

poisoned.'

'Poisoned? How bad is he?'

'Paramedic reckoned he'll not make it.'

Sarah stepped back, the chill wind now gusting through the open window. 'Do they suspect foul play?' Foul play, Jesus who was she, Agatha Christie?

'I told him to switch to mains water.'

'He's still using the spring water?'

Ernest gave an imperceptible nod. 'He gave your name.'

'What?'

'Reckoned you deliberately contaminated his supply. Said he'd seen you acting suspicious in the woods near Eileen's.'

'What?'

'Said he saw Jack digging up there again last week.' Ernest, having delivered his message, turned on his heel. 'Just giving you the heads up.' He disappeared into the darkness.

She stared after him. The penny rolled and spiralled and finally dropped. Oh shit.

Jack was already on the Melville Russet suspect list. Now there was a witness placing him at the scene. And his DNA would be all over the body. There was only one option. Her idea wasn't entirely altruistic; she too was in deep and she couldn't afford the cops looking into her past. She shut the window and grabbed her phone.

'Eileen, have you spoken to the police yet?'

'No, they haven't phoned back. They were up at Terence Johnson's but left with the ambulance. I'll call them first thing in the morning.'

'Change of plan. I'll be right over.'

The boys were fast asleep. Curled up with Moth. She hated leaving them alone but there was no time to lose.

Eileen was very flustered. She patted her curlers. 'I look a fright.'

'There's been a development.' Sarah tried to choose her words carefully – how much more could the poor woman take? 'Perhaps we should sit down.'

Eileen turned off *Beechgrove Garden* and took her time settling into her riser-recliner.

Sarah looked away from the photographs of Melville on the mantelpiece. 'I've been rethinking the situation and wondered whether, under the circumstances, we should perhaps deal with Melville's exhumation ourselves.'

Eileen took a floral scarf from her dressing gown pocket, tied it around her head and blinked at her. 'I'm sorry, dear, I have no idea what you are talking about.'

'The thing is.' She cleared her throat. 'We need to move the body.'

'I don't understand.'

'Terence Johnson is critically ill. Likely due to water contamination. Likely due to Melville being buried over the water course.'

'Goodness.' Eileen crossed herself.

'If the police find out that we knew and kept it quiet we could be looking at culpable homicide.'

'Goodness.'

'Cumulative effects. I should have told the police a week ago.' She held her head in her hands. 'Terence thinks I have a vendetta against him because of the abattoir and Jack's accident.'

'I'm sure many people have a feud with him. A vicar is hardly going to be the prime suspect.'

'Unfortunately, I've made a number of complaints against him. Even the police think I've got it in for him.'

Eileen blinked at her. 'Oh dear.'

'Terence has given my name. The police have sightings of me in the area and they have a video of Jack digging in the vicinity... an animal... it's a long story. It seems they now have further intelligence of him digging at the exact spot where Melville is buried.' Also, if they dug into her background her cover story would quickly unravel, her identity would be revealed and she'd end up in prison.

'It's a lot to take in.' Eileen rubbed her rheumy eyes.

'We'll just move him until the poisoning investigation is over. There'll be a forensic examination of the water course.' Sarah could smell alcohol. An empty brandy bottle glinted from under the armchair.

'I suppose it would mean no police, no investigation, no media circus. That would be best for Ben too.' Eileen knitted her fingers together.

'Thing is, we need to move him tonight. If you agree, I'll call Jack.'

'Alright, dear. If you think it's for the best.'

49

Four forty-four is a nice number. It was the exact time that the sun rose that morning; nearly the longest day. Jesús had forgotten to draw the curtains so the tent had become an orange. Or a giant peach. The centipede and the earthworm and the old green grasshopper would be waking up. Ben was still fast asleep. Moth was curled at the head of the tent. Jesús stroked him under his chin. He did his extra loud motorbike purr, stretched out his little rough tongue and bumped his head softly against Jesús's cheek.

'Good boy,' he whispered.

A crow cawed from the oaks. Moth fluffed up and dashed under the chair.

Jesús zipped his sleeping bag right up over his chin. He was a caterpillar with silky soft skin. The most vulnerable stage of the life cycle; he would make a tasty snack for a passing corvid. He rolled onto his stomach and inched out of the illuminated peach looking for a place of safety.

Arr, arr, arr went the crows. Dad would always say 'Sounds like an attempted murder' when they heard crows. Murder was the collecting noun for crows.

Jesús picked up speed, his smooth carapace gliding across the polished floorboards. It was fun. Faster, faster, faster. Ow. Head first straight into the wall. *Tonto torpe.* He rubbed his head and struggled to his feet.

It was a lovely morning. If they had young goats they would've been gambolling. Miss Bickerstool gave that word its own little tick when they had to write about farm animals. He liked it when everything was still and quiet except for the animals waking up. Before people spoiled it. The birds would

213

be standing up in their cosy nests, stretching out their wings and flying off to find an early morning snack. The caterpillars would be munching away on their leaves trying not to become an early morning snack. That was the food chain for you.

Something was moving very slowly along the hedgerow. Stopping and starting and stopping again. Maybe it was an old horse or a sick cow or an injured deer. It was coming this way. It was two people carrying something very heavy between them – like when a player got stretchered off in football. Except the thing was being half-held half-dragged and there was a lot of stumbling.

They disappeared into the trees. When they reappeared it was Dad and Sarah and the heavy thing was a rolled-up carpet. They were all the same colour; the colour of the soil. Dad and Sarah must be friends again – maybe they had a new hobby.

Now they'd reached the churchyard and were trying to get the carpet through the little gate but they were making a bit of a mess of it. They tried to stand it up against the wall but it kept falling over. It was actually hilarious but they weren't laughing.

Finally, they manoeuvred it through the gate and up the path to the church. Dad propped it up against the yew hedge and it fell sideways in slow motion.

Jesús struggled out of the sleeping bag and ran to get his binoculars. They had mud in their hair and on their faces and all over their clothes. Swamp creatures, risen up to take over the planet. He adjusted the focus. The carpet had feet. Human feet. One foot even had a shoe on. The other was just a naked foot. Its bones were too near the surface. The thing rolled up in the carpet was a dead person.

Now they were dragging it round to the little side chapel. It was always freezing in there. It had a flat stone table but no one used it because it was nicer to sit outside.

Dad and Sarah came back out and stood by the chapel door sharing a cigarette. Even the cigarettes were muddy. Dad put his arm around her shoulder which was nice. Definitely friends again. But they both looked spooked. It wasn't a new hobby; they'd been through something huge together. A trauma.

Dad looked up at the window. Jesús dropped down and

crawled back into the tent. Ben was still asleep. The back door creaked open. Dad's clop, clop, clop, up the stairs. The shower started running in the main bathroom and then in Sarah's little on-sweet. You weren't meant to use both showers at the same time because the pipes clanged and also the water ran cold too quickly. This must be an emergency. When there's a dead body it is usually an emergency.

Something was very wrong. You aren't meant to roll a dead body in a carpet and hide it in a chapel. You are meant to phone nine, nine, nine and tell the operator which service you require. The police. Jesús wasn't going to phone them in case he got massive officer Fletcher or Marky's beardy uncle.

50

After her shower Sarah ran a bath and topped it up with several kettles of boiling water. She might never feel clean again. The putrefaction of human flesh that hung in her nostrils could not be dislodged by the repeated application of geranium and lavender shower gel.

It had taken hours. The digging. She'd imagined that a shallow grave would be just below the surface but they kept digging and digging. At least she'd been spared that revolting resurrected dog. Jack said that the poor thing had been so degraded on his second reappearance that it was hard to identify what it had been in life. He'd chopped it up with a spade and dug it into Eileen's compost heap. There would be no coming back from that.

Sarah assumed that Jack's dog anecdote was an attempt to prepare her for the horrors to come. Nothing could. She would forever carry the sound of her spade hitting Melville with a sickening thud. While she was being sick behind a bush Jack had excavated the length of the corpse as if exposing an ancient Egyptian pharaoh. Removing it had been gruelling, it took all their strength to heave it out and manoeuvre it onto the leaf litter. The body had been tightly rolled in the rug and secured with reams of gorilla tape. A professional job. A two-person job. Of course, Terence wouldn't have done his own dirty work. With the right connections and the right bank balance you could procure any service. He'd probably hosted an alibi-rich dinner party the night of the murder and directed his hatchet men from afar.

It had taken another hour to refill the grave and disguise it with leaves, moss and fallen branches. Eventually she'd become accustomed to the stench. You can rise to anything if you have no option.

Jack had surprised her. His focus, his direction, his pragmatism. He hadn't even told her off for leaving the boys home alone. Maybe he was keeping her on side for future babysitting duties however deficient her skills. Jack had inspired confidence with his methodical concealment of their tracks, attentive removal of their cigarette butts, and careful cleaning of the spades before returning them to Eileen's shed. She had found it strangely attractive. Now she could hear the whirr of the washing machine – the clean-up was complete. She'd burn her own shoes and clothing. They could never be untainted.

They had agreed to continue with their scheduled activities as if nothing had happened. As if they had not spent the night digging up a corpse, dragging it through the woods and dumping it onto a cold slab in the side chapel.

Jack had not slept for twenty-four hours and he was due at work in an hour. She checked her diary. Oh God, she was giving a talk to Year Three: How to be a good person. Christ, she wished she knew; the world was a hard place to be good in. Why on earth had she agreed to this? Oh yes, it was an opportunity to experience what it might be like to be a teacher. The Dean had hinted, with some embarrassment, that her tenure would be terminated should she not refrain from local politics. A polite warning to go with Terence's gun to her head. She needed a plan B.

Jesús was very quiet on the walk to school, perhaps he'd not slept well in the tent but Ben was chirpy enough. She just needed to get through this and she could go home and have another shower.

Three rows of wide-eyed innocent faces stared up at her. They sat crossed-legged, socks pulled up, hair brushed, shirts tucked in. The start of the school day. Miss Bickerstool gave her a warm welcome and instructed the children to listen carefully because they were going to learn something very important. Sarah had not prepared. How difficult could it be to talk to a group of seven-year-olds?

She clutched her hands together and beamed at them. 'What

does it mean to be good?'

Silence. Perhaps they thought it was a rhetorical question. She tried to formulate her own answer; actually, it was not so easy. A pale looking boy with blue-framed glasses raised his hand.

'Yes.' She pointed to him. 'Go ahead.'

'It's the opposite of being bad.'

'Well yes, it is. So, can anybody tell me what does it mean to be bad?'

Another silence. A girl in the back row with her hair in tiny pigtails shot her hand up. 'You are not a bad person, it's your behaviour that is bad.'

'Excellent point.' Why hadn't she thought of that? Because she'd been out all night digging up a corpse.

'So, can anyone think of any examples of bad behaviour? You don't have to put your hand up, just shout out.'

The girl raised her hand again.

'Yes?'

'Shouting out.'

'Well, yes, unless the person has told you that it's okay.'

'So, if someone tells you to do something then it's okay to do it?' This from a boy who looked as if he was assembling a case for his own defence.

This was a can of worms. 'No. You have to listen to yourself. To your conscience. If it feels wrong it probably is.' This could quickly get out of hand. 'Does anybody else have any examples of bad behaviour?'

'Like, if you've taken something off the baby.'

'Or walked mud through the house.'

'Or eaten all your sweets before dinner and don't want any dinner.'

'Excellent examples everyone.' She looked at the clock. Five minutes down, twenty-five to go. Good grief. Now what? Ah, she could always fall back on the ten commandments. 'We are lucky because we've been given rules to follow by God.'

'Miss, please may I go to the toilet?'

Miss Bickerstool escorted the boy out. Sarah took the opportunity to tap 'The ten commandments for kids' into her phone. Blimey, a lot of stuff about floods and droughts and locusts and killing all the first-born sons of Egypt. God's punishments were crazily disproportionate. The sort of thing kids loved.

'Moses was tending his sheep one day when a bush caught fire. Anyway, that bit doesn't matter too much.' She scrolled down. 'He walked up a mountain and God gave him a tablet with ten rules.'

'Was it an iPad Miss?'

'No, a stone tablet.'

Writing them up on the board would kill some time. Put God first. Only worship God. Respect God's name. Don't work on God's day. Obey your mum and dad. Don't kill people. Keep your promises. Don't take other people's things. Tell the truth. Be happy with what you have got.

She herself had broken all of them. Bar one.

She was beginning to feel faint. 'What do you think about these rules?' Oh dear, now she was asking them to question God's wisdom.

The pale boy raised his hand. 'The first four are just about God. They could all be one big rule so they'd be easier to remember.'

The boy had a point.

Pigtails was looking puzzled. She wiped her nose on her sleeve. 'Miss, what if you aren't happy with what you've got? You can't make yourself happy.'

Another good point. One that she herself had learnt the hard way. 'Being envious of other people makes you even more unhappy. If you have a plain digestive and your friend has a Jammy dodger, try to be pleased that you at least have a biscuit.'

'If they were a good friend they might give you half,' said the girl pointedly.

'Jammy dodgers are quite hard to break,' said her friend. 'You'd get all sticky.'

Miss Bickerstool was back. Jesús raised his hand, bless him he'd redirect this fiasco back to the point of the lesson.

'Is it ever okay to kill someone?'

A tsunami of nausea hit her, she steadied herself on the desk. 'No.'

A small boy swamped in an enormous blazer joined in. 'Is it

okay to kill someone if they are a baddie?'

'No, not even if they are very bad. It's not for us to judge.'

'What if they were going to kill you?' This from a stick-thin child who seemed unlikely to harm an ant.

'I think that would be okay,' answered a red-haired girl in the front row.

'Yes, if they had a gun and you had a gun and they were pointing it at you,' said the thin boy.

On the floor.

On the fucking floor.

It's not a fucking toy.

She looked out of the window. Focus on the lime tree. The leaves moving in the breeze. Breathe. Breathe. Breathe. What was up with these children? She looked to Miss Bickerstool who held a rictus grin.

The bell sounded.

Thank God.

51

Jack stood shivering like a wet goat under the freezing shower. Sarah had used all the hot water. At least she'd let him wash his clothes and use her place to get ready for work. It took a special sort of person to be able to do what she'd done and then go off to teach little kids as if the world was a good place. She'd been amazing actually, calm, focussed, strong – well apart from when she was throwing up but you couldn't help your constitution. She was either an outstanding human being or a complete psychopath. The torrent whipped his back like a flagellant. Good for the soul, but nothing could cleanse him of this sin. Digging up a dead man. He raised his face to the onslaught, needles burned his eyes and cheeks, reddened his shoulders. Physical pain to equal what lay beneath.

The thought of manning a deep-fat fryer for eight hours while last night's horrors replayed in his head was unbearable. The final warning for insubordination hung heavy. He couldn't afford to lose this job. Just suck it up.

Jack squeezed into Sarah's baby-blue dressing gown. It smelled of her: digestive biscuits, figs, vanilla. No one smelled quite like her. He retrieved his clothes from the washing machine and bundled them into the dryer. One of Jesús's little blue socks lay mouldering in the drum. She must be using the washing line that he'd strung between the poplars. The thought made him smile. They both agreed that the profligate use of electricity was a crime.

The kitchen cupboards held a tower of Kellogg's variety cereal packs – she'd saved all Jesús's favourites; bless her. Jack scooped several teaspoons of Nescafé into a mug and mixed in cold milk. He'd entered a twilight zone beyond tired. Lights flickered in his peripheral vision. A faint hum buzzed in his ears. He downed the coffee, made another and took it through to the living room. The rhythmic humming droned on, louder this time. It wasn't inside his head – it was coming from the top of the curtain. He stood on the armchair and reached inside the pelmet. His fingers explored the dusty innards of the wooden rail. Ah, there it was, chunky and vibrating; an old Nokia phone. The buzzing stopped and started again. Whoever was calling was very persistent.

'Hello?'

'Hello, it's me.' A woman's voice. Distant on the crackly connection.

'Hello, can I help you? Hello.'

She'd gone. He pressed redial.

She picked up straight away. 'Hello.'

'Hi, who are you after?' He tried to sound friendly.

A rustle of wind and a sharp cry, possibly a seagull, then nothing. He called her back. No reply.

Jack scrolled through the data. No saved contacts, no old messages, no photos. Nada. Who the hell had a burner phone apart from drug dealers, organised criminals and thieves? Actually, who had wads of notes stuffed inside a mattress apart from drug dealers, organised criminals and thieves? But if you were calling a burner, wouldn't you block your number? Idiots or amateurs. Old Nokias had a stellar battery life but they didn't last for months on end – it couldn't have been Gooseworthy's.

A lively tapping on the window startled him. Whoever it was could just bugger off. He replaced the phone and went to check on his clothes. Nearly dry. Carole's face loomed at the kitchen window.

'Hello,' she mouthed.

She carried on talking, her bright pink lips forming exaggerated shapes but he couldn't make out a word she was saying. She held up a pink and grey pashmina and shrugged her shoulders theatrically.

'No, not Sarah's,' he shouted.

It wasn't her style. She liked cardigans and fleeces and loose jackets. Clothes that would look frumpy and old-fashioned on anyone else but somehow she pulled it off. She'd look good in a potato sack.

Carole's face flushed. 'Left at the barbeque,' she mouthed.

Yes, he nodded, he understood. No, he shook his head, it definitely isn't Sarah's. In fact, it was very much Carole's style. Why didn't the stupid woman just go away? Now she was craning forwards and staring at him in a very weird way. Thirty minutes to clocking on time. She held out the pashmina at arm's length, twirled it around and let it drop to the ground in a parody of seductiveness. Now she was wetting her lips and smiling with a strange glazed look in her eyes. He closed the curtain. The woman was a fricken lunatic.

A gust of hot air hit him as he pulled his clothes from the dryer. Oh God, Sarah's dressing gown was wide open. It stretched taut around his shoulders revealing his naked body. Carole had had quite an eyeful for a Wednesday morning.

52

Sarah checked the door to the side chapel for the third time. Definitely locked. She had the only key, heavy bronze with a solid square foot and trefoil head. Not the sort you could have cut at Timpson's. She dropped it into her inside pocket. Reburying Melville in a parish whose population kept a collective running commentary on all activity was not going to be easy. At least it was freezing cold in the chapel but he couldn't stay there long.

Tiny white flowers dotted the grass between the gravestones. A screaming party of swifts chased each other overhead. The graves were etched in green and grey. Pale stars of lichen had become part of the stone itself. Comforting ancient markers of lives lived, mourned and forgotten. The swifts had been returning for centuries before and would do so for centuries to come. The twenty-first century plots were less appealing, the shiny black headstones assaulted the eye with unweatherable starkness. Some were adorned with faded plastic flowers. Their ostentatious gold lettering an affront to the long generations of master stonemasons. God, what was happening to her? The vicarage was seeping into her bones.

A screech of brakes heralded the arrival of the post van.

'Morning, Vicar.' Pat waved a letter out of the window. 'Your monthly from Ireland.'

Geez, broadcast it to the whole village why don't you? She signed for it. 'Any news on Terence Johnson?'

'Out of intensive care.'

'Oh, so he's improving?'

'Unless they just need the bed. He'll either die or get better.'

'I guess those are the options.'

'Keep you posted.' His customary reply.

The clip clip of shears. Ernest was up beyond the ancient yew clearing the unruly ivy from the walls. A reassuring man; methodical, practical, honest. If only he talked a little more. Lionel Gooseworthy, Terence Johnson, Melville Russet. She suspected that Ernest knew a lot more about them and their relationships, knew where the real truth lay.

Sarah walked over and watched him work. 'Making the most of the nice day.'

He lowered his shears. 'Rain tomorrow.'

'The grounds are looking lovely.'

'I'll be poisoning later so best keep your cat in.'

'Poisoning?'

'Mice, in the vestry.' He nodded over his shoulder. 'I'll put trays down in the side chapel too.'

'Oh, I'd rather you didn't. God's creatures and all that.' She modulated the alarm in her voice.

'Chew through the electrics see.'

'I'll take the risk.'

'I'll get over to Johnson's then.' He sounded disappointed.

'Even though he's at death's door?'

'He's paid me upfront. A month's notice. So I'll work it.'

'He sacked you?' What a complete bastard.

'Found out about the shredding bags.'

'I'm so sorry. I can give you extra hours if you want them.'

'Aye. I'll take 'em.' He clipped with renewed vigour. 'By the way, I seen him stick his front door key under the stone lion. Bloomin' obvious hiding place.'

An opportunity not to be missed.

Terence Johnson's house sat at the end of a newly tarmacked driveway in all its orange hideousness. A featureless 1980s box designed to maximise square-footage at the expense of charm or character. The garden was expansive, Ernest's hallmark topiary the only delight in an otherwise lawn-heavy desert. The entrance porch was guarded by two open-mouthed stone lions. Sarah checked for CCTV.

Oh Christ. The camera at The Grange. Trained on the church and the vicarage. How the hell could she have forgotten? She called Jack. No reply. She called again and sent a text *Disaster. Need to speak urgently.*

Sarah put on her black leather gloves and unlocked the front door. A putrid smell emanated from the kitchen. She decided not to investigate. The open plan living area was wall-to-wall magnolia with a soft lilac carpet and a dusky pink Ikea sofa; Terence was a man who liked pastels. A glass cabinet housed a collection of porcelain parrots. She didn't know exactly what she was looking for – anything that shed light on the murder of Melville Russet or betrayed Terence's role in assaulting Jack or framing Lionel Gooseworthy.

Terence was a hoarder; old bills, out-of-date warranties, cinema tickets, one whole drawer dedicated to plugs, cables and extension leads. Nothing of interest. Two goldfish with bulging eyes swam without enthusiasm around a small bowl. They gulped down a large pinch of flake food.

Upstairs yielded a horrible peach bathroom and four bland bedrooms. The study looked more promising. It contained a pine desk that was empty except for a glass paperweight with a trapped fifty-pound note inscribed: 'In case of emergency break glass'. A tidy desk is the sign of a sick mind.

The filing cabinet was locked but the desk drawer contained the keys. It was a treasure trove of financial documentation; bank accounts, share certificates and investment portfolios all labelled, alphabetised, and organised by category. A tag written in gold pen leapt out. CRYPTO. It housed a thin file containing several pages of crypto currency transactions. Sarah ran her finger down the expenditure-return columns. The profit figures were staggering. Like an addiction, the more the value rose the more he bought. It quickly got crazy. His last investment was over half a million pounds. Purchased from Mr Melville. B. Russet. The following day the currency crashed to zero.

Wow, Terence had been duped. Possibly bankrupted. February thirteenth. The last day Melville was seen alive.

The smoking gun. Terence had means, motive, and opportunity. It was possible that he would die before justice was served but at least Eileen would know the truth.

A piercing volley of screams broke the silence. Sarah dashed behind the curtain and pulled it closed around her. No sound except the thumping of her heart. No voices, no opening of doors, no step on the stairs. Only the distant coughing of an old sheep. She was being ridiculous. Sound travelled for miles in the still of the countryside – it must have been a distressed fox or a trapped cat or a psychopathic peacock. She emerged from her ludicrous hiding place, locked the cabinet and replaced the key.

Downstairs the acrid smell was unidentifiable; just a quick look in the kitchen and she'd get out of there. The source of the odour was a cage by the kitchen window ominously draped in a black cloth. She pulled it aside to reveal an African grey parrot.

'Danger. Danger.' It screeched. 'Danger. Danger.'

Its bowl was empty, the cage floor deep with guano.

'Poor thing, you must be starving.'

'Danger. Danger.' It hopped from the bars to its swing and back again.

She refilled its water dispenser.

The parrot drank noisily before training its eye on her. 'Daddy's home.'

'Looks like I was just in time, little fella.' She found a limp corn on the cob in the fridge and threw it into the cage. The parrot gnawed enthusiastically, his thick black tongue dislodging each kernel. She added a spray of millet. The bird went crazy with excitement, he rattled the cage door, bobbed a little dance and rattled it again. The door swung open and he was gone in a blur of grey and red.

Shit.

'Dinnertime. Dinnertime,' he screamed from the curtain pole.

'It's in your cage, idiot.' She'd give him five minutes, if he didn't return she'd have to leave him loose in the kitchen. Her mobile trilled from her pocket. Dentist.

'Hi, Sarah Wilson here.'

The rescheduling of her check-up took three minutes. The bird watched from his vantage point and left a deposit on the cooker. It was a very unsanitary pet. She rattled the millet.

'Dinner's ready,' she called.

He crawled down the curtain and eyed her warily. She made a lunge for him with a tea-towel. Gotcha. He struggled and pecked and flew squawking onto the top of the fridge. A flurry of downy feathers floated to the floor.

Jesus Christ. 'I'm trying to help, Mr Screechy.'

'Hi, Sarah Wilson here. Hi, Sarah Wilson here,' he squawked.

Oh shit, now she was going to have to kill the parrot.

53

M iss Bickerstool was helping Ben, Marky and horrible Craig with their reading during morning break so Jesús dashed off to their hiding hole in the hedge. There was a lot to think about. Well, one gigantic thing and it was making him feel a bit sick.

A dead human being in a carpet.

Conclusion one. The body was not an actual body, it was for a play, or a fancy-dress party, or Halloween. But they weren't doing a play, it was too gross for a party and it was June.

Conclusion two. Dad and Sarah found the dead body lying in the woods and brought it back so it wouldn't get eaten by foxes or badgers or pecked by crows. But why would they be walking around in the woods at night? Why didn't they call the police?

Conclusion three. They murdered someone in the woods and hid them so that they don't go to prison. Weirdly the craziest idea made the most sense. Except it wasn't the sort of thing Dad would do. Or an actual vicar.

There were only two people the body could be. Mr Johnson, the total banker, because he lived up that way and he hadn't seen him since he'd seen the body. Or Ben's dad who had gone missing in the woods. Maybe they mistook him for a beast.

If Dad and Sarah killed Ben's dad then apart from having a murderer for a dad and also a murderer for a vicar-slash-friend-slash-babysitter, Ben wouldn't be his mate anymore. They'd been friends since nursery. More than half of their entire lives. Ben was his only true friend. He'd be completely alone apart from murderers. He couldn't tell Ben. He couldn't tell anyone.

There were a lot of reasons why Dad might kill Mr Johnson:

he was a Tory land-grabber, he made them move out of their home and sell their goats, he was a bureaucratic bullyboy, and a palm-greasing banker. Mr Russet didn't seem like the sort of person Dad would kill on purpose. His job was something to do with business and money so he was probably a capitalist pig with his snout in the trough but there were loads of those and Dad wasn't a mass murderer; he wouldn't have the time. Also, they didn't really know each other. Mrs Russet always picked Ben up. Perhaps she didn't run off with a financial advisor, maybe Mr Russet killed her; Dad didn't like men who hurt women. Maybe Dad took revenge like they do in Westerns. More likely it was just an accident.

After school Ben would be going back to Eileen the spider grinder and Jesús would be going home to the shepherd's hut with his dad the murderer and his dead mum in the bed-in-the-cupboard. It was not a good day.

After lunch Jesús and Ben took their marbles over to the flat area by the bins. Jesús rolled his marmalade aggi to strike Ben's green cat's eye.

Marky loomed over them, all swagger. 'Guess what?'

'What?' Ben lined up his steelie.

Marky crouched down. 'I'm an actual undercover police officer.'

Jesús ignored him. It was just like the time he told them he'd seen a real dinosaur and had a photograph to prove it but it turned out to be a life-sized model in a theme park.

'Don't you believe me?'

'Yeah, right, because you can join the police when you're seven.' Ben flicked his steelie, it missed and rolled out of the circle.

'I was specially recruited.'

Jesús rolled his swirly. He was fed up of Marky going on about his uncle Kenny as if being a policeman was such a big deal. His dad made real crisps that you could buy in shops but he didn't bang on about it all the time.

'You can't tell anyone because it's about catching a peedo. I've been on a sting.'

'You're getting confused because Sting is an actual singer in a band called The Police.' Jesús's mum used to listen to them. Dad would go outside or put on his noise-cancelling headphones.

Marky drew his foot through the circle scattering the marbles in all directions. 'It's true, you prats.'

Ben and Jesús jumped up and retrieved their marbles.

'Have you got a photo of yourself wearing a police uniform?' Ben counted his marbles back into their drawstring bag.

'No, you moron. I was undercover as a little boy.'

'Prove it.'

Marky looked in one direction and then the other for dramatic effect. 'You have to swear to keep it top secret because it's top secret.'

Jesús and Ben exchanged glances. 'Okay then.'

They did a three-way pinky swear.

'I had to meet a man called Dave 101.'

'What?' Jesús gasped.

'Don't interrupt while I'm telling the story.'

'Sorry.'

'What happened was, uncle Kenny had been chatting to Dave 101 in a chatroom on the internet. Uncle Kenny pretended to be a boy called Michael and he arranged to meet Dave 101 in the park in Peaminister on Saturday morning.'

'Blimey.' Ben was very pale.

'Yeah, so I had to pretend to be Michael and there were loads of police in vans and behind bushes and there were helicopters and machine guns.'

This was what Dad called over-egging the pudding. There were probably a couple of coppers crouched in the shrubbery.

'I had to wear a red jumper and blue shorts because it would make me easy to spot and I had to hang around by the fountain.'

'Creepy.' Jesús wasn't exactly sure what a peedo was but he knew that he and Ben had had a lucky escape.

'It was dead exciting at first but I had to walk around for ages. Then I stood by the pond. Then I sat on the lion statue. But Dave 101 never turned up.'

'What happened?' Ben whispered.

'They reckon he might have seen a policeman or someone gave him a tipoff.'

Ben was as white as a sheep. Jesús felt wobbly.

'Now do you believe me?'
'Yes. Abserfuckinlutely.'

54

Sarah raced back to the vicarage. As she rounded a corner a black car pulled out in front of her – she slammed on the brakes avoiding a collision by centimetres. The driver was abiding by the speed limit so he couldn't be a local. She crawled along at thirty, her heart pounding. She checked her phone. Still no word from Jack. She'd have to disable Carole's CCTV by herself. The car slowed again, the couple in the back were pointing at the scenery as if they were tourists. A taxi? In West Tillington? What was going on? It indicated left and turned into her driveway. Sarah pulled her van up behind it. A tanned middle-aged couple emerged and waited as the driver unloaded their luggage and carried it up the stone steps. The man pressed a banknote into the driver's hand with practised discretion. Their suitcases bore an Italian flag.

Jesus Christ, no.

They rapped on the front door.

Okay, she could handle this. She approached with a smile. 'Hello, can I help you?'

'It seems there's no one home. We've come to visit our daughter, Sarah Wilson, the Vicar.'

'Are you sure you're at the right vicarage?'

The man took an envelope from his inside pocket. 'How fortunate to come across a postwoman.' He waved the letter at her. 'Surely there can't be two West Tillingtons?'

'Sarah Wilson. Sarah Wilson,' squawked a sack on the passenger seat.

'Goodness, it seems your parrot knows our daughter.'

'You'd better come in.'

Sarah carried their suitcases into the hall; they were the sort of people that demanded help without asking for it.

'Why on earth do you have a key to the vicarage?' Asked Mrs Wilson, toying with her string of pearls.

'Come through. I'll explain.' She ushered them into the living room buying time.

'This is rather nice. We had envisioned a draughty old manse.' Mr Wilson appeared to be conjuring false bonhomie in an attempt to appease his poker-faced wife.

Sarah remained standing; it helped her to think. 'I'm afraid she'll be away for some time.' Where would a vicar go? 'She's at the General Synod.'

'Goodness, she has risen through the ranks.' Mr Wilson looked astonished.

'She's attending as an observer.'

'Rupert, I told you to let her know we were coming.' Mrs Wilson lowered herself into the armchair. 'This whole trip is to be an utter disaster.'

'I sent her a text. It's hardly my fault if she refuses to have telephone conversations like every sane person on the planet.'

'Have you come far?' Sarah knew the answer.

'We have a villa in San Gimignano. We adore the churches and the choirs.'

'Ah, south-west of Florence, how lovely.'

Mr Wilson held out his hand. 'Sorry, you didn't give your name. Do you work for Royal Mail?'

'No, I'm Abi Green, I'm covering for Sarah.'

'Abi, what a perfect name for a vicar.' Mr Wilson appeared delighted with himself.

'Isn't it.'

'A locum vicar, whatever next,' sighed Mrs Wilson.

'I'm afraid I have a church meeting at two.'

'Well, I'm sure we could let you get on.' Mrs Wilson scanned the room apparently displeased by the quality of the paintings, or perhaps she thought the subject matter too heavily weighted to pigs.

'I'm sorry you've had a wasted journey. I would offer to put you up but we're housing the homeless at the moment.'

A grimace flickered across Mrs Wilson's face. She rubbed her finger tips together and examined them with distaste. 'No matter, we are booked in at The Castle on the other side of Peaminster.' She retrieved her leather gloves from her handbag and put them on. Rupert do recall the driver before he goes too far.'

Sarah and Mrs Wilson sat in uncomfortable silence. She'd imagined the parents to be more overtly devout, more sackcloth and ashes than Louis Vuitton although Mrs Wilson was proficient in her own version of holier than thou.

'Has Sarah settled in?' asked Mr Wilson, his mission accomplished. 'She says very little about her new job in her monthly letters.'

'Yes, she's enjoying rural life. Fits right in.' Sarah imagined that she would be doing a far better job than herself. By now she'd know everyone by name and likely be running drop-in sessions and religious support groups and giving harp recitals.

Jack appeared around the door bringing with him the smell of deep-fat fryers.

'Sarah, I rushed over as soon as I got your text.' He caught his breath, his eyes were puffy, his scalp glistened.

'Jack, could you give us a moment?'

'Yeah, sorry, I didn't know you had guests.' He looked bewildered. 'Also, did you know there's a parrot screaming in your van?'

'Sarah?' Mr Wilson raised an eyebrow.

She mimed a drinker. 'Perhaps you could bring the parrot in? Watch your fingers.'

'Mr and Mrs Wilson,' Mr Wilson extended his hand. 'We are Sarah's parents.'

'Oh, I thought you were dead.'

'No, we are very much alive,' Mrs Wilson bristled.

'Nice to meet you both.'

'Abi is updating us if you wouldn't mind,' said Mrs Wilson. She waved her hand as if dismissing a servant.

Jack opened his mouth and closed it. 'Shout if you need me.' He shut the door behind him.

'Jack can get a little confused. Too much dog alcohol over the years.'

'I see. And does Sarah regularly take in vagrants?' Mrs Wilson appeared mortified.

'Oh yes. She's very community spirited.'

'Abi, could you call the Synod and let her know we are here?' Mr Wilson strode to the french doors and surveyed the garden. 'Perhaps she could return early?'

Wheels on gravel. The taxi returning. Thank God.

'Leave me your number. I'll see what I can do.'

55

'What the hell's going on?' Jack paced the kitchen.

Sarah had never seen him so animated. This was going to be tricky. She would sit and say nothing. Let him run his course.

'What's the big emergency? Why did you tell me your parents were dead? Why do they call you Abi? What's with the feckin parrot?'

'I'm sorry.' She glanced through the window to double check that the Wilsons had gone.

'I thought something had happened to Jesús. I drop everything, leave in the middle of my shift, rush over to find you chatting away with your dead parents.'

'Sorry, I didn't mean to panic you, but it was urgent. It still is.'

'Jesús?' He stopped pacing.

'No. We have to destroy Carole's surveillance recordings.'

Jack stared at her. 'What are you talking about?'

She drew aside the net curtains to reveal the camera tracking its path from the vicarage to the church. 'It's been up there for at least a week.'

'Bloody hell. Melville.'

'Exactly, we have to destroy the footage.'

'Melvilllllle,' trilled the parrot from the top of the fridge. 'Bastard, dirty money grubbing bastard.'

'Geez, what's up with him?' Jack backed away from the agitated bird.

'He's disorientated. I think he might be happier in a cage, more contained.'

'Swindling bloody psychopath,' screamed the parrot. Blimey, that was some advanced articulation.

'You know you can watch the footage on a smart-phone, right?' Jack said.

'I'm guessing Carol is not tech savvy. If she'd already watched it we'd currently be sitting in a police cell.'

'True.'

'And now there's also a recording of you taking Terence Johnson's parrot out of my van.'

'That's Terence Johnson's parrot? You stole Terence Johnson's parrot? What the hell is wrong with you?'

'What the hell? What the hell? What the hell?'

'He's going to drive you nuts.'

'Anyway. I have a plan.' Sarah poured out a bowl of Tropical Nutrigrain parrot food that she'd retrieved from Terence's kitchen cupboard. 'How about we go over to thank Carole for the barbeque. I'll ask to use the toilet. You keep her talking while I steal the hard drive.'

'What? Come straight over from next door and need the toilet? Plus, the unit could be anywhere in that enormous house. And I wasn't invited to the barbeque. Carole and I have never said more than Hi and Bye. And there was an unfortunate incident that I don't want to discuss.'

'Well, what do you suggest?'

'Melvillllllle. Melvillllllle. Bastard. Thieving bastard.'

'I cut the electricity.' Jack shot a look at the parrot who was now stepping furiously from foot to foot. 'Carole comes over to ask for help. I go in and check all the cables and appliances.'

'Brilliant.'

'On second thoughts, you should probably accompany me. I don't want to be left alone with her.'

'That would look weird. A big boy like you doesn't need a chaperone.'

He hesitated. 'Okay, I'll do it now. If I'm not back in fifteen minutes, come and rescue me.'

'Little piece of shit,' called the parrot.

Sarah stood on the chair and reached into the brocade pelmet. She'd hidden the phone on her first day at the vicarage.

Emergency use only. She called the one saved number. The ringing tone bored on; she must have to find a safe place to take the call. Come on. Come on.

'Hello, is that you?' Wow, she'd picked up an Irish accent already. Or else she was putting it on.

'Yes, of course it's me.'

'Is it an emergency?'

'Yes.'

'Go on.'

'Your parents are here.'

'I know. They sent a text. I called to warn you.'

Had the isolation sent her mad? 'No, you didn't.'

'A man picked up.'

Oh God, Jack knew about the burner phone. 'What?'

'It's okay, I hung up.'

'They want to see you.' Sarah could detect the distant cry of a seagull. 'You have to speak to them, make them leave. Immediately.'

'I can't phone, I've told them I have a phobia.' There was panic in her voice.

'Skype? Zoom? FaceTime?'

'It extends to all electronic communication.'

'For Christ's sake. They could be Googling General Synod at this very moment and finding it's not on.'

'What are you talking about?'

'You need to get rid of them.' Sarah jumped down from the chair. 'This is an absolute disaster.'

'How am I supposed to do that from here?' The wind crackled the connection.

'Arrange to meet them halfway.'

'The middle of the Irish sea?'

'More than halfway then. Get the ferry to Liverpool. I'll tell them you'll meet them at The Titanic hotel tomorrow night.'

'I can't just drop everything.'

'You have no choice. We need to get them out of West Tillington. Book the bloody ferry.'

Jack returned looking relieved.

'Any luck?' Sarah slid the phone into her back pocket.

'She was out. I cut the electrics. Now we wait.'

56

Jesús left Miss Bickerstool's room with his head bowed. What had he done? She'd kept asking if he was okay and saying if there was anything at all that he wanted to tell her then 'You know where I am.' She was in the classroom. He didn't tell her about Dad and Sarah carrying a dead person rolled up in the carpet at four forty-four in the morning. But that must be the sort of thing she was getting at.

Everything had piled up, like when you're playing snap and there hasn't been a pair for ages and your hand is hovering over the stack. Jesús had been tired out and missing Ben and Sarah and Moth. He'd been thinking about the whole Miss Walker thing and being able to choose where he wanted to live and about the place of safety.

He should have listened to Dad and not got sucked into the weirdness. He should have just asked Dad if they could move. He should have pretended that everything was normal and he was okay with not being able to sleep because his haunty-ghost mum kept showing up because their bed was done up like a buggering bathroom. You can do one little thing and it can have a humongous effect.

But he'd done it now.

Told Miss Bickerstool that he wouldn't mind living at Vespiary Cottage with Eileen for a bit. He didn't tell her it was because Mum was haunting him because that sounded too weird. Miss Bickerstool got him to write it down. He reckoned Dad would come too because they always stuck together but he still felt like one of those baby ducklings, way up in a tree that jump out of their nest and don't know if they'll land safely or be squished. But that's what he'd done. Now he had to wait until their big adult meeting. He couldn't crawl back up the tree.

Jesús had been told to walk over to Sarah's after school because Dad was working a double shift but when he got there Dad was there too. Jesús didn't get a chance to tell Dad about moving to Vespiary Cottage because he was trying to calm down a very sweary parrot that was loose in the kitchen. It was scratchy and bitey so Jesús wasn't to go in there. More weirdness to get sucked into.

Then the posh lady from next door with the very long surname was standing on the doorstep speaking really fast in a high-pitched voice as if someone had pressed fast forward. Jesús stood behind Sarah because the lady was quite scary. Her hair was all messy and there were black marks under her eyes. She said that she didn't have any electricity and when her husband Ted tried to fix it, he fell off a ladder and now he was lying on the floor underneath the fuse box. Dad said he'd go.

Sarah went to make Mrs long-name a cup of tea while she sat in the living room and cried. Jesús reckoned she shouldn't be left alone in case she suicided, so he sat on the floor and smiled at her in an 'everything will be okay' sort of way.

When Sarah came back the lady couldn't stop talking, like Mum used to get, but Mum would just be talking to herself. The lady was very worried about Mr Johnson because he'd been poisoned and he might die. She was crying about him more than about her husband but if Ted couldn't work and had to stay at home all day long her life would become a living nightmare. She got more and more upset the more she talked. Adults always said that talking about things will make you feel better but they were definitely wrong about that. He'd learnt that twice today.

It was pretty cool the way Sarah was nice to the lady even though she didn't like her. She said things like 'poor you' and 'oh dear' and 'he might pull through' and 'have another cup of tea.'

When the lady finally calmed down they talked about cats because Moth had slinked in to see what all the weird noises were and had jumped up on her lap. Cats are a great healer; like goats. She loved cats but couldn't have one because Ted was allergic. One of his many faults. Other faults were; his conversation – he talked mainly about meat – his snoring and his lack of interest in the bedroom. Jesús wasn't interested in bedrooms either, he didn't think many people were. She didn't mention Ted's current problem of lying at the bottom of a ladder which seemed to him to be the most important one.

Sarah said that the CCTV made her feel uncomfortable and was it really necessary? Turns out that next door has a camera that films the outside of the vicarage and the church. The lady said that it had cost thousands of pounds so she couldn't tell Mr Johnson that she'd turned it off. The problem was that Moth – who was now purring on her lap being vigorously stroked – kept setting off the motion detector and it made a grinding noise which was very disturbing, especially at night. Sarah said the camera probably caused the electrical fault and it was best to disconnect it. The lady said 'Yes, well the whole thing is meaningless now anyway,' and started crying again.

Dad came back and said that Ted had hurt his back. He was now lying down upstairs and he might have to rest in bed for a few days but he'd be okay. That cheered her up a bit. Maybe staying there would increase his interest in the bedroom.

57

J ack stuck his finger under his shirt collar. The suit felt too tight; he must have put on weight since his wedding. Sarah was rooting through her bag pulling out tissues and antiseptic wipes and The Picture of Dorian Gray. For God's sake. Why was she even here?

'Vegan fruit pastille?' She pulled down the wrapper.

'Nah.'

'It'll be okay.' Her words as hollow as the empty corridor.

An anxious looking woman with green dangly earrings poked her head around the door. 'Please come through to the meeting room.'

Judging by the empty coffee cups, biscuit crumbs and stale air, the people sitting around the table had been ensconced for some time. Jack undid his top button and loosened his tie. Sarah sat next to him as the space was hurriedly cleared of files. Weak smiles dissolved in the acidic atmosphere. A pair of social workers who he'd never met before made their perfunctory introductions. The man wore a crumpled grey shirt, the woman a fluffy orange jumper and a stony expression that gave the impression of a sick fox. Debbie Walker explained her role in a sing-song voice as if she were addressing a small child. Annoying. An older woman in a lived-in suit introduced herself as the conference chair and legal representative for the Local Authority. Dangly earrings picked up her notebook and shielded it from Jack's view. She was apparently there to take minutes and didn't bother to give her name. She announced that Miss Bickerstool sent her apologies. He didn't even know she'd been invited.

'Mr Jack Stretton, Jesus's father and Sarah Wilson, the Vicar of West Tillington, with whom they lived. Until recently.' Earrings may as well have said 'for the benefit of the tape,' although apparently it was not being recorded.

The clock ticked to two-thirty. The chair cleared her throat. 'This Child Protection Conference has been called in order to examine all the relevant information and circumstances in order to determine how best to safeguard the child.' She checked her notes, 'Jesús Stretton.' She turned to Jack. 'Is there anything you would like to say before we begin?'

'No, I'll wait and hear what you have to say.' Keep your powder dry.

'Yes, actually.' Sarah adjusted her dog-collar. 'I wish to speak on Mr Stretton's behalf.'

Jack flashed her a 'What the hell?' look, but she ignored him.

'I understand that there have been concerns raised about Jesús being left unsupervised as well as his use of the church computer, again unsupervised.' She was using her pulpit voice. Where the hell was this going?

He tried to kick her under the table but made contact with the vulpine social worker who scowled and made a show of rubbing her shin.

'I wanted to say that it was I, not Jack, who is to blame. It is entirely down to me and I can assure you that it will never happen again. In my experience Mr Stretton is an exemplary father.'

'Thank you very much for confirming the alleged lack of supervision and Jesús's use of the now sequestrated computer, Reverend Wilson.' The chair put on the glasses that hung from a string of black beads around her neck and made an entry in the notes. 'Ms Walker, if you could please outline the Local Authority case.'

The fluorescent light hummed. Debbie consulted her file. 'Mr Stretton has recently moved out of the vicarage into low-grade temporary accommodation and without informing social services. There are a number of ongoing concerns.'

'You might call it low-grade but I'd choose it over a new-build semi in Rose Haven Mews any day.'

'How do you know where I live, Mr Stretton?' She narrowed her eyes to imply stalking behaviour.

'I don't.'

Debbie flicked over a page. Jack placed the backs of his hands on his thighs, palms upwards and spread his fingers. It was a technique Sol taught him yesterday – it helped to keep calm or at least made you less likely to whack someone. The character assassination continued unabated. Edited highlights broke through like heavyweight punches. Uncooperative. Disabled. Low-paid employment. Antisocial hours. No formal childcare. Criminal record. Bloody hell, he sounded like such a loser. The final condemnation 'single parent' hung in the air.

Sarah caught his eye and signalled her outrage. It helped.

Debbie took a sip from her plastic Evian bottle. She was evidently not bothered about the planet. Now she was reading from a thin brown file labelled 'Stretton mother. Deceased.'

'Mrs Sofía Rodriguez moved to the UK with Jack Stretton whilst pregnant. She married the purported father following the child's birth and immediately applied for British citizenship.'

'There's nothing purported about Jesús's paternity. And I don't like the insinuations. She left a beautiful country to live with me.'

'If you could let Ms Walker finish Mr Stretton. You'll have your turn to speak.' The chair indicated that she continue.

'Mrs Stretton was described in her medical records as "volatile with a possible Emotionally unstable personality disorder."'

'Sofía had bipolar disorder. Undiagnosed because her doctor was a...' he searched for a suitable word. Sol had advised against expletives. 'Useless git. Said her outbursts were cultural. "All Latinos are fiery," were his exact words. Racist prat.'

'Mr Stretton, please.'

'I'm sorry but this is all crap,' he shouted.

'If you are unable to contain yourself, I'll have to ask you to wait outside.'

He sighed and replaced his open palms on his legs.

'Mrs Stretton committed suicide by exsanguination.' Debbie tripped over the word. She'd probably Googled it. 'She had slashed her wrists and neck. She was discovered by then six-year-old Jesus who was left to call the emergency services.'

Jack would have to correct this misrepresentation too. He should really be making notes.

'Despite repeated opportunities, Jesus has been unable to verbalise the trauma of finding his mother lying naked and dead in a blood-filled bath.' She took another sip from her bottle and replaced the cap.

Good grief, the woman could paint a gratuitously graphic picture. What the hell was wrong with her?

'Thank you, Ms Walker. Perhaps this would be a good time to tell us about your sessions with Jesús?' The chair looked at her watch. Not subtle.

'Of course. On my first meeting with Jesus, at the vicarage, I found him in a filthy and dishevelled condition. He had sustained multiple cuts and bruises, his clothing was ripped and he was practically monosyllabic.' She pursed her lips and glared at Jack. Judgey McJudge face.

'Could you clarify the purpose of your visit?' The chair shuffled her papers.

'I was notified by police that Jesus had run away from home and had spent the night in the woods.' She turned to a printout of her session notes. 'After several painstaking interviews at the children's centre, Jesus made a series of worrying disclosures. These included: that he felt his life was in imminent danger, that he carried a bladed article for his own protection and that he had been attacked and assaulted in Montague Forest by a group of people wearing hoods.'

Jack felt a pounding in his ears. 'What the hell? None of this has been passed on to me.'

Debbie ignored him. 'Jesus has shown recent behavioural disturbance. Previously an exemplary pupil he was sent home from school for fighting. He has disclosed episodes of glue sniffing with his father. He has described drinking from so-called "sacrificial goblets" which have now been seized by police.' She paused before throwing down her ace. 'It is alleged that Mr Stretton made and provided little Jesus with Molotov cocktails and that together they fire-bombed a car.'

A collective gasp sucked in the sour air.

This was looking very bad.

At least the police's raid on the church pre-dated Melville's exhumation so they didn't have a decaying murder victim to add to the catalogue.

'If I may now turn to the witness statements.' Debbie located a page marked with a red sticker. 'A neighbour, concerned for the child's welfare, recently reported that Mr Stretton indecently exposed himself to her.'

'You have got to be fricken kidding me.'

'To support the veracity of her allegation she disclosed that he has a tattoo of a heart above his private parts and that he was very well endowed.' Debbie flushed and turned to him for comment.

'It's a birthmark,' he said defensively. 'And I was in my own home, well in Sarah's home. I was getting dressed. Carole looked through the window.'

Debbie wrote the word 'acknowledged' in the margin.

'The concerned neighbour further reports that she witnessed Mr Stretton hurrying from the vicarage late one night wearing a black hood. The informant has provided a log of the occasions when Jesus has been left unsupervised, including overnight. He has been locked out and had to crawl through a toilet window.' Debbie turned to Sarah. 'Thank you for confirming the accuracy of information that might otherwise have remained uncorroborated.'

For Chrissakes, this was getting crazy.

Everything about Debbie Walker was infuriating; her little girl voice, her incessant sipping of water, the red blotches that spread up her neck as she rifled through the file, her lies. Debbie pulled out a sheet embossed with a crown. What more could there be? Oh Christ, a police statement.

'Officers from Peaminster and District Constabulary have shared several concerns through our working together initiative. Red flags include allegations that Mr Stretton desecrated the grave of a dog.' Debbie took a sip of water. 'There is a well-documented link between cruelty to animals and cruelty to children.' She paused for the minute taker to catch-up. 'Further, it is alleged that Mr Stretton launched an unprovoked physical attack on local businessman Melville Russet although charges were later dropped.' She looked so fricken pleased with herself. 'Despite a thorough police search Mr Russet currently remains a missing person.'

Debbie paused again. How much more could he take? 'Sarah Wilson visited a known sexual offender and remains in correspondence with him.' Another sip. God, he could smash the bottle from her hand. 'Of particular concern, Jesus and his friend have been in contact with a suspected paedophile and had arranged to meet him in person.'

'What the hell?'

Debbie closed the file. Stitched up like a fricken kipper.

Jack rubbed his hand across his scalp. 'Now I've got something to say.' He felt the muscle in his jaw tighten. 'This is a fit-up.'

'Jack, do you want me to respond?' said Sarah.

'He's my son, he's nothing to do with you. This is all unsubstantiated bullshit.' He was shouting again.

'Please control yourself, Mr Stretton. It clearly is substantiated.' The chair spoke in a maddeningly calm monotone. 'The concerns come from a number of sources and have been corroborated by police investigation. We have evidence of email contact with a potentially high-risk paedophile and witness statements pertaining to the lack of parental supervision. We also have transcripts and video-recordings of Jesús's sessions with Deb... with Ms Walker. His disclosures are of the most disturbing nature.'

'None of this is true,' he shouted. He was vaguely aware of Sarah's hand on his arm. 'None of this is true,' he repeated. He needed to stay calm. At least not hit anyone.

'Is there anything else you'd like to add before we move to the decision of the conference?'

'Yes, I would like Jesús to have his say.'

Debbie looked triumphant. 'The chair felt that it would not be in the child's best interests for him to attend in person but Jesus has written a short letter to express his wishes.'

'It's Jesús. Hay-sous. You think you know so much about him, you don't even know how to pronounce his bloody name.'

The chair unfolded a sheet evidently torn from a school exercise book. It was written in Jesús's unmistakable rounded cursive.

'If I could choose where to live, I would choose Vespiary cottage with Ben's Granny Eileen. Yours sincerely, Jesús Stretton.'

Sarah took his hand. He withdrew it. The note was passed solemnly around the table. How did this happen? Had they made him write it?

The chair's voice came from miles away. 'I recommend that a child protection plan be put in place on the grounds of potential risk of physical harm, potential risk of sexual harm and risk of neglect.'

He couldn't move. He couldn't breathe. People were talking around him.

'Mr Stretton?'

'Sorry?'

'Do you have any final remarks?'

He got to his feet. He needed air.

'Mr Stretton, please sit down.'

He sat down.

'The threshold to issue court proceedings has not yet been reached. The recommendations are voluntary at this stage.'

'What are the recommendations exactly?' Sarah sounded shocked.

'The child protection team recommend that Jesús stays with Eileen Russet while investigations continue. We note that Mrs Russet has agreed only on the grounds that it is temporary and that it is the child's own request. She herself expressed no concerns for his welfare.'

The silence hung like a shroud.

'Would it help if they moved back into the vicarage?' asked Sarah.

'No. Not at all.' The chair removed her glasses and held his gaze. 'Mr Stretton, if you agree, Jesús could go this afternoon.'

Jack looked out of the window. A small boy was holding up a stick for a barking terrier. He threw it. The dog chased after it. The boy followed. 'Will I be allowed visits?'

'Yes, visitation can be arranged.'

'Okay, let him go.' He stood to leave.

'No,' Sarah whispered.

He let the door slam.

58

J esús and Ben sat side by side on the bog oak. Jesús handed over the binoculars and clicked his stopwatch. They got five minutes each. The birch copse was a good place for birds. A jay was doing its funny ha-ha ha-ha call. Dad could imitate it so well that the jay would answer back. Hopefully there were some up at Lingen field today so he wouldn't be too lonely.

When you feel sad you're meant to list the good things in your life:

Hanging out with Ben all the time.

Collecting beans and peas and baby new potatoes from the veg-bed.

Hearing owls at night.

Sleeping in the top bunk bed.

Eileen's lovely cakes.

The ground-up spider jar was empty.

The lights were on in Mr Johnson's house so he wasn't dead so Dad didn't kill him.

But that means it was Mr Russet who was rolled up in the carpet.

That was the thing about listing positives; negative stuff always pushed into the queue.

Ben passed the binoculars back. Jesús focussed on the jay chattering up in the rowan. Probably looking for fledglings to eat. Even the best animals could do horrible things. Same as humans. Mum was being even worse here. She must have been annoyed that he'd moved from the shepherd's hut. Last night she was lying in the bath with her hair all floating around and her starey eyes and her neck open. She sat bolt upright and screamed. Jesús had screamed too and leapt out and shoved a flannel in his mouth. Luckily, Eileen had been in the summer house. He told Ben there was a massive spider.

The jay flapped away with a limp body in its beak. A baby woodpecker. It made the sweary parrot's behaviour seem not so bad. Sarah had stolen Mr Johnson's parrot! She was hard to figure out. Perhaps she was trying to teach the parrot to be good. Stealing a parrot was a small thing compared to killing someone, but still, it wasn't behaviour you'd expect from a vicar.

The sound of humans whooping came through the trees. Hardly anyone used these woods – sometimes a dog walker but they were always quiet except for yelling the dog's name. The last time there was a group of noisy people it didn't end well. Jesús signalled to get down. Ben hunched on the ground like a tortoise, or maybe a rock. A whirring sound right over head. Jesús peered through the cracks in his fingers. Wow, a drone. Cool. He stood up to see it better.

'Hey there, kiddies.'

There were five of them but they weren't wearing hoods. Well, one was but it was a normal hoody not a weird black cloaky one. They looked pretty normal, just teenagers, one was a girl.

Plus, he and Ben had pointy sticks so they'd be alright. 'Is that yours?' he asked.

'Yep.' The boy moved the stick on the control box. 'Stand back guys.'

The drone glided above the canopy and wove its way down between the trees landing right next to their feet. So cool.

'Wanna pick it up?' said the guy in the hoody.

Jesús took it in both hands, it was heavier than he expected. It was amazing. Four propellers, LED lights, a camera and a remote controller like an Xbox.

'Can I have a go?' asked Ben.

'Battery's nearly dead.' The fat one with the baseball cap took it back. 'I need to run through the footage to check we've got what we need.'

They gathered round the screen. Jesús went in front because he was the smallest. The smell of stale cigarettes was a bit off-putting. First there were some bumpy close-ups of branches then a smooth climb until they were above the trees. Now they were whizzing up Bradbury Hill. Wow, a deer running, then another one. The drone turned and dipped and came back down the hill. It was like you were flying in an actual plane. A grey bird zoomed past, probably a pigeon. Woah, there was Vespiary cottage, the veg-beds and the washing hanging on the line. There was him and Ben sitting on the bog oak way below. It circled and came closer. They were crouched down like tortoises; they stood up holding their pointy sticks. More blurry branches and a close up of their trainers.

The guys all patted themselves on the back like they'd just scored a goal.

'It's in the can,' said the one in the baseball cap.

The one in the hoody looked at them funny. 'Hey, are you the lads who were up here last month?'

'Yep.'

'I'm Johnno, this is Kev, Adam, Sid, Tracey.'

They all nodded.

'Jesús and Ben,' said Ben.

'You were perfect extras so we just kept rolling.'

Jesús didn't ask what that meant.

They all sort of looked at each other and grinned. 'So, guys, how would you like to be in a movie?'

'Cool.'

59

P repare to navigate off-road.
    Oh no, not again.

Sarah shifted down a gear, revved the engine and bumped along the edge of the meadow. She was going to ruin the suspension and God knows what Jack would think of her driving. What did she care? But she did. The van stalled under a copper beech; it could pass as her chosen parking spot.

The shepherd's hut was much smaller than she'd imagined but it was sweet, dwarfed by the row of beech trees in full leaf. The soft green paint made it vanish into the landscape. The sun illuminated the wildflowers surrounding it, the whole effect that of an advert for alternative living. Sarah sighed. How little one needed to be happy.

Anyway, back to reality. She was here to clear the air. Hmm, who was she kidding? Truth was she missed him. Maybe they could still be friends. Plus, they had the pressing problem of the dead body in the chapel to deal with. She couldn't solve that one on her own.

Jack appeared from a rickety shed, wiping his hands on his trousers, a baked bean clinging to his shirt. God, he looked rough. He hadn't shaved his face or his head. He'd taken on the appearance of a discarded kiwi fruit.

'Composting toilet,' he said by way of greeting.

'Oh, right.'

Sarah glanced inside the shepherd's hut. It was pretty much one room with a double bed inside an open cupboard. Jesús's neatly folded dinosaur pyjamas hit like a train. An empty bottle of lager stood beside an ashtray overflowing with spent roaches. So much for their healthy living drive – Jack had gone to pot, literally and metaphorically.

He gestured to a carved mushroom and she sat down. It was surprisingly comfortable. Jack sat by the wicker table, threaded a band of willow through a skeletal dome and tapped it down. The tension in his shoulders and the grip of his jaw suggested this wasn't going to be easy. He didn't offer her a drink. Maybe just as well; she really didn't want to use a composting toilet, whatever the hell that was. She took a deep breath and jumped in.

'Thanks for letting me come over. How're you doing?'

He peered at her with bloodshot eyes. 'Pastoral visit is it, Vicar?'

'I'm sorry if things are tough for you at the moment.'

'If?' His eyes flashed. 'Are you kidding me?'

'I'm so sorry about leaving Jesús unattended. And I honestly didn't know the vestry computer even worked, let alone had internet connection. I'm helping Lionel because I know he's innocent.' Her rehearsed apology sounded thin. Disingenuous.

The dying sun bruised the sky indigo. It was so peaceful here but Jack's melancholy soaked into the chill of the evening and stole into her soul.

'Had my visit yesterday.' His words hung heavy with defeat.

'How was he?'

'Wary.'

'Sorry. I know the meeting was a disaster but their investigation isn't going to find anything. He'll come home soon, I'm sure.'

'I'm not sure of anything. I'm worried what the hell they'll find once they start digging.'

'Such as?' Oh no, he wasn't going to make a confession was he? Meeting at his ridiculously isolated hut suddenly felt like a very bad idea. She was questioning everything these days, even her own judgement. Especially her own judgement.

'Let's see, there's the bundles of cash in your mattress, your burner phone, and the corpse we dug up that is currently decaying in the chapel.'

When the truth was spoken aloud it sounded crazier than ever. At least his choice of pronouns suggested that he was sharing some responsibility. She handed him the strip of willow that had fallen from the table. He took it and wove it through the supports. The task seemed to calm him a little.

'I'm still waiting for an explanation. The money? The phone? Your parents coming back from the dead? Why they call you Abi? What the hell is going on Sarah?'

The poor guy was still trying to give her the benefit of the doubt. She couldn't ask him to trust her. She didn't trust herself.

'It's complicated, I didn't want to burden you with my toxic relationship with my family. It was easier to say they were dead. I never liked the name Abi, I prefer to use my middle name.'

Jack looked up. 'Sorry. That's bullshit.'

She ran her hand over the smooth cap of the mushroom. She could summon no defence. When you don't know what to say, say nothing.

'Are you a drug dealer?'

'No.'

'Are you involved in organised crime?'

'God, no. What is this, twenty questions?'

She was being unfair. She owed him the truth but once he knew it their relationship would be over. Their friendship; there was nothing more but God knows she needed a friend. So did he. They needed to team up. And that's how to justify not telling the truth – she'd become a master of justification. And obfuscation.

'I hate to ask but did you find out any more about what happened in the woods or the alleged paedophile?' It broke her heart to think of poor Jesús keeping it all to himself. People who targeted kids must know how to silence them.

'Bloody social worker is still being very cagey. Obviously thinks I'm in on it. I'm not even allowed to talk to him about it.'

'The truth will out.' God, she sounded trite. Where did she get these ridiculous phrases?

'By the way, Johnson's back home.'

'Oh God, he survived? What about Juju?'

'Juju?'

'My parrot.'

'Terence Johnson's parrot. Yep, that's a big problem.' Jack

stopped weaving and stared at her. 'He'll call the police. Your fingerprints will be all over his house. Breaking and entry, theft. They make an example of people who abuse their position. You could be looking at three years. Another West Tillington vicar behind bars.'

The image of herself sitting on a plastic mattress in a prison cell was harrowing. The sentence for armed robbery would be much higher. Ten years, maybe more. Unbearable. Would he visit her? Would anyone? She wouldn't survive.

'I left the cage open. Made it look like he flew away.'

'With all the doors and windows locked? Well, at least you're not a criminal mastermind.'

'I couldn't leave a window open. What if someone broke in?'

'Can you hear yourself?' He continued weaving. 'And by the way, everyone knows you have the parrot, you can hear him screaming "Hi, Sarah Wilson" halfway across Adfordley.'

'It wasn't breaking and entering. I used the key.' Miss Innocent. 'I was in his house investigating a serious offence. That's a legitimate mitigating circumstance. We just need sufficient evidence to get him arrested.' Miss Self-righteous.

'Yeah, right. Because that worked perfectly last time.'

'If Lionel Gooseworthy is exonerated his testimony will be overwhelming. He knows about the murder.'

'You're deluding yourself. This isn't some American courtroom drama where a star witness walks in and saves the day.' He bent another rod of willow through the dome and tested its strength. 'Anyway, with the SS sniffing around and the coppers investigating Terence's poisoning we need to get rid of the body. Urgently.'

'Melville is evidence now. If Terence isn't dying, we need to hand the body over to the police.'

'And say what? Here's a body we found earlier.'

'We tell the truth. Well, not the whole truth.'

'We give them evidence that Terence was poisoned by a body that we knew was buried on his water course? Evidence of grave desecration. Evidence that we perverted the water course as well as the course of justice. Evidence that will get us both jailed. Then what'll happen to Jesús?' He spoke without a breath.

'We rebury him in a different spot and tip off the police.' She heard how ridiculous this sounded.

'That would be insane. Even if we got away with it our DNA will be all over the body.'

'Then how do you suggest we get rid of him?'

'I'm still working on that.'

He added a top band of flattened willow and held up the finished cage. 'Anyway, this might at least calm down the bloody parrot.'

'Wow. It's brilliant, he'll love it.'

'It'll show he's been well looked after when Johnson calls the cops on you. You could say you heard he was in hospital and you were caring for his parrot until he was discharged.'

'Friends?' Sarah held out her hand. A hug would have been nice.

'Sure.' He shook her hand with a matey bounce. Or did he hold it just long enough to imbue more meaning? No, she was reading in. What the hell was wrong with her?

'I really am sorry, Jack.'

'Thanks for trying to help at the meeting. Even if you didn't actually help. In fact made things a hundred times worse.' He looked gorgeous when he smiled.

Jack stood up, disappeared into the hut and returned with two bottles of lager. 'Fancy a sundowner?'

'Lovely.' A black shadow flitted overhead. Another. And another. She stared in horror. Bats.

'Noctules,' he said proudly. 'I knew you'd love them.'

She flinched. Try to stay calm, do not look at them, do not react in any way.

'They roost in the beeches. Must be a couple of hundred. Bad place to park your van by the way, it'll be covered in bat shit.'

A shadowy form swooped to take an insect from the grass. Another cut away inches from her face. Jesus Christ. She screamed and sprinted into the hut slamming the door behind her.

She was shaking. Half a spliff lay stubbed out in the ashtray. She lit it and inhaled deeply. God, that was good stuff. Okay, she would compose herself, go back out, walk calmly to her van and go home. She took another long drag. It was cosy in the hut. Very chilled. The woven wall hangings emanated wellbeing. Everything was cool, it was all going to work out just fine.

Jack poked his head around the door. 'It's okay. They've gone.'

She held the spliff behind her back, a curl of aromatic smoke rising from her fingers.

He came in and took it from her. 'I'll roll us a new one, shall I?'

'Sorry, I freaked out.'

'They forage up at Lingen Beacon so they won't be back for a few hours.'

'I think maybe I have a phobia.'

'Yeah? So, what's with Save Our Bats?' He took a bag of green buds from a container marked 'Flour' and sprinkled it along a patchwork of cigarette papers.

'Animal conservation can be very factional. Bats don't get a look in, what with all the baby pandas and cute koala bears and stuff.'

'This is me you are talking to, the guy who's planning on disposing of a murder victim with you.' He lit the joint and handed it to her. 'The truth will set you free, Vicar.'

Actually, the truth could get her locked up but she trusted him. It was easier to face him in a dark hut in the middle of a field. An intimate confessional. Time to tell him the truth, well not the whole truth, she wasn't an idiot. She took a long draw and exhaled slowly. Truth drug. 'It's a launderette.'

'Sorry?'

'The bat charity. It's a front for cleaning the five hundred and eleven grand that I stole from NatWest bank in Smethwick.' She took another drag and passed him the joint.

'Bloody hell.'

60

Jesús and Ben sat on the sacrificing rock and ate their chocolate spread sandwiches. It was much further away from Eileen's than they were allowed but there were no good sacrificing rocks around the cottage. Luckily, they'd brought a packed lunch because everything was taking ages; setting up the camera, checking the lighting, endless talking about angles and sound and wind direction.

They weren't named characters, they had 'bit parts' but if the scenes worked out, they'd get an end credit. That was probably like a token you could exchange for sweets and stuff; fair enough. Their role was 'scared-little-kids-slash-third-victims.' It turned out they'd already done their first scene which was running away through the woods and hiding for real. Johnno said it looked brilliant – just like The Blair Witch Project which was a cult film from before they were born. They had to wear the exact same clothes they wore last time for continuing purposes.

In their second scene they were going to be sacrificed on a rock so that the vampire-slash-beast would leave the girl alone and not eat her, although later the girl gets eaten anyway, but they didn't have to worry about that just now. Tracey sat about in her white nightie flicking through her phone and looking bored.

'Okay, guys, shooting in five.' Johnno signalled for them to stop eating.

Jesús liked the way he talked. It was just like a real film set.

Adam and the other guy Sid, who didn't say much, put their jackets on because it was meant to be winter. Jesús guessed they hadn't thought about the leaves on the trees but he didn't say anything.

Johnno had a cool clapperboard with The Digge, Date, Scene, Take, written on it in white letters. Very professional. The Digge was the name of the vampire-thing. Johnno positioned him and Ben by the wych elm. 'Okay, lads, it's best if you don't know exactly what's going to happen because it'll be more real. Just go with it.'

'Do we have any lines?' asked Ben.

'Christ, you'll be asking what's your motivation next.' Johnno was a bit stressed. 'I don't want any acting, we're not in a fricken school play.'

Kev stared up at the sun and walked around looking through a square in his hands and moved him and Ben further round the tree.

Johnno stepped forward. 'Take one. Action.'

Sid and Adam ran forward and grabbed their legs. Ben fell crashing onto his back throwing up a cloud of dust. He kicked and wriggled free and ran off. Adam was clinging onto Jesús's leg like a limpet. He tried to shake him off but he wouldn't let go. He bashed Adam on the top of his head with his fist. They fell to the ground. Jesús felt a hard lump under his back. He grabbed it. A log. He whacked Adam hard on the kneecap.

'Argh.'

'Cut.'

'Bloody hell.' Johnno put his hands on his head. 'Christ, you're not meant to fight back.'

Ben crawled out from behind a bush. 'Just going with it.'

Adam limped over holding his knee. 'You're supposed to be scared little kids, not fricken ninjas.'

'Sorry.' Jesús patted the dust from his trousers.

Johnno puffed out his cheeks. 'Do it again but this time don't resist. Pretend to be little girls or something.' He rubbed out Take one and wrote Take two. 'Right, starting positions everyone. And Action.'

Sid ran forward and grabbed Ben's legs.

'Help me, help me, help me,' Ben screamed, all high pitched, waving his arms. It was hilarious.

This time Jesús was ready for Adam. He jinked sideways. Adam tripped over a root and crashed to the ground.

'Cut.' Johnno threw down his clapperboard. 'Okay, listen up. You don't have any lines. No talking. At all. Alright? Just wriggle around a bit and absolutely no laughing, you're about to be fricken sacrificed.'

Ben wanted the toilet so he ran off to find a suitable place. By the time he came back the wind was picking up. There was a long argument about sound quality and abandoning the shoot until tomorrow.

'That might be difficult because we're helping Eileen to tie up the runner beans,' said Jesús.

After more debate they decided to ditch the sound and add creepy background music later. Johnno wrote Take three on the board.

'Action.'

Jesús ran, Adam dived and pulled his legs away. He whooshed forwards and cracked his head hard on the wych elm.

Oww. God, it hurt.

Warm blood ran down his face.

'Keep rolling.'

Jesús hung in mid-air. The trees were upside down and they were moving. The sky bobbed with big dark clouds. He felt seasick, perhaps he was in a bouncy dingey. No, he was going across a cow field because there was mooing. He was being carried like a dead deer with its legs tied to a stick. Blood trickled into his eyes but he couldn't wipe it because someone had hold of his arms, another had his legs. Maybe he was being stolen. No, it was okay because Ben was walking along beside him.

'He's awake.' The voice came from far away.

He was lowered onto the grass. His back was soaking wet. Someone shone a light right into his eyes.

'Get him to stand up.'

It was hard to hear. Blood in his ear. His legs had no bones. He sat back down. A banana was shoved into his hand. Warm and squidgy but tasted alright. Someone was crying. His body was not his own. He sicked up the banana. Now there was rain. He'd like to stay here getting wet but there was someone shouting about the camera equipment then they were off again.

He was upright, Kev and Johnno were dragging him, his arms slung around their shoulders and his legs trying to walk but it was too fast. Ben was trotting along beside him saying the same thing over and over. 'It's okay, mate, we're nearly there.'

Now he was on Eileen's sofa with a blanket over him and his head wrapped in something tight and an ambulance was coming so he just needed to lie still and rest and not to worry, it will be here soon.

61

It was a one-hour drive to Peaminster General Hospital; Sarah and Jack made it in forty-five minutes. They parked up without bothering with a ticket and raced into Accident and Emergency. It was packed. Eileen and Ben stood bewildered beside a panel of signs pointing to scary sounding departments. There was no sign of Jesús.

'Where is he?' Jack demanded.

'They took him for a brain scan,' said Eileen, expressionless.

Sarah took Ben's hand and squeezed it. 'You okay?' He was as pale as a moth. One of Jesús's sayings.

Ben nodded.

'Is he conscious?' asked Jack.

'In and out. He spoke briefly in the ambulance.' Eileen's voice a monotone.

'What did he say?'

'Place of safety.'

'Oh.'

'It could be a while.' Sarah tried to sound business-like. 'Should I get us some drinks?' No one replied. 'Would you like to come, Ben?'

He nodded.

She followed the signs to the League of Friends cafeteria. A dismal room with flammable looking ceiling tiles and incongruous framed photographs of sand dunes. Two ancient ladies stood behind the counter. She ordered three coffees, two to take away. Ben asked politely for an apple juice.

'What a lovely boy you have.'

Sarah smiled weakly and didn't correct her.

The cheap tables bore the smears of inexpert wiping.

She chose the one furthest from the thrum of the vending machine.

They sat and looked out at the carpark. She should really go and buy a ticket. The tepid coffee was revolting; she spat it back into the cup. Ben poked the plastic straw through his carton and drank in one long suck. The aerobic hoovering of the last drops made her smile.

'Thirsty,' he said in apology.

'It must have been pretty scary.'

'I thought he was dead at first and then again when he was on the sofa.'

'Blimey.'

'Yeah.'

'He's not though.' She exchanged glances with a woman comforting a crying teenager.

'He ran hair-first into a tree.'

'Hair first?'

Ben mimed a runner bowing over the line for a photo finish.

'Ah, that would do it.'

'He had blood coming out of his ear. I didn't know you had blood in your head.'

'Not good.'

Outside two men were arguing over a car parking space. Her race with Jack to the hospital had been equally tense. Silently united in their fears for Jesús. The kiss that had felt so right now so wrong.

'Do you know how to contact the guys making the film?'

'No.' Ben made an igloo from the sugar cubes. 'But the sticker on the clapper-board said Peaminster College, Dept of Film Studies.'

'Okay. Ready to go back?'

'Yep.'

Sarah left the coffees on the table.

Eileen and Jack had managed to get two chairs by the wall from where they could watch the double doors through which Jesús had been wheeled. The green exit light cast a sickly hue on their faces.

'Any news?' asked Sarah.

'No.' Eileen retrieved a packet of liquorice Allsorts from her handbag.

Ben took a Bertie Bassett, looked at it wistfully and returned it. 'Save that for Jesús, it's his favourite.'

Sarah rubbed his arm. 'You have it, we'll buy him a whole new bag.'

Eileen passed her an ornate silver hip flask like something from the Antiques Roadshow.

'What's this?'

'Brandy, medicinal purposes.'

'I thought you were teetotal.'

'Just for the shock.'

Sarah took a mouthful and passed it to Jack who swigged recklessly.

'Mr Stretton?' A woman with a severe haircut and a hound's tooth jacket stood over him.

'Yes.'

'Margaret Ratalov from the safeguarding team. May I ask you to come through to room six?'

'I'm staying here until I can see my son.'

'I understand that he's had his CT scan. He's had a neck-brace fitted and will be admitted to paediatric neurology. They are waiting for a bed.'

Jack stood up. 'I need to see him.' The brandy on his breath was not helping.

'That will be for me to decide.'

'You're kidding me?'

'It is routine when a child on a protection plan is admitted with a serious head injury.'

Several people turned to stare. Someone tutted.

'He wasn't even there,' said Eileen.

'And you are?' Ms Ratalov studied her as if she were in a police line-up.

'Eileen Russet, his current guardian.'

'Then if you could also come through.'

'I'm Reverend Sarah Wilson.' She put her arm around Ben's shoulder.

'Perhaps you could stay with the boy.'

Sarah stood with the gaggle of smokers opposite the No Smoking sign at the main entrance. The majority were nurses. A queue of ambulances waited with their cargo, the paramedics leaning against the bonnets sharing anecdotes and swigging Red Bull. There was a general air of comradery from which Sarah felt excluded.

Ben was sitting on the grass eating the packet of marmite crisps that Eileen had produced from her fathomless bag. Another pang of exclusion – she'd never have kids. She was destined to spend her life on the periphery. Had she ever done anything of consequence? Being a vicar was the closest she'd come and that was all a farce. A pretence that could be exploded at any moment. She inhaled deeply on her Silk Cut and offered the packet around.

A blaring ambulance screeched past the line of waiting vehicles and pulled up in front of A & E as a team of medics ran out of the automatic doors. The nurses stamped out their cigarettes and rushed to assist. Sarah followed hoping to contribute whatever help might be afforded by a passing vicar. The doctors climbed into the ambulance. She stood by the open doors trying to radiate goodwill.

'CPR given en route, patient unconscious and unresponsive. Substantial blood loss,' the paramedic stepped aside.

A young doctor in a stained white-coat bent over the patient. 'Stand back.'

Everyone stopped talking. Sarah held her breath. The minutes ticked by.

'Okay, thanks everyone, nothing more to do here. Dead On Arrival. Two-thirty-five.'

The urgency dissipated as the stretcher was wheeled past its subdued guard of honour. A wing of black hair protruded from the top of the cellular blanket that covered the patient's head and chest. His tight mustard trousers were splattered red. A paramedic rattled the body past the opening and closing doors of A&E and down the path signed Mortuary.

Terence Johnson was dead.

62

Sarah positioned herself by the kitchen window with a clear view of the church behind her to lend moral authority. She moved her rum out of view of the webcam. The Zoom call connected. A man with a crumpled face appeared on the screen in front of a promotional poster for Casablanca – his slicked back hair and 1940s jacket suggested that he modelled himself on Humphry Bogart. She let him chat away for a minute before telling him he was on mute. Get the upper hand. She pressed record.

'Thank you so much for your time, Mr Langur.'

'Not at all.'

'I wanted to ensure that you were aware of the police investigation into the injuries sustained by seven-year-old Jesús Stretton as a result of being an unpaid, unsupervised, unchaperoned extra in a film made by your students.' Go in early, go in hard.

Mr Langur's shoulders slumped as the opening volley hit their target. 'How is the little boy?' Chastened with a hint of shit-scared.

'He is in the paediatric neurology ward. His father is by his bedside.'

'Oh goodness, I'm so sorry.' Shocked, veering towards distraught.

'He has regained consciousness but according to Dr Dhooma, the consultant with a penchant for the double negative, he has suffered a not insignificant intracranial haemorrhage.'

'We will of course cooperate fully with the police investigation.'

'Thank you, it would certainly help Mr Stretton to understand exactly what happened to his son.'

'Of course.'

'Melvillllllle, Melvilllllle.' Juju bobbed on his perch. 'Bloody bastard.'

'Sorry?'

'It's just the radio.' She should really keep him upstairs but he enjoyed looking out of the kitchen window and he was actually rather good company.

'Play for today?'

'Yes. Mr Langur, I also wanted to ask you about the manipulation of video images and whether it was possible to simulate the illusion of behaviour that did not actually occur.'

He took on the expression of a beaten dog. 'I can assure you that we would never try to cover up what happened.'

'I meant as a general principle.'

Mr Langur relaxed slightly. 'An interesting question, Reverend. Yes, creative editing and image engineering are skills that we teach on our cinematography course.' He was back on firmer ground. 'Did you have a particular manipulation in mind?'

'Let's say, for example, if one were standing behind a piglet dressing it in a tutu. Could a sexual behaviour be inferred?'

His heavy jowls fell further. 'Oh, the Reverend Gooseworthy.'

'Yes, the Reverend Gooseworthy, who is currently serving a three-year custodial sentence for offences against piglets.'

'I see.'

'Good riddance,' screamed Juju. 'Wanker.'

'Gosh, that is a little rich for Radio Four.'

'I'll turn it off.' She threw a cloth over the cage and returned. 'A couple of things that you might wish to know. Firstly, if you are willing to testify at Lionel Gooseworthy's appeal you will be immune from prosecution for perverting the course of justice in his original trial.'

'I see.' He flushed. 'I really would like to help but...'

'Fabrication of evidence is a very serious offence. It carries a custodial sentence.'

Mr Langur rubbed the nape of his neck. 'I see.'

'Secondly, you should know that councillor Terence Johnson

died last Tuesday.'

Sarah allowed the implications to permeate.

Mr Langur sat motionless. It was possible that his screen had frozen although she could just discern a twitch in his left eyelid.

'It was something of which I am deeply ashamed. Mr Johnson made me an offer I couldn't refuse. A part-time lecturer's salary, you know...'

'Then I'm sure that you now wish to do the right thing and provide a detailed testimony.' Her most ecclesiastical voice. 'Righting of wrongs is the path to salvation.' Perhaps she should listen to herself; she gave excellent advice.

'Of course, I would be happy to.'

'Wanker.'

'Thank you, Mr Langur. I'll send across the details of the lawyer acting on behalf of Reverend Gooseworthy.' She squinted for the Leave button.

'Sorry, Vicar, just one thing before you go. How did you know that it was me who manipulated the piglet video?'

'I didn't.'

'Sarah, dear girl, how are you bearing up?' The Dean was a master of the resonant tone reserved for the recently bereaved. 'It's been such a jolt to us all.'

'Yes, it has.' She took the phone through to the hallway – Juju was particularly expansive in his condemnation of the clergy.

'I just wanted to let you know that Terence's body has been released.'

'That's good.' She had no idea why he was telling her this.

'He can now be laid to rest.'

'Yes.'

'Quite a shock, especially as he had so recently been restored to rude health.'

'Did he ever get a diagnosis?' she asked.

'Bacterial septicaemia I believe.'

'So he had another relapse when he got home?' How odd, perhaps trace contamination had remained after Melville's removal. In a way it was karmic symmetry. Terence poisoned by the man he had killed. Old Testament justice. An eye for an eye, a tooth for a tooth.

'Not a relapse, no. He was shot.'

'Shot?'

'Twelve-bore shotgun. Sawn off. Point blank range.' Geoffrey delivered the facts as bullet points. Literally.

'Good grief.'

'Both barrels apparently. Straight into the chest.'

'Who could have done such a thing?' She perched on the elephant's foot umbrella stand trying to make sense of what she was hearing.

'I understand that several leads are being followed.'

'There can't be many people who own a shotgun, had a vendetta against Terence and could actually fire bullets into a human being.'

'An interesting Venn diagram, sadly I think it may not rule out as many as you might imagine.'

'A horrible way to die.'

'Fell on his rhubarb apparently.'

'Goodness.'

'He has left this mortal life, as must we all, to be welcomed into the arms of our ever-loving Lord.' The Dean slipped back into generic minister mode.

'Thank you for letting me know.'

'Also, I have reconsidered your tenure and would love you to continue at St Osmund's after your probationary period.'

'That is very kind of you.' She registered a dull stone in her chest.

'The funeral is next Thursday, twelve noon. I myself will be in Bognor Regis on a minibreak. Perhaps you might preside?'

'Of course.'

A violent end to a violent man. Two slugs in the rhubarb patch. A good line but not one she could use in her sermon. It appeared that Terence had enemies even more ruthless than himself.

Terence had left detailed posthumous instructions to include a visiting wake. He wanted his constituents to have the opportunity to pay their last respects in the local church that had been so central to his life. Who was he kidding? He wished to lie in state for two days. Narcissistic creep. Sarah doubted many would come.

Tony Scutt of Scutt and Daughter, twenty-four-hour funeral care, had sounded very casual on the phone. As if he were arranging a delivery of firewood. He was even more informal in person. Denim jeans, a faded Led Zeppelin t-shirt, a roll-up dangling from his lower lip. His cracked-vein cheeks suggested a lifelong drinker. He had left the hearse idling in the lane.

'Alright love, where do you want him?'

'The chapel is a little dingy. Perhaps pride of place in the central nave.'

'Right you are, babe. I'll drive him up to the front door if you don't mind. He's in our heaviest mahogany. Brass handles the works. It's a bugger on the lower back.'

'Of course. Do you need help?'

'No, I've got our Ellie. Strong as an ox.'

Scutt and daughter slid the ridiculously large coffin onto a casket trolley and rattled it through the porch. They deposited it head-first beside the altar rails.

'Be easier for wheeling him back out. We'll be taking him up the crem straight after the service.'

'Perfect. Thank you. I'm not used to holding visiting wakes.' It would be her first.

'Not much call for them these days. Just a head's up love, you're best keeping the lid closed. Don't want any additional bodies getting in there if you know what I mean.'

'Mice?'

'You'd be surprised. We've had squirrels, rats, even a ferret one time.'

'Not nice.'

'Righty-ho, see you Thursday for the pick up.'

She walked him to the door.

What a brilliant idea. Two bodies, one coffin, one cremation.

63

Jesús lay in a giant's bed. It was hard to move his head. He opened his eyes. The lights were too bright. He shut them tight.

'Hi, are you awake?' It sounded like a little kid.

'No,' he replied, just to be contrasty.

'I'm asleep too. We're sharing the same dream.' The little kid was nice.

'Are we dreaming that we're in hospital?'

'Yes. In Daisy ward, Paediatrics, Bay Four. And your dad who has been sitting by your bed for three days has just gone to talk to the nurse.'

Jesús forced his eyes open.

'Hi, I'm Reuban. I'm five.'

'I'm Jesús. I'm seven.' His neck felt weird. It was encased in a hard plastic tube like a sort of exoskeleton. 'Have I turned into a giant insect?'

Reuban did a little kid giggle. 'Yes. And I'm a giant spider but I'm not going to eat you.'

Dad appeared above him and hugged him tight. Dad seemed to have forgotten how to speak. He hugged him for a long time and when he stopped he had tears in his eyes.

'Hey, Dad, you okay?'

'Yeah.'

'What's wrong with my neck?'

'Well, that's what happens when you run into trees, mate.' He wiped his eyes with the back of his hand. 'But you're going to be okay.'

'This is Reuban.'

'Oh yes, penguin boy. We've met.'

'I got a head injury from being a penguin on an icefloe. I lay head-first on a kitchen tray. The icefloe was the stairs.'

'Cool. I don't remember running into a tree.'

'That's Daniel.' Reuban pointed at the boy in the bed opposite. 'He came in yesterday but he sleeps a lot. And the girl is Mary, she's from a foreign country.'

Mary put down her My Little Pony magazine. 'I'm from Newcastle, actually.'

'Does anyone want to play What animal am I?' said Jesús.

Jesús was On Obs which meant that nurses kept coming over and asking him what day it was, and what month it was, although it was written on the noticeboard.

He liked being in hospital; the pings and beeps of the machines, the nurses adjusting his pillows and tucking him in, and being able to choose his own meal by ticking little boxes. Today there were chocolate cracknell hedgehogs for pudding but the man nurse said he'd be better off with jelly or ice cream because of his swallowing thing. He didn't like having to go to the toilet in a sort of giant cat bowl but as Dad said, that's what happens when you run into trees.

Dad had brought in his dinosaur pyjamas, his moth book and a bunch of red seedless grapes. He'd peeled them for him because it was hard to chew. He also brought an amazing magnetic chess board, but the weird thing was he'd forgotten how to play. Dr Dhooma didn't like the sound of that.

Jesús discovered that doctors didn't tell you important stuff, even when it was about you. Even when it was that you might die. But if you pretended to be asleep, they'd chat away like crazy. He'd learned all sorts of things. He'd had a bleed on the brain; that definitely did not sound good. Also, the next few days were critical; again, not a good word. And he had fractured a vertebrate. They'd done that in science; it was an animal with a backbone. When you have a head injury it's common not to remember what happened before or afterwards. That's why he didn't remember fracturing the vertebrate. He felt very bad about it, he really hoped it wasn't Moth.

Dr Dhooma let Jesús play with her penlight as long as he didn't shine it in her eyes. She shone it in his though, super close up. She was a type of peedo, but a nice type, not the sort that got beaten up. She had taken photos of his actual brain. They were very cool but he wasn't allowed to keep them because they had to stay in the file. The pictures showed that his brain was quite normal – phew. But there were tiny areas of damage – uh oh. So, because he had forgotten how to play chess he was going to stay in hospital.

Now Bay Four spent most of the time playing What animal am I? Reuban was pretty good for a little kid. Mary had been to Australia once and kept shouting out wild guesses like possum and kangaroo and wallaby that were way off. Daniel kept asking the same question – have you got four legs? – so it was better when he was asleep. When they weren't playing, Jesús taught Reuban all about moths. He held up his book so Reubs could see the pictures. He read him the whole section about owl moths because they were Reubs's favourite. It was fun being a teacher.

Jesús slept a lot. One time when he woke up Dad was behind the big window with pink and red balloons painted on it. Miss Walker was there too. And a nurse. Jesús pinched himself hard – it really hurt so it was real. There was a lot of nodding and glancing towards his bed and shaking of heads and then more nodding. Miss Walker was talking and Dad was listening. He looked very serious and he had his arms folded which was not like him. Maybe he was trying not to murder her.

The next time he woke up Sarah was holding his hand. She was wearing her normal clothes.

'People don't want to see a vicar sitting next to a hospital bed,' she laughed.

Jesús laughed too; she had the sort of laugh that made you join in. 'How's Moth?'

'Crazier than ever.' She showed him some photos on her phone. Moth climbing the curtain. Moth curled up in the wastepaper basket. Moth licking a toy mouse with his little rough tongue. 'He goes crazy when he sees Juju. He growls and Juju screams at him.'

'Is he still sweary?'

'Yes, very. You need to come and teach them both to behave. They're a handful.'

She did have a lot of scratches to be fair.

'Moth's been in your tent looking for you. He went right down inside your sleeping bag.'

'I hope he isn't worried that I've been kidnapped or murdered or suicided.'

Sarah gave him one of her nice long hugs. 'No, Sweetie, cats don't think like that.'

'I wish I was a cat.'

'Ben and Eileen are coming to see you later.'

'We're not in trouble, are we?'

'No, it's all good.' Sarah smiled. 'The nurse said you could have a bath today.'

'No thanks.' Mum would be building up for a big haunting because he hadn't had a bath for ages.

'It's one of the things you have to do before they let you go home.'

'I prefer the sponge thing.'

'No one prefers the sponge thing.' Sarah leant in close, she smelled nice. 'What's up, buttercup?'

He looked at his hands. Somewhere a clock was ticking that he hadn't noticed before. 'I'm having vegetarian shepherd's pie and ice cream for dinner.'

'Nice try.' She smiled that funny sort of smile she had. She was just going to wait for the real answer. She was clever like that.

'Hmmm.'

'Whatever it is, it's okay.'

He took a deep breath. 'Whenever I have a bath, Mum turns up. She's lying in the water like when I found her. Only it's getting worse now because she was even in the bed-cupboard because it's very bathroomy. That's why I wanted to leave the hut. Sometimes she sits up and screams and it freaksthebejesus out of me.'

'Wow, that's a lot.' Sarah rubbed his arm. 'Thanks for telling me, Sweetie.' She actually looked pretty shook up herself. 'Okay, so that also explains why you always had a bath in five minutes flat.'

'It's pretty scary.'

'Sounds it. I'm going to have a think about that.'

'Do you think I'm being haunted because I did something wrong?'

'Absolutely not.' She looked a bit weird, like she was remembering something really bad. 'But I do know that you have to face the monster. The more you hide, the more it comes for you.'

'It would be scary to face a monster on your own.'

'Then we'll do it together.'

64

O ud, myrrh, frankincense; the clash of scented candles failed to mask the odour of decomposition that hung in the chapel. Sarah took the feet, Jack the head end. Despite his state of decay Melville was heavy. It was all a bit much. The bandana tied cowboy style around her mouth and nose wasn't helping.

'You look like a bank robber,' said Jack.

'Funny.'

'One, two, three, lift.' Jack took control, she liked it.

They heaved the body from the marble slab. A flash of brown fur. Sarah screamed and jumped back in horror. The cadaver rolled from the rug and hit the floor with a sickening splat. Pallid, rotted, chilling.

'Christ.' She steadied herself against the stone pillar.

The rug had been thoroughly gnawed. Woollen fibres sprouted like thistle down. Jack hauled it back over the body. 'Mice.'

'Now what?' Sarah wiped her hands against the wall.

No reply. Jack was staring at Melville.

'What is it?'

'His head. It's pretty disintegrated but it looks like the cause of death was one hell of a whack.'

She forced herself to look. A shocking sunken hole was embedded in his temple. What weapon could have left such a perfect geometric square?

Jack seemed to have read her mind. 'Looks like a club hammer. Or a claw hammer. Or a sledge hammer. Or an engineer's hammer.'

'So, a hammer.' She could really have done without seeing

that.

'I'm guessing.'

'That doesn't actually help to identify the perpetrator.'

'No, everyone has a hammer. I've got four.'

'Now what?' He had no sense of urgency. He'd better not be stoned, this operation required a clear head.

'We can't drag him in this condition, he'll come apart.'

'Jesus, Jack.'

'We'll have to bring Terence's coffin into here.'

They walked in silence to their task. She gulped in the cool air of the nave in a vain attempt to dislodge the tang of decay.

'So, are you going to tell me the truth about who you really are?'

'This definitely isn't the time or the place.'

'Never is.' He took hold of the coffin. 'But I could do with an explanation.'

'It's best if you don't know too much.'

'Best for you, you mean.'

'You don't want to be an accessory.' She took hold of the brass handles and tugged at the coffin. It was ridiculously heavy.

'An accessory, she says while we're disposing of a murder victim.'

'The money is clean. The launderette is closed. That's all you need to know.'

They guided the huge coffin towards the chapel, the wheels skating crazily over the Purbeck marble. 'God, it's like a bloody Tesco trolley.' Sarah tried to manoeuvre it over a raised grate. It veered hopelessly off-course and smashed into the archway.

The polished mahogany sustained a hairline fracture. The mediaeval stone was chipped. She guided the coffin forwards as Jack steered from behind.

'Who were that couple you said were your parents?'

'Just drop it Jack, please.'

They looked at the coffin, then to the solid oak door and back at the coffin. It was clearly not going to fit.

'We'll need to take the door off. I'll get my tools.' Jack headed up the aisle.

'Christ, don't leave me here alone with two dead bodies.'

'Get a grip, bank robber. I'll be five minutes.'

Sarah sat in the front pew. The stained-glass windows were spotted with rain. Making their vibrant vegetable crisp windows seemed so long ago. The sun burst through throwing a lightshow of colours across the floor. Like a crazy disco ball. Like a miracle. Sometimes she regretted her atheism, it must be a comfort to be a believer. She had never really looked at the altar windows before. They depicted the Garden of Eden. An angry God pointed at the apple tree where a green snake curled malevolently around the trunk. A naked Adam and Eve clung to each other. It imparted a fearful message to the illiterate masses – you carry the burden of original sin. No, she hadn't been born bad; you can't lay that charge on a baby. She had gone astray. Somewhere deep down she felt the stirrings of a good person waiting to be resurrected.

65

J ack returned brandishing a large screwdriver and set to work twisting the rusted heads that had not been turned in decades; possibly centuries. It took a full twenty minutes to loosen both hinges. Sarah watched him work. Jack was a good person. Gorgeous too. Blimey, what was wrong with her? They were desecrating a corpse and she was eyeing up her accomplice.

Finally, he looked up. 'Okay, you steady the door while I tilt it onto the floor.'

She did as instructed, Jack taking the weight, huffing and puffing, his arms straining across the width of the ancient oak.

The clip of kitten heels echoed down the nave. Sarah turned in shock. What the hell? The door crashed down on top of Melville in an explosion of dust and dirt and cracking bones.

'God, Jack, you didn't lock the damn door.'

The woman continued towards them, her long red hair billowing in the draft. 'Hello.' Her manicured accent held a whisper of Irish lilt. 'I'm back.'

'What the hell are you doing here?' Sarah stared in disbelief.

'I might ask you the same question.'

'Where are your parents? Did you meet them in Liverpool? Why didn't you call me? What the –?'

Jack stepped between them. 'It looks like you two have some serious catching up to do but there's a shark a little closer to the boat.' He gestured to the feet and hands of a flattened Melville Russet protruding from beneath the door like a cartoon drawing. 'This has become a three-person job.'

Credit where credit was due; Jack was unflappable in a crisis. The three of them slowly raised the door and leant it against the wall. Mercifully, Melville remained covered in the Axminster but congealed fluids lay spattered all around him, marking his shape in a macabre crime scene outline. Sarah was becoming immune to the horror.

'Who on earth is that and why are they not in their coffin?'

'It's a long story. The funeral is tomorrow.' Jack looked at his watch. 'And the bereaved could show up any time for the wake, so we really need to get a wiggle on.' He pushed Terence's coffin through the doorless arch and slowly opened the lid.

Terence had evidently gone for the deluxe package; he was dressed in a navy pinstripe suit with a blue spotted tie. His hair had been coiffured; his nails manicured. The coffin lining was of the finest cream silk. He actually looked quite peaceful.

'Surely they are not sharing a coffin?' said the newcomer.

'There's no choice, the family can't afford a funeral. It's this or an unmarked grave.' Jack took hold of the rug. 'And you know that means under the footpath, right?'

Sarah marvelled at his inventiveness; he was becoming an accomplished liar. A bizarrely attractive quality.

They lifted Melville's body and lowered it on top of Terence's with as much solemnity as they could muster. Perhaps it would have been better to top-and-tail them; cheek-to-cheek was a little unnerving. They wheeled the coffin back to the nave and stood silently for a moment to recover from the task. The woman recited psalm twenty-seven. It was actually comforting although the quiet gravity of the narration was somewhat compromised by Jack clattering around with a metal bucket.

'Right, job done.' He fastened the lid. 'I'm due at the hospital so if you two wouldn't mind cleaning up the remaining remains.'

'Err, not so fast, what about the chapel door?' Sarah nodded at the open arch.

'Typical man, do one job and they're away and wanting an award.'

Sarah scowled at her; no one criticised her Jack. 'Actually, he's very hard working.'

'Grab a side each,' said Jack.

They pivoted the door into place and he screwed the hinges

tight.

'Can I go now please, Miss?' He gave her a schoolboy grin.

'Give Jesús my love.'

Jack waved goodbye.

Sarah watched him leave, pulled on a pair of yellow Marigolds and picked up the bucket. 'Okay, spill.'

'Sorry to barge in unannounced, that must have been a shock.' Her accent ratcheted up to royal family diction.

'What's going on?' Sarah handed her the Flash three-in-one.

'My parents are moving back to England.' She squirted the liquid across the floor releasing the bitter tang of artificial lemon fragrance.

'You're kidding?'

'No. Also, I'm afraid Donal was a dud. I've left him.'

'After giving up your career? It's only been four months.' Sarah let the mop flop over the congealed mess.

'Sadly, he turned out to be a drinker. It was all a terrible mistake.'

'So now what?' Sarah's accent rose in competitive enunciation.

'There's only one option.'

'I don't see it.' Sarah swished the mop in a figure of eight.

'I want my life back.'

'What?' Sarah froze.

'I want to be a vicar again. I want to rededicate my life to the Lord. I want to stop living a lie.' She sprayed the floor again. The thickened mass was proving hard to dislodge.

'Are you crazy?' Sarah scrubbed with renewed vigour.

'We have to tell the Dean the truth. We have to ask him for forgiveness.'

'No way.'

'I could start again as a curate. Demonstrate my repentance.'

'And what happens to me?' Sarah swiped the mop over her feet.

'A life of deceit is not a good life.'

'Now you're my moral guardian? We've both been living a lie and I'm quite happy to carry on. I actually like living in West Tillington.' The realisation surprised her.

'Being a vicar is no job for an atheist.'

'I can't go back, you know that.'

The entrance door swung open. Could nobody lock a bloody door behind them? High heels ricocheted down the aisle like gunshots. Sobs echoed through the chancel. Sarah peered through the chapel door. Carole was draped over the coffin, her body heaving with distress.

'Stay here,' Sarah hissed and closed the door tight behind her. She laid a gentle hand on Carole's back and waited for the sobbing to subside. 'Terence has gone to a better place.'

'Too soon,' she sniffed.

'He is no longer suffering.'

'The poor man endured such a terrible time in his last months.' Carole dabbed at her eyes with a lace hanky.

'He had been recovering.'

'And then the loss of his parrot. Can one die of a broken heart?' she wailed.

She was unsure whether Carole was referring to herself or to Terence. 'I don't think so.'

Carole shrugged Sarah's hand from her back. 'You as good as killed him.'

'What do you mean?' Surely she couldn't know about the contamination?

'You stole Milo. He was bereft.'

'The parrot? I was just looking after it while he was in hospital. I was going to give him back. He's quite a handful to be honest.'

'His heart was broken,' she whined.

God, histrionic people were annoying. 'You cannot die from a broken heart, but you can die from a bullet through it.'

'What do you mean?' Carole looked alarmed.

'I'm sorry, that wasn't very sensitive. But the truth is he was shot.'

'Oh Lord.' Carole made the sign of the cross. She was evidently ecumenical.

'He's at peace now. I'm sure heaven is full of parrots.'

Carole buried her face in her hands.

'Come on now, let's get you home.'

66

J ack carried a tray of Twining's English Afternoon tea and a plate of French fancies into the living room. Sarah burst out laughing. The islands of normality in her increasingly bizarre existence now struck her as hilarious. He must think she'd finally snapped. Perhaps she had.

Jack placed the tray on the side table and passed a cup to their guest. 'Right then, does anyone want to tell me what is going on?'

Sarah led the introductions. 'This is Jack Stretton who lived here for a while and now lives in Lingen field.' Was that really all he was?

'Oh, you must be the vagrant my parents mentioned. You're not all what I imagined.'

He raised an eyebrow but said nothing.

The clocks ticked.

With her co-conspirator genteelly taking her tea in the living room, ready to hurl a hand-grenade into her life, she was left with no choice. She was going to have to tell the truth. The whole damn truth.

Just go ahead and say it.

'This is Sarah Wilson.'

'Sarah Wilson?' Jack looked from her to Sarah Wilson and back again. 'So, who the hell are you?'

She took a sip of tea as if in slow motion and replaced it quietly on the saucer. 'My name is Jess Walters. I'm a former bank clerk from Smethwick.'

Jess Walters.

She had not said those words for so long. Even her own name sounded alien. It did not belong to her. She had gradually morphed into a new person. Jess Walters had been left so far behind she could have been a crazy fantasy.

Jack had entered some form of torpor. He deserved a full explanation but she didn't know where to begin. Perhaps the real Sarah would.

'Sarah, why don't you tell Jack how we got here?'

Sarah Wilson tucked her hair behind her ears revealing crucifix studs that matched the large gold cross around her neck.

'I grew up in a rather controlling, religious family. I went to Cambridge and studied theology, straight after which I was offered this parish. Then I had a crisis of faith.' She nibbled the fondant from a pink French fancy. 'Well, that's not strictly accurate, my faith was shaken by an overwhelming and idiotic infatuation.'

'So, you are a vicar?'

'Qualified, not practising. I ran away to live in Donegal with a harp teacher called Donal.'

'Okay.' Jack blinked.

'Jess and I came up with a plan so that my parents would believe that I took the job.'

'Okay.' The poor guy was evidently struggling to process the information.

'I know it sounds preposterous but my parents – you met them so you know what I'm dealing with – would've been devastated if they knew I'd given up the ministry.'

'They are your parents? They live in Italy. You live in Donegal. And you pretend that you are a vicar in West Tillington?'

'Exactly.'

'So as not to hurt their feelings?'

'Yes. And to keep my allowance. And so that they don't cut me off.'

'From what?'

'The family. My inheritance. They are very wealthy...' she tailed off.

'Surely if you explained they would come round?'

'They completely disowned my sister when she came out.'

'As gay?'

'No, as a Baptist.'

Jess gave him a weak smile. It was a lot to take in. She pictured a snake trying to digest a goat. Perhaps a little insensitive given his former occupation.

'So, you two hatched a plan?'

'We met at elocution lessons. We kept in touch.' Jess spoke slowly to allow the information to permeate. 'Sarah was looking for a way out and so was I.'

'Wait up, so you're not an actual vicar?'

'God, no. I'm an atheist.'

'This is crazy.'

'Yeah, I know right. But a pretty good gig for a girl with five GCSE's and a certificate in needlework.'

Jack gestured to the vicarage. 'How are you pulling all this off?'

'Most people don't see past the dog-collar. You become a type, I play to it. It's pretty easy actually, be a good listener, smile, try not to swear in public.'

'I did have some doubts when you never talked about religion. Also, the drinking and the smoking and the swearing and the robbery.'

'To be fair, Jess was very consoling to the grieving widow back there. Much more honest than the whole "Welcomed into the arms of our ever-loving Lord" thing that we tend to parrot.'

'Die, die, die,' screamed Juju from the corner.

They all stared at him.

'Can't you put him back upstairs?'

'He likes it down here and he's company now you're gone.' Damn, she shouldn't have said that.

'I'm glad a psychotic parrot fills my place.' He held her gaze.

'So, anyway, I needed to disappear after the robbery. Sarah here wanted to keep both Donal and her inheritance so I took her job. I became Sarah Wilson and she became Maggie O'Farrell. You know, like the author.'

'Total fricken madness.'

'It all made perfect sense,' said Jess.

'At the time.' Sarah Wilson clasped her hands together.

'And now? asked Jack.

'I want my life back.'

Jess put down her cup with finality and stood to leave. 'I've got an appointment with Jesús. We'll have to resolve this later. Jack will keep you company.' She looked back over her shoulder. 'Don't talk to anyone. Don't go outside.'

67

There had been a lot of kerfuffle and running and beepers going off and Reuban got wheeled out in the middle of the night. Jesús shouted, 'Bye, Reubs' but he must have been asleep because he didn't reply. Jesús stayed awake waiting for him to come back, staring at the empty bed space. Started worrying that he'd died. He didn't like it when his brain did that, always thinking the worst.

After breakfast Reubs was back but not so chatty because he'd had a sub-dur-al-haem-a-toma. Jesús had heard the doctors talking – pulling a curtain around a bed doesn't mean you can't hear. They kept saying the long word. Fun to say but not fun to have. Now the curtain was open again and Reubs was fast asleep.

'You okay, Jesús?' The man nurse took his temperature and wrote it on his chart.

'Being in hospital is becoming a bit boring.'

'That's a good sign. Try to stay positive.' He patted his hand and walked away. Jesús made his brain think about all the good things.

Dr Dhooma said he'd shown 'marked improvement'. The same type of improvement that he'd got in maths after Sarah showed him how to do division.

It had been fun pretending to be a caddis fly larva emerging from its carapace when he'd had his neck thing taken off, but that only killed half an hour.

He could get out of bed without feeling like he'd just come off the waltzers.

Eileen had knitted him a dark brown beanie hat with very soft wool that was the exact same colour of his hair. It was cool except he couldn't try it on because his stitches were covered with a big dressing so he didn't scratch them and get an infection and die. The dressing was a sort of positive thing, sort of negative thing. A mixed dressing.

At least no one ruffled his hair now.

Sarah came in, in a big hurry. Dad had been in a hurry too. He had smelled a bit funny like when a mouse dies under the floorboards. There was definitely something going on. Maybe with the dead body. Best not to ask.

'I hear you're doing well.' Sarah took a seat and put her massive bag on her lap.

'I'm allowed out of bed if I'm... something beginning with 'S.'

'Sober? Sedate? Sensational?'

'Chaperoned,' called the nurse in the next bay. 'I'll bring a wheelchair.'

Uh oh. He could see his swimmers rolled in a towel and they definitely weren't going swimming.

'I'm having a bath, aren't I?'

'Yep, but not just any bath. A marathon, world record-breaking bath. Come on.'

Sarah helped him into the wheelchair and pushed him down the ward and through the door with the scary word BATHROOM in big black letters.

'I've booked it for an hour. The nurses know to come in if there's any prolonged screaming.'

Jesús laughed. It was cool the way she made weirdness sound so normal.

'There's also a panic button, you know if either of us panics.'

The bath was ginormous. Sarah turned on both taps full blast and unpacked her bag: a CD player, a revolving disco ball, crazy foam, bubble bath, dinosaur bath bombs.

Just looking at the frothy water was making his heart beat like crazy. Mum was going to show up and do something terrible. He didn't want to let Sarah down after she'd been to all this trouble. She pulled the blinds and set up the disco ball above the bath as he changed into his swimmers. Red and green and purple stars revolved around the room. It looked brilliant.

'Ben told me Britney was your favourite.' Sarah turned on the CD player. '... *Baby, one more time*,' blared from the speaker.

She turned it down a notch.

Jesús put one leg in the water. He was trembling already and Mum was still on her way from wherever ghosts hang out when they're not haunting.

'Okay, wait up.' Sarah touched his arm lightly. 'So, here's what's going to happen. Your mum is going to show up. We're going to let her. She can do whatever she wants. You're not going to jump out. You're going to stay in there with her, keep her company. And we're going to sing along to Britney.'

'Okay.'

'At the top of our voices.'

That sounded pretty hard but he was going to try.

The bath was lovely and deep, the water came right up to his neck. He was one of those Japanese macaques bathing in a hot spring like on David Attenborough, except they didn't have disco balls and music.

It's all cool. Nothing bad is going to happen. Sarah is here, singing along, she has a nice voice. He joined in on the chorus. Their voices sounded really good in the echoey bathroom.

Mum was not here. Maybe the bath was too big or she only turned up when he was on his own. Or she didn't like hospitals.

A new song started. *Oops, I did it again.* Yeah, he liked this one.

The water turned red with blood. There she was. Under the water. Hair floating. Eyes open. Mouth open. Neck open. Screaming.

'Keep singing.' Sarah sounded far away.

He couldn't sing. Mum had stolen his voice like mermaids do.

Splash. A stegosaurus bath bomb landed right on Mum's head.

'Sing, Jesús sing.'

Mum lifted her arms, showed her cuts, blood ran from her neck and from her wrists, pouring down her body and into the water.

He could hear Sarah singing. He sang. Sarah sang louder. They both sang louder.

Mum was shaking. Her dark brown eyes staring right at him, jiggling up and down. Some sort of fit. He gripped the bath.

Don't get out. He shut his eyes tight but she was still there. His heart had stopped. Everything was slow motion.

Bam. Another bath bomb fizzed. Tyrannosaurus Rex. His favourite.

'Dance with me.'

Sarah was a brilliant dancer. She danced in time with the music. He swayed his body from side to side and splashed with his hands and sang at the top of his voice. Mum laughed. Not the scary laugh. The real laugh she used to do when she was happy.

And suddenly she was gone.

Just his arms waving.

Just his legs kicking in the mountain of bubbles.

He lay back. The song changed to *Stronger*. He sang along softly. Sarah sat on the edge of the bath and hummed.

Red and green and purple stars danced on the floor and walls and seeped through his skin into his brand-new heart.

68

'Dearly beloved, we are gathered here today to remember our brother Terence Ignatius Johnson, to give thanks for his life and to comfort one another in our grief.'

Sarah liked the way her authoritative clerical tone resonated from the pulpit. She held up her palms preacher style and counted the meagre mourners. Thirteen. There were several faces she'd never seen in church before, including Ted Adlington-Wyndham who sat straight-backed next to a sobbing Carole. It was apparently common knowledge that Terence had enjoyed a steady supply of Cumberland sausage, ham hock and pork scratchings and had allegedly given Carole much more in return. Ted had probably come to make sure he was dead.

'We brought nothing into this world and it is certain we can carry nothing out.'

Poor Eileen, flanked by Betty and Jean, must be thinking about her deceased son lying face down on top of his murderer. She was rooting in her oversized handbag. Instead of the assumed tissues, she brought out a bumper bag of wine gums and passed them along the pew. At least she got to attend Melville's funeral. And didn't have to pay for it.

'Whosoever liveth and believeth in me shall never die.'

A small party of middle-aged white men perched like albino crows in the fifth row. Presumably fellow councillors. They looked rather bored. Two were scrolling through their phones.

'Repent, for judgement day draws near.'

Somehow every word held meaning. Could one become a believer by stealth? Perhaps the heightened vigilance caused by the commission of heinous acts was adding salience to the words. She thought of Jack back at the vicarage with Sarah Wilson – they'd agreed a rota to ensure that she was not left alone to go rogue and call the Dean.

'Father, we have sinned against you and against our neighbours.'

She looked at Terence's plump face grinning from the photo frame next to the coffin. That severely abridged nose was a crime for a start.

'Sinned in thought and in deed.'

Sarah nodded to Betty who tottered over to the organ and struck a violently discordant chord. The congregation rose to sing a stumbling rendition of *Nearer My God to Thee*. Betty had insisted that she play the ancient organ rather than the piano, for added gravitas. It certainly added volume. From the physiognomy of the congregation, she could discern no identifiable relatives. Terence had never married and his parents were presumably deceased. She too had no living family. At least it cut down on the eulogies. Perhaps she should skip the next lines as not applicable. No, she would say them anyway. For Eileen.

'We ask that the family and friends of our brother may be consoled by the Lord, who wept at the death of his friend, Lazarus.'

Given Melville's epic journey to the coffin she felt that Lazarus deserved a mention.

Eileen had given her some pointers so that she could deliver an oblique eulogy for Melville, it was as much his service.

'He served his community for many years. He knew everyone, everyone knew him, he knew how to get things done. He worked tirelessly, often late into the night.'

A strained whimper from Carole.

'He could be controversial, he had his share of detractors and he suffered many personal setbacks. But he was loved.'

An audible sob – Carole was the only person showing any emotion.

'Let us all stand to sing his favourite hymn. *How Great Thy Art*.'

Betty blasted out the robust introductory bars. Eileen gave a faint smile; it was she who had selected the hymn.

The church door swung open admitting a tall man in a burgundy polo-neck along with a warm gust of air. The man took up the final verse, his voice rising above the others in a fulsome baritone. *When Christ shall come, with shout of acclamation, and take me home, what joy shall fill my heart.*

As Betty drew out the final chord Tony Scutt – unrecognisable in full funereal coat and hat – wheeled the coffin slowly past downcast eyes. Sarah followed the procession with her hands in prayer before her chest. Escorting the evidence to the hearse. The tall man held her gaze and grinned with the teeth of a horse. She knew him from his photograph, and from his startling resemblance to Eileen and Ben.

It was Melville Russet.

69

Jack wanted to dance, whoop, punch the air. But this was a hospital and he was an adult, so instead he smiled and nodded and walked down the ward. Everything was going to be okay. He'd had the best news possible and now there was his brilliant boy, sitting up in bed, eating pineapple rings and waving at him.

Jack kissed his forehead and pulled up the blue plastic chair. 'How're you doing, mate?'

'The doctor says I'm progressive. And also, I'm out of the woods.'

'Excellent.'

'She probably thinks that I think I'm still in the woods because of my head injury,' he said, through a mouthful of pineapple.

'Hello, Mr Stretton,' called Reuban from the neighbouring bed.

'Are you out of the woods too, penguin boy?'

'I was never in the woods. I was on an icefloe.'

'Oh yeah.'

'I had a hole drilled in my head.'

'Very cool.' Jack fished out a red jelly worm from the paper bag on the cabinet.

'Never take anything that is not freely given,' said Jesús.

He smiled and put it back.

'Please help yourself to a worm, Dad.'

'Thanks.' He chose a green one; nobody liked the green ones.

Jesús threw one to Reuban who caught it one-handed.

'Sarah said visiting the sick is part of her ministry but they don't all get jelly worms.' Jesús looked so pleased with himself.

'That's true,' said Jack. It was nice how close they'd become but a duplicitous bank robber pretending to be a vicar wasn't exactly a great role model.

'She's helping me have a bath. We're going to do it until I can have one on my own with nae bother.' The girl from Newcastle was evidently making an impression too.

'That's cool.' Wasn't that a nurse's job? The NHS was ridiculously understaffed.

'She caught me up with all the stuff's that happened.'

'Oh, right.' Jack winced. Had her new found honesty become a compulsive need to disclose everything to everybody? 'Like what?'

'She's got a friend staying from Ireland who is also called Sarah Wilson. I said "Wow, what are the odds?" and Sarah said we could work it out if we knew the names of everybody in England and Ireland.'

'Crazily low, I'd guess. Anything else?'

'That Mr Johnson died and is in his coffin and she's doing his funeral today. Probably at this exact minute.'

'Yeah, I'd heard.' He should get back to supervise the real Sarah Wilson although she seemed to spend most of her time crying on the phone rather than planning a coup.

'Dad.' He drank the pineapple juice from the bowl. 'Is it ever okay to kill someone?'

'How'd you mean?'

'Like, if they're land-grabber Tories and have taken your farm so your goats had to go to Wales and Shropshire.'

'Hey, what's brought this on? Mr Johnson wasn't killed. Well, okay he was but I didn't kill him.'

'You did say that you could kill him. A couple of times actually.'

'That's just something people say when they're upset.' Poor kid must have been fretting. That was some heavy load.

The nurse appeared with a wheelchair. 'You can go out into the courtyard if you like.'

'Fancy it? There's something I want to tell you. Something very cool.'

'Sure.'

Jack wheeled his son down the corridor. He really needed to

be more careful what he said; the boy was a memory sponge. And maybe reduce the time Jesús spent with Sarah – who, it seemed, could do no wrong – it would be a lot to deal with when the truth came out. He was still reeling himself.

The courtyard bench was rotten and lopsided. It was covered with the scratched signatures of the sick and the bored. A thrush hopped along a scrubby patch of lawn that consisted mainly of weeds and fag-ends.

'So, you want to hear some good news?'

'Always.'

'The police have sorted the Dave 101 thing.'

'Is he in prison?'

'They couldn't say too much, just that they'd been onto him for a while and not to worry, it's all over.'

'He's a peedo.'

'Oh, okay, I didn't know you knew that word.'

'Dad, everyone knows that word.'

Jesús seemed blissfully unaware of the danger he'd been in. If he ever met Dave 101 he'd fricken kill him. Best not say that to Jesús. The sun stretched their shadows across the scabby lawn. 'Look, the thrush is sitting on your head.'

Jesús laughed and dangled a jelly worm above the shadow-bird's beak. 'Here thrushy, thrushy, thrushy.'

'The brilliant news is that your little foray into the film world has saved our bacon.'

'How'd you mean?'

'The police came down to the hut. Cap in hand, literally. They were all chummy, and sorry pal, and no hard feelings mate.'

It had been a shock to see the squad car bouncing across the field. He thought they'd found the extra body in Terence's coffin. He'd dropped his spliff out of the window. Was going to make a run for it. Remembered he couldn't actually run.

'What's it got to do with the film?'

'The police and Miss Walker sat down and watched the footage.'

Jesús let the worm dangle from his mouth like a snake's tongue and sucked it in. 'Footage means everything, even the rubbish bits that'll be cut out when it's made into a proper movie.'

'Look at you, the cinematography expert. Give us a worm, mate.'

Jesús fed him like a baby bird. 'Do you think they had popcorn and ice creams?'

'Probably.'

'I bet it was hilarious. There'd be all the things that went wrong, like Johnno saying "For Chrissake," all the time.'

'The coppers showed me clips on their laptop. Drone shots of trees and people in hoods and the girl who was going to be eaten by a vampire screaming a lot. Then you and Ben running through the conifers. One of them says "Keep running" but meaning the video camera not you.'

'Is it scary?'

'Very. You and Ben are hunched inside a bush and they're being all creepy and saying "Come out, come out, wherever you are". Then you and Ben leg it and there are some shaky shots of you disappearing into the night which is super scary. The copper thought it could make a pretty good film if they're allowed the footage back.'

'Can I see it? I don't remember anything after sitting on the sacrificing rock.'

'Maybe. The scene of the accident is pretty hard to watch to be honest. It takes three takes. You crash into the tree and someone says "Oh shit" and the camera goes off.'

'How come that means you're not in trouble anymore?'

'They suspected I was involved in some sort of satanic thing. Adults can do some pretty bad stuff to kids. Once that was cleared up the other concerns didn't add up to much. None of their inquiries lead to anything. Miss Bickerstool put in a good word for me too.'

'So, I can come home?'

'Yep. You can definitely come home. Also, Walker the stalker apologised. She won't be hassling us anymore.'

'Yes!' Jesús punched the air.

'It wasn't really her fault. She was just doing her job. If there were real rituals and abuse and stuff it would be hard to uncover.'

'Better safe than sorry. That's what Miss Bickerstool says.'

'True.' At least he'd stopped with the Sarah Says. 'That's

why it's important to tell me if you ever feel worried about anything. I wish you'd told me about Mum pitching up in the hut. I could've painted the walls black, stuck up some glow-in-the-dark stars.'

'There is something. It's about Eileen.' Jesús stuffed another worm into his mouth. 'Now I'm leaving I think Ben might need a place of safety.'

'I'm all ears.'

Jesús chewed very slowly. 'She crushes up spiders and puts them in the coffee-morning brownies.'

'Jesus fricken Christ.' Eileen had always been eccentric but this was craziness. 'Thanks for telling me, mate. Maybe there's a reasonable explanation.'

Jesús nodded uncertainly. They both knew there was no chance at all of a reasonable explanation.

'Can Ben come and live with us in the hut?'

'No, it doesn't work like that.'

'Maybe Eileen's a witch. There's a ducking stool in the Peaminster museum that they used to put women in the river to find out who was a witch so they could kill them. But the innocent ones drowned so it wasn't a good test.'

'I don't think Eileen's a witch, mate.'

'Sarah said all those women were innocent because witches never existed. Doing horrible things to women was all part of patriarchy, like it is today. Maybe doing horrible things to spiders is too. Maybe Eileen is part of the patriarchy.'

'Well, Sarah's pretty cool and knows a lot of stuff but she's not the second coming.'

70

A warm breeze rippled Sarah's cassock, birds chirped, the sun emerged, daisies shone in the green grass. The hearse drew away on its slow pilgrimage to the crematorium. The sight did not elicit the relief she had anticipated; it heralded the start of another nightmare.

Eileen and Melville, arms linked, hurried from the churchyard. It would be unseemly to run after them so Sarah inhaled deeply and turned to bid farewell to the mourners. Betty and Jean were the last to leave; both wore identical expressions that she hadn't seen before. Shifty, definitely shifty.

'Lovely service, Vicar.'

'Thank you, Betty.'

'A shame there's no afternoon tea. Eileen would have made her famous brownies. Terence would have liked that.' Jean showed her tiny yellow teeth. Shrew-like.

'I've just seen Melville Russet.' Sarah scanned their faces for reaction. None came.

'Yes, Eileen has taken him home for a nice bowl of soup and a catch up.' Betty took Jean's arm. 'Which reminds me, I've an apple cake in the Aga.'

'Don't you think we should tell someone that he's alive and well?'

'I suspect Eileen will call off the manhunt,' said Jean, as if she were discussing the contents of a sandwich. 'The police investigation was rather lack-lustre, truth be told.'

Sarah stared after them in disbelief as they bustled down the path.

So, they knew.

Sarah strode towards Vespiary cottage becoming angrier with every step. Eileen must have deliberately misidentified the shoe as Melville's. She must have known all along that he was safe. Who on earth had been killed and buried in the woods? Who had they dug up and cremated with Terence for God's sake?

She rat-a-tat-tatted the fox head knocker. She really needed to calm down. A vicar would not come bowling over and shout at a pensioner recently reunited with her long-lost son. She knocked again. No reply. Through the letterbox she could see Eileen's croquet mallet in the umbrella stand. The metal face glinted in the sunlight. A perfect square. Whacked on the temple.

Oh, God. The murder weapon.

The body buried metres from the cottage.

The hanging dog.

The spider brownies.

No one knew she was here. She turned to leave as the door creaked open.

'Sorry to keep you, Vicar, I was in the bathroom. Melville is heating soup.'

'I shouldn't have disturbed you. You must have a lot to catch up on.'

'Nonsense, come in.' She held the door wide.

They sat on either side of the empty fire grate.

'Melville is such a help.' Eileen was shameless.

'Where has he been?' She managed to maintain a neutral tone. Underneath she was seething.

'He had a breakdown. Suffered a fugue state. Couldn't remember who he was.' Her answer was too rehearsed. Sarah recognised the practised tone from her own fabrications.

'Eileen, you identified his shoe. You told me his favourite hymn. You attended his funeral. You sat and wiped a tear.' Blimey, the worry and compassion she'd wasted on her.

'I'm allergic to lilies.'

'Eileen.' The woman was unbelievable. 'Who is sharing

Terence's coffin?' she shouted.

Melville appeared wearing an apron spattered red with beetroot soup. 'Mum, for goodness' sake, have you told the vicar as well?'

'No, but she knows about the body, it was Sarah and her friend who so kindly disposed of it for us.'

'Not kindly, unwittingly.'

Melville hung uneasily in the doorway. He would have been handsome had he not inherited Eileen's teeth and developed a tall man's stoop.

'Would you like to stay for lunch, dear?' asked Eileen.

'No, I would prefer the truth. This is making no sense.'

'Oh, I haven't introduced you, this is my son, Melville.'

'Yes, I'd worked that one out. Who the hell did we exhume?' She needed to calm down.

'I'm sorry, Vicar. I didn't mean to upset you.'

Melville lurched to the window. 'So, who else knows apart from Betty and Jean?'

'No one. I do feel bad lying to a vicar, especially as you've been such a help, dear.'

'Jack and I are now both fully implicated. Aiding and abetting, disposing of a body and Lord knows what other offences. I think we deserve to know the truth, Eileen.'

'We could call it a confession, then you won't have to report it.' Eileen looked to her son. 'That would be alright, wouldn't it?'

'Well, yes. If need be, we can always deny everything now the evidence has been cremated.' He picked up a toy dinosaur he had trodden on and sighed.

There was one last remaining piece of evidence; the man's leather shoe that currently lay wrapped in a Tesco bag under her kitchen sink. Sarah wouldn't mention that to them.

Eileen cleaned her glasses on a cotton handkerchief. 'There were rumours. Horrible rumours. About children. I told social services over a year ago, they talked to Ben and said there was no evidence that he'd been harmed in any way. Assumed I was senile.'

'That's why you haven't been cooperating with them.'

'Exactly. I told Melville I was worried and he launched an

investigation.'

'I thought you were in finance?'

'I am.' He placed the dinosaur on the windowsill. 'My son was in danger, so was Jesús. They were being groomed.' His voice wavered.

'Who by?'

'Terence Johnson.'

'Oh, God.'

'He took an interest in Ben once my wife left. Always coming over with little presents. They pick out the vulnerable.'

'Oh, God.' She must stop saying that.

'I did some digging. Found him on a chat-site, he went by the name Dave 101. There were two others. Peter 123 and John 666. I inveigled my way in, eventually joined their perverted online chats.'

'They accepted you as a paedophile, just like that?'

'I'm afraid being the father of a seven-year-old boy was the golden ticket.'

'Good grief.'

'I invited Peter up here to the cottage. A honey trap, without the honey obviously. I was going to record our conversation and give it to the police.'

'He wasn't a nice man.' Eileen removed her black cardigan. 'The sort that gives paedophiles a bad name.'

'As opposed to their otherwise good name?' snapped Melville. The flow of adoration between mother and son was evidently one way.

'You know what I mean, dear.'

'When Ben wasn't here Peter started to get suspicious. Things got out of hand. He got angry. Threatening. I asked him to leave. He got me by the throat. I hit him with mother's croquet mallet.'

'Blimey.'

'Thought I'd just knocked him out.'

'What a terrible shock.' She imagined Peter collapsed on the stone floor, blood seeping from his temple. 'What did you do?'

Melville looked away. He was shaking.

Eileen took up the story. 'I put a mirror to his mouth to see if he was breathing, like they do in the films. He wasn't.'

She recited the details as if describing a Victoria sponge recipe. 'He'd toppled onto the hall rug, quite a stroke of luck, no pun intended. We rolled him up and dragged him into the woods. It wasn't too hard once we got the momentum going, even with my hip.'

'You decided to get rid of the body?'

'We didn't discuss it. Just got the spades out and started digging.'

The corpse would still have been warm, perhaps bleeding, eyes open. Sarah felt queasy. They had dug such a deep grave, God, it must have taken hours. It had been hard enough work for Jack and herself to exhume the body. The image of Melville and Eileen rolling the blood-drenched corpse down into a freshly dug grave took a moment to dissipate. 'Has no one missed him?'

'Peter was unemployed, he lived alone up at Lington Valley, had no real friends.' Melville had regained his composure.

'So why did you run?'

'Like mother said, I had a breakdown. The murder, well manslaughter, was too awful. I couldn't cope.'

'I can understand you panicking and doing a runner, I really can, but you don't suddenly enter a fugue state and then get better the minute the body is cremated.'

'Coincidence.'

'No, I'm not buying it. Was it something to do with the crypto currency?'

Melville looked flustered. 'How do you know about that?'

'I thought I'd discovered Terence's motive to kill you. Being duped out of one's entire life-savings seemed like a pretty good one.'

Melville paced the room, ducking his head under the beams. 'I wanted to bankrupt him, that was his punishment. It was ridiculously easy to lure him with financial returns that were far too good to be true. Greed trumps reason.'

Sarah admired his audacity. 'The last transaction was fifty grand on the thirteenth of February. Unlucky for some.'

'When Peter died on the fourteenth I fled. I assumed the police would examine their computer histories and link the two crimes. I'd be the prime suspect. I had to disappear.'

It did make logical sense; she would probably run too. Indeed, she had. 'What about the third paedophile?'

'John 666. Oh, he turned out to be another vigilante. Ernest Farmer. Nice chap. We still chat online. Mostly about tractors.'

'Blimey.'

A spider on the ceiling caught in Melville's hair. She wished he would sit down.

'Mother told me that Terence had been poisoned recently. Several bouts of a rare bacterium.' Melville looked impressed. 'I did wonder whether it was down to Ernest.'

'Ernest told me it was the contaminated water course, but I suppose he would.' God, she could kill Ernest. No, she wasn't going to jump to conclusions, look where that had got her. Terence had many enemies.

Eileen took her son's hand. 'Well, it is lovely to have you back.'

It was brave of her to cover up her son's crime without hesitation. If Jesús committed a murder, would she do the same? Probably. And Jesús wasn't even her son. Anyway, she would destroy the shoe; the last evidence linking them to Peter. Something else niggled, oh yes. 'The spiders in Terence Johnson's brownies?'

'I'm not a poisoner, that was just for fun,' smiled Eileen. 'The least I could do.'

'And Peachy?'

'Peachy has disappeared from my shed. Do you know what happened to him?'

Of course, Eileen wouldn't hang her own dog. 'I'm sorry, we found him in the forest in a poor state, someone must have stolen him. We buried him. He's at rest.' It was best Eileen didn't know the full details and that she was currently using the poor macerated creature to mulch her herbaceous borders.

One large elephant remained in the room. Sarah addressed it. 'So, who shot Terence Johnson?'

'Not me,' said Eileen, emphatically.

'Definitely not me.' Melville held up three fingers in scouts' honour. 'In fact, the timing couldn't have been worse. Ernest told me the police had finally gathered enough evidence that he was grooming boys. The email correspondence with Ben was the clincher. They went to arrest him at his home but the ambulance beat them to it.'

'There's no justice.' Eileen shook her head.

'Well, being shot is a kind of justice,' said Sarah.

71

J esús hung upside down with his lower legs tucked under the mattress of the bed-in-the-cupboard. It was so great to be back in the roost, especially now it was painted black with glow-in-the-dark stars.

'Hey, noctule, you're meant to be recuperating.'

'Sorry, Dad, I forgot.'

'And when Ben and Marky come over after school don't be running around going crazy.'

Dad was being extra parenty. He must be worried about him having a seizure. The doctor said there was an outside chance but Jesús reckoned it wouldn't happen in the shepherd's hut because they didn't even have the windows open.

Since he'd been back home Dad was different. He was more hummy and smiley and cheerful even without his happy cigarettes. And he'd bought new black jeans and a cool multicoloured shirt for when he went to the vicarage. Maybe he'd fallen in love with Sarah Wilson, or with her friend Sarah Wilson. Jesús hoped it was their Sarah Wilson.

Ben burst into the hut, Marky trailing after; he was annoying but Ben couldn't get here without a lift. They'd brought homework from Miss Bickerstool. Rewrite a well-known nursery rhyme or story to give it a surprise ending.

'Like, if it was Cinderella, you could have her shoot the ugly sisters, bam, bam, bam,' said Marky, waving his arms wildly, his fingers the barrels of guns.

'I guess that's not Miss Bickerstool's example.'

Ben uncrumpled a worksheet. 'No, hers was the princess and the pea, where the princess starts up her own mattress factory.'

'Lame.' Marky was looking in the cupboards. 'This house is

307

sooo tiny.'

'It's a hut,' said Jesús. 'It's meant to be small. Maybe I'll do Chicken Little but the chicken turns out to be absolutely right and the sky falls on everyone and it's the end of the world.'

'Blimey, mate, they'll be phoning social services again.' Dad gathered his woodwork tools from under the table. 'Are you staying on with your Granny Ilene, Ben?'

'Yes, Dad's busy with his business. I'll see him on Sundays.'

'Cool. There's chocolate spread sandwiches in the fridge. Don't be too raucous, lads, this one's in sick bay. I'll be outside if you need me.'

Jesús dished out the sandwiches and everyone started eating really fast.

'Okay, listen up, we've got some crazy news.' Marky was all swaggery like he was in a gangster film. 'Mr Johnson didn't just die, he was murdered.'

'Wow.' Jesús did his astonished face. 'Mr Johnson? Murdered? How? Why? Wow, this is brand new news to me.'

'It's the first ever murder in West Tillington,' said Ben.

Counting the person who Dad and Sarah murdered it was the second. Also, there might have been other ones where the baddies didn't get caught. There could be loads of bodies in the woods just waiting to be dug up. Nobody seemed upset that Mr Johnson was dead, him neither. But still. 'It was mean of him to turf us off the farm but he could be nice sometimes. He used to buy me KitKats and Twix and stuff. He'd slide them into my pocket and say "Best not tell your dad"'.

'Same,' said Ben.

'Uncle Kenny is "on the case" so I can't say too much but you'll never guess what happened in a million years.'

'We've only got an hour so you'd better just tell us,' said Jesús through a mouthful of sandwich.

Marky did his look left, look right, pause for dramatic effect. 'He was shot, but before he was shot, drumroll; dum, dum durrr... he was being killed by a pig.'

Jesús and Ben burst out laughing. A bit of sandwich went down the wrong way. Ben whacked him on the back really hard and they rolled around laughing again.

'It's true,' said Marky, all huffy. 'Don't be divs.'

Jesús wiped his eyes. It was nice to laugh but it wasn't nice to make fun of someone. 'Okay, let's think of all the ways you could be killed by a pig.'

Ben cut his sandwich into little pieces; probably didn't want to choke. 'It could run at you and knock you onto something hard, like a trough.'

'It could bite you and you could get an infection and die.' That was the reason he couldn't touch his stitches.

'A load of pigs could stampede and trample you to death,' said Marky, perking up again.

'A frozen pig could fall on you in a butcher's shop.' Ben had a pretty good imagination.

'You could slip over and fall face down in a muddy pigsty and a pig could sit on you until you couldn't breathe,' said Jesús.

'Nice one,' said Ben.

Dad came back and gave Jesús a carved noctule. 'So have you got any ideas for your story?'

'Yes, This Little Piggy goes to Market, but instead of going to markets and staying at home and eating roast beef the piggies all do different kinds of murder.

'Blimey, mate, if you do that one, I'll be calling social services myself.'

72

'Hi, Jess Walters. Hi, Jess Walters.' Juju was an unnervingly fast learner.

It was nice to hear her own name, even if it was being screamed from the kitchen by a mad parrot twenty times a day. Jess stood in the hallway and listened to Juju and looked in the mirror and smiled.

'Hi, Jess Walters.'

She looked pretty good. Nancy had done a brilliant job with the cut and colour; a choppy crop, blue-black like a starling. There you are girl. Welcome back.

Jess was ready to face the question that had run through her head since that day. What the hell did you do? She had fobbed herself off for too long with pat answers; impulse, fate, destiny. Not true. No, it was a choice. A decision. Her call.

Would she do it again? Knowing the cost? Definitely not. Probably not. Hopefully not. Regret was a monster and a fickle one. Smethwick had been a hard place to be good in but so was West Tillington. But she had changed, grown calmer, grown wiser, grown up.

She had been unhappy; no, she had been trapped. A dead-end life, bloody Groundhog Day just to pay the rent on a shitty flat plagued by rodents and Mongolian throat singers. Still, that was no excuse. The truth was that she had made the wrong decision because she thought that money was the answer. Simple as that.

Three-fifteen, nearly closing time, planning supper; lentil Bolognese again. A woman was exchanging Euros, Jacqui on counter two being helpful. The man at her hatch was polite, herringbone jacket, he paid in a cheque, turned to leave. Home time.

Three men in balaclavas, holes for the eyes and mouth. Guns. A bloody film set.

Hands in the air. You are meant to press the alarm. Sod that.

Put your fucking hands up. You bet.

On the floor, face down. Not you bitch. She would do exactly as she was told.

Jacqui on the floor, sobbing quietly. She had a nice boyfriend, she had a baby, what was its name? Margaret, an adult name for a baby. The customers both on the floor, doing as instructed, no heroes here. No way.

Do what you're told and we won't blow your fucking heads off. Wasn't it meant to be 'And no one will get hurt?' These guys meant business. Just do what they say.

Disable the alarm.

Get in the back.

Open the door to the vault.

Put the money in the bags.

All of it.

Stuffing the notes in as fast as she could. Focus on the task, not the cold metal pushing into the back of her head.

Now on the floor bitch, face down, don't move a muscle. This jacket is dry clean only, funny what you think about. The buttons pressing into her chest with every breath.

Police cars wailing. God, now they were dead. Stupid bloody Jacqui must have pressed the alarm.

But the men panicked. Ran for it. Out the back. Kicked the door wide open. Gone, in a confusion of crashing and calling and curses.

Jess scrambled to her feet and made it to the open doorway gasping for breath. Lit a cigarette. The cavalry was coming with all sirens blazing. But the cop cars flashed by; one, two, three. Turned out they were going to a fight on Tile Street. A golden opportunity – weren't you meant to make the most of them? She watched herself picking up the duffle bags, heavier than expected, walking out of the back door, heaving them into the boot of the Clio.

Driving home on auto pilot. So calm. For days.

Depersonalisation. She'd looked it up online – thought she

was going crazy – but it was a real thing; the experience of being outside yourself, observing your actions, feelings and thoughts from a distance. It helped her to get through the police interview. They must have taken her detachment for shock. Anyway, they were very nice to her, tea, biscuits, the works. The victims became heroes. Brave just for lying on the floor.

Jess stayed in bed for days, prostrate on a mattress stuffed full of banknotes where she dreamed of soaring through a clear blue sky; a female Icarus, but a better judge of distance.

There was no way she could go back to work and pretend that everything was okay.

One trip to the G.P. was all it took. Trembling, staring into space and a quick burst of histrionic sobbing had the impassive Dr Devine-Wright reaching for his prescription pad before you could say post-traumatic stress disorder. She was shepherded out of the surgery with a supply of sertraline and four weeks sick leave. Bingo. She handed in her notice; felt bad about the whip-round – got a toaster, a bottle of prosecco and a basket of fruit.

Then who should she bump into but Sarah Wilson. They went for coffee for old times' sake. Jess confessed that her life was a mess – she needed to get away, a new start. Sarah laid her hand on hers; she had a proposition. Becoming a vicar was fulfilling her parents' ambition, not her own. She too wanted out. It all made perfect sense; a mutually beneficial arrangement. Why the hell not? And, just like that she left herself behind. Headed off to West Tillington. Willingly buried herself under Sarah Wilson.

Jess Walters had finally dug herself out. She was back and she knew exactly what she had to do. What she wanted to do. But first, she had to talk to Carole.

It was the first time Carole had seen her since the funeral. She did not conceal her shock at Jess's appearance. She gestured to follow her through to the 'orangery.' Carole too was a changed woman, casual in her blue slacks and nautical striped jumper. If it weren't for the grey line of neglect in her auburn hair, the smudged lipstick and the wild eyes, one might imagine that she was doing okay.

'How is Ted?'

'Why do you ask?' Carole had taken defensiveness to a pathological level.

The enormous orangery seemed to lack citrus fruits of any kind. Jess cast her eye around hoping to find a neutral topic. None came to mind. What the hell, she was being honest now and it felt good. Just go for it.

'I wanted to tell you that I know it was you who dobbed us into social services. And I know you were feeding information to Terence to try to get me sacked.'

Carole sat stony faced.

'And to say that in a way you were right, on both counts. So, no hard feelings.' She extended her hand.

Carole did not take it. Instead, she picked up The History of Glass Houses from the table.

'Shouldn't throw stones, right?' Jess smiled.

Carole retrieved a magazine cutting from between the pages and placed it on the mosaic tabletop between them. It was the original article on Cambridge Theological College with the photograph of last year's ordinands. Blimey, so it was Carole.

'Why did you stick that on my car?'

'To warn you off. Stop you from hounding poor Terence. I kept the original in case you made further waves. I was ready to defend him to the end. Much good it did me.'

'Why are you showing me this now?'

'Ammunition.'

'You kept your powder dry for too long. I resigned yesterday, hung up the ole dog collar. Geoffrey already has a new vicar lined up.'

Carole flicked to the final chapter. She removed a series of black and white photographs and laid them out like poker cards. She sat back with the air of a Bond villain.

The images were grainy, presumably downloaded from CCTV footage. They told a sinister story. Jack and herself dragging a dead body rolled in an Axminster rug into the side chapel. Christ. 'What do you want?'

'To avert mutually assured destruction.'

'Go on.'

'On the afternoon of June 15th you, Ted and I were at the vicarage enjoying afternoon tea and discussing the planting regime for the Villages in Bloom competition.'

'On the afternoon of June 15th, I was at Peaminster General visiting Jesús. I recall it very clearly because it was the day that Terence Johnson was shot.'

'You have an excellent memory.' Carole seemed to be relishing her new criminal persona. She could be stroking a white cat.

Jess looked at the flourishing palm trees and allowed the information to sink in. 'So, what did we decide about the planting regime?'

'That is not important.'

'On the contrary, details are the key to a convincing alibi.'

Carole snapped the book shut and looked her straight in the eye. 'The village hall, Church Lane lamp-posts and Adfordley Cross wishing well were to have hanging fuchsia baskets. A display of dwarf hollyhocks, geraniums and assorted lupins were allocated to Borten Wood Rise.'

'I did wonder if it was Ted who shot Terence. Jealous rage?'

'Ted is not a violent man. Quite the opposite. Spinelessness is not an endearing quality.'

'He seems like a decent guy to me.'

'As it happens, I had underestimated him. After Terence's funeral he confessed he'd been waging a covert campaign to debilitate him by supplying sausages, loin chops and pork medallions of a questionable bacteriological nature.'

'Good God.'

'The undercooked pig roast was to be his final triumph. Streptococcus suis leading to severe sepsis. Astonishingly, Terence survived.'

'Blimey. But everyone at the barbeque was tucking into that poor pig. Except me.'

'Ted put an under-cooked plateful aside for Terence. The fool-man wolfed the lot.'

'Oh yeah, I saw it. Looked revolting.'

'Ted thought that you were on to him when you popped over

the other day wearing that ghastly t-shirt.'

'Which one?'

'Meat is murder.'

Jess looked at Carole with a newfound admiration. 'Can I ask why you shot him?'

An automatic sprinkler released a fine mist over the majesty palms and tree ferns as the ceiling fans hummed into action – that was some misappropriation of community funds.

'Terence was using me. Dropping hints to everyone that we were having an affair. He never touched me.' She patted her hair. 'Not through want of trying.'

'I'm sorry, but also not sorry.' The image of Carole and Terence in flagrante was deeply unpleasant. 'Why would he pretend? Jeopardise your marriage?'

'It transpired that I was his cover, a patsy, an image enhancer. Womanisers are rarely suspected of being child molesters.' Carole produced an embroidered hanky and dabbed at her mascara-smeared eyes.

'Geez, what a psychopath.'

'All those promises. We were going to purchase a villa in the Algarve, run away, start a new life. All lies.'

'Honestly, you're much better off with Ted.'

'I discovered that parrots and little boys featured more heavily in Terence's plans than did I.'

Jess took a bag of jelly worms from the pocket of her biker jacket and offered one to Carole. 'You know I would have been happy to give you an alibi even without the blackmail.'

73

The early morning sun lit the grass emerald green. It was greener than before. The fallow period had done it good. Borten Wood Farm was alive once more with the bleating of goats. Jack strode his old turf with proprietorial pride. It was hard to believe it had only been six months since they'd left here. So much had changed. He was the same but better too.

Jack twisted a length of chicken wire over the hole in the fence where Pixie had squeezed through; Pat had found her on Adfordley Lane this morning and brought her back in his post van. The goats crowded around him, jostling and butting and chattering like crazy. Happy to be home. It had been a bit sneaky showing the Welsh couple Jesús's goat book and telling them about his head injury before asking if he could buy the goats back. Shakira had sealed the deal – jumping up and putting her skinny legs on Jesús's shoulders. Him hugging her tight.

The trip to Shropshire was successful too. They returned with all except Milly and Miley because the lady couldn't part with them. Jesús was okay with it because he knew the meaning of a pet. He'd taken a couple of photos to update his goat book. They hadn't changed much.

Jack checked his watch and headed back up to the farmhouse. The joy of walking through his own front door was tangible. The place looked amazing with his handcrafted furniture – Sofía had liked that crap from Furniture Warehouse. The goat paintings from the auction were perfect too. They made it their home, not some haunted house mired with memories.

He tapped on the bathroom door. 'Jesús, you still in there?

You'll be dissolving.'

'Five more minutes.'

'We need to leave by ten-thirty. Smartest clothes remember.'

It was weird how Jesús loved soaking in the bath now; those dinosaur bath bombs that Sarah bought were a miracle. That Jess bought. He must get used to using her real name. A name that came with a frisson of excitement that he tried to suppress. It had been pretty weird fancying a vicar. But Jess Walters. Wow. Jess Walters. She was something else.

Truth was, he was scared. His judgement had been clouded by love before. Wasn't everyone's? Bloody oxytocin. But not everyone had chosen a bipolar woman they'd met in a tequila factory in Chihuahua and had known for three weeks. Whose own parents told him she was a pesadilla. He'd loved her craziness before he realised it was actual craziness.

Not everyone would choose a pretend-vicar, ex-bank robber, who used a false identity and laundered money through a bat charity. But he was one hundred percent certain.

Now he just had to tell her.

Jess's red van was already in the hospital car park. Jack's heart skipped. He hadn't asked her if she wanted a lift in case he made a fool of himself and it was awkward on the way home. The atom bomb of their kiss was so long ago. Had she felt it too?

They'd arranged to meet in the foyer but she wasn't there. Jack checked his phone; nothing. Jesús pulled at his sleeve and pointed. There she was rushing into the hospital shop with a stack of leaflets. She came out empty-handed.

'Sorry, just distributing the new hospital-shuttlebus timetable.'

'You've certainly thrown yourself into your new job. Never off-duty hey?' God, she looked amazing.

'There's a hell of a lot to do after twenty-four years of neglect. Hi Jesús, you look nice. New shirt?'

'Especially for today.'

They walked together down the familiar corridor that had

held so much dread and so much joy. A raucous round of applause greeted them as they opened the double doors. The paediatric staff stood in a crescent around a tiny velvet curtain. Dr Dhooma stepped forward.

'Jesús, Jack, Jess, welcome back to Daisy ward. The team wanted to formally thank you for your incredibly generous donation. Five hundred and eleven thousand pounds will make an enormous difference to our service. It's already improving the quality of our patients' stay.'

Jess had assured him the money had been sufficiently laundered to leave no trace to NatWest Smethwick. She'd even replaced the money she spent on the post van with her own earnings.

'We plan to buy new state-of-the-art equipment. The courtyard has also had a makeover so please visit it afterwards. As you can see, we've already made some fabulous cosmetic changes to the ward.'

The outdated balloon paintings had been replaced by beautiful designs. One wall was covered in an astonishing mural of day and night flying moths, the other zinged with tobogganing penguins. Jack took a photo to show Reuban when he next came over for tea; it was great that Jesús had made a new friend.

'Now, may I ask Jesús to step forward.'

Jesús pulled the cord to reveal a plaque with his name on it. He looked so proud. Everyone clapped. A few people got teary. Jack got something in his eye.

The courtyard had been transformed into a sensory garden complete with a soothing water feature, medicinal herbs and a butterfly-covered lavender border.

Jack cleared his throat. It was the perfect place. 'It's really amazing what you've done.'

'It's a burden lifted, I can't lie.' Jess sat on the new oak bench and put her arm around Jesús's shoulder. 'It's fabulous but I don't want to have to visit you in here ever again, Sweetie.'

'Would you though? If I got injured or something.'

'Of course.'

'Oh, a dinosaur plant.' Jack pointed out a fan of green spirals. 'That's cool.' Jesús touched it lightly.

'Also known as the resurrection plant. They grow in the Chihuahuan desert.' He cleared his throat again.

'Are you okay, Jack?'

'Um, sure. I just wanted to ask you something.' He loosened his tie. 'The thing is...'

A woman wheeled a small girl with a neck-brace into the courtyard.

'Go on.'

He waited for the pair to move off to smell the lavender. 'Well, with you having to leave the vicarage and everything. I wondered if I could return the favour and offer you a place to stay.'

She looked away. 'Thanks, but I'm earning decent money. I can find somewhere to rent.'

'Oh, okay.' Damn, why couldn't he just say it?

'You could come and live with us anyway,' said Jesús.

'I wouldn't want to cramp your dad's style,' she smiled.

'I haven't got any style. I mean, you're my style. Jess, would you move in with us? Properly, I mean. You know what I mean.'

'Yes.' She kissed his cheek. 'I thought you'd never ask.'

74

Jesús combed his hair in the bathroom mirror in case he had to stand up and take a bow or something. Betty and Jean would be here soon with Ben for the film premiere of The Digge at Peaminster college. Eileen wasn't coming because she didn't like horror films. As well as premiere tickets, he and Ben had been paid for being actors. Jesús had wanted to give his money to the bat charity but Jess said it was closed now and instead she'd set up a monthly direct debit to the Bat Conservation Trust. So he put it in his orange skull for a rainy day.

The six of them sat on the back row near the door in case the film was too scary. A man in a white jacket and bowtie stood up and went on and on about the facilities at the college and then he talked about the film. Then he said if anyone had found a stuffed orange-coloured dog in the woods, please could they contact him because the students had 'borrowed it' from a shed but before they could return it the dog had disappeared.

Jesús looked at Ben and they did their puffed-out cheeks. Dad looked at Jess and did his raised eyebrow.

'Mary-and-fricken-Joseph,' said Jess. She was a lot more sweary now she wasn't a vicar.

Then Johnno, Kev, Adam, Sid and Tracey stood up and took a bow and the audience clapped.

The lights dimmed and everyone stopped talking. The screen turned from white to black and panned out to slow-motion pictures of Montague Forest from the air. The music was very creepy. Wow, there were their names going up in scrawly red letters like they were written in blood. Ben Russet, Jesús Stretton, Children of the forest. Brilliant.

Dad passed down a bag of liquorice Allsorts. There were a

lot of long arty shots of dark figures moving silently through dark trees. Betty must have had a long day because she was fast asleep and Jean had to keep nudging her to stop her snoring. She soon woke up when the screaming started. Now a hooded man was carrying something slung over his back like a hump. It was the camel they'd seen that first night. The man made a noose and hung the thing from a tree. It had been sacrificed. The sudden closeup made everyone jump; Peachy.

The liquorice Allsorts scattered across the floor.

'Best not mention this bit to Eileen,' Jess whispered.

The next morning Jesús took Jess down to Bottom Meadow to continue her lessons. Being back on the farm was a dream come true. It happened because Mr Johnson died – sometimes good things come out of bad situations. The farm had gone back to the big estate who were also land-grabber Tories but nicer ones. Something to do with claws. Anyway, because he and Dad had been excellent tenants, they'd got first dibs.

Jesús shook his head the way Miss Bickerstool did when she couldn't believe a behaviour, and showed Jess how to brush straight down, not along the body. Especially with Beyoncé who was still quite bitey. He was going to be a teacher now rather than a detective. Teaching was much more fun than dead bodies.

Jess was making progress. To be a good goatherd you needed to be calm but firm. To begin with she was all screamy and 'What the hell' and 'Oh my God, they're crazy,' but now she was getting the hang of it and was pretty good at feeding and moving them. She left the milking to Dad though because she was busy with her new job. It was something to do with filling in potholes and opening day centres and starting up meals-on-wheels, which sounded fun.

Jesús held Jess's hand and they walked back up the field. He still thought of her as Sarah.

'Jess.' He was walking fast now to keep up with her long strides. 'Do you prefer being Sarah or Jess?'

'Definitely Jess. You always have to be true to yourself.' She sounded even more vicary now than she did when she was an actual vicar.

'Except you weren't though. You know, when you were Sarah.'

'That's true. I made a big mistake and I got a bit lost.' She stopped and looked at him. 'Sometimes the life you have doesn't suit you.' She gave his hand a squeeze. 'If that happens you should change it.'

'Mum should have changed her life rather than suiciding.'

'Maybe she thought she'd run out of options. There are always choices, Jesús, but sometimes you have to search hard to find the right one.'

Shakira was shouting for them from Bottom Meadow. Jesús looked over his shoulder and gave her a wave so that she knew he'd be back. 'It's hard when someone leaves you.'

'She didn't leave you, she left herself.' Jess started walking again.

It was nice holding her hand, she was swinging it now. 'You won't leave, will you?'

'No, I'm very happy here with you and your dad.'

'Me too.'

75

'**B**astard.' Juju greeted their return from the top of the curtain pole.

'One big happy family,' called Jack from the living room, a laugh in his voice.

Jess helped Jesús out of his duffle coat, he could do it himself but she enjoyed unfastening the chunky toggles as he stood stock-still for her. Yes, the fifty-five of them were one big family now. Although it wasn't always happy because Moth and Juju kept falling out and there was a lot of hissing and screaming and running to separate them. Juju's language showed little sign of improvement but he was trying – sometimes he'd say 'banker' when a Tory came on the TV and they'd all praise him.

Sundays were special now. Jack had prepared all the veggies and trimmings for his meatless roast dinner and was clearing space for game time. He looked up and grinned as they came in. God, he was beautiful in his crisp white shirt.

'What d'you fancy playing, mate?'

'People Pictionary, please.' Jesús ran to retrieve the small whiteboard and marker pens from the cupboard.

Jess lay back on the sofa and watched father and son preparing for the game. It was hard to believe it had only been three weeks; it felt like home. It was home.

Jack came and sat beside her. 'Okay, mate, you start.'

Jesús stood beside the glass case that now housed her collection of porcelain whippets and drew an old woman with a cake.'

'Mary Berry?' called Jack.

'Judi Dench?' said Jess.

'Why would she have a cake?' asked Jack.

'She's got to eat.'

Jesús shook his head in that funny way of his and added a croquet mallet.

'Eileen!' They both shouted, then exchanged glances.

'Why a croquet mallet, mate?'

'Because she likes to play croquet and she's just bought a new mallet.' His innocent eyes made her choke-up.

'Ah, cool.' Jack took the board and sketched a circle with swept back hair.

'Nick Cave,' shouted Jess, before he could add anything else.

Her mobile trilled in her pocket; the vicarage number. 'Sorry guys, I need to take this, you carry on.'

She stepped outside. The goats were chasing each other up and down the meadow, their calls ricocheting across the valley in a happy chorus. 'Hi, Lionel, thanks for getting back to me. How's life as a free man?'

'Wonderful, dear thing, wonderful. I'm forever in your debt for clinching my appeal.' His clerical tone resounded as if from a pulpit. 'I must say the vicarage looks divine. I just love what you've done with the guest room.'

'It must be good to be back. How was your service today?'

'Splendid. I brought along darling Pandora, my new poodle, for added interest. Geoffrey gave me the runt of his litter. An adorable little girl. Quite suine in both looks and temperament. Ideal now that the vicarage is a pig-free zone.'

Jess recalled that it was very easy to drift off-track with Lionel. She needed to ask the question that she should have asked him as the prison bell rang all those months ago. 'Listen, I hate to bring it up again but the murder that you said Terence committed. I evidently got the wrong end of the stick. If Melville wasn't the victim, who was?'

A silence, filled only by the bleating of joyful goats.

'Lionel, are you there?'

A sigh, a sniff. 'That is a trauma that is hard to relive,' his voice wavered.

'I'm sorry, I didn't know it was someone close to you.'

The scrape of a chair on slate. He must have taken a seat at the kitchen table. She waited.

'The double murder of my girls. Janice and Janet.'

'Who?' She struggled to assimilate the information.

'He spit roasted them and served them at a council luncheon.'

'Your piglets?'

'My dearest companions and confidants.' The trumpeting of his nose being vigorously blown.

The sweet little piglets from the photo album. 'I'm so sorry, Lionel, that's really awful.'

'One has to confess that the pain is somewhat lessened by Terence's own violent demise.' He achieved his ecclesiastic tone again. 'We are all on the side of justice, dear thing. In all its many forms.'

'We are indeed.'

'Speaking of which, my hearty congratulations to you on your appointment as Terence's replacement.'

'Thanks, I had a lot of backing from westtillingtonwtf. Also no one else applied. The other councillors are a bit work-shy, tend to spend a lot of time on the golf course.'

'You are very modest. I'm sure your appointment was based upon your highly successful Stop the Abattoir campaign. How marvellous that the parish is to remain slaughter-free.'

'Thanks, Lionel, that's kind of you. I have to dash, I'm in the middle of something.'

'Do thank Jack for his goat's cheese. It was absolutely delicious with roasted beetroot and a black olive tuile. Quite a change from prison food.'

'I bet.'

Jess brought through two lagers and an orange juice. Jack and Jesús were deep in discussion about whether David Attenborough would ever wear a ring-tailed lemur t-shirt.

'Everything okay, love?' Jack raised his eyebrows.

She passed him a bottle of Peroni. 'Yes, just Lionel. He says thanks for the cheese.'

'Cool. Thought it might be Sarah Wilson.'

She settled down beside him. 'Last I heard all was going well in Donegal. Happy as a pigeon now that Donal's stopped drinking.'

'Happy as a goat.' Jesús handed her the white board. 'Your go.'

Jack clinked his bottle against hers. 'Glad it's working out for her. I guess getting that vicar job in Letterkenny means she's not disinherited. Must be happy as a parrot.'

'Apparently nearly everyone's Catholic so she spends most of her time helping Donal with his harp recitals.'

'Effing bastard,' screamed Juju.

Moth came skidding in and leapt onto Jesús's shoulder. He stroked her neck until loud purrs filled the room.

Jess raised her bottle. 'Here's to being one big happy family.'

'Cheers,' they said.

ACKNOWLEDGEMENT

My love and thanks to:

Debi Alper, editor extraordinaire, for keeping Moth the kitten safe and telling the whole truth.

Liz Binch for policing of botanical irregularities and grammatical inaccuracies.

Jasper Williams, for his enthusiasm, support and cover advice.

The Mill Street five o'clock club: Barbara, Daniel, Cy, Stan, Max, Miriam, Allan, June, Liz, Marilyn, Francis, Alan and Julian for regular reality orientation during my months of living in fictional West Tillington.

BOOKS BY THIS AUTHOR

The Tortoise

As two women celebrate New Year's Eve across town, a mutual acquaintance lies dead in her apartment.
Can a missing tortoise lead the way to the truth?

Former G.P. Dr Clara Astrell is content at home reading Animal Farm to her whippet. But when she inherits a tortoise with a past she becomes the prime suspect in a murder investigation.

Jo turns amateur sleuth find her best friend's killer. She is charmed by conman, Ludo, and her desperate attempts to solve the case put her own life in jeopardy.

A gruesome discovery turns the tables.
A gripping tale of friendship, murder and betrayal.
One tortoise, two strangers, three lives changed forever.

The debut novel by Emma Williams is available in ebook and paperback.

Amazon reviews.

'A fine balance of compassion and comedy.'

'Great story, great dialogue and very funny.'

'Absolutely loved this book from start to finish.'

'A thoroughly enjoyable read - warm, funny and twisted.'

Visit My Website:

To comment or ask a question please go to:

https://emmawilliams.online

We'd love to hear what you think
so please leave a review of Nothing
but the Truth on Amazon.

Prosimian Press

Printed in Great Britain
by Amazon

27627219R00191